P9-CZV-077

KAREN ROBARDS

The Midnight Hour

Delacorte Press

Published by
Delacorte Press
Random House, Inc.
1540 Broadway
New York, New York 10036

This novel is a work of fiction. Names, characters, places, and incidents either are the product of the author's imagination or are used fictitiously. Any resemblance to actual persons, living or dead, events, or locales is entirely coincidental.

Copyright © 1999 by Karen Robards

All rights reserved. No part of this book may be reproduced or transmitted in any form or by any means, electronic or mechanical, including photocopying, recording, or by any information storage and retrieval system, without the written permission of the Publisher, except where permitted by law.

The trademark Delacorte Press® is registered in the U.S. Patent and Trademark Office.

Library of Congress Cataloging in Publication Data
Robards, Karen.
    The midnight hour : a novel / by Karen Robards.
        p.   cm.
    ISBN 0-385-31971-1
    I. Title.
    PS3568.0196M53   1999   98-35730
    813'.54—dc21   CIP

Manufactured in the United States of America
Published simultaneously in Canada

Design by Claire O'Keeffe

January 1999

10 9 8 7 6 5 4 3 2 1

BVG

This book is dedicated to my parents,
Pete and Sally Johnson,
with love.
It is also dedicated, as always,
to the men in my life:
my husband, Doug;
and my sons,
Peter, Christopher, and Jack.

The Midnight Hour

CHAPTER 1

"**W**HERE DO YOU THINK YOU'RE GOING?"

The sound of his mother's voice affected him like fingernails scraping across a blackboard. His skin prickled, and he shuddered slightly. Turning to face her, he felt oceans of hostility surge through his veins. *He hated her. . . .*

"Out." His hand rested on the doorknob. She stood there glaring at him, arms crossed over the chest of her pink-flowered cotton robe. Her dyed-black hair was short and spiky with interrupted sleep. Her olive skin was creased with fifty-five years' worth of sun worship, and worse. Without makeup to hide them, the bags under her eyes were as big and purple as grapes. Her neck was thin and wattled like a turkey's. She wore little white sock-things on her feet, and above them her legs were bare and scrawny, with big varicose veins twining like vines just below her knees.

She was ugly. . . .

"It's after midnight. You're not going anywhere!"

They were standing in the old-fashioned kitchen. It was long and narrow, with a faux brick linoleum floor and faux marble countertops. The cabinets were of plywood stained to look like oak. A scarred round table with four rickety-legged chairs took pride of place in the center of the room. On the table, there was a bowl of green plastic apples, the same apples that had been there since he could remember. Overhead, the illumination was provided by a single fluorescent fixture.

"You off your Prozac, Ma?" The drawled question was mocking. He turned away from her, turning the knob. He had thought to get out without waking her. Usually she slept like the dead, snoring like a drunk in the master bedroom just off the kitchen. Maybe she'd been listening to Jay Leno. She had the hots for Leno, preferred him to Letterman. But usually she fell asleep before he came on.

"I said you're not going anywhere! You're seventeen years old, and you're living under my roof, and you'll do as I say! I'll tell your father. . . ." She was shriller than ever, shrieking shrill, as he ignored her, opening the door and running down the back steps into the welcoming night. The door slammed behind him, cutting her off in midtirade.

I'll tell your father . . . Big threat. It almost made him laugh. His father, the big-shot attorney who made his living suing people for a percentage of the award, was gone five days a week—in a slow week. When he got home, all he wanted to hear about was how many points Donny, jr., had scored in his basketball game, or whether Donny, jr., was gonna make the all-A honor roll again, like he usually did.

Big Don barely spared a glance, much less a word, for his younger son.

He'd known for years that as far as most people—including his parents—were concerned, he was the moon to Donny's sun. Nobody saw him when the golden boy was around.

But the long hours after midnight belonged to *him*. The warm, windy darkness embraced him as he rolled his Honda 250 from the garage, straddled it, and took off with a roar down the driveway.

He smiled faintly as he pointed the bike toward his destination.

The sun had set now, and Donny's little brother had come out to play.

CHAPTER 2

It was just after two a.m., and Jessica's bed was empty.

Light from the hall spilled over the tumbled bed, leaving the rest of the room deep in shadow. Grace Hart didn't even bother to switch on the overhead light. Her tall, thin figure cast an elongated shadow across the pale rose carpet for no more than an instant. Then she moved. Three quick strides brought her to her daughter's bedside. She yanked the covers clear to the foot of the bed just to make sure, but she already knew what she would find: nothing.

Jessica was not curled up in a tight little ball beneath the primrose comforter. A hasty glance around confirmed that Jessica was not in the tweedy pink armchair in the corner, or at her white-and-gold desk, or sprawled out with a pillow on the carpet. Grace didn't even have to check to know that Jessica was not in the connecting bathroom, or downstairs in the kitchen. . . . or, in fact, anywhere in the house.

Her fifteen-year-old daughter had snuck out.

Again.

Oh, God, Grace thought, staring blindly at the empty bed, *what am I going to do?*

There was no one but God to ask. She and Jessica lived

ℝ

alone. Grace loved her daughter more than life itself—but lately she had grown terrified that she was losing her. This was the third time in the past two months that she had been awakened—by what? a stealthy sound? a bad dream? she didn't know—and risen from her bed to check on Jessica, only to find her daughter gone.

It was Monday night—no, Tuesday morning now. A school day. Jessica had to be up at 6:45 A.M. She had a Spanish test first period. Just before bedtime, Grace had spent an hour listening to her daughter conjugate verbs. The test counted double, and a good score could bring her *C* in that class up to an *A,* which would be enough to get her on the honor roll. They had both agreed that making the honor roll in high school was important, and Grace, at least, had been psyched about Jessica's chances. But how was she going to do on the test with no sleep?

Of course, Grace realized even as the question formed in her mind, that was the least of her worries at the moment.

The overriding one was, *where's Jessica*?

She had a pretty good idea who her daughter was with, if not where she was. Now four weeks into her first year of high school, Jessica had fallen in with a new crowd, a "cool" crowd, she said, whose acceptance made her popular. The girls all wore flared jeans, midriff-baring tops, platform shoes, and neon-striped hair. (Talk about déjà vu all over again: Grace had worn the same kind of thing, minus the Day-Glo hair streaks, when *she* was in high school. But as Jess pointed out, the seventies were hot again.) Anyway, as far as Grace was concerned, this particular gaggle of girls was bad news rushing headlong toward a bad end. It scared her to realize that Jessica, her own sweet Jessica, was going to find that bad end right along with them if Grace couldn't manage to stop her.

So far, in the war for Jessica's allegiance, the score was dishearteningly lopsided. Mom had lost every battle.

A rattle followed by a soft whirring sound made Grace jump. She glanced around.

"Jessica?"

There was no answer.

It took only a moment for Grace to identify the source of the sound: Godzilla in his exercise wheel. The fat golden hamster whose cage sat atop Jessica's bookshelf was running busily, oblivious to the absence of his mistress or her mother's distress.

"Where is she, buddy?" Grace asked.

Godzilla ran blithely on. Grace grimaced at herself. Talking to a hamster was sad, she thought, and having nothing but a hamster to talk to at a time of crisis like this was even sadder. At age thirty-six, she had, besides her daughter, a sister, a father, an ex-husband, and a raft of friends and acquaintances, but no one she could pick up the phone and call at two A.M. The pattern had been set for years: she listened to their problems, not vice versa.

She was the strong one in all their lives. The fixer, the problem-solver, the one whose life was always under control.

Usually she was okay with that. But not tonight.

Crossing to one of the pair of tall windows that overlooked the front yard, she parted the ruffled pink-plaid curtains, rested her forehead against a cool glass pane, and shut her eyes. Her knee-length blue nylon nightgown had long sleeves, but still she was cold. She folded her arms over her chest, but that didn't help.

What am I doing wrong? The unspoken question repeated itself over and over in time with the pulse throbbing in her head. Trying to ease the pounding, she massaged her temples with her fingertips, then ran her fingers despairingly through her short, blond-streaked brown shag. *I love her so. I'm trying my best. What am I doing wrong?*

In her position as a Franklin County Juvenile and Domestic Court judge, she dealt with problem children on a daily basis. It was a rare session in court when she was not confronted with teens who were out of control.

Usually the kid's problem mirrored some kind of breakdown in the family.

Was that why it was so hard to acknowledge that *her* daughter was rocketing down the same path as the kids who appeared before her every day? Because she would then have to blame herself?

Was it not the unpalatable truth that she was as much a failure as a parent as any of those whose children were hauled into her courtroom?

She loved her daughter so much. She would kill for her. She would die for her. Every success she'd ever had in her life had been achieved for Jessica. How, then, could they have come to this? How was it possible for her to have succeeded in providing Jessica with everything she herself had longed for as a child, yet still have managed to lose Jessica along the way?

Was Jess out there somewhere drinking? This new reason for fear suddenly popped full-blown into Grace's mind, washing over every other consideration like an ocean swell hitting sand castles on the beach. Jessica had to be so careful—but she wasn't. She refused to be.

The last time she'd snuck out with the crowd, she'd come home smelling of booze. Although of course she had denied drinking more than a couple of sips from a friend's can of beer; someone had spilled the rest over her clothes, she'd said, to account for the smell.

Yeah, right. As much as Grace longed to believe it, that story didn't ring true. If a kid told her that in her courtroom, she wouldn't have swallowed a word.

It hurt to acknowledge that Jessica was lying to her. It hurt then, and it hurt now. But then, she'd let her daughter get away with it, on the off chance that she was telling the truth.

Big mistake, and one that she would not repeat.

No more Mr. Nice Mommy for Miss Jess. This time, Grace meant to lower the boom.

But she could do nothing but wait and worry until Jessica came home.

Grace opened her eyes. From her second-floor vantage point, she could see half a dozen darkened houses stretching to the east and west along their street, Spring Hill Lane. All were two-story, deceptively unpretentious residences built in the '20s and '30s, nestled cozily into tree-dotted grounds of half an acre or more per house. Their own house was of narrow white clapboards, with ten-foot-tall ceilings inside and green-painted shutters outside. It blended with its neighbors harmoniously, though none of them was in precisely the same style. A suburb of Columbus, Ohio, Bexley was an old neighborhood, well established, moneyed, safe. Which was why she had chosen it as the ideal place to bring up her daughter.

The tall oaks and elms standing sentinel in her own front yard swayed as a gust of wind caught their branches. A flurry of dislodged leaves swirled through the air, then drifted ghostlike toward the ground. Long shadows cast by a high-flying moon shifted and blended into the line of blackness that was the four-foot-tall privet hedge bordering the street. It was September, and the wind would be warm. Moonlight washed the landscape.

Behind her came the continuous whir of Godzilla on his exercise wheel. The sound was oddly comforting now. At least she was not totally alone in the house.

Jess was okay. She had to keep telling herself that. After all, Jessica was not out in the cold or the rain. She was not lost, and she probably was not alone.

It was Jessica's mother who was alone. And lost. And scared.

Out on the lawn, the shadows danced with the wind. One separated itself from the others, moving with seeming purpose toward a far corner of the yard. Grace blinked with surprise, then realized that she was watching someone walk away from her house toward the small, wrought-iron gate in the hedge.

Jess, or one of her friends. It had to be. This time she had caught her daughter in the act of coming in—or going out.

Before the thought was finished, Grace whirled and ran for the stairs. Her bare feet moved soundlessly over the thick, moss-green carpet that covered the upstairs hall and the steps themselves, and made scarcely more noise as they encountered the oriental runner and highly polished hardwood floor of the center entrance hall. The front door was unlocked, she discovered as she turned the knob. Jess would never go out and leave the house unlocked. As two females living alone, they were both extra careful about that.

Had she been no farther away than her own porch, or yard, all this time?

Grace yanked open the door and burst through the unlatched screen onto. the covered front porch. The concrete slabs that made up the porch floor felt cold to her feet. The wicker swing suspended from chains at the far end creaked as it was caught by the wind. The matching white rockers moved too, as if pushed gently back and forth by unseen occupants. A lightning glance around told Grace that her daughter was not there. She ran to the top of the half-dozen brick stairs that led down to the yard.

"Jessica!" Her hand curled around the cool wrought iron of the banister. Embarrassment at the prospect of waking the neighbors moderated her volume to some degree. Though it was hard to be certain amidst the obscuring shadows, Grace thought the figure heading toward the gate paused at the sound of her voice. Certainly it glanced back. Moonlight glinted briefly on a pale oval face.

"Jessica Hart, you come back here this instant!" If there was a cross between a hiss and a shout, that was the voice Grace used as she descended the front steps, beckoning imperiously to her daughter.

Jessica heard, and saw. The stillness of her, and the fact that she continued to look back, told Grace that. Grace was thankful that she didn't need to scream at the top of her lungs to get her message across.

Although she would have, if necessary.

Two yards over, the Welch's dog began to bark. It was a Scottie with an unmistakable, high-pitched yip. Someone must have forgotten to let it in for the night, as they sometimes did, to the consternation of all the neighbors.

Just as Grace reached the brick sidewalk at the base of the steps, Jessica moved. She turned, leaped like a deer over the remaining few feet of lawn, snatched open the gate, and ran headlong down the street.

Jaw dropping at this blatant act of defiance, Grace needed

only the space of a pair of heartbeats to respond. Unconcerned with her bare feet or the fact that she was wearing only her nightgown, Grace pounded across the yard in hot pursuit.

"Jessica!"

The grass was firm and faintly prickly underfoot, the ground damp but not overly cold. The scattering of fallen leaves was slippery when stepped on, like magazine pages on carpet. Wood smoke from an afternoon of leaf burning lingered in the balmy night air. She trod on a sharp stick and yelped, but didn't stop. Unbelievably, Jessica was running away from her, fleeing down the road.

"Jessica!"

Grace reached the gate at the corner of the yard, jerked it open, and bounded through it. Her right foot came down squarely on something soft and squishy and round and furry. Something that didn't belong in a grassy yard. Something that rolled as she stepped on it.

What . . . Grace thought even as she lost her balance and fell, landing heavily on the asphalt road. The impact to her knees and palms was instantaneous, jarring, and painful. She cried out.

At the sound, Jessica glanced back, but didn't stop. She had almost reached the bend in the road that would hide her from her mother's sight. Gasping with exertion and pain, Grace could do nothing but gaze furiously after her.

The fleeing figure ran through a bright patch of moonlight that spilled in a narrow swath across the road. At last it was clearly illuminated.

With a thrill of disbelief, Grace realized that the person she had been pursuing so desperately was someone she did not know.

The hip-length dark coat and dark knit watch cap did not belong to Jessica. Jessica was not that tall, or that bulky. Jessica did not move like that. *It was not Jessica.*

Whoever it was ran on around the bend, and out of sight.

It was a long moment before Grace was able to glance away from the spot where the figure had disappeared. The next object that registered with her confused senses was the soft, squishy, furry thing she had stepped on to cause her fall, which now lay just a few inches from her right hand.

It was a teddy bear.

Jessica's teddy bear, to be precise, the one she had owned since she was a tiny girl. The one she loved. The one that, up until at least tonight's bedtime when Grace had seen it there as she bade her daughter good night, had been perched on Jessica's bed-side table ready to watch over Jess as she slept.

Now it was lying in the grass beside the road, button eyes staring sightlessly up into the dark night sky.

CHAPTER 3

"WHAT TIME DID YOU LAST SEE YOUR DAUGH-
ter, Judge Hart?" The gray-haired, sixty-ish patrolman—J. D. Gelinsky, according to the name badge on the breast pocket of his
blue uniform—was polite, even deferential, as befitted Grace's
status as a member of the local judiciary. She didn't know him,
although he looked vaguely familiar, and she guessed that she had
seen him around the courthouse once or twice. Bexley had its
own police force to tend to traffic matters and the other petty
crimes that occasionally occurred in the small city, and she
doubted that its officers made many appearances in Juvenile and
Domestic Court. At any rate, he seemed to know who she was,
which was both good and bad. A stickler for paperwork and
punctuality, she had a reputation as a tough, no-nonsense jurist.
Not all cops appreciated that. Especially if they had a tendency to
be late, or ill prepared, when they came to court.

Licking her dry lips, striving to present a calm, professional
demeanor, Grace thought that, at the moment, she didn't feel
much like a judge. What she felt like was a mother, an increasingly frightened mother whose beloved only child was missing. A
mother who had awakened in the middle of the night to find her
daughter gone and a stranger fleeing her house.

It was possible that the two circumstances were not connected.

She shivered, icy with the acute sense of foreboding that had caused her to call the police.

Had Jessica merely snuck out again—or had something far more sinister befallen her? The former was still possible, but her mother's intuition was on red alert.

She felt that Jessica was in danger.

"Around ten. I went into her room to say good night." The careful evenness of her voice was belied by the nervous movements of her fingers digging deeply into the nappy brown fur of the teddy bear, which she held on her lap. Her palms, scratched in her fall, burned; her skinned knees stung. Wearing hastily donned khaki slacks, a black turtleneck, and black flats, Grace sat on the gold damask couch in the formal living room, perched on it, really, on the very edge, as if she would spring up at any moment. Officer Gelinsky sat solidly in the armchair opposite her, pen in hand, pad on knees, his gaze on her face. His stolidness was driving her insane. He behaved as if Jessica being missing was of no greater importance than a report of a burglary, or one more stolen car.

Grace felt as if the cold were sinking clear through to her bones. The house had seemed warm earlier, she remembered. Before she had discovered Jessica was gone. Now it felt like the inside of a refrigerator.

Perhaps, she thought, striving to maintain self-control, the chill in the room had something to do with its cool color scheme: the walls were painted a deep Wedgwood blue, the heavy silk curtains were blue-and-gold striped, and the carpet was an Aubusson that was predominantly blue. The floor around the rug was highly polished dark wood, and the fireplace mantel was of carved white marble. Everything was well polished, immaculate, and looked cold to the touch. The only warm note in the room was the painting above the fireplace.

It was a pastel likeness of Jessica at six. Jessica with her light brown hair in two braids, wearing a white pinafore over a yellow gingham dress, her blue eyes—so like Grace's—huge and solemn.

Grace could not stop glancing at that portrait. The tightness in her chest intensified another degree every time she did.

Where was Jessica?

"And she was in bed at that time?"

They had gone over this once already, when Officer Gelinsky and his partner had first arrived. Now the partner, a blond woman in perhaps her mid-thirties whom Grace was sure she did not know, was upstairs checking out Jessica's room, while Officer Gelinsky led Grace through the events of the night for a second time.

"Yes. She was in bed."

"What made you decide to check on her when you did?"

"I don't know. I . . . woke up. I don't know why. And I went in to check on Jessica. And she wasn't there." Grace clutched the stuffed bear on her lap tighter, oblivious to the tingling in her sore palms. Mr. Bear, that was what Jess had always called him. She stole a sidelong glance at the portrait, and felt her throat constrict. "Jessica—this is her teddy bear. It sat on the night table by her bed. It was lying outside, near the road. I stepped on it. Whoever I was chasing must have dropped it. He must have been in her room. *I'm afraid he may have done something to Jessica.*"

Burgeoning fear added urgency to her words.

"Don't worry, Judge Hart. If she's out there, we'll find her. I've already called it in, and by now the whole force should be aware that your daughter's missing. She'll be priority number one until she's found." His gaze dropped back to his pad, and he cleared his throat. "You say that the man you chased—it was a man?—was alone, is that right?"

Grace took a deep breath, fighting to remain calm. Hideous visions of Jon-Benet Ramsey were starting to dance in her head. A tale of a predawn intruder, a missing child, then later, a body . . .

You're being ridiculous, she told herself sternly. It was just this mother-sense she had that something was wrong.

"Whoever I chased was alone. I think it was a man. I . . . can't be one hundred percent sure. It looked like a man. But I can't be sure."

"But you are certain your daughter was not with him?"

"Yes, I am certain of that."

"And you say your daughter has left the house at night before without telling you?"

The admission was just as humiliating the second time as it had been the first.

"Yes. She's snuck out at night twice in the last few months. She's a freshman in high school this year, and . . ."

Her voice trailed off as the blond officer came back into the room, shaking her head significantly at Officer Gelinsky. Grace closed her mouth and felt her muscles tense.

"Do you mind if I take a look through the rest of the house?" the woman asked her. Sarah Ayres, read her name tag.

The Ramsey child's body had been found in the basement. . . .

Stop it, Grace told herself fiercely. Jessica was all right. Of course she was all right. She had to be all right. Grace swallowed, fighting to keep her voice steady. "No. I mean, please do. Do you—shall I show you around?"

Officer Ayres exchanged looks with her partner. "No, thanks, I can find my way," she said, and left the room.

Grace felt cold sweat break out on her forehead.

"When you went out the front door—you said you went out the front door, didn't you?—was it locked?" Officer Gelinsky glanced down at his notes again as he spoke.

"No. It was not locked. It was locked when I went to bed, but it wasn't locked then."

"Which led you to assume that the . . . individual . . . you were chasing had been inside your house."

"That—and the teddy bear. It's Jessica's teddy bear. Whoever it was must have taken it from her bedroom and then dropped it when I started chasing him. I don't see any other way it could have ended up where I found it."

"Maybe your daughter carried it outside and dropped it. If not tonight, then earlier."

Grace shook her head. "She loves Mr. Bear. He was on the night table beside her bed when she fell asleep, I'm sure of it. And she wouldn't take him outside in the middle of the night, much less drop him and leave him."

"Hmmm." Officer Gelinsky looked down at his notes again. When he glanced up at Grace, his gaze was sharper than it had been before.

"How would you characterize your relationship with your daughter, Judge Hart?"

Grace was surprised, yet not surprised. This was the turn the conversation had to take to uphold the nightmare. She wet her lips. "Why . . . good. Very good. Most of the time. Well, we've had a few . . . differences of opinion . . . since she became a teenager, but . . ."

There was a knock at the front door. Both Grace and Officer Gelinsky glanced toward it and rose at the same time.

"I'll get it." Dropping Mr. Bear onto the couch, Grace hurried into the front hall. Officer Gelinsky followed her.

The knock sounded again, just as Grace's hand curled around the cold brass knob. Turning it, she pulled the heavy door open. The porch light was on—every light in the house was on by this time, and the neighbor across the street had called to ask if everything was all right—allowing her to clearly see the man who looked at her through the fine steel mesh of the old-fashioned screened door. A glance told her that he was maybe an inch over six feet tall, stocky, with thick black hair and a bushy black beard that obscured his lower face. With his back to the light, she could see the glint of his eyes but not their color. He wore a shabby green army jacket, a pair of jeans, and ancient-looking white sneakers.

"Mrs. Hart? Uh, Judge Hart?" His gaze moved beyond her as he spoke, presumably to acknowledge Officer Gelinsky, before returning to her face.

"Yes?" One hand rose to the base of her neck. Was this bad news? It came like this, she had heard. The cop at the door . . . Dear Lord, please no, she prayed. Not Jessica . . .

"Detective Dominick Marino, Franklin County Police. I have a young woman I think may be your daughter in my car."

"What?" A wave of relief so strong it made her knees go weak hit Grace. For a moment her hand tightened around the knob, clinging to it for support. Then she let go. "Thank God! Is she okay?"

Pushing through the screen door, she rushed past him toward the cars in her driveway even as he answered. He turned to follow her progress with his gaze.

"Ah, basically."

The wind had picked up, Grace noticed distractedly as she ran down the front steps and along the sidewalk to where first a police car and then, behind it, a battered blue Camaro were parked. The police car she ignored. It had been there earlier. Officers Gelinsky and Ayres had arrived in it. Reaching the Camaro, she touched the still-warm hood, tried the locked door on the driver's side and the passenger door behind it, then bent down to peer through the rear window.

It was impossible to see anything in the nearly pitch-black interior of the car.

A dark-haired man in a brown leather bomber jacket got out of the front passenger side, standing in the vee formed by the open door and the car, one arm resting on the roof. She straightened to speak to him.

He forestalled her. "If that's your daughter in there, you better start keeping closer tabs on her. What is she, fourteen, fifteen? She needs to be home in bed at night, not out roaming the streets."

Taken aback by the blunt censoriousness of his words, Grace merely blinked at him for an instant without replying. He was as disreputable looking as the cop on her porch, she registered, though he was beardless.

What did he know about anything?

"Could you unlock the door?" Recovering her power of speech, Grace ignored his words completely, then was distracted by the sight of her daughter as she glanced down. The car's interior light was on now, illuminating Jessica in the rear. Dressed in jeans, sneakers, and a skimpy blue sweater, shoulder-length hair with its center hot-pink streak falling away from her face, her daughter was curled limply in the far seat, her head pillowed on the blue vinyl arm rest in the middle. Her eyes were closed, and her arms dangled off the seat toward the floor. From all appearances, she was either asleep or unconscious, and only the fastened seat belt kept her in place.

Grace's fear, which had been swamped by relief for the few brief moments since the announcement that Jessica had been found, returned full force, though in a scary new form.

"Jessica?" Grace tried the door handle again without success. She rapped on the window. "Jessica?"

Her daughter did not respond in any way. The small dome light in the roof of the car provided just enough illumination to enable Grace to see the artificial rosiness of Jessica's cheeks. The fragile bones of her slender, pointy-chinned face appeared almost skeletal in the ghostly light. Her parted lips were dry and chapped looking, which they hadn't been when she had gone to bed only a few hours earlier.

"Jessica!" she said again, then, straightening: "Unlock the door, please!"

This time it was a command, addressed to the cop—she assumed he was a cop—across the roof of the car. He had been watching her without making a move to help as she tried to get to Jessica. Now his gaze met hers, his expression impossible to read in the shifting shadows.

"Don't get in a panic. She's drunk, not dead." His voice was dry.

"She has diabetes." The tightness in Grace's chest grew until it felt like an iron band squeezing her lungs. She sucked in air, fighting against the compression that threatened to cut off her breath. For Jessica's sake, she had to stay in control, both of her emotions and the situation.

The lock popped up with an audible click. Opening the rear door, she leaned into the car, touching Jessica's flushed cheek. The familiar fruity breath that signified high blood sugar was as unmistakable as the smell of booze that hung around her daughter like a cloud.

"Jessica! Jess!" On her knees on the car seat now, Grace took hold of her daughter by the shoulder and shook her. Jessica's lashes fluttered.

"Mom?" It was a drowsy, slurred question.

"Jess!"

Jessica's eyes closed again, and she seemed to sag. Grace shook her, gently slapped her cheek. "Jess!"

This time there was no response.

The door on Jessica's other side opened.

"Jesus, lady, if she's diabetic, you sure shouldn't be letting her run wild." The cop was looking at her with disapproval across Jessica's limp body. He was black-haired, swarthy-skinned, unshaven, and unkempt looking. His eyes were narrow as they met her gaze. The brows above them were thick and bushy and almost met over his nose as he frowned at her. "That's neglect, pure and simple."

"I did not *let* her do anything." Jessica's needs were too urgent to allow her to waste time on this imbecile. "Look, her blood sugar's too high. She needs to go to the emergency room. Right now. Can you help me put her in my car?" Grace's outward calm was at odds with the burgeoning panic she felt inside.

The cop stared at her for an instant.

"Get in. We'll drive you."

He withdrew from the car, slamming the door, then bellowed, "Dom!" as Grace clambered into the back seat, sliding close to her daughter. Jessica's skin felt cool and dry, with a slight roughness like a snake's hide, a roughness that was not usually present.

Oh, God, please let her be all right!

"Jess?" Her voice quivered.

"She needs to go to the hospital?" The cop from her porch—Dominick Something—looked in the open rear door through which Grace had entered. His obnoxious partner was already sliding into the front passenger seat.

"Yes," Grace said firmly. She had herself in hand again.

"Put on your seat belt," the obnoxious one ordered, as Dominick Whatever-his-name-was slammed the rear door and got into the front seat. The inside of the car went dark as he closed his door. Grace put on her seat belt and reached across the small space separating her from her daughter to clasp Jessica's unresponsive hand.

"Is she in shock or something?" Voice uneasy, Dominick looked at her through the rearview mirror as he started the car and reversed down the driveway. Apparently his partner had alerted him to the diabetes before he got into the car.

"I don't—Oh, I forgot to lock the house!" Only as the car pulled out onto the street did Grace remember her open front door. Ordinarily it wouldn't have concerned her much—Bexley was very safe—but given the events of the night . . .

It surprised her to discover that, from the knock at her door until now, she had almost forgotten the intruder. Her concern over Jessica was paramount.

"The officers who are there will see that everything's closed up tight." This was the second cop, Mr. Obnoxious himself, who was in the process of shrugging out of his leather bomber jacket. "Here, put this around her."

He passed the jacket to Grace over the back of the front seat. It was still warm from his body and smelled faintly of leather and man. His gaze met hers. His expression was impossible to read in the darkness of the car's interior, but Grace could sense his disapproval. It was palpable.

"Thank you." For Jessica's sake, Grace accepted the coat gratefully, despite the donor's urgent need for an attitude adjustment, and tucked it around her daughter, who had not moved.

Had it not been for the faint, regular sound of her exhalations, Grace would have been terrified for her daughter's life.

"You're welcome." Mr. Obnoxious had slewed around with his left arm resting along the top of the seat so that he could watch them.

"So how bad is she?" Dominick kept glancing at Grace through the rearview mirror. She wished he would keep his eyes on the road. His job was to get them to the hospital in one piece, not to monitor her mothering skills.

"I don't know." It took tremendous effort to keep her voice even, Grace found. She looked at her daughter's huddled form. Jessica was either deeply asleep or unconscious. If she had been aware, if she had even an inkling that she was being rushed to the hospital, she would have protested furiously.

Jessica hated to surrender to her disease in any way. And she considered going to the hospital surrendering.

"You don't know?" Uttered by Mr. Obnoxious, the words were sharp with disbelief.

"I'm not an expert on diabetes. It's hard to tell." Grace glanced from her daughter to the men in the front seat. Except for the occasional streetlight, it was dark inside the car. She sensed rather than saw the cops exchange speaking looks. "A lot depends on if she took her insulin on time, and when she last ate. I don't know how much of this—the way she is right now—can be at-tributed to alcohol, and how much to the disease. I don't think she's going into a coma, but I can't be sure. She might be, and I don't want to take that chance."

"No, ma'am," Dominick said fervently, and stepped on the gas.

Grace dropped her daughter's unresponsive hand and tried to brace her as well as she could, to keep her from being flung about as the car sped through a blur of dark, twisting streets toward the hospital.

CHAPTER 4

OHIO STATE UNIVERSITY HOSPITAL WAS A COM-
plex of towering, fifties-modern buildings that sprawled over at
least a couple of city blocks at one end of the vast college campus.
At night it was easy to spot, glowing like an electric torch against
the inky-blue sky, its brilliance reflected in the dark waters of the
nearby Olentangy River. A chunky white-and-orange ambulance,
having discharged its human cargo, rolled silently away from the
emergency room entrance as they pulled in. Scrubs-clad orderlies
moving at a near-run bundled a white-covered shape on a gurney
through the sliding doors and out of sight. The red EMERGENCY
sign beckoned newcomers toward the well-lit interior.

"I'll let you out here, then park," Dominick said, stopping
the car under the carport that sheltered the wide steel-and-glass
doors. A sign affixed to the roof warned, AMBULANCES ONLY. Ignoring it, Grace unfastened her seat belt, then turned to do the same
for her daughter.

"Jessica?" She smoothed back the few strands of hair that had
fallen over her daughter's face. "Jess, we're here."

Jessica's condition was unchanged. She was limp, but breathing regularly. Not by so much as the flicker of an eyelash did she
acknowledge her mother's voice or touch. Fear began to build
anew in Grace, but she forced it back.

They were at the hospital now. Medical assistance was at hand. Giving way to panic would only hurt her child. But she—almost—couldn't help it.

"Jess!" Gently, she shook her daughter's shoulder. Jessica didn't stir. "Jess!"

Mr. Obnoxious got out of the car and opened the rear passenger-side door. The interior light came on. For an instant, as he leaned inside, his gaze met Grace's. He was frowning. His eyes, she saw, were a clear golden brown.

"Let's go." Without waiting for either emergency room workers to appear or Grace's expressed or implied approval, he scooped Jessica out of the seat and into his arms. She lay with her head lolling back and her arms and legs dangling, totally boneless, as he bore her away toward the emergency room entrance.

"Wait!" Taken by surprise by the suddenness of his action, Grace scrambled out the opposite side of the car, and was left to hurry behind as the cop carried Jessica across the pavement. The sight of her daughter lying so limply in a stranger's arms made Grace feel sick. It reinforced what she knew but tried not to think about: Jessica was chronically ill. She was afflicted with this damnable disease, with all its implications for her long-term health, for life.

As she acknowledged that, the despair Grace had felt upon first learning the cause of her daughter's troubling symptoms threatened to return in full force.

What made the situation almost unbearable was the knowledge that there was absolutely nothing she could do to change things.

But despair was of no use to her, or Jessica, she thought, and she resolutely refused to wallow in it. She chose, instead, to hope.

Diabetes was a serious disease, but it could be controlled. The problem was, Jessica was very young. She refused to accept the reality of her condition, or the restrictions it imposed on her. She refused to take care of herself and resented her mother for trying to make sure she did.

For a diabetic to get drunk was akin to a person with a food allergy deliberately gorging on the forbidden substance. The consequence was foregone: sudden illness, maybe a coma, even possible death.

It was reprehensible for a fifteen-year-old to drink alcohol, and deserving of dire punishment. But that punishment should not include death.

What had Jessica been thinking?

The hospital smell, a combination of alcohol and other disinfectants and sickness, hit Grace as soon as she walked through the double doors that slid open with a gentle *swoosh* to admit them. She had smelled it too often of late, and now it sickened her. Crossing her arms over her chest, she attempted to ward off the cold. It was entirely possible, she thought, that she would never be warm again.

There were only a few people seated in the maroon-and-gray plastic chairs that lined the walls of the emergency room: a man holding a bloody washcloth to his head, a woman clutching a sleeping baby wrapped in a blue-and-white quilt, a nicely dressed elderly couple reading magazines side by side, another woman trying to contain an energetic toddler. The little boy's laughter as he climbed over a row of chairs while the woman tried vainly to catch him was, to Grace, an off note, an anomaly in this place of fear and suffering. Off to one side, a man in a janitor's uniform sloshed a mop over the gray terrazzo floor. Near where he worked, the empty escalator hummed almost silently on its never-ending journey to an unseen upper floor. Piped-in easy-listening music jarred Grace's nerves.

The woman behind the admitting desk watched their approach. She had chin-length dark hair in the grip of a lousy perm, a plump, unlined face, and she wore a pink lab coat with a gray plastic nameplate pinned to one shoulder. Liz Barnes, receptionist, it read. A large clock affixed to the gray-painted wall above her head blinked the time: 3:25 A.M.

The receptionist looked as if she meant to greet them, but the cop carrying Jessica forestalled her.

"I'm a police officer. We have a diabetic emergency here." His words were crisp, cold, authoritative.

"Oh. Just a minute." With a frowning glance at Jessica, who lay as if dead in his arms, the woman lifted the receiver from the telephone on her desk, pressed a button, and spoke in a quick, low voice into the mouthpiece.

"Someone will be right with you." Her words were addressed to the cop as she put the receiver down.

She had barely finished speaking when the gray double doors to the left of the desk swung open. A nurse came out, clearly identified as Mary Morris, R.N. by the name tag on her white lab coat. Short straight gray hair, no makeup, a little hippy in her white uniform pants and smock, was Grace's quick first impression as she joined them.

"She's diabetic?" Placing her fingers on the pulse point beneath Jessica's left ear, Ms. Morris addressed the question to the cop. "Type I?"

"Yes," Grace answered, moving in closer. Her heart was pumping fast, in classic fight or flight response, she supposed. It was all she could do to keep her voice even. She put one hand protectively on Jessica's shoulder. "She's been drinking, but I don't know how much. I think her blood sugar's way too high, and . . ."

"Did you test it?" Ms. Morris moved a stethoscope over Jessica's chest as she spoke.

Grace took a deep breath and shook her head. "I brought her right in."

Ms. Morris nodded, lifting the stethoscope from Jessica's chest and disengaging it from her own ears. She looked from Grace to the cop and back. "You the parents?"

"I'm her mother."

The cop shook his head. "I'm a Franklin County police officer."

"Bring her on back." Ms. Morris turned and headed back through the double doors, gesturing to the cop to follow, which he did. Grace was right behind him.

"Ma'am, excuse me, ma'am, if you'll just step over here for a second to give us the information we need . . ." The receptionist called after her and smiled apologetically as Grace glanced back. The woman had to be kidding—but of course she wasn't. Arrangements had to be made so the hospital would be paid. "It'll just take a couple of minutes."

Taking a firm grip on her composure, Grace returned to the admitting desk as Jessica was borne into the treatment area through the gray double doors, which swung shut again, closing Grace out.

"It'll just take a moment," the receptionist murmured again, soothingly, as Grace stared at those doors with pain-filled eyes. "I need your insurance card."

Glancing at the computer screen to which the receptionist turned, it occurred to Grace that she didn't have her insurance card, or indeed, anything else, with her. Rubbing her hands over her face, she fought back an urge to scream. It was important, for Jessica and for herself, that she remain calm and in control.

"I don't have my purse with me. Or my insurance card," she confessed. She could barely stand still, so anxious was she to rejoin Jessica. "We should be in the computer. We've been here before."

Five times in the fifteen months since Jessica's diabetes had been diagnosed, to be precise. Six if you counted the visit that brought on the diagnosis, which had been prompted by Jessica's collapse on a bright May day at field hockey practice.

"Name?"

Grace gave the required information as quickly as possible—sure enough, Jessica's name and the required insurance information were in the computer—and signed the necessary forms. Then with the receptionist's blessing she hurried into the treatment area to be reunited with her daughter.

CHAPTER 5

E XCEPT FOR A PAIR OF WOMEN IN WHITE UNI-
forms at the nurse's station and a man in a white lab coat who was
walking rapidly away from her, no one was visible in the treatment
area. A sea of closed white curtains faced Grace whichever way
she looked.

"May I help you?" One of the women—she assumed they
were nurses, but was too far away to read their name tags for
certain identification—looked at Grace inquiringly.

"I'm looking for my daughter. Jessica Hart. She was just
brought in. A man was carrying her."

"Diabetic?"

Grace nodded.

"Treatment Room B." She pointed along the white-cur-
tained corridor. "They just finished checking her."

Like the other cubicles, Treatment Room B was partitioned
off from the corridor by an almost floor-length white curtain
suspended from a metal rod. All Grace could see from the hallway
were about three inches of a pair of men's feet clad in black
leather basketball shoes topped with the slightly frayed hems of a
pair of jeans, and the wheels and steel legs of a hospital bed.

Grace pulled the curtain aside just enough to allow her to

enter. A quick glance found Jessica lying on a white-sheeted mattress, eyes closed. A Band-Aid held a cotton ball to the inside of her right elbow; the sleeve of her blue sweater had been pushed up above the Band-Aid. Her head and upper torso were supported in a semiupright position by the raised head of the bed. A small flat pillow was beneath her head. A gray blanket covered her to her armpits; her arms were pale sticks atop the blanket. Someone had removed the cop's jacket, which had stayed wrapped around her as he had carried her in, and taken off her shoes. The items lay bundled together on a nearby chair.

By the bright light of the overhead fixtures, Jessica looked even more ill than she had in the car. The flush in her cheeks was a bright, hectic red. Her lips were so dry they looked painful.

"A nurse just left. She took your daughter's blood pressure, temperature, and a blood sample. She said someone would be back with the results in a little bit." The cop was standing to the right of the bed, his hands thrust into the front pockets of his faded jeans, his feet in the black basketball shoes planted slightly apart. He wore a green plaid flannel shirt, tucked in. She guessed his age at somewhere around forty years old; the harsh light revealed lines around his eyes and mouth, and there were gray threads in his black hair.

Until he spoke, Grace had barely noticed him. Her attention had been all for Jessica. She met his gaze and saw that he looked disapproving still.

"Thank you." Grace spared him no more than a glance as she walked over to the bed and put a hand on her daughter's forehead. The fruity scent of Jess's breath was detectable even above the antiseptic odor of the hospital and the unmistakable smell of booze. Jessica's body temperature, gauged through her hand, told her nothing, though it seemed normal enough. She was no medical expert, and she felt her daughter's forehead more for something to do than in any real expectation of learning anything from it. Her hand moved from Jessica's forehead to curl around her cold, unresponsive fingers where they lay atop the fuzzy blanket. There was nothing she could do for her daughter now, she knew, except wait for the doctor's verdict. As always, in the face of Jessica's illness, she was helpless.

"Did she say—could the nurse tell if this is something to do with the diabetes, or? . . ." She hated to ask *him,* but there was no one else.

"She didn't say." His reply was terse to the point of outright unfriendliness.

"Oh. Thanks." Grace's knees felt suddenly weak. Stress was getting to her, she thought. Glancing around, she found a gray plastic chair near at hand, scooted it with one foot even closer to the bed, and sank down in it, her hand never leaving Jessica's.

"Did you call her father?"

"No." Her reply fell just this side of being outright curt. This guy's criticism, both overt and implied, was starting to get to her.

"Shouldn't you?"

Grace met his weighing gaze straight on. "Look, her father's in New Mexico. We're divorced. I have custody. He's remarried with a whole new family and, believe me, calling him in the middle of the night over something like this is completely unnecessary. Okay?"

"It's fine with me." His expression, his stance, his words, his tone were, every one of them, downright judgmental. "Doesn't seem to be working out too well for your daughter, though."

Grace's eyes snapped at him. She felt her temper stretch almost to the breaking point—it had been a hard day, after all—but she let go of the anger before it could control her. If the guy was an obnoxious jerk, that was his problem, not hers.

Jessica moved then, her legs shifting and her fingers stirring in Grace's hold. That brought her attention back to where it belonged: on her daughter.

Just looking at her scared Grace to death. Jess was so thin—too thin. It was a rare thing for Jessica to be still, and Grace supposed that it was her daughter's constant motion that had kept her from realizing just how fragile-looking the child had become.

Surely she had not been this frail fifteen months ago.

"Mom?" Jessica's eyes opened. The normally clear blue of her irises looked cloudy and blurred. Her pupils were tiny in the bright light.

"I'm here, Jess." Grace's hand tightened around Jessica's even as she leaned closer to her. Awareness slowly grew in her daughter's eyes as their gazes met. Her pupils enlarged to normal size.

"Mom, I feel so sick." It was a slurred whisper.

"Shh, baby. You're going to be okay. We're at the hospital. Everything's all right. Jess, did you take your insulin?"

"I think so. I . . . don't really remember." Jessica's mouth twisted and her nose wrinkled in a way that Grace knew from long experience meant trouble. Wildly Grace looked around and managed to produce a small, plastic-lined trash can from almost underneath her feet just as Jessica leaned over the edge of the bed to vomit.

"Can I help?" The cop took a step closer, watching with obvious revulsion.

"No."

Minutes later, her stomach emptied, Jessica rolled back against the pillow. The terrible smell emanating from the trash can made Grace's stomach threaten to rebel as well. She ignored the incipient nausea, tying the nearly full plastic bag closed. Standing, she carried the trash can to the hallway, where she handed it to a passing orderly. She washed her hands at the sink, wet a paper towel, and returned to her seat by Jessica, wiping her daughter's face and mouth with tender care.

"Is it the diabetes?" Fear and loathing combined in Jessica's question as Grace smoothed the paper towel over her forehead. Jessica hated her disease.

"At a guess, I'd say so. That, and the amount of alcohol you consumed." Speaking calmly, Grace wadded the paper towel up, and in the absence of a trash can, reached around to discard it on the nearby counter.

"Mom . . ." Jessica looked at her imploringly. Recognizing a lie when one was getting ready to be told to her, Grace shook her head at her daughter.

"You were drinking. You can't drink alcoholic beverages, Jess, you know that." Grace leaned closer, her hand once again finding and curling around her daughter's. Her voice was low, meant for Jessica's ears only, but urgent. Her eyes were intent. "To begin with, you're only fifteen. Drinking at your age is against the law. Even if you were old enough, which you certainly are not, you can't. You're not *ever* going to be able to drink alcohol to excess, just like you can't eat a dozen chocolate dough-nuts or three boxes of Girl Scout cookies at a sitting. You *know* that. You have to eat on schedule, and watch what you eat, and take your insulin. You can't just go wild, Jessica, with alcohol or doughnuts or anything, because you'll make yourself sick. You . . ."

"Oh, God, Mom, don't fuss. You always fuss." Jessica's eyes closed again, and her voice was weary. She tried to tug her hand from Grace's.

Grace broke off in midsentence, then clamped her lips to-gether. Hurt swelled inside her. Her eyes closed as her fingers clung tenaciously to Jessica's. What could she say that would get through to her? If only Jessica would listen! She had to be made to understand. . . .

But this was not the time, or the place, for the discussion she and Jessica needed to have.

When she felt better, they would talk. And more than talk. Guidelines had to be laid down. Consequences had to be im-posed.

Being a mother was a hundred times harder than Grace had ever imagined it would be. The responsibility was enormous, and the rewards were few. Even the endless, boundless love she felt for her daughter was in itself a painful thing.

"You in there?" The other cop, Dominick, stuck his head through the curtain. His voice was loud, inappropriately hearty, and caused Grace's eyes to pop open at once.

Her gaze flew from him to his partner, who was once again

leaning impassively against the wall. For a few moments, she had forgotten he was there. He looked almost pale beneath his tan, much paler than she remembered him being when they had entered the hospital, and she wondered if the sudden gray cast to his skin could be attributed to the harshness of the overhead lighting, or the sight—or smell—of Jessica being sick.

Savagely she hoped it was the latter.

For an instant, their gazes met. Again Grace got the feeling that he was judging her and finding her wanting.

Seeing at a glance that he was indeed in the right place, Dominick came on through the curtain. His size made the small cubicle seem suddenly crowded.

"How's the little girl?" he asked in that same inappropriately hearty voice.

His partner shrugged.

"They're waiting for the results of a blood test," Grace said.

The two cops exchanged glances, then, as if one, looked at Grace. She'd had about enough of those weighing looks, she decided.

"Don't let us keep you," she said politely. "I know you must have things you need to do."

Again the cops exchanged glances.

"Yeah, we oughta be going," Dominick said, and Grace got the impression that he was talking more to his partner than to her.

"You sure there's nothing else you need us for?" This was Mr. Obnoxious. His gaze met hers.

"I'm sure." Grace looked from one to the other. Standing side by side, they shared an obvious resemblance. Both were tall, dark, and disapproving. Were they related? She neither knew, nor cared. Common civility plus a healthy dose of honesty prompted her to add, "Thank you for all you've done. Both of you."

They *had* found Jessica, after all, and she *was* grateful. She just didn't much care for their bedside manner.

"You're welcome." Her thanks must have lacked something in the way of graciousness, because Mr. Obnoxious's acknowledgment was clipped. Dominick nodded, and fixed his partner with a meaningful look. Mr. Obnoxious's shoulders came away from the wall, and he headed toward the curtained exit with Dominick behind him. As an obvious afterthought, just as he was getting ready to exit the cubicle, Mr. Obnoxious added over his shoulder, "If you need a ride home . . ."

"We don't. Thanks." With him and his partner? He had to be kidding. She'd sooner ride with a pair of investigators from the Spanish Inquisition. "There's someone I can call. But thanks."

"You're sure?" Still he hesitated.

"I'm sure."

"We'll be in touch, then."

They left, the curtains fluttering in their wake. Grace was glad to see them go. Ever since the first one had arrived on her doorstep, their poor opinion of her as a mother had been a palpable thing.

She didn't need it. She felt bad enough about her mothering skills on her own.

Grace sighed. Looking back at her daughter, who to all appearances was now truly asleep, she had to ask herself again: where had she gone wrong?

Jessica looked like her. Her face, with its high cheekbones, wide mouth, and—the bane of her existence—long nose with the slight bump in its bridge, was identical enough to Grace's so that casual observers had no trouble determining that they were mother and daughter. Her almond-shaped, thick-lashed blue eyes were Grace's to the life. The pointy chin was her own, though, as was the scattering of freckles across her nose.

With aching fondness, Grace's gaze traced the butterfly pattern they made. Angel kisses, was how Grace had described them not so many years ago to a little girl who had come crying to her mother over what some other little girl had tauntingly called dirty brown spots all over her face.

Jessica had been entranced with the idea of angel kisses. She had gone back to the other girl and told her, smugly, that the brown spots meant she was special, because the angels loved her best of all.

Grace had secretly agreed.

But the face Grace knew better than she knew her own was that of a young woman now. Grace could not kiss all her hurts and make them better. Grace could not spin fairy tales to keep the sometimes harsh realities of life at bay.

She couldn't make the diabetes disappear, or take it on herself. In that regard, all the mother's love in the world did not change a thing.

What she could do was remind herself that the specters of kidney failure and blindness and limb amputations that so terrified her were just that—specters. Grim ghosts of frightening future possibilities that did not have to be.

Jessica had the power to prevent them from becoming reality. Grace couldn't do it for her. Jessica had to do it for herself.

So the question became, *would* Jessica take care of Jessica? Sometimes it seemed that she deliberately went out of her way to do the opposite. Until now, Grace had thought that the incidents that had brought on the various crises Jess had experienced since being diagnosed were the result of youthful carelessness.

Suddenly she wasn't so sure.

For the first time it occurred to Grace to wonder: was defying the restrictions imposed on her by her illness the ultimate act of teenage rebellion against her mother?

Oh, God, she hoped not.

Jessica stirred and her fingers moved trustingly in her mother's hold. Watching her, Grace's throat ached with the pain of unshed tears.

The curtains parted, attracting her attention, distracting her from her daughter and her thoughts. A thin, bespectacled man in a white lab coat entered the cubicle. A stethoscope hung around his neck, and he carried a manila file folder that almost certainly contained Jessica's medical chart.

"Mrs. Hart?"

Grace nodded.

"I'm Dr. Corey. It looks like we have quite a problem here. . . ."

CHAPTER **6**

"YOU OKAY, MAN?" DOMINICK MARINO ASKED,
clapping a hand on his brother's shoulder as they stepped through
the hospital's wide double doors into the blessed freshness of the
night. The moon, small and pale at such a distance, floated high
overhead, veiled by moving wisps of clouds. Tiny stars pocked the
midnight blue of the sky.

"Yeah." It was a brief answer, but the best Tony could manage under the circumstances. The sick nausea that had been
churning in his stomach was only just now beginning to recede.
The crisp breeze felt good against his damp skin, reviving him.
He'd broken into a cold sweat in that treatment room; he couldn't
believe he'd done that, that just being in that damned hospital had
affected him so, but it had.

He'd thought he was over it, by now.

Correction. He had *hoped* he was over it, by now.

He was never going to get over it.

"The mother was a real ball-breaker, wasn't she?" Dominick's hand was on his arm, steering him unobtrusively toward the
parking lot when Tony would have walked blindly off into the
night. He allowed his brother to guide him, concentrating on
getting his body back under control.

"Yeah."

It had been the smell that had done it, he thought, that unforgettable, indescribable hospital smell.

That, or watching the suffering of another sick little girl.

The halogen lights in the half-empty parking lot closest to the emergency room gave off an eery yellow glow. Insects by the dozen fluttered in the vapory illumination.

A small white moth flew directly toward him, targeting him with the precision of a kamikaze bomber. Tony dodged and felt its soft wings brush his cheek.

"Damned bugs," he said, swatting at it and missing. The moth circled back up toward the light.

"You gonna go see the mother tomorrow, or you want me to?" Dominick asked. They had reached the Camaro, and Dom automatically walked around to the driver's side. Ever the big brother, he thought it was his birthright to drive.

Not that Tony minded. Dom had basically pulled him from the darkest pit in hell, sobered him up, kept him alive. Dom could drive if he wanted to.

"I'll do it."

"You sure?"

"Yeah."

They got into the car. Its interior was stuffy, and Tony could still faintly recall the nauseating hospital smell. He didn't know if it was in his mind or on his clothes, but it had to go or he would be sick for sure. He rolled down the window, breathing deeply, inhaling the murky smell of the nearby river and the acrid scent of some fresh-laid asphalt and the lingering gaseous exhaust of an old clunker that had chugged out of the parking lot two rows over.

It didn't matter what the smell was. Raw sewage was better than hospital.

"You okay?" Dominick asked again.

"Yeah," Tony answered, with greater truth this time.

As the car moved out of the parking lot, neither of them noticed the white moth make another dive, this time soaring right through the open window.

For a moment, after that, the shape of a young girl appeared, sitting in the back seat. She was about eleven years old, small and thin, with straight black hair that reached her waist. She wore a frilly white dress, white ankle socks, and black Mary Janes. Her hands were folded primly in her lap.

Her eyes, wide and dark and haunting, were fixed with a kind of sadness on the man in the front passenger seat.

She was there for no more than a pair of seconds before she faded, becoming no more substantial than a shadow in the length of time it took to draw a single breath. Then she disappeared altogether.

Neither man saw her.

Tony took another, ineffectual swat at a small white moth as it flew past his cheek and out the car window, then soared upward into the great dark vastness of the night.

CHAPTER 7

IT WAS APPROXIMATELY FOUR-THIRTY IN THE AF-
ternoon. Grace was so tired she could barely move, so tired it was
an effort to focus on what was, fortunately, her second to last case
of the day. The courtroom was overwarm and smelled of Lemon
Pledge, musty carpet, and stressed-out human beings. The fluorescent lights concealed behind the translucent ceiling overhead
were so bright as to be blinding. The combination did nothing for
her incipient headache.

"My grandma died, see, and I couldn't get to school,
and . . ."

"Just a minute, Mr. Boylan. I fail to see what your grandmother's dying or your inability to get to school has to do with
your stealing a car." Grace's voice was dry as she interrupted the
sixteen-year-old boy who stood before her. He was a big boy,
close to six feet tall and two hundred pounds, she guessed, although it was hard to be certain of his height, at least, from her
elevated seat at the front of the courtroom. He was dressed in an
oversized white T-shirt with a blurry silkscreen of some rock band
on the front of it, baggy jeans, and untied sneakers. His greasy
blond hair hung limply to his shoulders.

My grandma died was the equivalent of the dog ate my homework, excusewise. She had heard that one so many times in her three years on the bench that it held no water with her at all.

Under her stern regard, he licked his lips and cast the lawyer standing at his side, a young black woman named Helia Shisler, a nervous glance.

"Robert was very close to his grandmother—" Ms. Shisler began.

Grace shook her head. "I want to hear it from him. Mr. Boylan? Would you care to explain how your grandmother's death and your inability to get to school are related, and how they forced you to steal a car?"

The kid chewed his lower lip before speaking. "Well, uh, my grandma, she drove me lots of places, and when she died she wasn't there no more and I needed to get to school, see."

The pause as Grace considered the logic of that lasted no longer than a few seconds. There *was* no logic.

"Correct me if I'm wrong, Mr. Boylan, but didn't you steal the car *on a Saturday night*? I wasn't aware that schools were in session then."

"There was a dance," the kid said. His lawyer looked pained.

"It was his stepdaddy's car, Your Honor. It weren't stealing, exactly. He just forgot to ask permission before he took it, and it made his stepdaddy mad, and he called the police. It shouldn't've happened."

Grace looked past the boy to the woman who had risen to her feet just beyond the railing. Heavy-set, bottle-blond, with a ruddy, jowly face, she was perhaps thirty-five. Her black polyester pants and pink flowered blouse were a size too small. The blouse gaped open a little between the buttons securing it above and below her ample bosom, affording Grace a glimpse of a sturdy white bra. She looked worn down, and her eyes were red-rimmed and bloodshot. From crying over her son? Grace wondered, then caught herself. It was just as likely to be from a totally unrelated cause, like allergies, or a need for glasses, or a late night and too much beer.

"You're his mother?" The resemblance between the two was unmistakable.

"Yes, ma'am, I am." The woman's voice was so soft that Grace had to strain to hear. "He's a good boy, Your Honor. He shouldn't've taken Gordon's—my husband's—car, but it wasn't really stealing. Honest it wasn't."

Grace felt an unwelcome stab of sympathy for the woman.

"Any priors?" she asked Herb Pruitt, the prosecuting attorney, brusquely.

"He has one conviction for shoplifting, Your Honor. And he's a habitual truant. Nine days absent so far this school year."

As school had been in session just over a month, that was an impressive total.

"Was it his stepfather's car he stole?"

The prosecutor looked down at his notes. "Yes, Your Honor."

"It wasn't stealing, Your Honor. Gordon lets him drive it sometimes. He was just mad." The mother's voice was pleading. Her eyes beseeched Grace. "Robby's a good boy. He just . . . don't think sometimes."

Ordinarily a parent would not have been allowed to speak out like that in Grace's courtroom. She prided herself on running a tight ship. But as an embattled mother herself, Grace felt an unexpected kinship with the woman. There but for the grace of God went . . .

The thought was unpleasant, and she dismissed it with determination almost as soon as it appeared. There was no comparison between Jessica and this boy.

Yet.

The sneaky little qualifier made its way into her head before Grace could completely close her mind to her own problems. She stifled a sigh.

"All right." Grace fixed the young offender with a gimlet gaze. "Taking a car without the owner's permission is *stealing,* Mr. Boylan, whether the owner is your stepfather or not. I want to make that perfectly clear. Nevertheless, I am going to give you one more chance. *One* more, got that? Under these conditions: You get yourself to school every day, come rain, shine, or the common cold, and you stay out of trouble. Any more shoplifting, car stealing, or the like and you will be taken away from your family and remanded to an institution until you are eighteen. Do we understand each other?"

"Uh-huh." The kid nodded eagerly, looking relieved. His attorney poked him in the ribs with her elbow. "Uh, yes, ma'am. Uh, Your Honor."

"A social worker will call your school every week to make sure you're attending and will report any absence to me. If I see you in this courtroom again, Mr. Boylan, I promise you, you won't like me."

It was a threat she used often. Every time she did, she half-expected a smart-alecky kid to come back with, *I don't like you now,* but so far none ever had.

"Yes, ma'am. Uh, Your Honor," the kid said again, breaking into a wide grin. Grace pursed her lips, wondering if she was being played for a sucker. Once again her gaze went to the mother, who was shedding tears for real now and wiping them away with the backs of her hands.

"Thank you, Your Honor," the mother said. For a moment their gazes met.

Grace nodded. The sense of fellow feeling the woman engendered in her was what had saved the kid from a probably well-deserved punishment. Grace didn't know whether she felt good or bad about her unaccustomed leniency.

At the moment she was too tired to worry about it.

"Case dismissed."

She closed her eyes briefly and rubbed her temples as the Boylan kid and his mother embraced, then left the courtroom, attorneys in tow. Her head hurt. It had been almost seven A.M. by the time they'd gotten home from the emergency room, and she'd been in court since nine, with an hour break for lunch.

"Next case," she said, opening her eyes.

It was an ongoing custody dispute, a particularly ugly one in which the father, a well-to-do dentist, accused his ex-wife, and former hygienist, of being an unfit mother because (he said) she was an alcoholic and entertained a succession of men in their home with their two daughters present. In retaliation, she accused him of being an unfit father because (she said) he physically, emotionally, and sexually abused her and their daughters. Both parties had appeared before her on at least half a dozen occasions, and by this time she believed neither one. Today's installment involved the father's request for lowered child support because, he said, he now had custody of the children more often than was specified in the divorce decree.

She listened to the opposing lawyers' arguments, unimpressed.

"Dr. Allen, I don't find that keeping your children over Super Bowl weekend while your ex-wife was out of town justifies a reduction in child support. I therefore rule in favor of the defendant. Case dismissed." Thank God, she was done for the day.

The dentist spluttered angrily, while his ex-wife looked smug.

"Just a minute, Your Honor." Dr. Allen's attorney, Colin Wilkerson, was better known to her even than his client. In fact, she had made the mistake of dating him for three months in the spring and early summer, before coming to her senses. "May I approach the bench?"

The question was moot, since he was already bearing down on her like a train on a crossing while the courtroom slowly emptied behind him.

"What is it, Mr. Wilkerson?" Grace asked wearily. He was tall, fair, balding, with a long nose and sharp features. She had once thought him handsome, in a William Hurt kind of way. His navy suit, like all his clothes, looked expensive. His blue shirt and tie had no doubt been selected to match his eyes, which at the moment were narrow with anger as they met hers. His fingers twitched at his sides in a compulsive way she had noticed before.

WESTCHESTER PUBLIC LIBRARY
CHESTERTON, IN

"This wouldn't be personal, would it, Your Honor?" he asked, voice soft so that he wouldn't be overheard. His mouth curled into an unpleasant smile. His fingers twitched again.

"What?" She was really, really not in the mood for histrionics at the moment. In a nutshell, that was why she had stopped seeing him. He took nothing lightly. Everything was a matter of life or death to him. Such as where they went for dinner, or what movie they saw, or whether it was the right weather for boating on the Scioto.

Life was too short to have to deal with that kind of personality on a daily basis. It was bad enough to have to deal with it in her courtroom.

"You've ruled against my clients every time I've appeared before you since you stopped seeing me. I don't think it's just coincidence."

Grace regarded him steadily. "It is, Mr. Wilkerson, I assure you."

"I don't believe it. What did I do to make you mad at me, Grace? Was it my ties? My aftershave? The way I drive? Not that I care. All I ask is that you don't take your personal animosity toward me out on my clients."

"You're skirting very close to contempt of court right now, Mr. Wilkerson." Her voice was cold, her eyes hard. What had she been thinking, she asked herself, to get involved with this man, even for so brief a time?

All right, she'd been lonely. But as she had learned, and was still learning, loneliness was sometimes preferable to the alternative.

"Oh, that's right, hide behind your judge's robes. But I'm putting you on notice right now: I'm not going to let you punish my clients because you've got a grievance with me. I'll file a complaint with the Judicial Oversight Board first."

"File a complaint with anyone you please, Mr. Wilkerson. And now I'm putting *you* on notice: If you don't leave my courtroom *right now,* I will cite you with contempt of court, and you will spend the night in jail." She stared coldly at him. His face turned red, then purple. His hands clenched at his sides. For a moment the issue hung in the balance.

Then he swung on his heel and stalked away, pausing only to collect his client before exiting the courtroom.

As the heavy oak door at the rear of the courtroom closed behind them, Grace permitted herself a mental sag.

"Rough day," the bailiff said sympathetically. Walter Dowd was sixty-two, with the wrinkled, jowly face of a basset hound atop the massive build of an NFL linebacker. Grace considered him a good friend.

"Aren't they all." Grace's smile at him was wry as she stood up, eager to reach her chambers and indulge in a much-needed jolt of caffeine. She would allow herself ten minutes to relax. Then she needed to call Chief Mapother of the Bexley Police Department and inquire about the status of their investigation into the intruder in her house the previous night. On the way home she had to stop by the dry cleaners and the grocery. After that came supper and Jess's homework. And sometime tonight, she had to have a serious discussion with her daughter, to which she wasn't looking forward one bit.

All on the approximately three hours' sleep she'd had before discovering that Jessica was missing from the house.

That old saw about a woman's work never being done was certainly right on target in her case. Exhaustion on a daily basis seemed to be her lot.

The door at the back of the courtroom swung open, and a man walked into the now hushed and echoing chamber. Already on his way to lock that same door, Walter stopped in his tracks in the center aisle and looked at the man.

"Court's over for the day." He tended to be protective of Grace, which most of the time she appreciated. His voice was gruff, his stance meant to block the intruder from advancing farther.

"I know that. But I was hoping to catch the judge before she left." He looked over Walter's head at Grace, who still stood on the dais behind the bench. "Got a minute?"

Grace recognized him at once: the cop from the night before. Mr. Obnoxious himself. Grace's eyes narrowed and her lips compressed, but she nodded. To Walter she said, "It's all right. You can let him in. And you can go ahead and lock up and leave. I know you need to get home. He can go out the back with me."

"Thanks, Your Honor." Walter's wife of forty years, Mary Alice, was recuperating from a hip replacement and needed him at home, Grace knew.

As Walter again headed for the courtroom door, the cop walked past him toward Grace, who was stepping down from the bench.

"What can I do for you?" she asked coolly as he came up to her. He was still half a head taller than she was even though she was wearing heels, and as scruffy-looking in jeans and a battered army jacket as he had been the night before. His gaze swept over her. Grace thought with satisfaction that she must present a far different picture in her solemn black judge's robes than she had in her previous incarnation as a frightened, harried mother. A picture more deserving of respect.

"Sorry to keep you late, Your Honor," he said. Grace thought she detected a hint of irony in the honorific, and her frown intensified. But it was impossible to be sure. He continued, "I thought you might want to know under just what circumstances we found your daughter last night."

Grace sighed inwardly. She did want to know, of course. No, correction, she didn't really want to know, but she *needed* to know. Oh, the joys of motherhood.

"Come into my chambers," she said with resignation, and led the way through the door in the wall behind the bench.

CHAPTER **8**

CHAMBERS WAS REALLY NOTHING MORE THAN fancy judicial lingo for an office, and not much of an office at that. The floors were brown-speckled linoleum, the walls ancient plaster painted beige, and the furniture—a desk, three chairs, a credenza, and a pair of glass-fronted bookcases—was all of heavy dark walnut. There was an ancient black leather couch against the wall through which the door opened, a green-shaded pharmacy lamp on her desk, and a framed, faded print of a long-ago foxhunt in shades of brown and red and green on the wall over the couch. Except for the assortment of family pictures and mementos scattered on the shelves of the bookcases, and the photograph of herself and Jessica perched on one corner of her desk, the room was completely impersonal.

"You want a cup of coffee?" Glancing over her shoulder as she spoke, Grace headed directly toward the Mr. Coffee machine on the credenza directly behind her desk. If she didn't ingest caffeine soon, she would die, she thought.

"No. Thanks. You go ahead." Standing just a few steps inside the door, he was looking around the room.

Pouring herself a cup of coffee—the smell alone was to die for—Grace cradled the cup in both hands and then took a sip. God, it was strong, so late in the day! Beginning to revive, she sipped again and turned around to find that he was watching her now, in the same judgmental way that she remembered from the night before. What was with this guy, anyhow, she thought with growing resentment as she sat down in the chair behind her desk, placing the coffee cup on the glass-covered wood surface in front of her. If she was the worst mother he had ever run across, he sure didn't get out much.

She looked up at him. "You know, I don't think I caught your name last night." Her voice was cool, her manner very much that of the person in charge.

"Tony Marino. Detective."

Marino. That was the name of the other police officer, the one who had first told her that Jessica had been found. So they *were* related. Grace wasn't surprised. Their looks and mannerisms were very similar, although this one was the more unpleasant.

A quick tap sounded at the door, distracting them both. He looked around and she looked past him as Nancy Lutz, one of the pool secretaries she shared with the other four Juvenile and Domestic Court judges, appeared in the doorway.

"Need anything before I leave?" Nancy was a slender, attractive blonde of twenty-something with a wide, ready smile, which she turned on in full force after a quick appraisal of Grace's visitor. Recently divorced, she was vocal about her newly restored interest in men.

"No, thanks, Nancy. Good night." From somewhere Grace summoned up an answering, if somewhat dry, smile.

" 'Night, Your Honor." She turned and left, her pert bottom in its snug black skirt swaying with every step, her blond hair swinging saucily about her shoulders. Marino was so obvious about checking her out that Grace's smile vanished. By the time he turned back to her, faintly smiling in lingering appreciation, her mouth was set in a thin, straight line and her eyes were cold.

Pig's the word for you, all right, she thought, taking another sip of her coffee. Of the male chauvinist variety.

The coffee was faintly bitter on her tongue, but welcome nonetheless.

"Mind if I shut the door?" he asked, gesturing toward it.

"Not at all."

He closed the door, then turned back to face her. His army jacket was open. Beneath it he wore another plaid flannel shirt, this one in shades of brown and blue. Five o'clock shadow darkened the lines of a lean jaw and shaded the sides of his cheeks. His black hair was longish on top, short at the sides, and untidy. All in all, she decided, he was good-looking enough to merit Nancy's come-hither sway—if one liked blue-collar types. Personally, she had never been too partial to big, cute, and macho. In her experience, those elements usually added up to stupid. And arrogant. And anti successful, competent women.

"Have a seat." Her tone was not exactly that of someone making an invitation. It was too abrupt for that, and the nod with which she accompanied it was abrupt, too, but he sat in one of the straight-back chairs in front of her desk, leaning forward so that his elbows rested on his thighs. Without Nancy to prompt it, he had lost his smile. His gaze met hers, and suddenly he didn't look any more friendly than she felt.

"You wanted to talk about my daughter," Grace prompted.

He nodded. "For starters, she goes to Hebron, right?"

"Yes." Hebron was the big public high school that was the bright and shining star of the city's educational system. Grace would have preferred a smaller, private school, but Jessica had begged to go there. And Grace, as she usually did where Jess was concerned, had given in.

"You know anything about her friends?" he asked. The question was almost accusing. His tone was the final straw.

"Wait a minute." Grace held up a hand to stop the conversation right there. She fixed him with her judge's stare, perfected over three eventful years on the bench and guaranteed to pin miscreants to the spot like bugs in a collection until she saw fit to release them. "Stop right there. Your attitude ticks me off, Detective. I don't know you from Adam, and you don't know me. Who are you to sit in judgment of how I raise my daughter?"

For a moment he returned her stare without speaking or altering his elbows-on-knees posture by so much as an inch.

"I'm the narc who didn't bust your daughter last night, Your Honor," he said at last in a measured way. Straightening, he reached down into his jacket pocket. "Even though she had just paid twenty bucks for this when we came across her."

He pulled a Baggie from his jacket pocket and held it up so that Grace could see it. The clear plastic bag held a small amount of what appeared to be dried, ground-up grass.

Harmless looking, unless you knew what it was.

Grace knew what it was. She audibly caught her breath. All the vinegar went out of her, just drained right away along with her spine, so that she was left sitting there like a jellyfish, gazing speechlessly at him and the hideous, horrible, terrifying thing that dangled from his hand.

"I see you recognize it." His voice was dry as he restored the Baggie to his pocket. "Top grade Colombian by way of Mexico, by the way."

"Oh, my God," Grace said. She felt as if she'd been socked in the gut by a huge, invisible fist. She could hardly draw breath.

He nodded. "Hebron was more or less clean up until about five years ago. Then somebody figured out that these kids have the resources to buy drugs and started a campaign to penetrate the high school. Bingo! Now Hebron's got a real drug problem, and Dom and I got the job of catching the creeps responsible. I'm hoping your daughter can help us."

"Oh, my God." Grace felt as if she were suffocating. Jessica had bought pot. She was smoking pot. The night before, she'd been drunk. Grace saw all her bright dreams for her daughter wavering like a mirage in her mind's eye. One wrong move and they would vanish. "My God."

His lips tightened and his eyes narrowed as he registered her distress.

"If it'll keep you from hyperventilating, I'll start out by telling you I don't think your daughter's in very deep." His voice was not unsympathetic. "At least, not yet. I've never run across her before the last couple of weeks, and I would have if she was out there regularly."

"How . . ." Grace swallowed, then tried again. "Where did you find her?"

"We were following a car full of kids from Hebron last night. They drove to Brandeis Park, where they met up with a group of kids in another car. We had surveillance set up. Your daughter got out of the first car, walked over to the second. She handed a twenty through the window, got this in return, started to walk back to her group, and passed out cold on the ground midway there. A patrol car cruised by about then, and turned on its lights to go after a speeder. It must have scared the daylights out of everybody because both cars hightailed it out of there, leaving your daughter lying where she fell. One of our cars tailed them. Dom and I checked on your daughter. About the time we put her in our car, her description came over the radio, so we took her home."

"You're sure *she* was the one who bought—that." Her gaze touched on his pocket. Her lawyer's instincts were to search for the loophole, to find a way out for her daughter at all costs. Her mother's instincts were muddier. More on the lines of Jessica needing to take responsibility for what she had done.

"I'm sure."

"Why didn't you arrest her?" Grace was still having trouble talking.

He glanced away from her then, very briefly. Then he looked at her once more. "Like I said, I've never seen her around before. She's new to this group, and they're using her to score. Dom and I aren't out there to bust a bunch of kids, anyway. We want the big guy, the guy who's selling it to the little dealer who's selling it to them. I'm hoping your daughter might be persuaded to help us."

"How could she help you?"

"For starters, she could give us the names of the kids in the cars. A couple we know, the rest we don't. She could tell us who set up the deal. Who she gave the twenty to. Who that person gives the money to, if she knows."

"In other words, you want her to act as an informant."

"We're asking for her help."

"She helps you or you charge her, is that the deal you're trying to make?" Grace remembered the coffee then. Her hand moved to the cup, curled around it. But she couldn't summon up the will to lift the brew to her mouth. She felt numb, as if her body had been shot full of Novocain.

"Nope. Consider last night a freebie. We're not going to charge her. She can help us, or not. But if I were you, I'd think about that 'not.' She doesn't help us, that drug ring's going to stay right where it is, where she is exposed to it constantly. This time, when we caught her, she's not a stoner, not a cokehead or a crackhead, doesn't score smack, is not heavily involved in the drug scene. Next time, whether it's us or someone else, who knows? She could face big-time jail time—or worse."

"I'll take her out of Hebron. . . ." Grace was talking more to herself than him. Her right hand was clenched tight around the cooling coffee cup. Her left hand was clenched into a fist in her lap. .

He shrugged. "If you think that'll help."

"I'll put her in private school, and ground her for the rest of her life, and hire someone to be at home when she gets home, and . . ."

"Watch her every minute of every day?" he finished for her. "Not possible. According to what I read in the police report, she managed to sneak out on you just last night. For the third time in . . . what was it, three months? That you know about."

Silenced, Grace could do no more than look at him. The sheer impossibility of watching Jessica twenty-four hours a day until she was an adult overwhelmed her. It could not be done, not without locking her daughter up in some kind of prison. Anyway, given Jessica's nature, the more restricted she was, the more she could be counted on to rebel the moment she got the chance.

"So just how would helping you help her?" Grace asked finally.

"We'd be able to break up the drug ring that's targeting her school, for one thing. It would help us get rid of the bad guys. And it would put her on notice that she has already come to the attention of the authorities and had better watch her step in future."

Grace stared at him fixedly while she turned the problem over in her mind. In law school, her keen analytic ability had always been touted as one of her strengths, but for a moment, swamped as it was by terror and panic, it threatened to fail her. When it did begin to function, however, one thing became perfectly clear almost at once.

"My daughter would be in danger. If anyone found out that she was helping you, she would be in danger."

His eyes narrowed. "We would protect her. Guaranteed."

Grace laughed. The sound was short, staccato, unamused. "You can't guarantee that she would be protected. You can't watch her twenty-four hours a day for the rest of her life any more than I can. You think I don't know what happens to kids who rat on dealers? Get real. I'm a judge, for God's sake. I've seen it, and it's ugly." She took a deep breath. "No. I thank you for your forbearance in not arresting her last night, but no. She cannot help you. I'm sorry."

There was a pause as he digested this. His gaze as it met hers had grown hard.

"Your call." He stood up and turned to leave. Reaching the door, he glanced at her over his shoulder. "Remember, though, only one freebie per customer."

Then he left. The door closed behind him with an audible click.

CHAPTER **9**

GRACE FELT LIKE A PACKHORSE AS SHE SHOUL-
dered through the back door into the soft creams and yellows of
her kitchen. In one hand she juggled three plastic bags filled with
groceries and her purse. In the other was her briefcase and,
gripped by two fingers, the hanger hooks of the dry cleaning that
was sheathed in slippery plastic bags and draped over her shoulder.
The clothes kept slipping down her arm, impeding her progress as
she leaned more and more to the left to keep them from sliding to
the ground.

"Hi, Aunt Grace!" A piping voice greeted her as she
dropped grocery bags, purse, and briefcase on the white-painted
oval table at which she and Jessica ate most of their meals.
Straightening up with relief, she hung the cleaning on the antique
iron coatrack that stood against the wall just inside the door.

"Hi, Courtney." Rolling her shoulders to ease the cramping
caused by carrying all that weight in such an awkward position,
Grace greeted her niece with a smile as she darted past, a pony-
tailed four-year-old in a pink sweat suit. Then she glanced the
length of the long, narrow, charmingly old-fashioned kitchen to
discover her sister perched on one of the center island bar stools
talking to Pat Marcel, the woman who came in once a week to
clean. "Hi, Jax. Hi, Pat."

" 'Bout time you got home," Jackie said with a smile, breaking off her conversation with Pat, who usually left at four and was thus owed two extra hours' pay. Today Grace had asked Pat to stay until she got home so that Jessica would not be alone in the house. By the time they'd left the hospital that morning, Jess had already been much better, revived by the correct dosage of insulin. But she had stayed home from school under strict orders to sleep.

"Hi, Aunt Grace!" Paul, her six-year-old nephew—tall, thin, sandy-haired, and freckle-faced—skidded past, sliding like an ice skater in his stocking feet on the hardwood floor. He had a hole in the knee of his jeans and a big grin showing off a space where one of his front teeth had been just a few days before.

"Hi, Paul. He lost a tooth," Grace said unnecessarily to her sister. Having retrieved the groceries and her purse, she heaved them onto the island counter, which like all the others in the kitchen was of white ceramic tile. For a moment she abandoned the groceries to Pat's capable hands while she extracted her checkbook and a pen from her purse.

"This morning. It fell out just as we were getting ready to leave the house. You've never heard such a commotion in your life. It bled," Jackie said significantly, reaching into a sack for a white bakery box that revealed half a dozen blueberry muffins through a clear cellophane window. She put the box on the counter, opened it, and helped herself to a muffin. "He's all excited now, though, because the tooth fairy's coming tonight. I hear you had some excitement of your own last night, by the way. Jessica's diabetes act up again?"

Busy writing out Pat's check, Grace nodded. The full story of what had happened was not for Pat's ears. Grace wasn't even sure she would tell her sister. Her first impulse was to keep the embarrassing, terrifying truth strictly between herself and Jessica.

"How is Jess, by the way?" Grace asked Pat as she folded the check and handed it to her. Having just put away the milk and butter, Pat stood in front of the built-in refrigerator, which had been fitted with wood panels to match the cherry cabinets that lined the walls. One of the kitchen's four vintage brass-and-glass lanterns, fitted retroactively for electricity, hung over her head, bathing her in a pool of light.

"She's been real quiet all day, but I think she's doing okay. A friend's upstairs with her now. She brought Jessica's homework over, so I thought it would be all right if she went up." In her mid-fifties, with short dark hair gone to gray, Pat had deep wrinkles between her brows and around her mouth that made her look perpetually worried. When she had first come to work for them, Grace had braced herself every time she had talked to Pat, waiting for the bad news that seemed imminent. It had never come, and Grace had finally realized that the worried frown was the woman's habitual expression.

"That's fine." Just in case the worried look today was for real, Grace set Pat's mind at ease about letting Jessica's friend go upstairs on a day when Jess had missed school. "Thanks for staying. I appreciate it."

"You get any candy at the grocery, Aunt Grace?" Courtney appeared at her elbow, the wide blue eyes that were a family trait looking appealingly up at her. Courtney's hair was blond. Like her brother, aunt, and cousin, she was tall and thin. "Mommy always gets candy when she goes to the grocery. That's why she's so fat."

"No, honey, I didn't," Grace said, placing a consoling hand on Courtney's head, while Jackie swallowed a bite of muffin, grimaced, and said, "Hush your mouth, little girl, before your mommy throws you in the trash can, puts on the lid, and calls the garbage men!"

"No, Mommy!" Courtney ran off with a giggle and a shriek.

"I guess I'll be going, then." Pat retrieved her jacket from the coatrack and pulled it on. "You need me before next week, you call me, Grace."

"I will. 'Bye, Pat. Thanks again."

" 'Bye," Jackie echoed.

Pat waved and went out the door. It closed behind her, but not all the way. Grace frowned at it for a moment, gave up wishing that it would function as it was supposed to, and went to pull it tightly shut. It was an old door, and it had to be slammed in just the right way to get the lock to catch. After last night, she meant to be extra careful about that.

During the course of the day, it had occurred to her that perhaps the intruder had gained entry through the less-than-perfectly latched back door.

"I *am* fat, aren't I?" Jackie sighed as Grace retraced her steps and began putting the remaining groceries away. On the verge of telling her sister about most of the events of the previous night—she would keep the marijuana story to herself, she decided—Grace was sidetracked by the plaintive question.

"You're beautiful." In truth, Jackie was slightly overweight. She was tall, though, and carried it well, well enough so that she could truthfully be described as voluptuous rather than fat. Her light brown hair had been streaked with blond and fell in soft waves to her shoulders. Her face was lovely, with rosy round cheeks, big blue eyes, and a sweet expression. She had been spared the long, bump-in-the-middle family nose. Hers was short and pert above a well-shaped, usually smiling mouth. At twenty-eight, Jackie was the younger sister by eight years. Grace had always felt fiercely protective of her.

"Stan says I'm beginning to look like a sumo wrestler. He says if I keep eating maybe we should just move to Japan and I can have a career and he won't have to work."

Stan was Jackie's husband.

"Stan's an asshole." Grace's whole body prickled with anger at the slight to her sister. She had filled the bread box with a fresh loaf, and now she shut its lid with a snap.

"He's just trying to motivate me to lose weight." Jackie's tone was plaintive.

"He's just trying to make you feel bad so he can feel better. Has he found a job yet?" Stan had been laid off from the Honda plant eight months before. His unemployment benefits had run out a few weeks previously, and it was only then that it seemed to occur to him that he had better start looking for another job. In the meantime, Jackie had been working at a local day-care center to keep food on the table. It didn't pay much, but she could take Courtney with her and Paul could come after school. Even when Stan was not working, he refused to watch the kids. He was always "too busy."

Which, come to think of it, was probably just as well, Grace thought. Her brother-in-law had little patience with his lively offspring.

"He's still looking."

Grace started to say more, then swallowed the words. Jackie didn't want to hear about her loser of a husband. Grace had said it all before, to no avail.

"You staying for supper? We're having chicken, rice, and salad," Grace said instead. Jackie and her brood ate with them two or three times a week, usually when Stan had plans—such as bowling or poker—with his buddies.

Jackie shook her head. "We just stopped in to say hi."

"Mommy! Mommy! Save me!" Courtney came shrieking into the kitchen, diving toward her mother and trying to hide behind her body and the bar stool.

"I'm a garbage man! I'm a garbage man! I'm a garbage man!" Arms flailing wildly, bent almost double, Paul lurched after her.

"Paul Andrew, stop teasing your sister! Courtney, you know he's not a garbage man."

"Yes, he is! Mommy, you said you were going to call the garbage man on me for saying you were fat, and that's him!"

"I'm a garbage man! I'm a garbage man! I'm a . . ."

"All right, stop it!" Jackie yelled. "If you two don't go somewhere and play quietly for five minutes, I'll . . ."

She didn't have to finish the threat. Having driven their

mother to what was obviously the edge of losing her temper, the children scuttled off.

"Sorry I yelled," Jackie said, looking sheepishly at Grace when they were gone.

"I don't blame you," Grace said with perfect truth. She loved her niece and nephew, but at times they could be—and this was an understatement—a little loud.

"You never yell at Jessica, do you?" Jackie's voice was rueful. "You're so good at everything, Grace. You're a *judge,* for goodness sake, and a great mother, and you're thin and . . ."

"What's wrong, Jax?" Grace's voice was quiet. She had known her sister a long time—all Jackie's life, in fact—and she could tell when she was upset. Jackie's eyes flickered away tellingly at the question, but she shook her head.

"Nothing. I'm fine. Sometimes it's just hard to have a perfect sister."

"Oh, can it. Now what's wrong?" Grace paused in the act of filling a pot with water for the rice and stared hard at her sister. "Are you short of money? Do you need a loan?"

For a moment, Jackie didn't reply. She was seated on the opposite side of the center island from where Grace stood at the sink, her upper arms resting on the tile surface in front of her, the half eaten muffin—untouched since Courtney had called her fat—beside her left elbow. Her eyes were troubled as they met Grace's.

"I hate to ask."

"Sweetie, you're my sister. If you need money, ask. How much?"

Jackie named a sum, her voice low and shamed. "It's for the electric bill. If we don't pay it by tomorrow, they'll shut us off. And I don't get paid until Friday."

"It's not a problem." The checkbook and pen were still on the counter. Grace turned off the tap, dried her hands on a paper towel and wrote out a check, which she slid across the tile.

"Thanks, Gracie." Looking subdued, Jackie picked up the

check. Still, she tried for a light tone as she pocketed it. "If I ever get richer than you, which isn't going to happen, you can come to me any time for a loan."

Grace laughed, keeping it light, too, but aching inside for her sister. "I'll keep that in mind."

"Mommy! Mommy!"

"Run, Courtney! *Jessica's* the garbage man! She's going to get you!"

"Oh, for . . . Mom!"

Courtney appeared first, shrieking as she darted toward her mother. Paul was right behind her, grinning from ear to ear as his socks skidded over the floor. Jessica and her friend were last, both wearing identical disgusted expressions. Grace was relieved to see that her daughter looked completely recovered. Her color was normal, and her skin and lips no longer appeared overdry.

"Jessie's after me, Mommy!"

"I told you, *she's* the garbage man now! She's gonna get you!"

"They were playing with my *computer,* Mom." Jessica and her friend, both tall and lanky in faded jeans and cropped sweaters, crossed to the refrigerator. Jess glanced at her aunt over her shoulder. "Hi, Aunt Jackie."

"Hi, Jess. I'm glad you're feeling better. Okay, kids, that's it. We're going home." Jackie stood up. Jessica opened the refrigerator door. Both she and her friend regarded the interior intently.

"No! No! Come on, Mom, we were just playing!"

"Mommy, no!"

"I'm fixing supper right now," Grace said to Jessica, hoping to forestall snacking. To Jessica's friend she added, "Hello, Allison. Jess, aren't you going to introduce your friend to your aunt and cousins?"

"Oh, yeah. Aunt Jackie, Allison. The brats are Paul and Courtney."

As an introduction, it left a lot to be desired, but Grace had learned long ago not to sweat the small stuff.

"We are not brats!" This was Paul.

"Oh, yeah?" Jessica extracted something from the refrigerator and closed the door. Automatically, Grace checked out the item in her daughter's hand: a can of Diet Pepsi. Fine.

"Yeah!" Courtney said.

"Monsters, then."

"Jessica!" Grace reproved, as the little ones responded with loud protests. Removing the saucepan from the sink where it had been waiting, filled, while she wrote out Jackie's check, she set it on the stove and turned the burner on high. The great thing about chicken and rice was, it was quick. It was important that Jessica eat on time.

"Nice to meet you, Allison," Jackie said pleasantly as she herded her still-bellowing tribe toward the door. "Thanks, Big Sister. Love ya. You too, Jess."

" 'Bye, Jax. Love you, too. 'Bye, Courtney. 'Bye, Paul."

" 'Bye, Aunt Jackie. 'Bye, brats." This was Jessica, of course.

Jackie waved one last time, and the door shut behind her. Grace put two chicken breasts on the broiling pan, slid the pan in the oven, and shut the oven door. Then she added rice to the boiling water.

"Boy, are they loud." Jessica's comment was heartfelt. She sat on the bar stool vacated by Jackie, swigging Diet Pepsi from the can. "I don't see how Aunt Jackie stands it."

"You were loud, too, once upon a time, my child. And use a glass."

"Was not." Jessica ignored the glass that Grace slid across the counter to her, swigging from the can once more.

"Trust me, dear, you were. And *use a glass.*"

Jessica grudgingly splashed soda pop in the glass and drank. Allison perched on the bar stool beside Jessica, munching on an apple. Her hair was black and wavy, with neon-green stripes woven amongst the shoulder-length strands. She was a pretty girl, with olive skin and dark eyes, but her makeup was, in Grace's opinion at least, not far short of hideous. Sky-blue shadow so thick it looked clownish covered her lids clear to her eyebrows, and her lashes had been transformed by mascara into lethal-looking spikes. Black lipstick adorned her mouth. Next to her, barefaced Jessica with the single hot-pink streak in her hair appeared positively wholesome.

Allison was one of Jessica's new friends. Grace had met her perhaps three times previously and didn't feel that she knew her well at all. Had she been one of the kids in those two cars last night?

"It was nice of you to bring Jessica's homework to her, Allison," Grace said pleasantly, removing a bowl from an upper cabinet and then turning to the refrigerator for the salad fixings.

Allison shrugged. "I was coming over anyway."

"You're a freshman too, aren't you? Do you and Jess have many classes together?"

Allison shrugged again.

"English," Jessica said, looking hard at her mother. "Algebra. Choir."

A horn honked in the driveway.

"That'll be for me," Allison said, popping off the bar stool with a bright-eyed look of expectation and heading for the door. The apple core was abandoned on the counter. "See you at school tomorrow, Jessica. 'Bye, Mrs. Hart."

Grace followed her to the door, ostensibly to close it properly but more important to observe the car, and driver, that picked Allison up. Probably it would be one of her parents. She always liked to meet Jessica's friends' parents. Once you were acquainted with the parents, she thought, it was much easier to understand the child.

The driver was not a parent. An ancient-looking black jeep with a teenage boy at the wheel reversed down the driveway into the street, then peeled rubber as it shot away.

Grace closed the door properly, then came back to the cooking island and her daughter. Jess had taken over making the salad. Her slender hands efficiently tore iceberg and romaine lettuce and spinach leaves into bite-sized pieces.

She watched her daughter reflectively, only to find herself the recipient of a daunting frown when Jessica glanced up.

"God, Mom," Jessica said. "Did you have to give Allison the third degree?"

For a moment, caught by surprise, Grace was left with nothing to say. Then her jaw tightened, and she fixed her daughter with a stern look.

"Jessica," she said, "we need to talk."

CHAPTER **10**

LATE THAT NIGHT, AFTER JESSICA WAS ASLEEP, Grace crept into her daughter's room, moving quietly so as not to awaken her. The bedroom light was off, but the hall fixture was on, just as it had been the night before. The vee of light cut directly to Jessica's bed. Grace followed it and stood for a moment looking down at her daughter. Jess slept with her arms clutching her pillow and her body curved into a tight *S* shape beneath the bedcoverings. Her hair was swept back into a single braid and tied with a blue ribbon, leaving the gentle curve of her cheek and the clean line of her jaw and throat exposed. Her nightgown, of ankle-length white nylon with tiny blue polka dots and ruffles on the bodice and sleeves, was her favorite. In it she looked like a little girl again, sweetly vulnerable. Except for the soft hiss of her breathing and the continuous whir of Godzilla on his exercise wheel, the room, like the rest of the house, was silent.

The emergency room doctor had confirmed what Grace had suspected: Jessica was not taking her insulin on schedule, was not eating as she should. That, coupled with the drunkenness and the pot, had spurred Grace to action. She was the parent, and this was her child. She had to take control.

There were tear stains on Jessica's cheeks. The faint silvery tracks were only visible when Grace leaned down to pull the blankets closer about Jessica's shoulders. The sight of them stabbed Grace clear through to the heart. She ached with the need to wrap her arms around her daughter and hold her tight, to promise her that everything would be all right and reassure her that Mommy loved her still.

But she couldn't. This time, under this provocation, she had to hang tough. The disciplinary measures she had imposed had to stand. She could not weaken.

For Jessica's sake.

Grace's mouth quirked wryly. For Jessica's sake: was that not the story of her life?

A glance around the room assured her that all was well. The curtains were drawn. The door to the connecting bathroom was closed. Jessica's backpack waited beside the bed, unzipped but loaded with binders and books for the morning. Her sneakers had been placed near the backpack; of course, on Wednesdays she had gym.

Nothing was out of place, nothing was extraordinary at all. Yet something did not feel quite right.

Grace couldn't put her finger on what it was.

Her gaze swept the room more slowly. Computer off, backpack ready, shoes out. Godzilla busy in his exercise wheel. Alarm clock set: from where she stood, Grace could see the glowing red button that meant it had been turned on.

Her gaze lit on Mr. Bear, plump bottom planted as always on the bedside table next to the clock. In the place of honor, where he could look out for Jessica as she slept. The hall light just touched him, glinting off his shiny black eyes so that they seemed almost alive in the dark.

Grace shivered. Then she realized that of course Pat had taken him from the living room couch and returned him to his usual spot. Nothing strange or sinister about that.

She realized, too, what felt wrong about Jessica's room. The night before, it had been invaded. *A stranger had walked across the carpet, touched her daughter's belongings, left his imprint in the air.* He—or she—had stolen nothing. Nothing but Jessica's beloved teddy bear, which had been dropped like trash beside the road.

Although Grace seemed to be the only one who was prepared to believe that this was what had happened.

The police had found no evidence of a break-in, they'd said when she had called them before coming home. Officer Gelinsky, and then his superior, had listened to her patiently, but it had been obvious that they weren't going to pursue a crime that they didn't even believe had taken place, especially when the only thing that she alleged had been stolen was a teddy bear— which had been recovered.

Grace had not told Jessica about the intruder. There was no point in frightening her for no real reason, after all. Instead, she had mentioned finding Mr. Bear outside and asked Jess if she had carried him out or knew how he had gotten there. Jessica had professed no knowledge of Mr. Bear's nighttime ramblings. He had been sitting where he always did when she left the house, she said.

So the facts behind Mr. Bear's journey remained unclear. Grace had already reconciled herself to the notion that they were likely to remain so. No one—except herself—seemed particularly concerned; no harm had been done, after all.

But Grace looked at Mr. Bear now and felt uneasy. Moving on impulse, she rounded the bed and picked him up from his customary spot. He felt soft and furry and squishy in her hand, just as he always did. How many times, over the course of Jessica's life, had she picked him up? Grace wondered. The number had to be in the thousands.

His black eyes shone up at her through the darkness. Staring down at him, Grace gave an involuntary shiver, then chided herself for her idiocy. Still, she took him with her as she left the room and tucked him high up on the top shelf of her own closet before she went to bed.

She had the strangest feeling that Mr. Bear was not the same as he had been before. That he had been changed, no, *tainted* by the touch of something—someone—evil.

It was a long time before she finally fell asleep.

CHAPTER 11

CAROLINE HAD BLACK HAIR, BLUE EYES, A PAIR of dimples that twinkled like stars on a cloudy night, and a killer body. In short, she was *hot*. He looked at his brother's girlfriend sitting on the couch with her bare legs tucked beneath her cheerleader's miniskirt and felt himself harden to the point of painfulness. It was all he could do not to look down at the front of his jeans to see if she could *see*. How humiliating if she could!

She was giggling at some stupid sitcom playing on the big-screen TV that was the focal point of the living room. One hand was clapped to her mouth and she rocked slightly back and forth, shoulders shaking with laughter.

She looked good enough to eat. He *wanted* to eat her, to gobble her up like his favorite rice pudding.

"Yo, bro, you want me to bring you something back? I can stop by Mickey Dee's on the way home." Donny breezed into the room, fresh from a shower, his blond hair still damp, his skin glowing from the force of the water. Donny was tall, a good four inches taller than he was himself, and built like the athlete he was. It was ten-thirty at night, Donny had just finished basketball practice—Caroline had watched and cheered—and he had come home to shower before taking her home.

It didn't take a genius to figure out why Donny thought he needed to take a shower just to drive his girlfriend home.

The pictures his mind conjured up out of that just made him get harder.

"Uh . . ." he began, but before he could formulate an answer—admittedly it was taking longer than usual because Caroline had stood up, and the upward movement of her body had caused her breasts to thrust against her sweater—his mother butted in.

"Your brother's had supper. He doesn't need anything else to eat," she said to Donny. At this reference to his weight in front of Caroline, he felt his body go cold all over. His burgeoning penis deflated like a stuck balloon.

"Geez, Mom," Donny said. His brother's blue eyes met his, and he could read the compassion there. God, he hated Donny when he felt sorry for him. He hated everybody who felt sorry for him. And everybody did. Except his mom. And her he hated most of all.

"Go on and take Caroline home," his mother said to Donny, standing up. She hadn't undressed for bed yet because she had expected Donny to bring Caroline back to the house. Donny always did after basketball practice. The nylon sweatsuit she'd put on after work was white with a big pink stripe across the front of the zip-up jacket. In it she looked like the Goodyear Blimp. A real ugly Goodyear Blimp.

He often wondered if she made such a big deal over his weight because he looked so much like her.

Ugly as trolls, both of them. She said it herself, all the time.

"Okay, then," Donny said.

"Night," Caroline said to his mother. She walked to Donny's side, and he put his arm around her. Then she looked past Donny's shoulder straight at *him* and smiled so that her dimples danced. "Night, Little Brother."

That's all he was to her, Donny's little brother. Although she was in his class, a junior, not a senior like Donny. Although he had loved her from eighth grade on. Although Donny treated her like an accessory, something to hang on his arm, while he—he would treat her like a queen if she would just give him the chance.

She only had eyes for Donny, though. Just like everybody else.

"Night, Caroline," he said hoarsely, and watched her leave the house with his golden brother's arm around her slender waist. He stared into the dark front hall until he heard the slam of the car doors and then the sound of the car starting and reversing down the driveway toward the street.

Only then did he recollect himself and glance around. His mother was watching him from her seat in the recliner, a knowing gleam in her eyes.

She knew, he realized in a panic. She knew how he felt about Caroline.

"If you'd lose some weight, and do something about your skin—have you tried one of those benzoyl peroxide creams? I hear they work real well—you might be able to get your own girlfriend instead of ogling after your brother's," she said.

"You're nuttier than a Snickers bar," he told her, and stood up. He hadn't meant to go out tonight, but he was suddenly claustrophobic. In his mother's presence, in Donny's wake, in Caroline's afterglow, he couldn't breathe.

"You're not going out," she said, standing too. She knew him well, well enough to anticipate what he intended without him having to spell it out for her. "It's a school night."

"What difference does it make? I won't make the honor roll whether I get enough sleep or not. You know it, I know it. I'm not like Donny."

"No," she said sadly, "you're not like Donny."

That was it. The final straw. The nail in his coffin. The epitaph one day, without a doubt, on his grave.

You're not like Donny.

He turned away from his mother, ignoring her bitching, and walked out of the house, slamming the door behind him to cut off the sound of her voice.

Outside, he stopped in front of the garage and just stood for

a minute, trying to calm himself, to chill out. It was cooler tonight, and darker, with a thick canopy of clouds rolling across the
sky, and the moon and stars peeping out now and then, like they
were shy.

The dark wrapped itself around him like comforting arms,
enfolding him into the bosom of the night. Gradually the painful
knot inside of him loosened, and he could breathe.

Then he turned and walked into the garage. When he
emerged, he was feeling better, energized by the power of the
engine between his legs.

He, not Donny, owned the night.

CHAPTER 12

THE PRIVET HEDGE MADE AN EFFECTIVE SCREEN, blocking the view of all but the upper story of her house from the street, as Grace realized the next evening seconds after pulling through the open iron gates into her driveway. She hit the brakes of her gray Volvo sedan almost at once. Another car, a black Honda Accord, was already parked halfway up the drive. Beyond it, an unlikely pair were playing basketball in front of the garage, which was connected to the house by a covered walkway—Jessica and Tony Marino, the cop.

It was a sunny evening, windy and warm, with a good two hours of daylight left. Golden oak and beech and elm leaves floated lazily earthward all around. A trio of burning bushes on the left side of the double garage blazed crimson. Acorns and buckeyes littered the ground. The smell of grilling meat and charcoal wafted through the open window of Grace's car; one of the neighbors must be enjoying a late-season cookout.

They were playing one-on-one. As Grace watched, Jessica, her long hair flying, her too-long jeans puddling dangerously around her sneakers, dribbled around Marino, whirled, and made a layup. Her waist-length yellow sweater went up with her arms, baring her midriff. Grace was struck again by how very thin she was.

"Yes! Two points!" Jess pumped her fist in the air in a trademark gesture that brought a faint softening to Grace's face. Her daughter was nothing if not competitive. And she loved basketball.

Grace parked behind the Accord, turned off the ignition, and got out.

"Hi, Mom!" Jessica called, barely glancing up. She was guarding her man for all she was worth as he drove toward the basket. He shot, a textbook one-handed jumper—and the ball hit the rim and bounced off. Jessica crowed with triumph.

"She's good." Marino broke off the game by the simple expedient of catching and holding the ball, and turned toward Grace. He was wearing a short-sleeved navy T-shirt and jeans, she saw, with the same black basketball shoes he'd had on the other night. The casual attire showed off broad shoulders, bronzed, muscular arms, narrow hips, and long legs. His black hair was tousled, and a broad grin revealed even white teeth. Grace registered once again, unwillingly, that he was an attractive man—if one liked the type, which she did not.

"She was on the basketball team in middle school. She's hoping to make it onto Hebron's team this year." If there was a slightly sour note to her voice, Grace couldn't help it. What did he want? was the question. The obvious answer was: nothing good.

Briefcase and purse in hand, clad in her standard work attire of a knee-length skirted suit—today it was charcoal gray—a white blouse, and heels, Grace walked unsmilingly toward the other two. It was five-thirty, she'd had a long day, and she was tired. She did *not* feel like dealing with Tony Marino.

"What are you doing here?" she asked ungraciously as she reached him.

"I came by for my jacket. I'm assuming you have it. I left it at the hospital the other night." His smile was engaging. His brown eyes were all warm and twinkly as they met hers.

"Oh, yes, I do." As a matter of fact, she did have his jacket, the leather bomber jacket he'd given her to wrap around Jessica on the ride to the hospital. It was hanging in the front hall closet.

She'd put it there upon arriving home from the hospital and forgotten about it until now. But she mistrusted that smile, with its accompanying twinkle. He wanted something besides his jacket. She would bet the mortgage payment on it. "Let me change my clothes and I'll bring it out to you."

"Thanks," he said. Jessica reached in just then, whooping as she succeeded in knocking the ball from his hands, and the play resumed. Grace walked into the house to the beat of a basketball bouncing over pavement, with accompanying yells and the sound of pounding feet.

Usually she entered through the kitchen door, which was accessed via the passage that opened off the garage. Today, since she couldn't pull her car into the garage due to the basketball game in progress, she went through the front, picking up the mail as she went. Pat, whom she had asked to come in for the after-school hours only, looked surprised as she entered the kitchen.

"I didn't hear you come in."

"It's all the noise." It was a dry reference to the now slightly muffled sounds of the ongoing game.

"Is Jessica okay out there?" Pat sounded slightly anxious. As always, she looked worried. "A couple of her friends came by, but I told them she was grounded so they left. Then she went out on the porch to do her homework on the swing. I thought that would be all right, since it's such a beautiful day—but the next thing I knew that man was here, and they were playing basketball. I didn't know whether to call her inside or not. I stayed out on the porch for a while and watched them, but she seemed okay with him. If he'd been a kid I would have called her in or sent him away, but . . ."

"That's fine, Pat. He's a . . . friend." Busy writing out Pat's check, Grace hesitated only slightly over the lie. What could she say, that he was a cop who had fortunately chosen not to bust Jessica for drug possession? Not possibly. Pat also worked for several other local families, and that story would flash around Bexley with the speed of a grass fire.

"You've got some messages," Pat said, accepting the check

that Grace passed over. She pulled a piece of paper from beneath the magnet that held it to the refrigerator and looked down at it. "Let's see, there were three. Mrs. Gillespie called to tell you that basketball tryouts have been moved to next Saturday at nine. Ruth Ann called to see if you want to start walking in the evenings again. And your ex-husband called. He didn't say what he wanted, but he talked to Jessica. All the numbers are written down here. And there were a couple of hang-ups."

"Thanks, Pat." Grace took the paper, glanced down at it, and set it on the counter. So Craig had called to talk to Jessica, had he? She wondered what about. Jessica wasn't scheduled to visit him again until Thanksgiving break. "Did you think of anyone for me?"

Not wanting to leave Jessica home alone after school in future, Grace had asked Pat if she knew of anyone who might be available to work from three until six or six-thirty on weekdays.

Pat shook her head. "But I'll keep thinking."

"Thanks." Grace smiled. "And thanks for coming. I'm just going to run upstairs and change clothes."

"Have a good night." Pat waved and started for the back door as Grace headed for the stairs. Seeing which way the woman was going, Grace called over her shoulder: "I'd go out the front if I were you. Otherwise you're liable to get beaned by a stray basketball."

"Good advice." Pat changed directions with a chuckle. Grace headed up the stairs. Her room was directly opposite Jessica's, overlooking the spacious backyard. It was decorated in restful shades of green, with a rose-and-green bedspread covering the queen-size bed and celery-striped curtains with sheers beneath shading the windows. A white-tiled bathroom and a walk-in closet completed the bedroom suite. The first thing Grace had done upon buying the house six years before was reconfigure the upstairs, reducing four bedrooms to three, one of which now served as Grace's study, and providing herself and Jessica with abundant closet space and a private bathroom each.

That was when she had still been making pots of money as a

hotshot young attorney with Madison, Graham and Loew, the city's premier law firm. She'd had the world by the tail then, or thought she'd had, she reflected with a wry smile as she took off her work clothes and hung them in her closet. Jessica had been an adorable nine-year-old who still thought her mommy was perfect. She herself had been well over the trauma of her divorce, and Jessica seemed to be handling it just fine. She'd been so *proud* of herself, then, for making it through law school and getting hired by such a great law firm and doing so well in her chosen profession and being able to provide such a good life for Jessica.

At the time, she'd been sure that, if she was only prepared to work hard enough, she could have it all.

Now she knew better. Now she knew that life was a series of trade-offs. At the law firm, she had been expected to work all the hours God sent. After school, Jessica had gone to day care until Grace could pick her up. There had been babysitters at home at night. There had been plays Grace had missed, field trips she hadn't gone on, homework supervised by someone other than herself. She loved her daughter, always, and she knew Jess knew it, but she hadn't been there lots of times when Jessica had needed her. Little by little, they'd become, not distant, exactly, but separate people. Jessica stopped confiding everything in her mother, stopped expecting her to be there, stopped even wanting her to be. And that was the worst thing of all. By the time Grace realized the enormity of what was happening to them, Jessica was twelve. The catalyst for change had been the afternoon that Jess and a group of friends were caught, during school hours, shoplifting at Eastland Mall.

Grace hadn't known Jessica wasn't at school that day. She hadn't known Jessica had started hanging out at the mall every chance she got. She hadn't even known the names of the friends Jessica was with when she was caught.

And she realized that she should have known. All those things.

After that wake-up call, she started looking around for a job where the hours were sane. A job where she could come home every night at the same time, and fix supper, and supervise homework, and in general be there for her daughter. A job that was more family friendly than the one she had.

Then Thomas Pierce died unexpectedly, and his position as a Juvenile and Domestic Court judge was left vacant. With the help of her boss and mentor at the law firm, George Loew, she had been appointed to fill the remaining five years of Pierce's term. That had been three years ago. The position had seemed ideal at the time, from Grace's perspective. She wouldn't even need to run for reelection when her term was up, she'd thought, because Jessica would be seventeen then. Grace could, if she chose, return to Madison, Graham and Loew, and her lucrative career, her duty to her daughter largely done.

Only nothing had worked out as she had imagined it would.

Pulling on a pair of slim khaki trousers, Grace sighed. When did life ever work out the way it was supposed to? She yanked a white T-shirt over her head, tucked it in, and slipped on a navy cotton cardigan sweater, which she left unbuttoned. Thrusting her bare feet into a pair of loafers, she headed back downstairs.

Thanks to her reduced work schedule, she and Jessica had regained some of that wonderful closeness they'd shared when Jess had been little. Then everything had happened at once: Jessica had become a teenager, she had been diagnosed with diabetes, and her father and his new wife had had twins down in New Mexico. Any of those events by itself would have been enough to send a sensitive child careering out of control. All three together were practically guaranteed to. Grace had tried reasoning with Jessica, talking to her, pleading with her, bribing her. Now, in the face of this latest catastrophe, she was applying tough love. If that didn't work, she didn't know what she would do.

Sometimes it seemed to Grace that she was living with a hormone-driven, teenage version of Dr. Jekyll and Mr. Hyde. One minute Jessica was her familiar sweet self, and the next she was a monster. Over the last few weeks, since Jessica had started high school, Grace had felt as if they were more adversaries than anything else. Basically, Jess told her nothing and blamed her for everything.

Grace sighed again. Motherhood was the hardest job in the world.

Jess and Tony Marino were in the kitchen. They glanced up in unison as she entered. He at least had the grace to look faintly guilty for being there.

"Your daughter was kind enough to offer me a glass of water." Standing by the sink, one hip resting against the counter, he held up the glass he'd been drinking from as proof. He was sweaty, his hair curling slightly, his skin shiny with a faint moist sheen.

"I'm going up to take a shower," Jessica announced, swallowing the last drops in her own glass and setting it down on the counter. She looked at her mother. "Have you see Mr. Bear, by the way? He's not on my nightstand."

"I took him to the cleaners. There was something yucky on his fur," Grace lied. She didn't want to admit the truth—that Mr. Bear was hidden away in her closet because she felt he had somehow become tainted with evil. For one thing, it sounded ridiculous. Besides, there was no point in frightening Jessica.

"Oh." Jessica accepted that without difficulty and smiled saucily at Marino.

"You're pretty good, for an old man."

"So are you," he said, "for a little girl. Maybe next time you'll beat me."

"Maybe nothing. I *will*."

Grace thought with pride, there's my confident girl. Then Jessica's gaze switched to her mother again. "We need to eat soon. I have to be over at Maddie's at seven."

"Darling, you're grounded, remember?"

Jessica was already heading for the door. She stopped, turning, her eyes widening on her mother's face.

"But I have to go! Talent show tryouts are Friday after

school, and we have to practice our act! We're going to do a dance routine!"

" 'Fraid not, sweetie pie."

"I *have* to go!" Jessica's voice grew shrill. Her eyes were as big as quarters in her whitening face. Her hands clenched into fists at her sides. "I promised Maddie and Becca and Allison and Jenna I'd be there. We're going to be the Spice Girls! If I'm not there, it'll ruin it! We need *five*!"

"I'm sorry about that, but you can't go."

"I *have* to. I promised them. They'll get somebody else if I don't show! Mom, please!"

"No."

"Mom! . . ." It was a wail.

"We'll talk about this later, Jessica," Grace said in a low, even voice, acutely conscious of Marino leaning against the counter watching every gesture and listening to every word.

"No! There's nothing to talk about! I'm going over to Maddie's at seven! I don't care if I'm grounded! Being grounded is stupid! What good does it do? Do you think it will keep me from doing anything I feel like doing? I'll drink beer if I want, and I'll smoke pot if I want, and I'll go out with my friends in the middle of the night if I want! And you can't stop me!"

"Jessica Lee Hart, that's enough!"

"You can't! You can't!"

"Watch me," Grace said through her teeth, patience lost, her eyes snapping as they met Jessica's turbulent gaze. "For starters, young lady, you can go to your room. Right now."

"I hate you!" With a sob, Jessica whirled and fled. Eyes closing, Grace listened to her feet pounding up the stairs and then running along the hall. Seconds later the slam of a door reverberated in the air.

It was a moment before Grace had recovered enough to turn and look at Marino. He was studiously watching something through the window over the stove, his face in profile to her, his expression as innocent as if he hadn't witnessed anything so agonizingly personal as a quarrel between mother and daughter. He must have felt her gaze, because he turned to meet it.

"Grounded her, did you?" he asked. "Think that's going to work?"

"That's my problem, and my business," she said bitingly, walking toward the front hall. In the few minutes she was out of his sight, she retrieved his jacket from the closet.

"Here," she said, returning to the kitchen and thrusting it at him. She knew she was being ungracious, knew this latest upset was not his fault, knew that nothing that had happened was his fault, but still she was furious at him. Because of the way he looked at her—as if he judged her mothering skills and found them wanting. Again.

Because maybe the truth was that they were wanting.

"Thanks," he said, accepting his jacket.

"So why did you really come?" she asked, striving for a measure of calm. Her gaze challenged him.

"I told you. For this." His glance indicated his jacket, which was now draped over his left forearm.

"Bullshit."

He smiled a little, as if amused by her bluntness, and shrugged. "All right. To check on your daughter, to see if she was doing okay. And to see if you'd changed your mind. About her helping us."

"The truth comes out." Grace had known it. "No, Detective Marino, I have not. I will not. It's too dangerous. I'd appreciate it if you would just leave her alone, please."

"You're not going to be able to keep her away from her friends forever, you know."

"Like I said before, that's my problem."

"Yeah, I guess it is." Reaching into the back pocket of his jeans, he came up with his wallet, which he opened. Extracting a business card from it, he handed it to her.

"What's this for?" she asked, accepting it and looking at it with suspicion.

"If you change your mind, my pager number's on this. All you—or she—have to do is call."

"I won't change my mind."

For a moment their gazes locked.

"That's up to you," he said, heading for the front hall. Just before he walked out of the kitchen, he looked over his shoulder at her.

"Good luck with the grounding. For your daughter's sake, I hope it works."

His tone told her he doubted it would. Grace was left to grit her teeth and glare after him as he disappeared into the front hall. A moment later, the sound of the door opening and closing told her he had left.

Grace stood where she was for a moment, taking a deep breath, trying to get her emotions under control. For a moment she thought about heading upstairs to confront Jessica. But then sanity reasserted itself. The necessary discussion was far better postponed until she was calmer. Until they were both calmer.

She went to lock the front door. Then she returned to the kitchen, stuck Marino's card in her purse, and headed toward the coffeemaker.

What she needed before she did anything else was a strong cup of coffee. Her body cried out for a jolt of caffeine.

CHAPTER 13

W EARING NOTHING BUT A PALE–BLUE NYLON
nightgown, one bare foot tucked beneath her as she sat on the
porch swing, Jessica took a deep drag on her cigarette and immediately felt better. God, she'd needed that. She'd had a real nicotine jones going. She'd just started smoking at the beginning of
the summer and already she loved nicotine, craved it, lived for it
really. With her mom on her case so much these days, plain old
cigarette smoking was getting to be as hard to manage as scoring
dope. Once she was out of school for the day (smoking at school
was *easy,* in the restrooms or out behind the gym, where everyone
went; none of the teachers cared) she had to sneak out of the
house like a criminal for a quick puff whenever she could squeeze
one in. Her mom had the nose of a bloodhound. If she dared to
light up in the house, she'd be caught. And her mom would have
a shit fit. Better to come out here on the porch, like she was doing
right now. It was just after midnight, her mom was asleep upstairs,
and there was nothing in the whole wide world but herself and
the cigarette and the swing on which she sat and the tinkling wind
chimes for mood music and the darkness all around.

The smoke as she drew it in steamed over her tongue, rolled
down her throat, curled into her lungs. For a moment she held it
there, the red tip of her cigarette glowing bright through the

shadows, and then she let it out, practiced blowing it out her nose so that it made cool twin streams of smoke like a dragon exhaling.

Allison had taught her how to do that. Allison could blow smoke rings, fat round circles that floated through the air like ghostly Cheerios. Jessica had tried, but she hadn't quite gotten the knack yet.

Damnit, she was old enough to smoke. She'd been smoking on the porch when that cop had stopped by. He'd seen her, she knew he had, and he'd been cool with it. He hadn't said a word, hadn't told her mom either or she would have heard about it when they had their "little chat" before her mother went to bed. Instead he'd talked to her like one adult to another, said hi, asked her how she was feeling. Then he'd picked up a basketball and started shooting hoops and challenged her to a game—which she'd missed winning by two points. While they'd played, they'd talked like two ordinary people, not about dope or being in trouble but about normal things, like the weather and basketball and her friends.

Not like her mom talked to her: *She was grounded. The police were watching her. She had to be careful. Please, please don't do dope.*

Holy hell. Her mom treated her like a baby. She just couldn't let go. And the diabetes thing had made it worse. She hadn't been able to so much as go to the bathroom without her mom in her face ever since they'd found out she had it.

Did you take your insulin? Did you test your blood? You know you shouldn't eat that. You need to get more exercise. If you don't take care of yourself, you're going to die.

Well, all right, her mom had never actually said that last thing. But she thought it, all the time. Jessica knew that she did.

The thought of dying scared her. She shouldn't have to think about dying yet. She was young, a kid. Old people worried about dying. Not kids like her.

Once her friends found out about the diabetes, they treated her differently. *Should you eat that Jessica? Jessica can't do that, she's sick. Jessica, are you going to die?*

It was always there, that dying thing. Once people knew, they all treated her like they thought she was going to die.

She just wanted to be treated like everybody else.

She didn't think Rusty knew about the diabetes. He didn't act like he did. He treated her like she was perfectly normal, like he kind of liked her, even. Rusty was *so hot*. All she had to do was think about him and her insides melted. He was tall, with a big, broad-shouldered body and dark brown hair with kind of a reddish tint to it that accounted for his nickname, and real light blue eyes. He was a junior, he had his driver's license and *his own car,* and he was on the basketball team. Becca liked him too, and Allison kind of did. Maddie was friends with a girl he had broken up with last year, and she said you had to have sex with him if you wanted to be his girlfriend.

She would have sex with Rusty anytime.

Her mother would *die*, though. Her mother thought she was a virgin. She wasn't, not anymore. She'd had sex with Drew Kennedy in the tree house in Christy O'Connell's backyard last summer, twice. Both times she'd snuck out of the house after her mom was asleep. They did that a lot, she and her friends, because their parents were all *hopeless,* trying to keep their children babies forever, refusing to allow them to grow up.

Sex hadn't been all Christy and Katie Morris, her old best friends, had made it out to be. At least, sex with Drew hadn't. Truth was, it had hurt, and it had been kind of icky and embarrassing and just plain gross. She didn't like to see Drew now, remembering. But that was probably because he was only fifteen, he didn't know what he was doing, and anyway she'd never really *wanted* him like she wanted Rusty.

Rusty was seventeen. He wasn't a little boy like Drew. Sex with Rusty would be different. Allison and Becca and Maddie and Jenna all said so.

She wasn't stupid, though. She was prepared. Christy had stolen a pack of her mother's birth control pills before the thing with Drew and given six to Jessica. If she wanted to have sex more than six times, she was on her own, Christy said. So far she had used only two, for Drew. Jessica figured that she would worry about where to get more when she ran out, because she and Christy weren't really friends anymore. What worried her more than running out was the possibility that there might be something in birth control pills that would cause a reaction with insulin or diabetes or something. She was supposed to tell her doctor about any prescription medicine she needed to take, and birth control pills were prescription medicine. But if she told him, he would probably tell her mom, and if he did the shit would hit the fan for real.

She'd already decided to just go ahead and take the birth control pills when she needed to and hope for the best.

So far nothing had happened, except she'd bled a little.

People with diabetes had sex. They had to take birth control pills, didn't they? And nobody died, so worrying was stupid.

Bonnie, the Scottish terrier that lived two doors over, started to bark suddenly, interrupting her thoughts. The dog's yaps were loud enough and shrill enough to almost completely drown out the wind-blown melody of the wind chimes. God, couldn't the Welches ever remember to let that dog in at night? One of these days somebody was going to call the police.

Must be a fox around or a deer or something—they got those from time to time in Bexley—because Bonnie was really going to town. Jessica spit on the tip of her cigarette to douse it, and flicked it over the porch rail into the big snowball bush beside the steps. Her mother would never find the butt there, not in a million years. The snowball bush had been growing in front of the porch forever, longer than they had lived in the house by far, and no one ever bothered it. There was no reason anyone, especially her mom, ever would.

Her mom was *not* a gardener. Whatever the opposite of a green thumb was, she had it. She couldn't even keep houseplants alive. Every single flower and piece of foliage in their house was silk.

She looked toward the Welch's to see if she could see what was agitating Bonnie so. The night was dark, so dark she could barely see to the end of her own yard. The canopy formed by the treetops largely blocked stars and moon from her view and created a shifting, formless mass of shadows that turned her own beloved front yard into a suddenly alien place.

Jessica froze on the swing. There was something—someone—standing in the darkness by the iron park bench beneath the big oak in the center of the yard. The shifting shadows had allowed her just a glimpse, before once again swallowing up whatever or whoever it was.

It looked like a man. Or a dog or a deer standing on its hind legs. Or something very, very weird—and out of place.

She had the terrifying conviction that unseen eyes were watching her. The hairs rose on the back of her neck.

In a flash she leaped from the swing, sprinted for the door, got inside, and locked it behind her. For long moments she stood there, her hand still on the lock, getting her heart rate and her breathing under control.

Stupid, of course. Who—or what—would be in her yard at this time of night? If anything, it had been a deer. Maybe a buck with antlers. It had certainly not been what it had most resembled—a man.

Had it?

Shivering, Jessica checked the lock again, then scurried up the stairs and into her mother's bedroom. She carefully shut and locked the bedroom door behind her. Her mother slept on the left side of the bed near the alarm clock, lying on her right side in a semifetal position as she nearly always did. Jessica could just make out the shape of her by the clock's neon glow. Just the sound of her breathing made her feel safer. Trying not to make any noise, Jessica crawled into bed beside her as she had done when she was sick or frightened since she was a tiny girl. Unable to help herself, needing the comfort of her mother's touch, Jessica snuggled up against her back, so that they lay front to back, like spoons in a drawer.

"Jess?" Her mom's voice was sleepy.

"Mmm-hmm."

"Nightmare?"

"Mmm–hmm." If she told her the truth, she would have to explain what she was doing on the porch in the middle of the night. Bad idea.

"You okay now?"

"Yeah."

"Okay. Go back to sleep."

"I will. Night, Mom."

"Night, baby. Love you."

"Love you, too," Jessica said, curling close. Her mother's even breathing told her that she had already fallen asleep again. But it was a long time before Jessica felt safe enough even to close her eyes.

CHAPTER 14

THE SQUAD ROOM WAS, FOR THE MOST PART, A
study in grays: light gray concrete-block walls, gray-speckled tile
floor, charcoal-gray metal desks with gleaming silver legs. Even
the molded plastic chairs pulled up beside the desks looked gray
from age and usage, although their original color had been off-
white. Only the police officers' desk chairs were a different color:
they were upholstered in black vinyl. They were comfortable
chairs, as that type of chair went, chairs that swiveled and tilted
easily and were mounted on casters.

Tony Marino occupied one of those chairs, which was tilted
back a little as he sat with hands linked behind his head, staring
with some concentration at the glowing screen of the computer
on his desk. On it appeared, in the upper right hand corner, the
mug shot of a balding, middle-aged man in an orange prison
jumpsuit: Lynn Voss. Tony knew him well, had helped bust him in
fact.

Not that it had done any good. Voss had gotten a life sen-
tence for murder, plus twenty-five years for running a drug ring.
He was still running the same damned drug ring from the federal
penitentiary where he was incarcerated, unless Tony missed his
guess.

"Hey, man, how come you're not out there with your

brother tonight?" Darryl Withers entered from the booking area, shoving a skinny little handcuffed white man in front of him. An undercover cop, Darryl was tall, athletic looking, and black. He'd been working vice for the past two weeks, trolling the men's rooms of the local parks, which was everybody's least favorite assignment. Tonight he wore a navy knit watch cap pulled down low over his ears, ripped jeans, and a stained army jacket. It was after midnight, and the sickos were out in force. They'd been bringing them in steadily for the last hour.

"We're going," Tony answered, as Darryl shoved his prisoner into a plastic chair, unfastened one side of the handcuffs with a quick turn of the key, and just as quickly secured the open cuff to the metal ring set into the side of his desk. The prisoner was thus handcuffed to the desk.

"Mo'fo', you makin' a mistake!" the prisoner protested, looking earnestly at Darryl. "I wasn't doin' nothin' but takin' a piss! I got this prostate problem, see—"

"I sure as hell don't want to hear about your prostate problem," Darryl said, sitting down at his desk and turning on his computer.

"But I wasn't jackin' off, I was pissin'; it just takes me a long time and—"

"Man, you say one more word like that and I'll write you up for murder one, so help me God I will."

"You can't do that! I tell you, I was just pissin'—"

"Hellfire, I hate this job," Darryl complained, looking over at Tony as his collar continued to explain the particulars of his plumbing in excruciating detail.

"Listen to the man, Darryl, you might learn something," Tony said, grinning. Darryl flashed him the bird and started typing over his prisoner's bleats.

"Withers, you got anything?" Captain Sandifer stuck his head out of his office to ask. It was located at one side of the squad room, its glassed-in walls shaded by closed, gray miniblinds.

"Another indecent exposure," Withers called back.

"I was just *pissin'*!" the collar protested.

Exchanging glances with Tony, Sandifer grimaced and withdrew.

"You ready to go?" Dom emerged from the rest room at last.

"Yeah." Tony saved his file, turned off his monitor, and stood up. "What'd Jenny feed you tonight, anyway?"

Dom had visited the rest room three times in the past two hours.

"I don't want to talk about it." Dom shook his head as the two of them headed for the door. "I love the woman, but she can't cook worth a crap."

Tony laughed. "Didn't you invite me over for supper tomorrow? Guess I can't make it."

"You guys get anything out of that little girl you picked up last night?" Sandifer stuck his head out of his office to ask.

Both Tony and Dom paused. Tony shook his head.

"She's not going to be any use to us. She doesn't know anything."

Sandifer nodded and withdrew.

"You gave that kid a major break, you know," Dom said as they walked out of the police station into the parking lot. "We had her solid on possession."

"Yeah, I know." Tony shrugged. "She's only a kid. Hell, if we tried we could bust half the kids in the city. We'll do better concentrating on the big boys."

"Like Voss?"

"Yeah. Like Voss."

"Her mom *was* kind of cute, wasn't she?" Dom asked with a laugh; then before Tony could reply he got into the driver's side of the blue Camaro.

CHAPTER **15**

Iᴛ ᴡᴀꜱ ᴡᴇᴅɴᴇꜱᴅᴀʏ ᴏꜰ ᴛʜᴇ ꜰᴏʟʟᴏᴡɪɴɢ ᴡᴇᴇᴋ.
Grace called home at exactly three-thirty ᴘ.ᴍ., just as she had
done every school day since Jessica had been grounded, to make
sure her daughter was in the house.

"Judge Hart's Reformatory for Wayward Young Women,"
Jessica answered pertly. The Caller ID machine beside the phone
would, of course, have revealed that her mother was on the other
end of the line.

"Good afternoon, Inmate Number One." Grace responded
to Jessica's needling with unimpaired good humor. "Did you eat
your snack?"

"Yes."

"Check your blood?"

"Yes."

"Good. How was school?"

"Oh, just peachy-keen," her daughter said in a syrupy voice.
"Nobody will talk to me now, but that's okay. I like being the
butt-girl of the school."

Grace laughed.

"It isn't funny, Mom."

"What homework do you have?" Grace asked, determined
to ignore Jessica's grumblings. If she was no longer accepted by

the "cool" crowd, Grace for one was certainly not going to complain.

"Algebra. Spanish. Read a short story for English."

"Better get on it."

"I *will*. Mom, I'm serious. Everybody hates me now. They think I squealed on some of the kids to the cops."

"Oh, Jessica, why would they think that?"

"Because it's all over school that I got caught buying pot and nothing happened. They think because you're a judge, you made some kind of deal with the cops."

"Jessica, that's absurd! I don't have that kind of clout."

"Mom, that's what they think. They hate me, they really do. Somebody even followed me home from school today."

"What?"

"It's the truth, I swear it. The whole time I walked home, I could feel somebody behind me. I kept looking around, but I never did exactly *see* anybody. I mean, there were some people on the street, but I couldn't tell who was following me. But somebody was watching me the whole way. I could *feel* it. It made my skin creep. Of course, I was alone, because none of the kids would be caught dead walking with me now, which made it even worse. It really freaked me out, Mom."

"Oh, Jess, are you sure you didn't just imagine it?" Jessica's vivid imagination, coupled with a strong desire to punish her mother for grounding her for three months, might just prompt her to make up a story that she knew would worry Grace to death.

"Swear to God. It was creepy."

"Jessica . . ." It was a warning.

"Don't believe me. When I wind up murdered on my way home from school, then you'll see I was telling the truth."

Grace took a deep breath. Whether someone had actually followed her home or not, Jessica believed what she was saying. Grace knew her daughter well enough to be sure of that. "Is Linda there with you?"

Linda was the college student Grace had hired to be there in the afternoons with Jessica. No more staying home alone after school for her, because it meant too much unsupervised time to get into trouble.

"She's down in the family room watching some dopey soap opera."

"Where are you?"

"Up in my room."

"Are the doors locked?"

"How do I know? I guess."

"Check when you get off the phone. And stay in the house."

There was a pause. Grace could sense Jessica's growing uneasiness even over the phone lines.

"Taking this kind of serious, aren't you, Mom?"

"That's what you wanted, isn't it, Jessica? Now get off the phone, check to make sure that the doors are locked, and stay in the house. Do your homework. If somebody knocks at the door . . ."

"Don't let any strangers in the house. I'm not five years old, you know."

"If anything strikes you as really odd, like you see someone you don't know hanging around the house or something, call 911."

"Oh, Mom, I think you're overreacting as usual."

"Probably. Still . . ."

"I know. Better safe than sorry." Grace could almost see Jessica rolling her eyes.

"Right," Grace agreed. "Let me speak to Linda, please."

"She's all the way downstairs," Jessica protested.

"I don't care. I need to talk to her. Get her, please."

"God, Mom, you're a lot of trouble. 'Bye."

" 'Bye," Grace said, but she doubted that Jessica heard her. A bellowed *Linda, telephone!* from Jessica echoed over the line a split second later.

After finally getting her on the line, Grace talked to Linda for a few minutes, repeating what she had told Jessica about mak-

ing sure the doors were locked and not letting anyone in the
house. Then she had to go back to work. She still had a half-
dozen cases left on her docket before she could call it a day.

The whole rest of the afternoon, she worried about Jessica.
Was she being targeted by someone who thought she was talking
to the police? Was she into the drug scene more heavily than
Grace knew? Who, if anyone, was following her?

What had really happened, after all? The hard facts didn't
really add up to much: Jessica had been caught buying pot and had
not been prosecuted, she herself had chased someone from their
yard on the same night, and Mr. Bear had been found lying by the
road. Everything else was subject to interpretation.

Still, Grace was disturbed. Disturbed enough to call Tony
Marino.

When he called her back, she was in court. When she called
him back, all she got was his pager again. Checkmate.

His car was parked in her driveway when she got home. She
recognized the black Honda immediately. He was nowhere in
sight.

Eyes narrowing slightly, Grace stopped behind his car, got
out, and headed for the house.

Godzilla greeted her. Or, rather, a clear plastic sphere rolling
noisily across the front hall as she came through the door greeted
her. From experience, she knew it was Godzilla in his exercise
ball.

Nimble despite her two-inch heels and the slim cut of her
navy skirt suit, Grace did a quick two-step to avoid the hamster,
who careened on into the dining room. A savory smell from the
roast and vegetables she had thrown in the Crock-Pot before leaving that morning reminded her that she was hungry. That smell,
coupled with the sound of laughter and people talking, drew her
on toward the kitchen.

Sure enough, Marino was there, looking right at home. He
was leaning against the center island, munching an apple, wearing
jeans with a white T-shirt tucked into them and a blue-and-gold
flannel shirt hanging loosely over all.

Also dressed in jeans, as usual, and a gauzy fuchsia smock, Jessica sat on a bar stool, her Spanish text open in front of her, a pencil lying forgotten on the notebook beside the book, and a not-on-her-meal-plan apple in her hand. Linda sat on the other bar stool, laughing.

"Hey, Mom!" Jessica waved with the hand holding the apple.

"Your Honor." Marino's tone was, to Grace's ears at least, sardonic.

"Judge Hart." Linda sounded slightly nervous, as if laughing on the job was something of which her employer might not approve.

Three very different greetings, delivered in three very different voices. Three pairs of eyes fixed on her with very different expressions.

"Hi, baby. Linda. Detective Marino." Her answering salutations descended the scale of friendliness as they were uttered. Her warm smile for Jessica (in the few minutes since she had spotted it, she had decided not to nag about the apple) became a hard, straight look by the time it reached Marino. His brows lifted in response to that look, but he didn't say anything, waiting for her to take the lead.

"Oh, gosh, is it that time already?" With a glance at the clock over the pantry door, Linda jumped up and came around the island toward Grace. She was an attractive brunette with a chin-length bob and a no-nonsense manner, dressed today in green hospital scrubs that were all the fashion with the current college crowd. Grace had liked her upon meeting her, and so had Jessica, which made the situation somewhat easier. Grace knew it would probably happen sooner or later, but so far Jessica hadn't accused Grace of hiring Linda to act as her jailer.

"I've got to go," Linda continued, retrieving a hunter-green backpack from the coatrack. "I've got a seven o'clock class."

" 'Bye, Linda! Thanks for the help with Spanish!" Jessica called as Linda opened the back door.

Before Linda could exit, Paul burst through the open door,

just missing crashing into Linda as he bounded inside. He was dressed in jeans and a purple T-shirt with a picture of a tiger on the front, his short fair hair ruffled and his blue eyes sparkling mischievously. Right behind him came Courtney, her blond hair done up in twin pigtails, wearing a black Mickey Mouse T-shirt and black-and-white polka-dotted leggings.

"Hi, Aunt Grace! We've got McDonald's!" Paul whooped.

"I wanted to get some french fries for you and Jessica, but Mom said you don't like junk food," Courtney supplied earnestly.

"*I* do," Jessica said. "But Mom won't let me eat any anymore."

At that moment, Paul spied Godzilla in his exercise wheel as the unsuspecting animal rolled with a clatter across a corner of the kitchen on his way from dining room to family room.

"Look at that!" Paul cried, and sped after the gyrating hamster.

"What is it? What is it?" Courtney was right behind him. "Paul, let me see!"

"Godzilla!" Jessica exclaimed protectively, jumping up from her seat and darting after her cousins.

"Goodness," said Jackie, appearing at the back door with two small bags from McDonald's in one hand. She was wearing a loose-fitting denim blouse embroidered across the yoke with flowers, and a pair of stretchy black pants. Black sneakers were on her feet. "What's going on?"

Her gaze swept from Linda to Grace, then touched on Marino and widened.

"Hi, Jax." Grace's voice was dry. "They're after Jessica's hamster. Come on in."

"I'm out of here," Linda called, and left with a wave to a chorus of good-byes.

"Is it loose? Her hamster?" Jackie came on into the kitchen, letting the back door close behind her and advancing toward Marino and the counter with another quick look for Grace. She gave an exaggerated shudder. "Those things give me the creeps."

"Sort of. He's in his exercise ball, which gives him free run of the house. This is Detective Tony Marino, Jackie. My sister, Jackie Foster."

"Hi," Jackie said to Marino, placing the food bags on the counter and beaming at him. She was looking tired today, Grace thought, noting the faint shadows beneath her sister's eyes that remained despite her wide smile, and the pallor of her skin. Once again Grace felt a spurt of anger at Jackie's husband, for not doing more to provide his wife and children with an easier life.

"Nice to meet you." Marino smiled back. He had, as Grace had noticed before, a really nice smile.

While Marino's gaze was focused elsewhere, Grace gave her sister a look. From long and intimate acquaintance, she could pretty much divine what Jackie was thinking. Grace's single state bothered her. Almost from the moment Grace's divorce had been final ten years before, Jackie had been trying to fix her up.

What was it they said about misery loving company?

Forget it, Jax, Grace thought, and tried to silently convey that thought with her eyes.

A shriek, a crash, and pounding feet cut the wordless exchange short.

"She's gonna kill me!" Paul darted into the room, running for his mother, comic terror all over his face.

"Who?" Jackie wrapped her arms around Paul as he leaped the last few feet into her embrace.

"Jessica! She's gonna kill me! She's gonna tear my head off and feed my insides to the worms! She's gonna rip out my heart! Don't let her kill me, don't let her kill me!"

Paul's tendency to overdramatize was well-known within the family. Marino, however, looked startled.

"Mom, help!" It was Jessica, from the other room.

Courtney echoed the cry. "Help! Help!"

"What did you do?" Jackie's voice, as she addressed her son, was resigned.

"All I did was kick that stupid old ball. . . ."

The rest of Paul's confession was lost to Grace as she hurried into the family room to assist Jessica.

Jessica and Courtney were down on their knees. Both were holding up opposite ends of the sofa's tailored kick skirt and were peering into the darkness beneath. Half of a clear plastic sphere lay on its back in the middle of the oriental carpet. The other half was facedown near the wall.

"Oh, dear," Grace said, comprehending in an instant what had happened.

"Godzilla's under the couch." Jessica's voice was urgent. "Mom, get down there by Courtney. Don't let him get past you. Here he comes!"

It was a screech. Courtney screamed, too, and threw herself back away from the couch as, apparently, the hamster headed in her direction. Her end of the kick skirt dropped.

"He's getting away! He's getting away! Mom, grab him! There he goes!"

Jessica sprang to her feet just as a small, furry ball of gold-and-white lightning scurried from beneath the couch right in front of Grace's navy leather-shod toes, heading as fast as it could go toward the bookshelves that lined the far wall. Unable to stop herself, Grace jumped back.

"Oh, gosh, I hate doing this! Jess, he doesn't bite, does he?" Despite her wail of protest, Grace, who liked Godzilla fine in his cage but wasn't crazy about him out of it, recovered her nerve, swooped and snatched—and missed. The hamster continued his hell-bent-for-leather flight toward freedom.

"Get him, Mom! Get him!"

With Jessica's screams for encouragement, bent almost double, Grace scrambled after the rodent, grabbing at the speedy little creature who eluded her half a dozen times by dodging beneath and behind an end table, a wooden rocker, and a green ceramic planter holding a silk potted plant.

"I'll catch it, Aunt Grace!" Hands outstretched, Courtney came to her assistance, lunging for the hamster as it darted from behind the planter. There was a *thunk* as her head made solid contact with the edge of a bookcase. She fell back with a cry, one hand clapped to the top of her head.

"Head him off, Mom! I'll get him! Herd him toward me!"

Jessica was beside her now, at knee level really, grabbing for the hamster to the accompaniment of Courtney's whimpers, which in the heat of the moment went ignored. Jess missed, and Godzilla turned in Grace's direction once again, prompting Jessica's shrieked instructions.

"Oh, Jess, I hate doing this!" Grace moaned, but followed her daughter's orders nonetheless and thrust both hands downward to block the rodent's path to safety behind the bookcases. Instead of turning back toward Jessica as it was supposed to, however, the thing kept coming. Grace screwed up her courage and grabbed it, snatching it up into the air, holding the warm, squirming little body cupped between her two hands, careful not to hurt it. Then it bit her.

"Mom, you got him! You got him! You *dropped* him!"

"He bit me!" Grace thrust her wounded index finger into her mouth, and glared after the absconding creature.

"Mom, you let him go! Grab him, Courtney! Mom, you *had* him! How could you let him go?"

"He bit me!"

"He only has little tiny teeth, they don't hurt! He's bitten me lots of times! Paul, stop!"

This last was shrieked at the top of Jessica's lungs, in response to the emergence of her cousin at the forefront of the chase—armed with an upside-down saucepan, which he promptly slammed down on top of Godzilla.

The hamster squealed once, then fell silent.

"Paul, no! You hurt him! Get out of the way! You little . . ." Jessica thrust Paul aside. The force of her push sent him teetering wildly toward the big-screen TV against the far wall, but to Grace's relief he managed not to crash through it. Jessica, meanwhile, dropped to her knees beside the overturned saucepan. Despite Jessica's fury, the fact remained that, however crude his method, Paul had gotten his man, er, hamster—dead or alive.

Grace winced at the thought.

Jessica gently lifted one edge of the pan a little way up from the carpet and peered beneath it. Then she slammed the pan down again.

"Get me the exercise ball, Courtney."

From this Grace deduced that Godzilla was alive. Courtney scrambled for the exercise ball and handed both halves to Jessica. Jessica glanced around, dismissing both her cousins with evil looks.

"Mom, when I tell you, lift the pan."

Grace moved to Jessica's side, hunkered down, and placed both hands on the pan's cool aluminum bottom.

"Now!" Jessica said, and Grace lifted the pan. Jessica dropped half the exercise wheel over Godzilla, who was looking stunned. Then she scooped him up in it and screwed the other half onto the base. She had him.

"Is he hurt?" Paul asked.

Jessica glared at her cousin. Before she could say anything, Grace intervened, putting an arm around his shoulders.

"I don't think so. Jess, go put Godzilla back in his cage. Jackie, didn't you bring McDonald's? Let's feed these kids, shall we?"

She glanced up to find her sister and Marino both standing in the doorway between the kitchen and the family room. One hand clapped to her mouth, bent almost double, Jackie was convulsed with laughter. Marino, more reserved, was still grinning from ear to ear.

CHAPTER **16**

STRAIGHTENING, GRACE BECAME IMMEDIATELY
conscious of the fact that she had a run in her pantyhose. Not just
a run, but a ladder, that started with a large hole in her right knee
and descended in a series of smaller, interconnecting holes to her
ankle. Almost an entire calf's worth of pale bare skin showed
through the rips in the silky, dark blue nylon. To add insult to
injury, her face was flushed, her hair mussed, and she was perspir-
ing.

Not to mention that her index finger was bleeding. And it
throbbed.

Not exactly the kind of dignified image she wanted to convey to Marino.

"Poor baby," Jessica crooned to Godzilla, brushing past her
mother and the pair in the doorway and heading toward the stairs,
the hamster in his exercise ball held carefully in her hands.

"I don't see why you don't get that child a *real* pet," Jackie
said, half under her breath so Jessica would not hear. "That thing
is disgusting. It looks like a rat without a tail."

"Godzilla *is* a real pet," Grace said, taking a deep mental
breath and responding with measured calm. Glancing around for
Courtney, she shooed both children in front of her. "Let's go into
the kitchen, children. Jax, if you're planning to feed these two,

you'd better be doing it. The food you brought is getting cold. Detective Marino, I'm sorry to keep you waiting so long. I just need to talk to you for one minute."

"No problem," he said. He wasn't grinning any longer, but there was laughter in his eyes. "I always wondered about the most efficient method of catching an escaping hamster. Now I know: drop a pot over it. If you don't miss and turn it into road pizza, you've got it. I'll remember that."

Although Grace did not say *oh, shut up* as she would have liked, her eyes said it for her.

"All right, kids, let's eat." Jackie moved back into the kitchen, with Marino following in her wake. Grace and the children brought up the rear.

While Jackie set out her children's meals, Grace grabbed a paper towel from the roll near the sink, wet it, wrung it out, and wrapped it around her injured finger. She then took Marino out onto the porch. It was the only place where she felt (fairly) safe from interruption.

"Your sister live nearby?" Marino asked as the screened door swung shut behind him.

"In Whitehall."

The city of Columbus was actually a loose conglomeration of smaller cities, each with its own identity. Bexley, Worthington, and Upper Arlington were the wealthy districts. Whitehall was one of the working-class ones nearby, with small, mostly one-story houses crowded close together. The joke was: Whitehall was where Bexley's household help lived.

"Oh?" Marino's eyebrows went up as he recognized the significance of the address. Grace chose not to elaborate on her sister's life. That Jackie had chosen not to finish college, had made a bad marriage and compounded it by having two children while still in her twenties, whom she loved but couldn't afford, was no business of this man.

"I wanted to talk to you about Jessica."

Grace stood by the porch rail, glancing away from him for a moment as he waited just beyond the door. It was coming on twilight now. Shadows in shades of lavender and gray stole across the front yard, robbing shapes of crispness and colors of clarity. The scent of autumn was everywhere. A cool gust of wind rattled the remaining gold-and-crimson leaves on the big oaks and elms and beeches, sending some half a dozen spiraling toward earth. Deep purple clouds were piling up on the western horizon, promising rain before morning. The air felt like rain, heavy and moist. At the far end of the porch, the swing moved gently back and forth on its chain, as though an invisible occupant gently propelled it. The wind chimes that hung behind the swing, an oxidized copper whimsy of a long-tailed rooster with five slender metal tubes dangling from its toes, tinkled melodiously. The still-green leaves of the ancient snowball bush beside the steps rustled in harmony. A green Ford Explorer drove down the street, lights on, turning left into the Taylor's driveway at the bend in the road and then disappearing behind the bank of tall junipers that separated their yard from the Welch's.

"She thinks someone followed her home from school today." Grace crossed her arms over her chest and looked him square in the eye. "She says none of the kids will talk to her at school. They know she was caught with marijuana in her possession and not charged. She thinks they think the reason she wasn't charged is that she's cooperating with the police in a drug investigation."

"So they think she's cooperating with us, do they?" He stood with his feet slightly apart, his hands thrust into the front pockets of his jeans. He looked altogether too casual, *sounded* altogether too casual, for Grace's peace of mind.

"Yes, they do," she said curtly. "And, not being totally stupid, I realize that you wheedled the names of her friends out of her when you were here before. I want you to know that I know that. I also want you to know that I feel you are endangering her by using her in that way, and I won't have it."

"Telling me the names of her friends is pretty innocuous, don't you think? She just mentioned a few of them in passing conversation, like she would to anybody. I checked out the kids she named, by the way. She's running with some pretty hard-core druggies, but she's not one of them—yet."

"Oh, God." Grace lifted a hand to her throat. "Listen, I don't want her to be a part of this. She's a good kid. She really is. She just . . . wants to be cool right now. It's a phase. I've talked to her. I've grounded her. I think she understands how dangerous this whole scene is. I want you to leave her out of it, too. I want you to leave her alone."

"Your Honor, *you* are the one who called *me* today. I was totally leaving your daughter out of it."

"She thinks someone followed her home from school." Grace's hand fell away from her throat to cross over her chest again. "That scares me. Is there enough of a drug scene at Hebron for this to be real? Could she possibly have become a target because someone thought she was telling on them?"

He shrugged. "Anything's possible, but I don't see why someone would think that. I wouldn't expect Jessica to be marked as a snitch simply because she wasn't arrested for possession. A lot of times kids will be let go with a warning to them and their parents for a first-time offense if the amount involved is small. Is your daughter truthful? Is she imaginative?"

"Do you mean, could she be lying about somebody following her home? She wasn't. I can tell when she's genuinely disturbed by something, and she was disturbed by this. Could she have imagined it? Possibly. What concerns me is that maybe she didn't."

He studied her in silence for a moment. "I don't think you have anything to worry about. I'd be almost willing to bet that she imagined it. She's probably reading too much into the fact that the kids are being mean to her at school."

That was a possibility, of course. A good possibility. But Grace could not shake the uneasiness that had gripped her ever since Jessica had told her that somebody had followed her home. Call it intuition, call it sixth sense, call it anything you like, but she just felt that something was wrong.

But what could she say? What, really, did she expect him to

do? Write a note for her daughter to show to her friends stating that Jessica was not cooperating with the police, so let her alone?

Get real.

"If you should hear something, find out something, about her being in danger . . ."

"Believe me, we would protect her, and you would be informed."

Grace supposed she would have to be satisfied with that.

"Thank you." She said it almost grudgingly.

"No problem." Then he moved, heading toward the porch steps. "I'd better be going. It's getting late. If you have any more concerns, call me."

"I will," Grace said in such a grim tone that he laughed.

When he was gone, backing his car down the driveway and heading east toward Eastland Boulevard, she turned and went back into the house.

Jackie was alone in the kitchen. From the sound of the TV, which had not been on when she had stepped onto the porch, Grace deduced that Courtney and Paul were in the family room. There was no sign of Jessica. In the wake of her cousins' invasion, Grace was not surprised that she had elected to stay in her room.

"Where'd you find the handsome cop?" Jackie asked with a teasing look when she saw that Grace was alone.

Conscious of an aching need to share her growing worries with somebody, Grace started to confess exactly who Marino was, how she had come to know him, and why he had been present at the house this evening. Then, with a look at her sister, she decided against it. Jackie had enough problems of her own. She didn't need anything more to worry about, and she would worry about her niece. She loved Jessica, just as Grace loved Paul and Courtney, noisy and boisterous though they were. Besides, Grace didn't want to tell Jessica's loving aunt anything too negative about Jessica. Such as the fact that she'd snuck out in the middle of the night, gotten drunk, and been caught buying marijuana.

For Jessica's sake. Because Grace couldn't bear anyone, even her own sister, thinking badly of Jessica.

And, if she was honest, also because Jackie thought she, Grace, was such a good mother. Grace didn't want to spoil her sister's image of her, illusory though it might be.

"He's not a friend. He's a police officer whom I wanted to question about a case and couldn't get hold of during business hours. He answered a couple of questions, and then he left," Grace said, heading for the stairs. Her explanation was true enough, after all. She just had neglected to mention that the case involved Jessica. "There's roast and potatoes and carrots in the Crock-Pot, and dinner rolls from the bakery in the bread box. If you'll set it out on the table, I'll change clothes and fetch Jessica, and we can eat."

CHAPTER 17

WHEN GRACE CAME BACK DOWNSTAIRS, CLAD IN
an ancient OSU-gray sweatsuit with socks on her feet, Jessica was
in the kitchen and the food was on the table. The three of them
ate together comfortably, as close relatives who see each other a
great deal are comfortable together, sharing tidbits about each
other's day. Grace talked about some of the more interesting as-
pects of the cases that had appeared before her, Jackie described
the antics of her children and those at the day-care center where
she worked, and Jessica chatted about her schoolwork and the
state of Godzilla's health. Grace noticed that Jessica, too, said
nothing to Jackie about the trouble she'd gotten into or the kids
not speaking to her at school or her feeling that someone had
followed her home. Her daughter's reticence made her feel that
she had done the right thing in keeping their troubles to herself.

When supper was over, Jessica helped clear the table. After
Jackie and the kids left, Grace and Jessica went for a run, as they
did several times a week after supper.

It was full dark by this time. There were few street lights in
Bexley, and the ones that existed were only on the corners of the
busier intersections. Once off Spring Hill Lane, which had no
sidewalks, they kept to the sidewalks whenever possible. Cars and
vans and an occasional motorcycle were parked along the sides of

the streets. The sky was covered with a heavy dark blanket of clouds that completely blocked any glimpse of the moon or stars. Except for an occasional dog-walker and one prepubescent boy frantically pedaling his bicycle in the opposite direction in what Grace assumed was a race against the clock to get home, there was no one else out.

Still, Grace could not forget Jessica's feeling that someone had followed her home that day, or that she herself had chased an intruder the preceding week. She did not feel as comfortable as she usually did on their runs. She was plagued by an almost compulsive need to glance behind bushes, parked cars, and trash receptacles for someone who might be hiding and watching them. It was stupid, she knew, and she took care not to infect Jessica with her own anxiety.

But stupid or not, she could not dismiss it entirely from her mind.

Side by side, talking about nothing really in desultory spurts, they jogged down Spring Hill Lane, up Bellewood, over and across the railroad tracks to Hobbs Station Road, and then down Evergreen to Spring Hill Lane and home again.

All in all, they covered a distance of about two miles. Usually their run was pure pleasure for Grace because this was an activity that she and Jess could share without strife or stress and because of the sheer joy she took in her daughter's company. Tonight, because of the uneasiness she could not banish, it was something less than that.

"Whew!" she gasped, winded, as they reached their front porch and she collapsed in a rocker.

"You're getting old, Mom," Jessica told her cheerfully. Jessica, star forward for her basketball team last year, was not one whit out of breath. She wasn't tired, either. Instead, she propped one ankle on the porch rail, using it as a kind of ballet barre to stretch her leg muscles.

Did I ever have that much energy? Grace wondered, watching her.

"Oh, by the way, I got my Spanish test back today. I got a 93. You need to sign it."

"That's great. I'll gladly sign it. Put it on the kitchen table and I'll do it before I go to bed."

Jessica switched legs. "Mom."

"Mmm?"

"How come you and Aunt Jackie are so different? I mean, you're sisters and all. I always thought sisters were pretty much alike."

"Aunt Jackie's a lot younger than I am—eight years."

"So, what difference does that make? I mean, look at you two: she's fat, and you're thin. You're real successful at what you do, and she's not. You were in a bad marriage, and you got a divorce. She's in a bad marriage, and she's not ever going to get a divorce as long as she lives. You know that as well as I do."

Grace was silent for a moment, rocking slowly back and forth as she contemplated the question. The wind chimes tinkled, the swing creaked, the leaves on the snowball bush rustled. The brisk breeze felt good against her overheated skin. Jessica was still working the porch rail like a ballet barre. Her wiry body was backlit by the light, coming from the front hall and kitchen, which streamed out through the windows in golden blocks of illumination that defied the night.

"Jackie and I had very different childhoods, you know, despite the fact that we're sisters. I was fourteen—just a year younger than you—when my mother died. Jackie was six. I can remember her at the funeral home, with Mom lying there in her coffin, laughing and playing with our cousins who were her age. She didn't know, didn't *understand,* what had happened, what we had lost. Then Dad got married again in less than a year. Jackie and Deborah really hit it off. I have to say, Deborah was good to Jackie, treated her pretty much like she was her own daughter. I, on the other hand, hated Deborah. Looking back, I can see that I was pretty bad to her, but at the time I thought I was standing up for my mother, defending her place in the family, so to speak, even though she was gone. That made Dad mad at me, so he and I fought all the time, too. Our house was pretty much a battleground until I finally left home."

"For college?"

"Mmm-hmm."

Jessica's leg dropped, and she stood with both feet flat on the ground, knees straight, and bent at the waist as she placed her palms flat on the floor.

"What did your mom die of?" she asked, her voice faintly muffled from her bent-over position.

"Ovarian cancer." To this day, Grace could not think about it without pain.

"Was it bad? For you, I mean?"

"Pretty bad."

In truth, it had been devastating. Her mother's death had been swift, brutal, unexpected. One January day she went to her doctor for a routine checkup. Six months and countless surgeries, treatments, and hours of suffering later, she was dead. Grace had felt as if the sun had been ripped from the sky, as if her life had been swallowed up by a black hole from which there would never be any escape.

"But you got over it."

"I got over it." Grace smiled slightly, ruefully, affectionately, at her daughter as she confirmed this gross oversimplification. "Actually, I didn't really start to get over it until I had you. You were the first thing I ever loved as much as I loved my mother. From the moment you were born, I loved you even more. Better than anything in the whole wide world."

Jessica straightened, and turned to grin at her, hands on hips. "And I was the most beautiful baby in the whole wide world, right?"

"Well . . ."

"If you loved me so much, Mom, the least you can do is tell me how beautiful I was."

"You grew into your beauty," Grace temporized. Jessica loved the story of how long and skinny and red and wrinkly and, yes, homely, she had been as a newborn. Craig, an idealistic twenty-two-year-old at the time, had taken one look at his infant daughter and burst into tears, appalled at how ugly she was.

Craig had told Jessica that. Fortunately, Jessica thought it was funny.

"I love you, Mom." Jessica bent, dropped a kiss on Grace's cheek, and held out her hand. "Give me the key. I'm going to go take a shower."

"I'll be in in a minute. Don't use all the hot water."

"I won't—if you're lucky."

The banging of the door behind her marked Jessica's departure. Grace continued to rock back and forth in the white-painted wicker chair for a while, staring out into the darkness. There were so many ghosts out there for her, ghosts from her past, that Jessica's questions had given renewed form and substance to. Ghosts that she couldn't bear to remember, and, equally, couldn't bear to forget. . . .

"Mom!" Grace could hear Jessica's shriek all the way from upstairs, through the closed door. "Mom!"

Stark terror laced Jessica's voice. Grace sprang to her feet, yanked open the door that Jessica had left unlocked for her, and sprinted down the hall. Clad only in a towel, Jessica was almost at the foot of the stairs by the time she reached her. Her face was white as paper and her eyes were huge.

"Mom! Mom! Oh, my God, Mom!"

"Jess, what is it?" Grace caught her daughter's arm, looking her frantically up and down for any sign of injury. There was none that she could see. "What's wrong?"

"It's in my room." Jessica was still wet from her shower. Her skin felt cold as ice beneath Grace's hand. "Oh, God, Mom, it's in my room! You've got to come and see!"

CHAPTER **18**

O FFICERS PHILLIP PETERS AND AARON STEIN
were the first ones on the scene. Grace took the two uniformed
young men upstairs to Jessica's room. Dressed now in jeans and a
white sweatshirt, Jessica went with them. Grace realized with a
pang that she was afraid to stay downstairs alone.

The primrose comforter with its ruched ruffle all around the
hem was still on the bed. The twin pillows with shams that
matched the comforter still leaned against the headboard. The
curtains were drawn over the windows. The bedside lamp was
turned on. Except for Jessica's jogging clothes, which were lying
across the back of the armchair in the corner, the bedroom was
undisturbed.

Jessica's hand crept into Grace's as Grace pointed the way
into the bath.

The officers pushed open the white-painted, paneled door.
The bathroom light was still on, brightly illuminating the small,
pink-and-white space that contained, in a roughly triangular
shape, a shower, sink, and toilet. The steam from Jessica's shower
had almost completely dissipated. The shower door stood ajar.

The white porcelain pedestal sink stood directly opposite the
shower. Above it hung a rectangular mirror-fronted medicine cabinet. The mirror had an arched top.

In order to view the sink and the medicine cabinet above it, it was necessary to step inside the bathroom and then partly close the door.

Officer Stein went first, followed by Officer Peters. Grace and Jessica, hands linked, brought up the rear.

The tiny bathroom was crowded with four people crammed inside it.

"See," Grace said, pointing. "On the mirror."

On the surface of the glass had been drawn the rough outline of a tombstone. *Jessica, R.I.P* read the legend inside the outline, with *Jessica* on one line and *R.I.P.* below.

Some sort of oil had been used to compose the drawing, so that it remained invisible until steam from a shower clouded the rest of the mirror, leaving the illustration in sharp relief. With the steam almost gone now, the marks had grown faint, but were still visible.

"We were out running. Someone must have come into the house while we were out and written that," Grace said.

For a moment Officers Peters and Stein simply stared at the mirror. Then they exchanged glances.

"Did you lock the doors before you went out?" Officer Stein asked Grace.

"Yes, of course."

"We'll check the windows and doors for signs of forced entry," Officer Peters said. He was a nice-looking man of about thirty, tall and slim, with regular features and tobacco-brown hair. Officer Stein was shorter, stockier, with a ruddy complexion and short blond hair.

"Whoever it was might have gotten in through the kitchen door. It doesn't always latch properly," Grace said.

"We'll check it."

The quartet trooped down the stairs. While the officers looked around, Grace and Jessica waited in the kitchen. In less than ten minutes the officers joined them there.

"No sign of forced entry," Officer Stein said, shaking his head. "We can take a report."

"I want you to do more than take a report," Grace said with authority, her hand tight around Jessica's. "I want whoever did this caught."

"Yes, Your Honor. We'll do our best, ma'am." Officer Stein's tone was respectful.

The doorbell rang. Knowing who it had to be, Grace hurried to answer. Jessica was right behind her, and the two police officers were behind Jessica.

Grace opened the door. Tony Marino looked at her through the screen. Behind him stood Dominick Marino. Grace had called Tony Marino's pager number even before she had called the Bexley police.

Meeting his gaze through the fine black mesh, she realized that she was surprisingly glad to see him. At least he knew enough to put what had occurred into its proper context, she thought.

"Hi," Tony Marino said to Grace, reaching for the handle of the screen door even as Grace pushed it open. He stepped inside. Dominick followed. Both looked past her to Officers Peters and Stein.

"You're Phil Peters, aren't you?" Tony asked.

"That's right, Detective. This is my partner, Aaron Stein."

"Dominick Marino," Dominick said, and the men shook hands all around. Then Tony's gaze slid to Grace.

"What's up?"

"Somebody got into the house while Jessica and I were out running and wrote . . ." Grace hesitated, thinking of Jessica behind her ". . . a very unpleasant message on Jessica's bathroom mirror."

"A death threat," Jessica said in a small voice. Her hand in Grace's was very cold.

"A death threat?" Marino did not sound—quite—skeptical. But his tone was close enough to rouse Grace's ire.

"Come upstairs and I'll show you," she said, her voice tart. This, she considered, was largely his fault, though she didn't mean to say so in front of her daughter and the others.

With Jessica in tow, Grace led the way upstairs. Tony and Dominick Marino and the other two police officers followed.

With six people in the bathroom, Grace could barely draw breath. Standing directly behind Tony Marino, with Jessica squashed against her side, she was surrounded by men, all of whom were larger and taller than she. In the sneakers she wore, to see the mirror, she had to look over Tony's shoulder, the top of which was on a level with her eyebrows. As a woman who prided herself on being in control, Grace found the unaccustomed sensation of being femininely "smaller than" disconcerting.

"There's no sign of forced entry, Detective," Stein volunteered. "We already checked."

"Judge Hart told us the lock on the kitchen door doesn't always work right, though. Somebody could have come in that way, maybe," Peters added.

"It looks like some kind of oil," Dominick said, leaning close to the mirror and touching the drawing with a questing finger. He rubbed his fingers together, testing the substance. "It's oil. I'm sure of it."

"Take pictures. Take a sample of the oil for testing. Then dust for fingerprints. Everywhere in the bathroom, the bedroom doorknob, the kitchen door, and the front door," Tony directed the two uniformed officers. To Grace, who stood close against his back, he added with a glance over his shoulder: "This could be a prank, you know. Let's get out of this bathroom and talk about it."

"I don't think it's a prank." Grace led the way downstairs. Jessica still clung to her hand. Tony and Dominick Marino followed. At the base of the stairs, the two uniformed officers headed out the front door in search of a camera. Grace steered the remainder of the party into the kitchen. "I think it's a continuation of what's been happening to Jessica at school."

"Maybe," Tony said. Prudently left unspoken, but obvious to Grace nonetheless, was the corollary: maybe not.

"Sit down, baby," Grace said to Jessica, pushing her gently

in the direction of a bar stool. "I'll make you some hot chocolate." To the Marinos, who had stopped rather awkwardly in the middle of the kitchen, she added, "I'm making hot chocolate for Jessica, and I'm going to have a cup of coffee. Would either one of you like something?"

"I'll have coffee," Tony said, while Dominick shook his head.

"Nothing, thanks."

"Sit down. Please."

Dominick did, settling onto the bar stool beside Jessica, while Tony leaned against the counter. They were both wearing dark sweat suits and jogging shoes. Grace wondered, vaguely, where they had been. Running, like Jessica and her? Somehow it didn't seem likely. Dismissing the issue from her mind as unimportant, she poured chocolate milk into a mug and put it in the microwave to heat. Then she poured out two cups of coffee.

"Cream? Sugar?" she asked Tony just as the microwave pinged.

"One spoonful of sugar," he said. Grace retrieved the hot chocolate from the microwave and passed it to Jessica, then added a spoonful of sugar to one of the coffees and handed it to Tony.

"Okay," Tony said, taking a sip of coffee. His gaze was on Grace. "You think somebody broke in here while you were gone and wrote that message to Jessica, right?"

"Right," Grace said. She was already on her third sip and was feeling marginally more able to cope.

"How long were you gone?"

Grace looked at Jessica. "About . . . twenty minutes?"

Jessica nodded.

"So whoever it was had twenty minutes to break into your house, go up to Jessica's room, and write that message in oil or whatever on her mirror, worrying all the time that you might return at any second," Tony said. "Let's think about that. Twenty minutes is not a very long time."

"Long enough, apparently," Grace said darkly, sipping her coffee.

"In that twenty minutes, the perpetrator would have had to enter your house, either with a key or through your possibly improperly latched kitchen door or by some other means not yet discovered, go up to Jessica's room, write the message with a substance he either found in the house or brought with him, and get out of the house again without either of you seeing him—or her. Possible, I suppose, but the timing's tricky."

"We stayed out on the porch for a few minutes after we got back," Grace recalled. "Maybe five minutes. Maybe even ten."

"I think it was more like five," Jessica put in. Her voice sounded a little stronger, too. "Then I went in to take a shower."

"Obviously you saw no one in the house, right, or nothing that would make you suspect someone was in the house?"

"If I had, I would have screamed the place down." Jessica gave Tony a lopsided little smile. Grace was glad to see that smile. It meant that Jessica was starting to recover.

"That's what I thought." Tony smiled back at Jessica. "So the message already had to be on the mirror and the perp out when you came into the house. That means that whoever wrote it had to be watching you and your mom pretty closely to know that the house was empty. Do you go running every night at the same time?"

Grace and Jessica both shook their heads.

"About three nights a week, usually, but we don't go on specific days, or at specific times. Just whenever we feel like it," Grace said.

"So whoever it was couldn't have known you would be gone at that time."

"I don't see how." Grace took another reviving sip of coffee.

"So for this scenario to work, you had to be under direct observation."

Grace shivered at the thought.

Jessica said, "That's scary."

Tony looked from one to the other of them. "Do either of you ladies possess any oil that could have been used to write the message?"

"I have bath oil beads," Jessica volunteered. "I keep them right in the medicine cabinet. I've never used them, though. I usually take a shower."

Grace thought. "I have some bath oil. And some baby oil. And some makeup remover that's kind of oily."

"Let's go check it out."

The four of them went upstairs again. The Marinos and Jessica went on into Jessica's room, while Grace collected the required items from her bathroom.

"We've got pictures of the mirror." Standing in the bathroom doorway, Peters was talking to the Marinos, who were in Jessica's bedroom. He looked past them as Grace entered. The Marinos glanced around, too. Stein was inside the bathroom clicking away with a black, 35-millimeter camera. He lowered the camera and also glanced toward her as she joined them.

"All done," he said, waving the camera as he turned toward the others.

"Go ahead and fingerprint the front and back doors," Tony said. "Leave fingerprinting the bathroom for last."

"Okay."

Peters and Stein left the room, heading downstairs. Tony and Dominick entered the bathroom. Jessica was reluctant to go back inside her bathroom, so she sat down in her chair to wait. Grace stood in the doorway between the bedroom and bathroom so she could watch both Jessica and the men.

Using a towel and very gingerly gripping the edge of the mirror, Dominick opened the medicine cabinet and extracted the clear plastic container of brightly colored bath oil beads that Jessica had found in her stocking at Christmas.

Tony, meanwhile, touched the message, then sniffed the oil on his fingers and rubbed his fingers together to test the texture. Dominick crushed a bath oil bead between his fingers, and both men grimaced at the strong floral scent that resulted.

"That's not it," Tony said positively. "We would have smelled that a mile away." Then, to Grace, "Let's see what you have."

Grace handed over the cumbersome collection of objects she had retrieved from her bathroom.

Carefully pulling the stopper from the smoky-rose glass bottle of bath oil that Grace rarely used, Tony poured a little on his fingers. The resulting smell of lavender was less overpowering than Jessica's floral, but unmistakable nonetheless.

"Nope," Dominick said.

Tony then dribbled a little baby oil on the back of his hand, sniffed it, then tested its texture with a finger.

"This is it," he said. "Or something real similar. We'll need to run tests to be positive. Check this out, Dom, and see what you think."

Dominick touched the oil on the mirror, smelled it, then touched and smelled the oil on Tony's hand.

"Yeah, I agree," he said. "We need to have this bottle finger-printed."

"It could have come from another bottle. One the perp brought. Or it might be something else altogether."

"You're right."

As they spoke, both Marinos wiped their hands on the towel Dominick had used to open the medicine cabinet and headed for the bathroom door. Grace stepped out of their way.

"You realize," Tony said, stopping just inside the bedroom and looking at Grace, "that there is another possibility."

"Such as?" She crossed her arms over her chest, her brows lifting.

"That this wasn't done while you two were out jogging. That it was done earlier."

"We would have noticed it, surely," Grace said.

"Would you? Jessica, when was the last time you took a shower in your bathroom?"

"This morning. Before school."

"You obviously didn't notice anything on the mirror then."

"No."

"Did you look in the mirror after you got out of the shower this morning so you would have noticed?"

"I . . . I don't remember, but I'm sure I did."

"Believe me, she did. She *always* looks in the mirror," Grace supplied dryly.

"Shut up, Mom," Jessica muttered in an aside.

"Then this could have been done any time today. Who has had access to your house today?"

Grace frowned. "Well, let's see. Linda. Jackie and her children. You. That's it, I think, except for Jessica and me." She looked inquiringly at Jessica.

"That's everybody I can think of," her daughter corroborated.

"Is it possible that one of your cousins wrote that as a joke?" Tony asked, looking at Jessica. "I've met them, remember. They look like they might think that kind of thing is funny."

Struck by the possibility, Grace and Jessica exchanged glances. Then Grace looked back at Tony.

"I don't think so," she said, shaking her head. "They're too young. Paul is only six, and Courtney's four. I don't think they can write that well, either one of them, even if they wanted to."

"You sure? My little girl's in first grade and she can write real good," Dominick put in.

"I'll call Jackie and have her ask them." Grace moved toward the door. She knew it wasn't possible, knew Paul couldn't write that well, but it was such a neat, unfrightening solution. . . .

"Mom!" Jessica broke into her thoughts. "Godzilla's gone!"

"What?" Grace looked toward the bookshelf where his cage was kept. Jessica was already out of her chair and heading around the foot of her bed toward it.

"The door's open." Jessica lifted the door in the top of the hamster's cage easily, without have to unlatch the spring hook that usually held it shut, making it obvious that the cage was unlocked. "He's gone."

Grace moved to stand beside her daughter, looking down at the double-decker wire cage that was Godzilla's home. The exercise wheel was there. The red-tinted but still transparent plastic house that he loved to sleep in was there. His wooden chews were there, his food dish was there, his water bottle was there.

Grace reached down and poked the nest of paper towels that he sometimes hid beneath.

Everything in the cage was where it should be, except the hamster.

Godzilla was definitely gone.

CHAPTER 19

"O H, DEAR, YOU MUST HAVE FORGOTTEN AND left his cage unlocked," Grace said.

"I didn't! I know I didn't! I *never* leave Godzilla's cage unlocked." Jessica's lips trembled and her eyes filled. This, coming on the heels of the fright she had experienced, was too much for her composure.

"Godzilla?" In the background, Dominick's low-voiced question sounded mystified.

"Her hamster." Equally low-voiced, Tony filled him in.

"Oh."

"Don't worry, we'll find him." Ignoring the sotto voce conversation behind them, Grace put a soothing arm around her daughter's thin shoulders. Jessica was already visually scanning the floor, paying particular attention to the shadowy angles where floor and walls joined, blinking back tears. "He has to be here somewhere."

"He could be anywhere in the house!" Jessica looked at Grace despairingly. "My bedroom door has been open this whole time!"

"We'll find him," Grace repeated, then glanced up as a hand curled insistently around her arm just above the elbow.

It belonged to Tony Marino. With a jerk of his head he indicated that he would like to speak to her privately, in the hall.

Message delivered, he let his hand fall away from her arm, and she followed him out of the room. As Grace left, Jessica was dropping to her knees beside the bed, getting ready to look beneath it. Clearly not particularly concerned about the case of the missing hamster, Dominick had disappeared into the bathroom again.

Once in the hall, Tony stopped walking and turned to face her. Grace stopped, too, frowning up at him. They stood several feet away from Jessica's doorway, with Grace's back to the door so that her daughter could not read anything untoward in her face. If he had bad news to impart, she wanted to keep it away from Jessica for as long as possible.

"I don't want to make your daughter mad at her cousin again, but it seems fairly likely to me that your nephew is our culprit." As he spoke, his gaze slid past her toward the bedroom, as if, like Grace, he was concerned that Jessica might overhear.

"Paul?" Grace's frown deepened. She crossed her arms over her chest. She still wore the same gray fleece sweat suit with the OSU logo on the front that she had worn to run in. It was a warm outfit, too warm for the house really, but she felt chilled. "What makes you think so?"

"Leaving a message like that on your daughter's mirror is something a kid would do." The small, many-faceted chandelier that illuminated the upstairs hallway picked up silver threads in his black hair, Grace noticed. It also emphasized with shadows the tiny lines that radiated out from the corners of his eyes and the deeper ones that bracketed his mouth. "And now with the hamster missing—I'd say that makes a pretty strong case against your nephew."

"Why would Paul do such a thing?"

He shrugged. "To get revenge because your daughter took the hamster away from him? As payback because he got in trouble? Just to tease? Who knows? Before we go any farther with this, why don't you call your sister and have her ask him?"

.

Grace looked at him for a moment without replying, while she turned the possibilities over in her mind. It *was* just possible that Paul might have . . . Oh, she hoped so!

"I will," she said and, walking around Marino, headed toward the phone in her bedroom. Marino followed her. While she talked to Jackie, explaining the situation as well as she could without revealing the pivotal fact that a drunken Jessica had been caught buying marijuana, she saw him look around her bedroom.

While Jackie went to question Paul, Grace, on hold, surveyed the room through Tony Marino's eyes. As she did, she felt increasingly self-conscious. A bedroom was very personal, after all, revealing much about the person who slept there.

The ornate mahogany four-poster was queen-size, with a scallop-edged rose-and-green floral spread and a cream lace skirt. The dresser, night table, and lingerie chest were, like the bed, crafted of elaborately carved mahogany. The walls were painted soft green. The brass lamps, two on the dresser, one on the bedside table, had dark green shades and provided soft pools of illumination. Celery-striped curtains were drawn over the large window behind the bed and the even larger bay window at the far end of the room. Two armchairs covered in the same floral print as the bedspread stood before the bay window, with a small table bearing a bowl of deep pink silk roses between them. Silver-framed family pictures stood on her bedside table. Three books that she was currently reading, her place in each marked by turned-down corners, were stacked beside the pictures. One was a heavy-duty biography of LBJ (for help when she couldn't go to sleep), one was a thriller by a popular author, and one was a parenting tome entitled *The Chronically Ill Child*. The navy pumps she had taken off earlier and neglected to put away stood at the foot of the bed; one had fallen over on its side on the dark green carpet. A tuft of lace from a nightgown peeked out of one improperly closed dresser drawer. The pearl earrings she had worn earlier lay atop the dresser, along with her hair brush.

A gilt-framed oval mirror hung above the dresser, flinging her own stressed-out looking image back at her. She stood with one arm clamped tightly across her chest, her head tilted slightly over the white plastic receiver that she held to her ear. She was pale, with dark shadows under her eyes and cheekbones so sharp she looked almost gaunt. Her lips, devoid of lipstick or any soften-ing hint of color, were clamped tightly together, revealing a trio of C-shaped lines on either side of her mouth that she had never noticed before. Another line, a small vertical one, snaked between her eyebrows. Shocked at how old she looked, she immediately relaxed her face. The lines disappeared, but that was the only improvement. She was still, she acknowledged to herself with some chagrin, a not particularly pretty woman of thirty-some-thing, dressed in ancient, unbecoming sweats—too tall, too thin, with a too-long nose and short, untidy hair.

In short, no sex goddess she.

Since there was nothing to be done about that, Grace quit looking at herself and continued her inspection of the room, still attempting to view it through Marino's eyes. The door to her bathroom was ajar, revealing her cream quilted robe hanging on a hook inside the door, her toothbrush in its holder, and her night cream on the edge of the sink. A fluted blue lipstick tube lay on its side next to the pink jar of night cream. There was the faint smell of flowers and fruit in the air, which Grace had become accus-tomed to and usually did not notice. It came from the small china dish of fancy soaps that she kept—just because she liked them— on the other side of the sink.

She noticed the smell tonight because Tony Marino was in her bedroom, standing at the foot of her bed near her discarded pumps, his nostrils slightly distended as he seemed to sniff the air, his eyes hooded as he looked slowly around.

In his charcoal sweat suit, with the lamplight bronzing his skin and throwing an intimidatingly tall and broad-shouldered shadow against the far wall, he looked big and tough and out of place amidst her belongings.

As if sensing her eyes on him, he looked at her then and met her gaze. In that split second of eye contact, Grace felt a shaft of sexual attraction to him that set her insides quivering. A split second after that, when she realized to her horror what she was feeling, she very casually pivoted, breaking eye contact and turning her back to him. At that moment, thankfully, Jackie came back on the line. Concentrating fiercely, she was able to finish her conversation.

Then she had to hang up the phone and face him again.

"Paul says he didn't do it," she said crisply, her gaze meeting his as coolly as if she had never felt that sudden, sizzling bolt of awareness.

His brows lifted. "Is he telling the truth, do you think?"

Grace shrugged, walking toward him and the door. Her aplomb returned as she realized that of course he had no way of knowing what she had been thinking—or feeling. And anyway, she told herself, she was allowed to indulge in little spurts of sexual desire toward hunky men. She was a woman, after all, and single, and her senses were not dead even if she was not stupid enough to constantly indulge them.

The head-to-toe tingle she had felt, looking at him, was harmless. It was even kind of fun.

As long as she recognized it for the purely instinctive thing it was and left it at that.

"Jackie thinks he is. To tell you the truth, I don't think Paul did it, either. He's too young, for one thing. He can't write that well. It wouldn't occur to him. It's just not something he would do."

"Somebody did it."

He stepped out of her way as she approached him, and followed her out the door. Once in the hallway, without the intimacy of his presence in her bedroom to distract her, she was able to turn and confront him with more force.

"Look, Detective, I don't think this is a prank. Not by Paul. Not by anybody. I think somebody is trying to intimidate Jessica. I think this whole thing has something to do with your drug investigation at Hebron High School. I think somebody thinks Jessica is endangering them by talking to you, and this is their way of warning her to shut up."

From the corner of her eye, she saw Officers Peters and Stein, armed with equipment she couldn't identify from that distance, entering Jessica's bedroom. Marino must have seen the same thing, because his gaze flickered past her for an instant before returning.

"It's possible, I guess," he said slowly. "But I don't think so. Jessica doesn't know that much, to begin with. At this point, she's not a real player. If this is not a prank, which I have to tell you I'm inclined to think it is, then we have to start looking at other possibilities. You said you had a break-in here, the night Dom and I picked Jessica up. Tell me about it."

"I . . ." Grace began just as Jessica emerged from her bedroom.

"Mom, Godzilla's not in my room *any*where!" Sounding distraught, Jessica spotted her mother and Marino and came toward them. Her face was flushed now instead of pale, and her eyes were red-rimmed and teary.

"Did you remember to take your last insulin shot?" Grace was sidetracked by the telltale flushed cheeks. In all the excitement, it would not be surprising if Jessica had forgotten to give herself the injection.

"*Yes,* mother." Jessica's eyes grew stormy, and her voice sharp. "And *yes,* I ate when I was supposed to, and *yes,* I tested my blood. I'm *fine.* Would you just please leave me alone about the damned diabetes and help me find Godzilla?"

"Jessica Lee!" Grace exclaimed, protesting both swear word and attitude, but her daughter had already stormed past her and was stomping down the stairs.

Grace's expression, as she looked back at Marino, dared him to comment. He didn't, merely meeting her gaze for a pregnant instant before harking back to their interrupted conversation.

"So tell me about the break-in."

Grace sighed. And answered the question. Reprimanding Jessica for her rudeness and helping in the search for Godzilla would both just have to wait.

". . . and so I picked Mr. Bear up and carried him into the

house and called the police," Grace concluded, feeling cold all over again at the memory.

Marino seemed to ponder for a moment. "You know," he said slowly, "stealing a teddy bear from a little girl's bedroom doesn't sound like something a drug dealer bent on intimidation would do."

"Then what else could it be?" Grace sounded angry. She realized that as she heard the words come out of her mouth. But she wasn't angry, not really. She was growing increasingly frightened.

"The time line's not right, for one thing. Dom and I hadn't even picked her up yet that night while you were running around outside chasing mystery burglars from your yard. Why would anyone want to intimidate Jessica before we had even picked her up?"

"I don't know. How could I possibly know? But she was already involved with these kids by then. She was already out buying marijuana, and maybe she already knew something she shouldn't, or they thought she did. Maybe whoever it was that night just wanted to show Jessica that she was vulnerable, that they could get into her house and into her bedroom any time they wanted. Maybe whoever it was meant to harm her; maybe they didn't know she wasn't there. Or maybe they did know, and they were just checking out where she lived for some reason or another. I don't know what the motivation was, exactly. How could I know? All I know is that on the same night Jessica snuck out, got drunk, bought marijuana, and was picked up by you, someone broke into my house and took her teddy bear from the table beside her bed. And earlier today, she thought someone followed her home from school. And tonight, when we got back from running, there was a tombstone with *rest in peace* and my daughter's name inside it drawn on her bathroom mirror. And all that's changed in our lives since this stuff started happening is that she's gotten involved with some druggie kids at school, and *you*."

Marino held up both hands as if to ward her off as she glared at him. "You know, everything that's happened could easily fall under the heading of pranks," he said gently.

"Pranks?" Grace's voice rose. "Pranks? They're scaring me to death!"

"I know they are." He said nothing more for a moment, his eyes warm with sympathy as he looked down at her. "And I don't want to say you're overreacting. But what's really happened here, after all? You chased someone out of your yard in the middle of the night. You don't know who it was. It could have been anyone, a neighboring teenager out wandering just like Jessica was doing that night, one of her friends who got separated from the main crowd and was looking for her, a bum, a neighbor, anyone. You don't have any proof that whoever it was entered your house; there was no sign of forced entry and nothing of value was missing." He held up his hand to stop her protest before she could even get the words out. "Okay, except a teddy bear that you found down by the road that was a favorite of your daughter's. But it could have gotten there any number of ways, it seems to me, the least likely of which is that it was dropped by someone who broke into your house and stole it. Also, today, Jessica never *saw* anyone following her home. She just *had a feeling* she was being followed. It could have been a friend playing a trick, an admiring boy too shy to approach her, or her own imagination. I grant that there is no doubt that someone wrote *Jessica, R.I.P.* inside a tombstone drawn on her mirror. We all agree on that. But was it intended as a death threat? I doubt it. It looks like a prank. Everything that's happened, even conceding that everything you think happened really did, could easily fall under the heading of prank. I'd be more inclined to look at your nephew and niece, or maybe some of Jessica's friends, than I would a pissed-off drug dealer out for revenge."

"You're not going to take this seriously," Grace said with disbelief. "Someone is threatening my daughter and *you're not going to take it seriously.*"

"It's not that——" he began.

"Leave," she said, interrupting. "Just leave. If you are not going to treat this incident with the respect it deserves, then you are of no use to me. Leave. Get out of my house. Now."

"Look, Your Honor, I know that you're upset, but we have to look at this realistically," he tried again.

Down the hall, Dominick Marino and the two uniformed policemen emerged from Jessica's room carrying a black case, a camera, and other paraphernalia.

"All done," Dominick said as the trio approached. Tony glanced around as they joined them, then looked down at Grace. The look she returned him was stony.

"Head on out, I'll be with you in a minute," Tony said to the other men. When they were on their way downstairs, he spoke to Grace again.

"If I thought there was any danger for your daughter or for you, I'd tell you, and we would leave no stone unturned until the perpetrator was caught," he said. "I know you don't agree, but I am almost one hundred percent certain that whoever did this tonight, and did the other things *if* they happened, had to be a kid. They're not meant as serious threats. They're pranks. The kinds of things a kid would do."

"I understand that you think so," Grace said icily, turning away. "I disagree very strongly. Thank you for coming. Good-bye."

"Look, . . ." Sounding tired and faintly exasperated, he followed her down the stairs. "If anything else happens, call me. I don't care if it's in the middle of the night, or whenever. I'll come. If you hear a noise at the window, I'll come. If you see a shadow on the wall, I'll come. I know it's scary for you and your daughter to be living here alone, and I know it's easy to blow things out of proportion when you're scared. I'll check out what-ever comes up, and I'm going to thoroughly investigate this thing with the mirror no matter what I think happened. Okay?"

"Good-bye, Detective." Reaching the front door, Grace pulled it open and stood waiting for him to leave. He stopped for a moment, looking at her. She met his gaze with stony anger. He started to say something, appeared to think better of it, shook his head, and walked out.

Grace closed the door behind him with controlled fury. For

a moment she stood there gripping the knob, fighting to get her emotions under control so Jessica would not see how upset she was. Then, carefully, she checked to make sure the dead bolt was locked and pulled on the knob to make sure the lock had caught. She walked around the downstairs, checking to see that all the windows and especially the kitchen door were secure. Jessica was in the kitchen, chopping an apple into fine pieces.

Jessica had to be so careful about eating fruit, and she'd already had an apple that day.

"You don't need to eat that," Grace said, the words out before she could catch them.

Jessica gave her a withering look. "It's for Godzilla. He loves apple. I thought if I put some in his cage and set the cage on the floor . . ."

Her voice trailed off, and she looked down at the apple in her hand as she continued to chop.

"Oh," Grace said, "good idea."

Opening a cabinet, she got out a couple of saucers and spooned some of the chopped apple onto each. Then she helped Jessica set hamster lures of cage and exercise wheel and red plastic hamster house bated with saucers of chopped apple in hopes that Godzilla would get hungry during the night.

Though she was careful to give no sign of it to Jessica, Grace was still, in almost equal parts, angry and scared. By bedtime, scared had won out. That night she and Jessica, by mutual agreement, slept together in her big bed. Or at least Jessica slept, curled against her side. Grace lay awake listening to the rumble of thunder and the patter of rain on the roof as the threatened storm finally hit. She was almost afraid to close her eyes even with her bedroom door locked. So far, locks had proved to be no protection against the evil that she was becoming increasingly convinced lurked without.

CHAPTER **20**

I T WAS FUN FREAKING THEM OUT.

He waited outside in the darkness, crouched in the shadow of the next-door neighbor's hedge, grinning as the police car and the other car, the blue Camaro, pulled out of the driveway and took off slowly down the street. The Camaro was a police car, too, he was sure. An unmarked one. Little brother had his faults, but he wasn't stupid. He knew a cop car when he saw one.

The night the judge lady had chased him, he'd been scared at first, afraid of being caught. What would happen to him if he was caught? he wondered. His mom would piss her pants, his dad would look at him like he had just crawled out from under a rock, and Donny, jr., would act sorrowful and supportive and superior all at the same time, which was a crock. The parents would probably get him some *help*. Or maybe they'd just leave him to rot in jail, hoping that he would learn his lesson.

But he hadn't gotten caught. He'd gotten clean away. A sense of exhilaration had filled him as he'd realized that the judge lady couldn't catch him. The police couldn't catch him. He had hung around that night and watched the boys in blue arrive, and it had been cool to know that he'd gotten the judge lady scared enough to call them, cool to know that he had upset their lives just like his had been upset, cool to know that the police were looking for him. The coolest thing of all was knowing that they didn't have a clue who he was.

Remembering how the judge lady had looked chasing him, kind of like a psycho scarecrow with her spiky hair standing on end and her arms and legs pumping and her nightgown flapping, made him snicker. Old ladies like that looked nasty in night-gowns. But Jessica had looked nice in hers. He'd liked looking at her that night on the porch, which was why he'd crept closer and closer—so he could get a better view. She'd seen him finally. He felt a quick surge of pleasure as he remembered how she had stared right at him through the darkness, then jumped up off that swing like she'd been shot, and run inside and locked the door. He'd heard the dead bolt slam home even as far out in the yard as he was.

When were they going to learn that they couldn't lock him out?

He'd expected the police to come that night, too, but they hadn't. He guessed she hadn't told her mother about him. Proba-bly because she wasn't supposed to go outside at night in the first place, in case the bogeyman should get her.

He snickered again, picturing himself as the bogeyman. He kind of liked the idea.

Jessica wasn't as pretty as Caroline, but she was pretty enough to get him excited. He liked being excited, liked the way it felt. Looking at her when she didn't know he was there got him excited, following her when she didn't know he was there got him excited, and scaring her when she didn't have a clue who he was got him more excited than anything else.

Scaring her was a rush.

But the show was over for the night, he thought with regret, and he had things to do. Picking up his backpack and heaving it over one shoulder, he turned his back on the house and headed toward his motorcycle, which he had parked two streets over. Each time he'd been inside their house, he'd chosen a memento of his visit, although he'd dropped the teddy bear he'd taken from beside Jessica's bed. He still regretted the loss of that. Tonight's memento was small and furry and scrambling around frantically as it tried to escape from the inner zipper compartment of his backpack.

He couldn't wait to get it home and play with it.

Maybe he'd put it in his mom's bed, right down between the sheets near the foot where her toes would feel it first. That would be a trip. She'd scream the place down. Or he could put it in the refrigerator, in the clear plastic compartment on the door where the butter was kept. She always had toast with butter first thing in the morning.

Or he could put it in her purse.

Just considering the possibilities made him laugh out loud. For the first time in a long time, little brother was really having fun.

CHAPTER **21**

"**M**AN, YOU DON'T THINK YOU'RE TAKING Judge Ball-Breaker a little too seriously, do you?" Dominick's question was a soft murmur, barely audible over the various parking lot noises that wafted through the air. Car doors opened and closed, people laughed and talked, engines started, a guy urinated on a nearby tree. They were doing a stakeout, hiding behind a rusty dumpster at one edge of the parking lot. The air around them smelled of rotting garbage and piss. It was almost one A.M.

"What kind of cop wouldn't take a woman calling the police to report a break-in seriously?" Tony was crouched beside Dom, camera at the ready, his gaze focused on the entrance to the seedy tenement opposite. It was a run-down brick building, two-story, composed of a dozen attached town-house apartments. Their mission was to record for evidentiary purposes everyone who entered or exited the target unit. One of the biggest drug dealers in Columbus had rented the apartment, strictly for the purpose of drug distribution (he actually lived in a lavish five bedroom house outside of town), and he was in there now, along with a couple of flunkies and some buyers.

"The kind of penny-ante stuff she's been reporting, you know you ought to let the uniforms handle it. Come on, a stolen teddy bear, somebody following her daughter home, some writing with oil on a mirror? It's got nothing to do with us or this investigation."

"She thinks it does."

"So?"

"So give me a break, will you? What does it matter if I go over there and check things out for her? It's no skin off anybody's teeth but mine."

"You like her, don't you?"

"Shut up, Dom." Tony said this perfectly amiably, one brother to another.

"You *do* like her. That's why you've got me running over there every time she whistles." Dom was grinning.

"You know where you can go." Again, this was perfectly amiable.

"Jesus, Tony, have you thought what you're lettin' yourself in for, man? That woman's used to getting her own way. She'll be telling you how to do her in bed."

"Fuck off, Dom."

"Now you're gettin' . . ." Dominick broke off as a white Ford Taurus, maybe a '93 or '94 model, pulled up in front of the town house and stopped. "Looks like we got customers."

Tony was already leaning into the open, camera clicking away. As the car doors opened, disgorging boisterous teenagers, Dom grabbed his own camera and followed suit. Eight kids— three more than the number the car was designed to hold— headed for the door.

"Hey, buddy, open up!" one of the kids yelled, pounding on the door with his fist while Tony was still busy counting heads. Five boys, three girls. At least, the smaller ones with long hair looked like girls. Sometimes it was hard to be sure, especially in the dark and at a distance.

"We wanna buy some smack!" A second boy joined in the pounding, bellowing his business. Still clicking away, Tony shook his head at their sheer stupidity. They were already high as kites on something, from the sound of it. The gentleman in the town house, with his preference for quiet, discreet illegal activity, was more likely to kick their asses for them than sell them anything.

"Open up!" The first boy bellowed, pounding again. Tony and Dom exchanged alarmed glances. If this didn't bring uniforms down on the whole operation, they could count themselves damned lucky. "Open up!"

"We want some smack!" A third kid yelled.

The town-house door jerked open, spilling light over the supplicants. The tall, rangy body of one of the flunkies was silhouetted in the doorway, legs spread, one hand on the door knob and the other on the jamb, barring any attempt at entry.

"What be wrong wit' you all?" he demanded fiercely. "You get away from here now. Go on away."

"No, man, we want smack." The first boy was swaying on his feet. "We got money."

"I don't know what you fools be talkin' about." He started to close the door on them. "Get, now."

"No! We want smack!" The first boy tried to push his way past the guardian of the door, and the two behind joined in.

"We want smack! We want smack!" The remaining kids chorused, rushing the door. The guardian fell back, the door fell open, and the kids tumbled over themselves rushing inside.

The sound of a gunshot, sharp and staccato, brought Tony and Dom to their feet with a single horrified exchange of glances.

"Haul ass, man!" Tony said. Drawing their pistols, crouching, they ran for the town house, approaching it separately from either side of the door.

Kids erupted from the door like rocks from an erupting volcano, screaming bloody murder as they ran. Behind them, Tim Fulkerson, the Marinos' primary target, was firing a .45. Behind him was what looked like a regular forest of bushy marijuana plants, most about five feet tall, under a ceiling of grow lights.

"Police! Drop your weapons!" Dom shouted.

"Drop your weapons!" Tony echoed, coming out into the open. He was still moving fast, trying to both dodge and shield the kids while keeping a bead on Fulkerson. Fulkerson turned his weapon in Dom's direction. . . .

"Police! Drop your weapon!" Tony screamed, and fired. The bullet thudded into the doorway, Fulkerson jumped back, Tony ran forward, gun drawn—and the flunky who'd answered the door in the first place jumped out with an automatic weapon and began firing.

Still in a crouching run forward, Tony had barely eyeballed the weapon when someone pushed him hard in the center of his back, sending him sprawling facedown on the concrete parking lot.

A hair-parting hale of bullets passed not two feet over his head. If he'd still been standing, he would have been cut in two.

Close call, but now wasn't the time to dwell on it. Tony rolled, coming up on his feet, and fired a single shot. The flunky ran.

Three marked cars came roaring into the parking lot, sirens screaming, tires squealing.

"We're police officers! We're police officers!" Tony and Dom both shouted as uniforms piled out of the cars. When in plain clothes, a police officer at the scene of any action involving gun play was most in danger from his own side, as every under-cover cop knew.

"Lay down your weapons! Lay down your weapons!" The uniforms yelled, approaching Tony and Dom with guns drawn.

"Jesus Christ, we're police officers!" Tony bellowed. "Hell, don't let that guy get away!"

But the flunky was already hightailing it down the street, picking up his heels so high he almost kicked himself in the butt with every step.

By the time the mess was sorted out, they had two flunkies under arrest—Tim Fulkerson had escaped, as had the guy who'd come to the door when the kids knocked—one high school kid down, shot in the thigh, another seven under arrest, and a town house full of marijuana, cocaine, and crack for evidence. Ironi-cally, there was no smack anywhere in the house.

Later, when Tony and Dom were back in their car heading in, Dom looked at his brother.

"Man, I thought you were a goner when that dude burst out of there with that automatic blazing. You sure picked the right time to fall on your face."

"I didn't fall. Somebody pushed me."

Dom shook his head. "Uh-uh. There wasn't anybody near you to push you. I saw the whole thing."

"I'm telling you, somebody pushed me. I felt a hand on my back."

"And I'm telling you there was nobody there."

This good-natured wrangling continued all the way to the station house.

In the backseat, the merest shadow of a little girl listened, and smiled.

CHAPTER 22

THE STORY WAS ALL OVER THE LOCAL NEWS THE next morning. However, Grace didn't hear about it until she was about to ascend the bench. Franklin County Courthouse, in the middle of downtown Columbus, was a busy place so early in the day. There were lines at the metal detectors set up at every entrance, and uniformed sheriff's deputies were busy poking through purses and briefcases that didn't pass the X-ray test. Fortunately, the deputies knew Grace by sight and she was waved on through. Charging along traffic-packed corridors and riding crowded escalators to her courtroom, she did not have time to do more than acknowledge with a called-out word or two and a wave the greetings of her colleagues and acquaintances. It had been a hectic morning: The alarm had failed to go off—in all the excitement she must have forgotten to pull out the little button on the back of the clock—which had made them late to start with. She .and Jessica rushed around, getting dressed, eating, doing the hundred and one tasks necessary before they could head out the door. At Jessica's insistence, they had also taken a few minutes to search without success for Godzilla, who had not, as hoped, been lured from hiding by the sweet smell of chopped apple. Finally, instead of allowing Jessica to walk to school as she usually did, Grace had driven her. The steadily falling rain had provided a convenient excuse, although they both knew the truth that neither cared to put into words: even if the day had been as dry as a bone and they'd had all the time in the world, Grace would not have permitted Jessica to walk. She had already called Linda to make arrangements for Jessica to be picked up after school and driven home.

She did not want Jessica to be alone, not even for a minute. Her mother-instinct was working overtime, telling her that something was wrong. Ridiculously, she pictured it as being rather like the robot in *Lost in Space,* waving its arms and warning: "Danger! Danger, Grace Hart!"

Whether Tony Marino and the police department took what was happening seriously or not, Grace did. And she meant to protect her daughter at all costs.

Her second phone call of the morning, after speaking to Linda, was to a home alarm company. They promised to come out and install a security system the following Monday. Her third call, to a locksmith, was equally productive: she would have the locks changed on Monday as well.

Four days to go, and then at least they would be safe inside their own house.

"I kinda thought you might be late this morning, with what's happening at Hebron and all," Walter said with a commiserating look as Grace emerged from her chambers right on time. The zipper on her judge's robe had stuck three quarters of the way up, which meant she'd had to wrestle with it so as to appear properly gowned. Therefore, she was pink-cheeked and irritated and still in the process of settling the white lace collar of her blouse over the neckline of the enveloping black polyester garment that was the symbol of her authority.

"What's happening?" Upraised hands stilling on her collar, Grace blinked at Walter with surprise. Had she forgotten a school program, or a parent meeting, or something? But how would Walter know about anything like that?

"The drug thing. The dogs. You know."

Grace stopped walking some three feet short of the bench and stood stock still, staring at him. "No, I don't know. Tell me."

"It was on all the news shows this morning. A late-breaking bulletin, they called it. Don't tell me you missed it."

"I missed it. Fill me in, please." Anxiety sharpened her voice.

"You didn't hear about the Hebron kid getting shot last night?"

"No!"

"Your Honor, with respect, shh." Walter glanced around significantly, reminding Grace that they were in the courtroom. Lallie Baker, the court reporter, was already behind her small desk in front of the bench, poised to go to work. About half the seats in the courtroom, a typical case load for a Thursday morning, were filled.

Everyone was waiting on her. Quite a few were looking at her expectantly. Of course, there was no mistaking the judge in her black robes.

Grace didn't care.

"Walter, please, tell me the whole story," Grace said in a lowered voice. "Quickly, if you don't want me to turn into a raving lunatic right here."

He looked surprised. "Okay, sure, of course I will. Well, let's see. Last night a group of kids from Hebron apparently drove to an apartment down by the university to buy drugs, and one kid got shot. A boy. I can't remember his name but I remember thinking that Jessica might not know him even though he was a Hebron student because he was a couple of grades ahead of her. He's in serious condition this morning at University Hospital. Anyway, the upshot is that the police are raiding the high school this morning. They've got dogs there and they're searching all the lockers. Supposed to be some big drug ring involving a lot of the kids. 'Course, I'm sure Jessica's not part of it, or any of her friends either, most likely."

"Oh, my God!" Grace was appalled. She should have been

told—Tony Marino should have told her. He had to have known what was going down. Under the circumstances, he should have called her and told her. She would not have sent Jessica to school if she'd known.

She didn't know what worried her more, the prospect that drugs might be found in Jessica's locker, or the prospect that some of the other kids—or someone who was not a kid—might blame Jessica for the raid.

Well, yes, she did. If Jessica was arrested for drug possession, personal use, first offense, it would be a misdemeanor and as a juvenile she would receive, at most, a referral to counseling and her record would eventually be expunged. If Jessica was targeted as an informer by someone involved in a drug ring, she could end up dead.

Terror, cold and stark, began to race through Grace's veins.

"Jessica at school?" Walter asked.

"Yes. I dropped her off. We were in such a rush . . . I didn't notice anything out of the way at all. There must have been police cars, something, but I didn't see anything."

"Well, likely they're making a bigger deal of it on TV than it is in real life." There was rough comfort in his tone.

"Walter, I need to make a quick phone call. I'll be right back." Grace was already turning toward her chambers. *Warning! Warning, Grace Hart!* her arm-waving mother-instinct shouted again.

"Sure, Your Honor."

Grace was barely conscious of the multitude of eyes watching her as she strode back into chambers, her robe billowing behind her. She shut the door, grabbed her purse, fished out the card he had given her, and called Tony Marino. Of course, she did not get him, but his pager. Seething, she left her number. Then she called Hebron High School. Mrs. Page, the principal, who'd always been very nice to her and Jessica, assured her that despite the locker searches, which were admittedly upsetting, the school day was proceeding as usual. Yes, Jessica was fine. Everything was fine. In case she was worried, which of course she had no reason to be, Jessica's locker had already been searched and nothing out of the way had been found.

Good. Fine. Thank you. Have a nice day. What more could Grace say? I'm coming to get my daughter right now? But she had a courtroom full of people waiting for her, and according to Mrs. Page, Jessica was fine. Pulling her out might just draw more attention to her, anyway, if any druggie types were looking for a scapegoat. Grace replaced the receiver slowly, stared into space for a moment, and then walked back into her courtroom.

"All rise. . . ."

With her thoughts full of Jessica, she was barely aware of the traditional opening of court as she took her place on the bench.

Just before the noon recess, Tony Marino walked in and sat down in the back of her courtroom. For a moment Grace was so glad to see him that she was shocked by the intensity of the feeling. It was as though a friend, an ally—someone she could depend on—had suddenly appeared. Then she remembered that she was furious at him, and why, and the warm rush of gladness disappeared. Frowning, she returned her attention to the case at hand.

It was a man who had broken into the home of his former girlfriend and assaulted her. She had taken out an order of protection against him earlier on the day of the assault, and the fact that she had thus publicly *dissed* him—his words—was his justification for the attack.

"Mr. Harmon, I find you in violation of a court order of protection and guilty of assault in the first degree. Six months in county jail," Grace said after listening to both sides of the story. The man's version of what had happened—he didn't deny hitting his girlfriend, but kept insisting she had it coming because she had humiliated him by making their private troubles public—sealed his fate.

"What? What?" the defendant howled as Walter and another bailiff started to clap handcuffs on him. "You can't send me to jail for this, you bitch! I got fuckin' rights!"

"So does the woman you assaulted," Grace said, dismissing the case.

"I'll get you for this, bitch!"

Grace was already looking down at her docket for the next case as the man, yelling threats, was hauled off.

It was 11:35. The next case was a custody dispute that threatened to be both lengthy and complicated, and Colin Wilkerson was the attorney representing the plaintiff. That, coupled with Tony Marino's presence in her courtroom and her urgent desire to speak with him, was enough to make Grace's decision easy. She banged her gavel on the wood surface in front of her.

"I realize that it's a little early, but I'm going to call the lunch break now. Court will reconvene at one P.M," Grace announced. Over the sea of heads, her gaze met Marino's. Without a word or gesture being exchanged, Grace knew that he understood that he should join her in her chambers as soon as she left the bench.

"Please clear the courtroom," Walter intoned as Grace stood up. Out of the corner of her eye she saw that Colin Wilkerson was headed toward her. What now? she thought as she stepped down. Colin had better watch himself; she wasn't in the mood for histrionics today of all days.

"Grace! Grace, wait a minute!" He caught up with her halfway to her chambers.

"What can I do for you, Colin?" she asked with resignation, turning to face him.

To her surprise, he smiled at her. His blue eyes were warm and coaxing. For a moment she glimpsed what had attracted her to him to begin with.

"I want to apologize for my behavior the other day," he said, taking her hand and clasping it earnestly between both of his. His hands were long and narrow and warm, and she had once enjoyed their touch. No longer. "I was out of line."

"You certainly were," Grace agreed, pointedly removing her hand from his hold. Fool me once, shame on you, she thought.

Fool me twice, shame on me. "But I accept your apology. Now if you'll excuse me . . ."

"I was hoping you'd let me take you out to lunch to make amends." He was trying to charm her, for what reason Grace couldn't fathom, but she was sure there was a reason. She would have to pay particular attention to the client he was representing after lunch, she thought. Something was up.

"Thank you, but I have a previous engagement." Grace was cool.

"But . . ." Colin protested, then glanced over his shoulder as Tony Marino walked up behind him.

"Hi," Grace said to Marino. His black hair was combed back off his brow today, and it was in waves probably because of the rain. His eyes were slightly narrowed as they met hers. Dressed in the ubiquitous leather bomber jacket over a T-shirt and jeans, broad of shoulder and heavy of muscle, he looked like the quintessential working-class stiff next to Colin's slender, pin-striped elegance.

How she had ever found Colin attractive when there were men like Marino in the world, Grace couldn't fathom.

"Hi." He was equally to the point. The very brevity of the unsmiling exchange spoke of familiarity, Grace realized. Colin's eyes focused on the newcomer, and his fingers twitched at his sides. Obviously he thought Marino was her "previous engagement" and didn't much like the notion.

Too bad, Grace thought. What Colin Wilkerson thought mattered to her not at all anymore.

"Excuse me." Her words to Colin were perfunctory but polite. To Marino she said, "Come into my chambers, please."

"Yes, ma'am," he answered, following her, his pseudorespectful tone a payback for her brusqueness, she knew.

Once they were both inside, she closed the door, leaned back against it, and glared at him.

CHAPTER 23

"**Y**OU DIDN'T TELL ME," GRACE ACCUSED angrily.

"It was a confidential police matter. I couldn't." Marino made no attempt to pretend not to know what she was talking about. Thrusting his hands into the front pockets of his jeans, he rocked back on the heels of those black basketball shoes and looked maddeningly nonchalant.

"Bullshit."

"It's the truth. What do you think I should have done? Called you up this morning and said, by the way, Your Honor, we're getting ready to conduct a raid on your daughter's high school, so be prepared? Number one, if she'd had pot or anything else in her locker, and you had told her, which I'd be willing to bet anything I possess you would have done, she would have had a chance to get rid of it, and that would have been an obstruction of justice on both our parts. Number two, she—or you—would have had time to tell someone else, *might* have told someone else, probably *would* have told someone else, thus compromising the raid. I'm a professional, just like you. I could not have told you."

"Last night, when you were so busy assuring me that there was no good reason that you knew of for anyone to want to scare or harm Jessica, you knew this was going down; you knew there *was* a reason. That's why that message was written on her mirror, isn't it? Because of this!"

Grace was so angry by now that she was practically hissing at him. The fact that he didn't seem one whit chastened, contrite, or even concerned just added fuel to the fire.

"Your timing's off again. The message came before the raid."

"Someone obviously knew about it!"

"No one knew about it. It happened too fast. When I was at your house last night, there was nothing planned. The kid getting shot triggered it. The powers that be felt we couldn't have any high school students getting killed just to further our investigation, so we had to end it. The raid ends it."

"You and your—what is he, anyway? brother? cousin? stepgrandpa?—whoever he is, you were wearing dark sweats when you came to my house last night. You were dressed for what was going down. Don't deny it."

"Dom's my brother. Older by three years. Thank you for asking. And did it ever occur to you that maybe we were dressed that way because we, like you and your daughter, were planning on getting some exercise?"

"Bullshit!" Grace said again.

He crossed his arms over his chest and cocked his head at her. To her fury, a twinkle appeared in his eyes. "You know, you might want to think about getting some help with that rampant paranoia you seem to be developing."

The lid blew off Grace's temper. Pointing an accusing index finger at him, she moved away from the door, her eyes narrow and as cold as steel as she closed in on him.

"Listen, Detective, *your antics are endangering my daughter and I won't have it.* Is that clear? *I won't have it!* You're aware of what's going on at my house, you're aware that Jessica's being stalked and threatened because of this drug thing, and proceeding with a raid at her high school without notifying me and giving me a chance to get her out of harm's way is nothing short of criminal irresponsibility! My inclination at the moment is to call the district attorney, call the chief of police, and call the police department internal-affairs unit and scream bloody murder about the tactics that you have used in this case!"

Practically vibrating with outrage, she came to a stop less than a foot in front of him, her finger jabbing the air with each point she made. She was tall, he was taller. She was also thin where he was muscular, but then, she was furious while he gave every evidence of being amused. That, she felt, was enough to balance the physical scales.

He reached out, caught the hand that was pointing at him, and held it fast. The feel of his hard, warm fingers wrapping around her slimmer, cooler ones was startling enough to be distracting. Their gazes met over their joined hands.

"Tell me something, Your Honor: Do you try to bully everyone you meet, or am I just lucky for some reason?" There was no mistaking the amusement in his face now.

Grace jerked her hand from his hold, her anger reenergized by his levity. On the verge of exploding at him, she managed not to. Taking a deep, calming breath, she said nothing for the space of several seconds. Remaining in control was the secret of wielding authority, she had found. Once you lost control, the other person gained the upper hand.

"I want my daughter protected." She used her judge's voice, the cold, clear tones that stated distinctly that she expected to be obeyed. "I want someone sent to her school to watch over her for the rest of the day. I want her—and the girl I've sent to pick her up—to have an escort home. I want a police officer in my house to provide protection for us until I am sure that Jessica is safe. If you don't have the authority to make the necessary arrangements, I will go over your head and find someone who does."

He looked at her for a moment as if he were considering how to reply. He crossed his arms over his chest, and lines appeared between his brows as he frowned slightly.

"Your Honor," he said, speaking slowly and distinctly as if he were addressing someone whom he considered a trifle thick. "Think about what you're asking here. At this point, there is no evidence that anybody at Hebron High School or anywhere else has connected your daughter with our drug investigation. Any threats to her from that direction seem to be strictly a product of your possibly overly vivid imagination and a set of coincidental circumstances. If we surround her with police escorts, we will make her stand out in a way that you don't want. *That* is what will target her as an informer, which, let me remind you, she has not been. If you want my advice, it would be to not draw attention to her in that way."

Grace was stymied. She had had similar thoughts herself, which had been overruled by her growing feeling that her daughter was in danger. *Was* she overreacting? she asked herself desperately. Should she just—and, oh, it was the hardest thing in the world to do—should she just wait and see what, if anything, happened next, in the hope that nothing would?

He sighed. "If it will make you feel better, I'll see that someone follows your daughter and her babysitter home from school. I'll see that there's a periodic drive-by of your house this afternoon and tonight. And I'll see that the whole thing is done very unobtrusively. You have my number and the general police number, and you and Jessica can call either one if you feel threatened in any way. But I don't think there's anything for you to be worried about. If, and you notice I say *if,* big if, our drug investigation at Hebron was in some way putting your daughter at risk, then you have nothing more to worry about, because it is over. *Over.* Got it?"

Grace stared at him. He met her gaze, his expression a combination of exasperation, humor, and understanding. This feeling she had that she could rely on what he was telling her, rely on *him,* warred with the more subtle promptings of her intuition. Maybe he was right, she thought, and her screaming mother-instinct was wrong.

She had always had a tendency to be overprotective where Jessica was concerned.

"All right," she said. "All right. Linda—you remember Linda—is picking Jessica up after school. She drives a tan Ford

Escort. Just—have somebody see that they get home okay. And have somebody do a few drive-bys this afternoon and tonight."

"I will," he promised, his lightened tone and expression telling her that he thought she was seeing reason at last. "Don't worry. I—"

There was a knock at the door. Before Grace could move to answer it, the door opened and Owen Johnston stuck his head in. Fiftyish and married, with a thick head of silver hair and a kindly expression, he was a fellow Domestic Court judge, and Grace had a standing date with him and the other three Domestic Court judges on the fourth Thursday of each month.

"You ready to go to lunch, Grace?" he asked, spotting her. She was still in her judge's robes, turned toward the door, with Marino standing behind her. Owen glanced over her head at the cop, and then back at her, frowning as though he thought he had intruded on something personal. "Sorry, I didn't mean to interrupt."

"I'll be with you in one minute, Owen," she said with a smile. He nodded and withdrew, closing the door behind him.

When she turned back to Marino, his expression had changed in some undefinable way.

"I'll take care of things, Your Honor," he said crisply and, just like that, walked past her and out the door. Grace was left staring after him for a frowning moment before a gentle knock reminded her that Owen and the others were waiting. Hurriedly, unzipping her robe, she joined them for lunch.

And refused to allow herself to remember the delicious little tingle she had felt when Tony Marino had held her hand.

As it happened, that day and the next were uneventful, even reasonably pleasant. When she anxiously (though, she hoped, subtly) questioned Jessica about what had gone on at school, her daughter reported that none of her friends had been caught with any drugs in their lockers, so none of them had been arrested. The kids who had been arrested, as well as the boy who was shot, were juniors and seniors, and she didn't know them. She was happy because most of the kids had started talking to her again, although some of them—like Allison—were still being kind of snotty. Listening, Grace thought with relief that Marino had been right. With the drug investigation at Hebron concluded, perhaps Jessica really was no longer in danger.

Reaching that conclusion, even tentatively, was such a *relief*.

Basketball tryouts were Saturday morning. Grace got Jessica to the gym early at eight A.M., then stayed to watch, chewing nervously on her knuckle when things got tense. The Hebron Ladybirds was one of the best girls' high school teams in the state, and the competition to make the squad was fierce. As a freshman, it would be difficult for Jessica to make varsity, but she had her heart set on it.

"Jessica's doing well," Ann Millhollen murmured encouragingly as Jessica went six-for-six from the free-throw line. Ann sat beside Grace in the bleachers, which were sprinkled with parents watching the tryouts. Ann's daughter Emily was a friend of Jessica's and was trying out as well.

"Thanks. Emily is, too," Grace replied. Emily had gone four-for-six from the free-throw line, but she was tall and sturdily built and murder on the boards.

"She was so nervous this morning. Was Jessica?"

"Jessica doesn't get nervous," Grace reported wryly, rubbing her chewed-on knuckle. "I do."

"Oh, look at that!" Ann exclaimed, her gaze caught by the action on the court. Grace's head whipped around, and her stomach twisted as she watched her daughter run the length of the court with a steal, go for a layup—and have the ball snatched from her hands at the last second by Tiffany Driver. No call from the coaches, who were acting as refs. The look on Jessica's face as she chased the ball downcourt again made Grace proud and despairing at the same time. Jess was determined to make the team, and she was playing her heart out. Jumping to block Tiffany's shot, she was knocked to the floor. Grace winced.

Once tryouts were over, Grace drove Jessica home to change clothes. In a one-time exception to the three-month grounding that was still in force, Grace had agreed to let Jessica go to the mall for lunch and a movie with a group of girls who had tried out for the team.

It was hard not to relent occasionally. Grace justified it by reasoning that they had both been under so much stress lately that Jessica really needed this time with her friends as a kind of release.

As for danger, there shouldn't be any. All had been calm for two days. The drug thing was over. Jessica's friends were speaking to her again. And it was broad daylight and a whole group of girls and the mall, after all.

If the mother-instinct thing wouldn't leave her alone, Grace thought, she could always go to the mall herself, stay out of sight, and keep an unobtrusive eye on her daughter.

Though Jessica would kill her if she was caught.

As she pulled into the garage, Grace was smiling faintly at the thought of skulking behind kiosks while trying to keep her daughter in view. Jessica leaped out of the car as soon as it stopped, then hesitated. Ordinarily she would have run in ahead of her mother, dropped her gym bag in the kitchen, and headed straight upstairs for a shower, but after her recent upsetting experience with the mirror, she was reluctant to go inside alone. Grace understood perfectly what she was feeling, without Jessica needing to say a word. In many ways, despite the recent ups and downs in their relationship, she and Jessica operated on the same psychic wavelength. Probably because it had been just the two of them for so long.

Therefore Jessica was only a little bit ahead of her as they entered the house through the kitchen door. True to form, she dropped her gym bag by the coatrack—and then stopped dead.

"Mom, you got me a *cake*?" Jessica asked in disbelief, inadvertently blocking Grace's view as she stood as if carved from stone, staring at the kitchen table.

"What?" Carrying her purse and a bag of groceries, Grace nudged her daughter aside, glanced at the table, and stopped dead, too.

In the center of the table was a layer cake, beautifully presented on a doily-bedecked paper plate, decorated as if it had been ordered for someone's birthday. It glistened with white icing and yellow roses with green leaves and apricot buds. Leaning closer, Grace saw that the top of the cake was adorned with a picture, drawn in icing, of a basketball going through a hoop. The message read, "Good luck, Jessica."

Grace had not ordered the cake, nor authorized anyone else to do so. In fact, she and Jessica rarely, if ever, ate cake.

More important, the confection had not been on the table when she and Jessica had left. And since then, no one else should have been in the house.

CHAPTER 24

"A CAKE." MARINO STARED DOWN AT THE CAKE
on the table, his hands closing around the back of one of the
green-painted ladderback chairs that made up the kitchen set. He
glanced at Grace, who stood on the opposite side of the table
watching him. "So what makes you think that a cake that says
'Good luck, Jessica' constitutes a threat?"

Officers Gelinsky and Ayres, who'd been on the scene for
about ten minutes, hovered nearby. Gelinsky appeared faintly
bored as he contemplated the cake, while Ayres looked downright
dour as she, like Marino, looked at Grace.

"I didn't order it. We don't eat cake. And it was not in the
house when we left," Grace explained for the second time, holding on to her patience with an effort. Marino had just arrived.
Gelinsky and Ayres had already been underwhelmed by the significance of a cake as a threat.

"Your sister probably brought it. For God's sake, it's a nice
gesture. Unauthorized delivery of a cake is not exactly a crime."

"My sister knows Jessica and I don't eat cake. My sister did
not bring it. No one who knows us would bring it. Jessica is
diabetic. We do not eat cake."

Grace spoke emphatically. On the surface, she supposed that
it probably did seem as if she was having a strangely negative

reaction to what could be construed as a charming surprise for Jessica. But the cake was sinister. She felt it with every iota of intuition she possessed, and regarded the beautifully decorated dessert with as much fear as if it were a live bomb sitting in the middle of her kitchen table.

Whoever had written the message on Jessica's mirror had left the cake, she knew.

"It's not over," she said aloud, crossing her arms over her chest. She wore a navy wool blazer over a white turtleneck and khakis, and still she was cold, cold to the bone. The kind of cold that had nothing to do with the heavy gray skies outside, or the rainy mist that hung like fog in the air.

"What?" Marino glanced at her, a hint of exasperation in his voice. His black hair was wavy today, too, adding credence to her theory that its latent curl was brought out by rain, and she thought maybe he'd had it cut, because it looked shorter around his neck and ears. Like herself, he was dressed in a blazer and slacks, the former tan tweed, the latter well-cut dark brown wool. He was even wearing a tie, of tan silk with thin black stripes. With the tiny part of her mind not consumed with mushrooming fear, she wondered where he'd been headed when she had paged him.

"It's not over," she repeated, crossing her arms over her chest to ward off the chill and glaring at him across the table. "You said it was over, and it's not. Whoever wrote on Jessica's mirror and stole Mr. Bear did this."

"Jesus." Marino shook his head at her. "You really are getting paranoid, you know that?"

"I am *not* getting paranoid." Grace fought down a bubble of rising hysteria so as to sound cool and collected and forceful. "You see the cake, don't you? It's real, and it's on my kitchen table although it wasn't here when I left the house, and my daughter and I don't eat cake and didn't order it. The writing on the mirror was real, too, and Jessica's teddy bear was really down by the road, and I really chased an intruder from my yard the night I found it there. So explain to me exactly how all those circumstances add up to my being paranoid, if you please."

"It's a *cake,* Grace."

His use of her first name, the first time he had called her by it, appeared to slip out unnoticed. Grace noticed, but she was too worried and upset and generally beside herself with concern for her daughter to do more than register in passing what he'd said.

"It's a *threat.*"

A horn blared in the driveway. Grace started, unnerved by even that homely sound. Marino and the other police officers glanced around toward the front of the house from whence the sound had come.

"Mom, Mom, it's them!" Jessica flew into the kitchen, fresh from her shower and dressed to go out, which meant the usual jeans and top with the addition of dangly earrings, shoulder bag, and a black leather jacket styled as a minitrench, which was belted around her tiny waist. Determined not to terrify her daughter, Grace had played down the significance of the cake. But she had thought Jessica understood that its arrival precluded any chance of her being able to go to the mall.

"Jess . . ." she began helplessly, shaking her head as she started to tell her daughter that she could not, after all, go.

"Oh, Mom, *please.*" Jessica must have read her intention in her eyes and from her body language. "*Please.* I want to go so bad! I haven't been out of the house in weeks, and I've been so good, and it's driving me crazy being cooped up here like this and everything's okay with my friends again and I don't want to screw it up. . . . *Please!*"

"Jessica, sweetie, I know I said you could go, but—"

"I don't care about the stupid cake," Jessica said passionately. "Or the mirror or anything else! This thing is ruining my life, and I'm not going to let it happen. I just can't stay cooped up in the house forever, Mother! I have a *life!*"

From the driveway, the horn sounded again.

"Oh, please, oh, please, oh, please," Jessica begged, her hands clasped prayerfully beneath her chin.

Without in the least meaning to do so, Grace glanced at Marino. He was watching the two of them with a sardonic expression that said more clearly than words that he considered her putty in Jessica's hands. Grace's lips tightened. Not that his opinion mattered to her in the least.

"Mom, *please*."

Jessica's eyes were huge, and beseeching. Against her better judgment, Grace felt herself caving in. She couldn't keep Jessica under guard forever, couldn't build walls around her no matter how much she wished to do so.

The truth was, she had a hard time denying her daughter anything, and always had.

"Will you promise, promise, *promise* me to stay with the other girls no matter what?"

"Oh, Mom, yes! Thank you, Mom! You are the best mother in the whole world!"

Taking Grace's question for consent, which in a tacit way Grace supposed it was, Jessica darted over, dropped a kiss on her cheek, and, to avoid Officer Gelinsky who was testing the latch on the rear door, ran out of the kitchen toward the front door.

Grace was already getting the terrible feeling that she might have made a mistake. One look at Marino's face told her he felt the same, although for a different reason. He was thinking about discipline; she was worried about danger. She shot him a defiant look: her daughter, her call.

"Excuse me a minute, I'll be right back," Grace said, to Marino and the others. "I just want to have a word with the mother who's driving."

She hurried after Jessica. Ann, who was driving the girls to the mall, was of course burning with curiosity about the presence of a police car (the one Ayres and Gelinsky drove was marked) in the driveway. Grace told her that they had had a break-in, without going into the matter in depth. She did, however, ask Ann to keep an eye on Jessica. This Ann promised to do. The conversation was short because the girls were in a hurry to get going and made no bones about their impatience. Still, when she watched the car pull out of her driveway, Grace felt a little better about her decision to let Jessica go.

When she returned to the house, rain beaded her hair and dampened her clothes. Her face was wet, and she could taste the cold moisture on her lips. The house's warmth enveloped her like a blanket. Its familiar smell, a mix of what she had decided long ago was furniture polish and old wood and the Love My Carpet powder Pat sprinkled on the rugs on Wednesdays, was comforting. She passed Officer Ayres, who was on her way outside, in the hall, and nodded to her. The woman nodded back, but did not smile. As it had been when she had come to the house before, her demeanor was so professional it bordered on unfriendly.

"There is no sign of forced entry," Gelinsky was telling Marino as Grace walked back into the kitchen. The overhead lights were on, although it was only early afternoon, to combat the darkness of the day outside. With its soft, warm colors and homey furnishings, the kitchen looked far too cheerful to be the scene of a police investigation.

"What about footprints? It's been raining all day. There should have been some footprints if someone came in from outside," Marino replied.

"I didn't notice any," Gelinsky said apologetically, looking around on the floor. If there had been footprints, Grace thought, following his gaze, it was too late to discover them now. If they had existed, they had been obliterated by more footprints as first she and Jessica and then the three police officers had walked around the kitchen without any thought for evidence that might lurk underfoot. The area circling the table and the paths to the front and back doors all showed traces of a damp, mud-smudged path, but it was clear even to her untrained gaze that no single footprint was distinguishable from the rest.

"Did you lock the doors when you left?" Marino glanced at Grace as she shook her damp hair with her hand to rid it of as much moisture as possible. Their eyes met.

"Yes, of course."

"What door did you come in?"

"The back door. Behind you." She nodded toward it.

"Was the door locked?"

"Yes."

"Isn't that the door where the latch doesn't catch right?"

"Yes. But it did this time. I had to use my key to unlock it."

"You're sure?"

"Yes."

"That doesn't mean much, though." Marino frowned thoughtfully. "If someone did find the door improperly latched, entered by it, and then left by it again, the latch might have caught when whoever it was left."

Officer Ayres returned at that juncture, her hair and clothes wet just as Grace's were. Her shoes made squelching sounds as she crossed the tile floor to the table. She carried a Polaroid camera and immediately began taking pictures of the cake. The continuous *click-whir* sound of the camera at work was loud in the quiet house.

Moving away from the area where she was taking pictures, Marino leaned a hip against the center island, drummed the fingers of one hand on the tile countertop, and focused on Grace, who stood just a few feet away, near the sink.

A lone cereal bowl that had not yet made it into the dishwasher waited in the sink, Grace noted absently. Jessica had had cereal for breakfast.

"Who has a key to your house? Besides your sister."

"The Allens do. They live next door." She picked up the bowl and put it in the dishwasher. Her breakfast dishes were already there, waiting to be washed until there was enough for a full load.

"What about your housekeeper?"

"Oh, yes. Pat does." She closed the dishwasher door without turning it on—it still was not full—and turned to face him again.

The look he gave her said as plainly as if he had spoken the thought aloud that almost forgetting that her housekeeper possessed a key did not enhance his opinion of the quality of her testimony. In other words, what else was she forgetting?

"Anybody else? The babysitter?" There was a slight edge to his voice now that spoke of impatience.

"Linda? No. Jessica has her own key, which she uses to let them in after school." Grace leaned against the island, too. The tile countertop felt cool and slick as her hand rested on it.

"Ah." There was a world of enlightenment in the syllable. "Jessica has her own key. Who's had access to it, I wonder?"

"What do you mean?" She frowned at him.

"I mean that it's entirely possible that she's had a friend or two make a copy."

"I don't think—why would any of her friends do that?"

"So they can write messages on her mirror and deliver a surprise cake," he said dryly.

"Oh." Grace hadn't thought of that possibility—that one of Jessica's friends might have copied Jessica's key. It would explain things.

"Yes, *oh*. Okay, that considerably increases our list of possible cake-delivery suspects with access to a key. Let's see, there's your sister. Your next-door neighbor. The housekeeper. And any or all of Jessica's friends. And their friends, ad infinitum."

"I'm having the locks changed on Monday. And a security system installed." But Grace was almost certain that the person she had chased out of the yard the night she had found Mr. Bear down by the road had not been one of Jessica's friends. At least, not one she knew.

"Good idea." Again his voice was dry.

"I've got the pictures." Ayres was holding several instant snapshots in her hands, waving them in the air so they would dry, and more lay in front of her on the table. The camera dangled from her neck by its strap.

"Great." Marino walked back over to the table, and stood looking down at the pictures for a moment. Ayres touched his hand and said something to him, smiling. It was the first time Grace had seen her smile. So Officer Ayres was flirting with Detective Marino. She was surprised at herself for being surprised. The policewoman was young and attractive. Why shouldn't she find Marino appealing? Grace did herself, whether she liked to admit it or not.

Marino, however, appeared oblivious to what was going on. He never even smiled back at Ayres. Instead, he was all business as he glanced over his shoulder at Grace. "What I want you to do now is call your sister, the next door neighbor, and the house-keeper, and see if they still have their keys and if any of them made you a gift of the cake." He held up his hand to stop her when Grace would have protested that none of them would have done such a thing. "Just on the off chance, okay?"

"All right. Fine." Grace called the Allens first and spoke to Judy. Who said the key still hung on a nail in her pantry. She personally hadn't so much as looked at it in months and from its dusty state didn't think anyone else had either, and she knew nothing about the cake. Called next, Pat said she'd used her key on Wednesday as always, but not since then. It was still on her key ring, and she knew nothing about the cake. Jackie was not at home.

Marino and the others had been looking through the house as Grace talked on the phone. Marino entered the kitchen just as she tried Jackie's number for the second time.

"None of them brought the cake. Jackie's not home, but I know she didn't," Grace said, hanging up.

Marino acknowledged her words with a nod. "Everything in the house looks fine. No one lurking in the closets or under the beds. Nothing seems to be missing, but you might want to check yourself."

Grace nodded. A quick tour of the house with Marino at her heels showed everything seemingly in its place. Officers Ge-linsky and Ayres were standing in the kitchen talking in hushed tones when they returned.

"There's really nothing else we can do except file another report," Gelinsky said apologetically to Grace.

Grace's mouth thinned. Filing a report was useless. "I want whoever is doing this *caught*." She looked at Marino as she spoke. Talking to Gelinsky and Ayres was, as she had already learned, a waste of breath.

"You've said that before," Marino said. "And, believe me,

we're doing our best. What I'm going to do now is have someone check with all the bakeries in the area to see if anyone made a cake like this, and for whom. It shouldn't be hard to find out where it was made if it was done locally, which it probably was. If you have no objections, I'm also going to take the cake and have it tested, just to make sure that it isn't poisoned or anything."

Grace hadn't thought of that. "That sounds good."

"Okay." He picked up the cake, looked down at it thoughtfully, then glanced at Grace again. "You have anything to put this in? A box or something?"

Grace shook her head. A shoebox wasn't going to do it, and she had nothing larger. "I don't have a box, but I have some plastic wrap. At least that would make it less messy."

"What about a garbage bag? One of those big plastic ones."

"I have that."

"If you don't need us any longer, Detective . . . ," Gelinsky said as Grace fetched a garbage bag from the pantry. It was obvious from the rather furtive glance he cast her way that he was not 100 percent certain how she would receive his desire to leave.

Marino shook his head. "Go ahead and take off. There's really nothing else to do except take care of the cake, and I'll handle that."

"If you need help, Detective . . . ," Ayres said, clearly offering. Again she smiled at Marino. Grace felt a quick stab of antipathy toward the other woman, and appalled by the implications, immediately strove to banish it. Marino shook his head no to the offer of help, and Gelinsky and Ayres left, the latter with obvious (to Grace at least) reluctance.

"You have any toothpicks?" Marino asked when Grace handed him the trash bag.

"I think so." She returned to the pantry, located the box of toothpicks she had used to spear olives and cheese for her last dinner party, and returned with them to the table. Marino extracted perhaps a dozen from the box and inserted them into the top and sides of the cake.

"What are you doing?" Grace asked, mystified.

"These'll keep the plastic off the icing," he explained, giving her a quick smile loaded with self-deprecating humor.

"Good thinking." Grace was impressed—both with the toothpicks and the smile, which dazzled her.

"My mother used to bake cakes all the time. Won prizes for them at the state fair. Believe me, I know about transporting cakes. Now hold the bag open for me, please."

Grace complied. Marino deftly slid the cake inside, and sure enough the toothpicks held the black plastic away from the icing. That done, Marino picked up the pictures, which Ayres had left on the table, glanced at them a final time, and put them into his pocket.

"I've got to go." He picked up the cake, holding the plastic-wrapped bundle carefully with both hands beneath it. "I'm due at my newest niece's christening"—he glanced at the clock on the wall—"in thirty minutes."

"Wait a minute," Grace said, her bedazzlement instantly torpedoed. Her hands curled around the top back rung of the nearest chair as she stared at him in disbelief. "That's it? That's all you're going to do? Look around, take a few pictures, ask some questions, and then just leave? What about this person who is breaking into my house and terrorizing my daughter and me?"

For a moment he just looked at her without speaking.

"Grace," he said finally. "I'll make sure this cake thing—and the other things—are thoroughly investigated, I promise. But I have to tell you that we don't have much to work with here. Gift cakes and messages on a mirror and stolen teddy bears are not enough to justify mobilizing the entire police department."

"They're *threats*." Anger was building in her voice again. Her hands tightened on the chair back.

"Maybe," he said noncommittally, turning toward the door. Glancing over his shoulder, he added, "I'll do what I can. In the meantime, keep the doors locked, whether you're home or not."

"That doesn't seem to do much good, does it?" There was a

slight shrillness to her voice. "Just like calling the police doesn't seem to do much good."

"We came, didn't we?" He headed toward the door with Grace at his heels.

"And you left." Her tone was definitely shrill now. "Without doing anything to resolve the problem. Like I said before, you're not taking this seriously."

"I'm keeping an open mind," he said, pausing in front of the door and nodding at it. "Could you get this?"

"Great." Grace opened the door for him ungraciously. A rush of cool air, the soft roaring sound of what was now a downpour, and the smell of dampness, of soaked earth and greenery and pavement, greeted her. "I'll keep reminding myself of that. Knowing you're keeping an open mind certainly makes me feel better, let me tell you, when my daughter is being stalked and threatened because of *your* drug investigation."

He stepped onto the porch, then turned to look at her, a slight smile tilting up a corner of his mouth in silent acknowledgment of her sarcasm. With the ephemeral grayness of a sheet of falling rain for backdrop, his broad-shouldered frame seemed suddenly very solid and substantial, and she realized how much she did not want him to leave. "All right, you made your point. As of this moment I am now, officially, taking this seriously, I promise. But I really don't think you or your daughter are in any physical danger. Whether these are threats or pranks or just a bizarre series of coincidences, nobody's confronted you or Jessica directly. I don't think anyone's going to."

"I certainly hope you're right." Her voice positively dripped sarcasm this time.

His smile broadened into a grin. "Call me if you need me."

He turned away.

Helplessly, angrily, Grace watched him cross the porch and then take off running down the steps with a left turn at the bottom toward the driveway, at which point the dripping snowball bush largely blocked him from her view. Mouth tightening, she shut the door and locked it.

As she turned to walk back into the kitchen for a much-needed cup of coffee, it suddenly struck her just how vulnerable she was, alone in her large, echoing, empty house.

Which someone with evil intent could apparently enter at will.

CHAPTER 25

"**J**ESSICA, LOOK, IT'S RUSTY CURRAN! OVER there, with Todd Williams and Andrew Sykes and Jason Ol-shaker!" Emily jabbed her in the ribs with an elbow. Her excited whisper was, Jessica feared, loud enough to be heard clear down to the opposite end of the crowded mall, where Emily's mother, Ann, was shopping in Lazarus Department Store.

"Shh!" Jessica warned, shifting away from the sharp-edged elbow as she shot a covert glance in the direction Emily indicated. Sure enough, there was Rusty, in baggy khakis and an untucked flannel shirt, laughing and talking in the middle of a pack of his similarly dressed friends. It looked as if they had just come out of the movies, which were the centerpiece of that section of the mall. Streams of people moved in front of and behind them.

"Quick, let's duck in here." Panicked, Jessica steered Emily and the others—Tiffany Driver and Polly Wells—into the nearest store, which happened to be an earring boutique. It was a mis-take. Allison and Maddie were in there—basically all the high school kids who weren't nerds hung out at the malls on the week-end—trying on earrings in front of the mirrored walls. Spotting them, Jessica almost backed out again. But it was too late. They'd seen her, too, through the mirrors.

"Why, if it isn't Jessica!" Allison said, too sweetly, as she turned away from the mirror. Like a lot of the kids in the cool crowd, Allison blamed Jessica for bringing the cops down on their heads. If Jessica were *normal*—translation, nondiabetic—their reasoning went, she wouldn't have passed out that night in Brandeis Park and they could have bought their pot and gotten out of there without the cops having any idea who they were. Thanks to Jessica, the heat was on now at Hebron, and it wasn't safe to bring so much as a Midol to school.

"Hi, Allison, Maddie," Jessica offered weakly, knowing herself scorned. The bright blue earring that Allison wore in one ear—she held the other in her hand—almost exactly matched the eyeshadow that swept from her lid to her brow. Unwillingly, Jessica admired the effect. From her chunky sandals to her tight black mini to the pumpkin-orange streaks that adorned her hair today, Allison was so *stylin'*. Jessica knew she couldn't look that good in a million years.

To handle the stress of the moment and stay cool, what she really needed was a cigarette. Not just for the nicotine, but because it would look so *right*. She didn't have any with her, though. She'd left her Winstons under the swing cushion on the porch.

"Are you hangin' with the girl jocks now?" Maddie's tone was patronizing. Unlike Allison, she was a blonde, with waist-length hair held back from her face by a leopard-print headband that exactly matched the scarf she had used to belt her tight black jeans. She was pretty, probably the prettiest girl in school, although she was not considered to be as cool as Allison, and she was totally aware of her place in the scheme of things. The look she swept over Emily, Tiffany, and Polly was openly contemptuous. In the hierarchy that every student at Hebron lived by, girl jocks were in a class just slightly above the total dweebs. Definitely *un*cool.

"Hi, Allison," Emily said in a small voice, while Tiffany and Polly didn't speak at all, merely nodded. Emily was broad-shouldered, with muscular arms and legs, a flat chest, and a bouncy, athletic walk. Tiffany was almost six feet tall, and broomstick-thin. Polly was shy, flat-chested, and wore both glasses and braces. All three of them were total zeroes with boys. To Allison and Maddie and their crowd, such social misfits just didn't count. Like every other nonperson at Hebron, Emily, Tiffany, and Polly knew their status and were intimidated by it, and by the two pretty, popular girls who confronted them.

Thanks to her damned diabetes, Jessica knew she was now reduced to the ranks of a nonperson, too.

"Jessica plays basketball. Didn't you know?" Allison said to Maddie. She completely ignored Emily's greeting, and, indeed, her presence, and Tiffany's and Polly's, too. Her focus was all on Jessica, the recently fallen.

"Eww, no, I didn't," Maddie said, in exactly the tone she would have used if Allison had asked her if she didn't know that Jessica had lice in her hair.

"Jessica's really good," Tiffany said loyally, making Jessica want to sink through the ground. "I bet she makes the team."

"Well, isn't that special?" Allison cooed. "I just bet she does, too."

"Hey, look, it's Rusty Curran and his crowd," Maddie said, spotting the boys through the glass window as they passed by.

"Jessica likes Rusty, don't you, Jessica?" Allison gave Jessica a malicious smile. "Does he know you're here, Jessica? I bet he came to the mall just hoping to run into you."

Of course former friends Allison and Maddie knew how she felt about Rusty, Jessica thought, willing her face not to turn red.

"Let's tell Rusty Jessica's here," Maddie said, giggling, and Allison nodded. Before Jessica could stop her—she would have thrown herself on top of a live grenade to stop her—Maddie darted out of the store.

"I've got to go," Jessica said abruptly, not caring what Allison thought if she could only get away before they humiliated her in front of Rusty. With Emily, Tiffany, and Polly trailing, Jessica practically ran from the store.

"Jessica, wait, here's Rusty!" Maddie called. A quick, involuntary glance back showed Jessica that Maddie, indeed, had Rusty in tow. Giggling, she had one hand hooked around his arm, pulling him onward. His friends were farther back, mere faces in the milling crowd. Rusty was frowning as he looked after Jessica. She wasn't surprised, Jessica thought, her body burning with humiliation. It wasn't every day that a guy like Rusty had a girl positively flee from him.

Without warning, her toe caught on something. She stumbled, flailed her arms, and fell. Just like that.

For what seemed like an eternity she lay facedown on the cold terrazzo floor. Her life passed before her eyes, scene by scene. Mortification was the mildest term for what she endured. It was so all-encompassing that it overrode any physical pain.

"Are you okay, young lady?" A man with cordovan wing tips and gray polyester trousers knelt beside her, his hand touching her back.

"Jessica! Jessica, are you all right?" Emily, Tiffany, and Polly came running up. Into her line of vision came jeans with frayed edges, sneakers, Polly's embarrassing lime-green laces.

"Should I call security?" A woman's voice. Tan hose, sensible black pumps.

Jessica scrambled up. "I'm okay," she said, her voice high-pitched as her trembling knees threatened to dump her back on the floor. "Really. I'm not hurt."

The man, silver-haired with glasses; the woman, a plump boutique clerk; and other passersby nodded and faded away.

"Are you sure?" Emily asked. Jessica barely heard her. Rusty was walking toward her, long hair thrown back from his face, grinning from ear to ear. Maddie clung giggling to one of his arms and Allison, also giggling, clutched the other. Neither of the girls reached higher than his shoulder. *Large and in charge* was how he was described at school. Just looking at him made Jessica feel dizzy.

"That was *so* funny," Allison said between giggles. "You must have been practicing."

"It takes somebody really clumsy to trip over a bench in the middle of the mall," Maddie said, her eyes snapping maliciously at Jessica.

"Shut up, you bimbos, Jessica might really be hurt," Rusty said in a voice that was only semijocular. Despite his wide grin, Jessica was stunned to see what appeared to be real interest as he looked at her.

"I'm okay," she said again in a tiny voice. Unbelievable that *Rusty Curran* was really looking at her like that. Rusty Curran, the hero of her daydreams—and fantasies. He was *so cute,* and he had the bluest eyes.

"I can give you a ride home, if you want," he offered. "That is, if you hurt yourself, and you don't feel like shopping anymore."

Maddie and Allison looked shocked. Rusty's friends, who had joined them in a cluster, looked surprised. Emily, Tiffany, and Polly were slack-jawed with amazement.

None of them was any more dumbfounded than Jessica herself.

Rusty Curran, one of the most popular guys at Hebron and certainly, in her opinion at least, the cutest, was offering to give her a ride home?

Unbelievable. Such a thing was the stuff of her wildest dreams.

Her life flashed before her a second time. That is, the most recent weeks of her life. Brandeis Park. Her being grounded. The mirror. The cake.

She had promised her mom that she would not, for any reason, leave the other girls.

"I can't," she said, feeling her heart break.

"Whatever." He shrugged, accepting the news with unimpaired good humor. All the girls, from Allison to Polly, looked even more shocked at Jessica's refusal. Jessica barely noticed them. Her eyes were all for Rusty as he turned away.

Of course, she thought, her acceptance or refusal had meant nothing to him. He had only offered to take her home to be polite. Not only was Rusty Curran a total babe, he was also—she could hardly stand it—a gentleman.

Her heart did a slow revolution in her chest.

"Oh, by the way," Rusty said, turning back to her, "there's a party tonight at Olshaker's here." He punched Jason Olshaker in the shoulder. Jason winced and playfully returned the favor. "His folks are outa town, and we're gonna have a keg. You oughta try to come, if you can."

"Thanks," Jessica managed. "What—what time?"

"We probably won't get crankin' till around ten," Jason said. "Then we'll party till dawn."

"Yee-haw," Todd Williams said.

"I'll—I'll try," Jessica stammered. Oh, God, she was being offered a second chance.

"You do that." Rusty's hand formed a pistol with his first three fingers folded in, his thumb straight up and his index finger pointed at her. "See ya."

He and his friends ambled away.

Jessica, in shock, barely heard Maddie's and Allison's catty comments before they, too, walked away.

Her whole body was warm from head to toe. She was smiling, floating on air, feeling light as a feather and beautiful as a star as she followed her friends around the mall in a daze.

For her, everything had changed in a single moment.

Because Rusty Curran had offered to drive her home and invited her to a party, however off-handedly.

Her mom would never let her go. She knew it as well as she knew her own name.

But, weird happenings or no weird happenings, she meant to · go anyway.

Rusty Curran. Rusty Curran. Rusty Curran.

Be still, my heart.

CHAPTER 26

INSTEAD OF GOING INTO THE KITCHEN, GRACE changed course, heading upstairs. Once in her bedroom, she locked the door behind her—although she usually never did so even when she was alone in the house—and turned on the overhead light, as well as all three lamps, to change into navy-blue sweats. She then turned on the closet light as well, pulled a chair over, stood on it, and rummaged around on the top shelf for the gun she had bought years ago when she and Craig had first separated. At the time, she had been scared to the point of sleeplessness over being alone at nights with only Jessica, who'd been scarcely more than a baby. Burglars, rapists, and murderers who broke in during the wee hours of the morning had routinely populated her nightmares when she did sleep.

Funny, she had gotten over that fear years ago. Until this.

The gun was in the very back corner of the top shelf, and she stood on tiptoe straining to reach it. Her fingers touched cold metal and curled around the slender barrel; she pulled it out. It was an old gun, a .22 caliber automatic, with a long, black barrel and a removable clip that could be filled with bullets and then loaded into the handle.

It had been at least six years since she had held it in her hand. She just barely remembered where the bullets were—tied in a knotted athletic sock in the bottom drawer of her dresser. Getting them out, she loaded the pistol, then checked to make sure that the chamber was empty and the safety on.

Funny how the mechanics of it came back to her.

Unlocking her bedroom door, she headed back downstairs, feeling marginally better now that she had a gun in her hand. At least she was not a sitting duck any longer, she thought. She could defend herself and her daughter, if it became necessary.

Taking a quick detour through Jessica's room, she checked to see if Godzilla had succumbed to hunger yet and had crawled back into the cage that Jessica had left, stocked with food and water and his favorite chopped fresh apple, on the floor for him.

No such luck. The cage was still empty. Grace was beginning to think that Godzilla would never turn up. But where, in a relatively well-cared-for house, could a hamster hide for days on end? Surely they must see some trace of him sooner or later. Droppings, or crumbs where he'd gotten into the pantry, or *something*.

Even if he was dead, there should, by now, be a terrible odor. Which, since the house smelled just as usual, was some comfort.

Grace shrugged, determined not to worry about it, and walked on down the stairs. The stairwell and much of the house— except for the kitchen and her bedroom—were gloomy and dark because of the rain, although it was only about four o'clock. Jessica should be home within the next hour and a half or so, and then it would be time to start supper and . . .

Her sleeve snagged on something, arresting her in midstep. Surprised, Grace glanced around to see what had caught her. The wall of the stairwell was hung with dozens of family pictures mounted in matching jade-green wooden frames, including yearly ones of Jessica from the time she was a baby and pictures of the two of them together. Her sleeve had caught on a nail where one of the pictures should have been.

Should have been. Freeing her sleeve, Grace proceeded slowly down the stairs, flipped the light switch at the bottom so that the stairwell was brightly illuminated, and retraced her steps.

A picture was missing. One of a trio of shots of herself and Jessica together. They were three-by-fives displayed in five-by-seven frames. She had mounted them herself.

The bottom one—the latest one—taken less than a year ago, was gone. A bare nail sticking out of the wall was the only mark of where it had been.

How long had the picture been gone? Had someone—one of Jessica's friends maybe, or Courtney or Paul—accidentally broken it and hidden it somewhere instead of telling her? Had someone—Jessica or Pat, maybe—moved it for some reason?

She couldn't remember the last time she had actually seen it. Surely she would have noticed if it had been missing long. But maybe not.

Whoever had left the cake must have taken the picture. Her blood ran cold.

Her first instinct was to call Marino.

Grace took a deep breath to calm herself and walked on down the stairs. Deliberately she went from room to room, turning on all the lights and closing all the curtains, the pistol clutched tightly in one hand. Then she went into the kitchen and made herself a cup of coffee.

So a picture was missing from her wall, Marino would say with a shrug. A recent picture of herself and Jessica, with no value to anyone but the two of them. Even the appearance of the cake in a locked house was more sinister than that.

The disappearance of a single framed photograph from a whole wall filled with dozens of similar photographs was not sinister at all.

She could not call Marino, or anyone else, over that.

Sitting at the table, Grace sipped her coffee and tried without success to concentrate on the newspaper. The missing photograph might mean nothing.

But she didn't for one minute believe that.

Giving up on the paper, she called Jackie, who still was not home. She hid the pistol in a cabinet where she could easily grab it, but Jessica was not likely to find it, and started supper. When Jessica walked in through the kitchen door at five-thirty, Grace was standing at the stove testing the broccoli for doneness. She was still so tense that it was an effort to summon a smile.

"Hi, sweetie. Did you have a good time?" One look at Jessica's face as she hung her jacket on the coatrack was enough to answer that. Her child was sparkling-eyed and glowing and looked happier than Grace had seen her in some time.

Letting her go had been the right decision after all.

"It was okay." Communicative as always, Jessica shrugged, took off her coat, and hung it on the coatrack. Her hair was only damp, not soaked, leading Grace to assume that the rain had slacked off.

"What did you buy?"

"Oh—nothing." Jessica looked and sounded blank, as though the notion of buying something had only just occurred to her. "We just basically window-shopped."

"You didn't buy anything?" Jessica had never been to the mall in her life without buying something.

"I don't always have to buy something." Jessica's tone was defensive.

So Jessica had bought nothing, but come home starry-eyed. In Grace's experience, that could mean only one thing: a boy.

"Did anything interesting happen?" Grace probed delicately, knowing that too-pointed questions would ruin any chance of getting her daughter to open up. Not that there was much chance of that anyway. Over the past year, Jessica had guarded details of her personal life as closely as if they were precious gems, allowing Grace only an occasional glimpse at the treasure.

"Not much." Jessica came into the kitchen, sniffing the aromas emanating from the stove. "Why aren't you getting dressed, by the way?"

"For what?"

"Weren't you going to some fund-raiser tonight?" Steam

rose around her as Jessica lifted a lid from a pot, peering down with evident satisfaction at the bubbling stew within.

"Oh, my God!" There was a clatter as Grace dropped the spoon she'd been holding and stared at her daughter with horror. "I completely forgot!"

"Linda's supposed to come at six." Jessica glanced at the clock. "You've got twenty-five minutes."

"I can't go." Grace bent to retrieve the spoon and tossed it into the sink. She glanced at the clock, too. "I'm not going. It's too late to catch Linda. I'll pay her and send her home when she gets here. I have to call John. . . ."

"Is that who you're going with?" Jessica asked interestedly, leaning against the counter and munching a carrot stick, which she had grabbed from the raw veggie platter Grace had already prepared and left sitting beside the stove. "John who? Is he cute?"

"John Parson. And not particularly. He's a judge I work with, and it's no big deal that I'm going out with him, so you can just get that look off your face, miss. We're both supporting George Loew for the Senate and this is his first fund-raiser, so . . ."

"You have to go," Jessica said positively.

"I'm not going." Grace was already headed toward the phone.

"Why? Linda will be here. I won't be all alone."

"I'm just not going." Grace thought of the cake and the picture, and shuddered. She started to ask Jessica if she knew anything about the picture, then stopped. Jessica looked so happy—there was no sense in frightening her more than was necessary. Picking up the phone book, she turned to the P's and began running a finger down the columns, looking for John's name.

"He must have an unlisted number," she said as she drew a blank.

"See? You have to go. Sheesh, Mom, I'll be all right. Linda will be here, and anyway you can't stand guard over me for the rest of my life."

Grace looked at her daughter. She hated to stand John up at the last minute—he was a friend as well as a colleague and this was an important event for someone with political ambitions, which he had. On the other hand, Jessica was her life.

"Have you ever heard the word *over-protective*?" Jessica asked impatiently. "Nothing's going to happen. And if Linda and I get scared, we can always call the police."

The police. Tony Marino. Grace thought of him, and her decision to stay home wavered. Being attracted to him was bad enough. But she was starting to rely on him, she realized, and that was worse. He was just a cop who came when she called because that was his job.

What she needed was a new man in her life to focus on. John could, possibly, fill the bill. He was good-looking enough, recently divorced, intelligent, funny, had a prestigious job. . . .

If he was not as sexy as Tony Marino, well, then, sexy was not what a thirty-six-year-old mother of a teenager should be looking for in a man, and it would behoove her to keep that in mind.

"Mom, give it up and go get dressed. I'll be fine." Jessica sounded impatient. In fact, she sounded like a mother trying to talk sense into a recalcitrant daughter. Like Grace herself, in fact.

Grace had to smile.

"Sure you'll be all right?" Still she hesitated.

Jessica rolled her eyes. "Mo*ther* . . ."

"All right. I'll be home early. Supper just needs to be dished out, so you go ahead and eat. If you get scared, or anything seems wrong . . ."

"Go take a shower, Mom." Jessica shook her head in disgust, pulled on an oven mitt, and started lifting pots from the stove.

Grace went upstairs. The doorbell rang while she was in the shower, announcing, she assumed, Linda's arrival. She blow-dried her hair—thank God for short cuts and hair gel!—and was applying makeup when the doorbell rang again.

John.

Hurrying into the bedroom, she shimmied into control-top

pantyhose—was it just her or were they starting to feel more like girdles every year?—and a bra, then pulled from her closet the white satin shell and oyster silk dinner suit that was her answer to big nights and put it on. Thrusting her feet into a pair of taupe pumps, she snatched up the matching taupe purse from her closet shelf, dumped the contents of her everyday purse into it, and headed downstairs.

Dressed in the male jurist's eternal dark suit, white shirt, and silk tie—this one was red—John was in the living room seated on the couch. He put down the drink he was holding and rose when he saw her, giving her an exaggerated once-over accompanied by a wolf-whistle under his breath. He was forty-five years old, about five-ten, stockily built with short reddish hair and a cocky grin.

The thing she liked best about him was that grin.

"I'll be right with you," she promised with a smile. "Just let me say good night to Jessica."

"Sure." He shrugged and sat back down again. "You look beautiful, by the way."

"Thanks."

Smiling, she turned and went into the kitchen. Jessica and Linda were seated at the kitchen table, eating and talking a mile a minute. Grace thought about reminding Jessica that, for politeness sake, she should have made an effort to talk to their guest until her mother appeared, but then gave a mental shrug and let it pass. At least she, or Linda, had provided John with a drink—orange juice from the look of it. Anyway, life was too short to lecture all the time.

"You look great, Mom," Jessica said as Grace walked over to the table.

"You really do, Judge Hart," Linda echoed.

"Thank you, both of you. Linda, I have my cell phone with me. If you need me, the number's written down under the phone. Jess knows it. The next-door neighbor's number is written down, too, the Allen's. Bob Allen could get over here fast if necessary. Jessica, you guys stay inside and keep the doors locked. If anything should . . ."

"*Go,* Mom. I know the drill." Jessica took a bite of stew. "We'll call the cops if we need to, don't worry."

"I'll be home early," Grace promised, and left.

As dates went, this one was pretty tame. She and John ate dinner side by side at one of the big tables, talked about nothing really, and then separated when dinner was over as he schmoozed his way around the room and she chatted with friends and acquaintances. By ten-thirty, Grace was ready to call it a night. Detaching John from potential future backers was tricky, however, and it was eleven o'clock before they were in the car headed home.

"Do you always leave parties this early?" he asked her with a teasing smile as he pulled into Spring Hill Lane.

"I'm sorry to drag you away," Grace said, "But there's something going on with my daughter and I really need to get home."

"How old is she? Sixteen? Seventeen?"

"Fifteen."

"I imagine kids that age are a lot of trouble," John said, commiserating. He was childless, Grace had learned over the course of the evening, and she realized from his manner when Jessica came up as a topic of conversation that he had no real interest in hearing about other people's children.

Scratch John from her list of potential men-friends, she thought.

"Sometimes," Grace admitted. They reached her driveway, pulling through the gates and past the hedge and stopping behind Linda's car, which was illuminated by the light in the black iron lamppost at the end of the walkway. When John reached for his door handle, Grace got out without waiting for him to come around and open her door.

The rain had stopped, but puddles on the pavement shone in the lamplight and the air was cool and damp. Rolling clouds hid the moon and stars from view, and made the world seem very dark beyond the yellow circle of light cast by the lamp. Grace walked around the car, braced for the awkward moment that always came at the end of dates.

"There's no need to escort me to the door," she said with a little laugh. Ending a date on the sidewalk was the most tactful means she had found to break it gently to a man that the evening was over. Though how any man could expect more, when they knew she had a teenage daughter in the house, was beyond her. Still, most if not all of them seemed to.

"I take it you're not going to be asking me in," John said with a rueful smile.

"Jessica . . ." Grace explained with pseudoregretfulness. If she was being strictly honest, she would have to admit that she would not ask him in even if Jessica did not exist. She liked him well enough, but she was not attracted to him.

"Maybe we can go out again," he said, catching her by her arm as she walked near him and drawing her close. He was going to kiss her, Grace knew. Not that she minded, not really. A kiss was small change in the currency of male-female relations, after all.

He did kiss her, holding her tight against him and invading her mouth with his tongue. As kisses went, it was perfectly pleasant. His lips were warm and soft, his tongue performed the obligatory maneuvers without being offensive, and his breath tasted faintly of Scotch, which he had been drinking. He was taller than her, though not by much, and his body was pleasantly firm. Grace kissed him back in an easy, relaxed fashion that said volumes about the lack of passion she was experiencing, then as soon as she decently could, eased herself out of his arms.

"How about lunch next week?" he asked, his voice slightly thickened.

Grace was already moving away from him. "I'll have to check the calendar in my office. Call me and I'll let you know," she said with a wave and a friendly smile thrown over her shoulder. "Good night."

"Good night." John got back in his car. As Grace went up

the steps, he reversed down the driveway, his headlights cutting bright swaths through the darkness.

Grace was grimacing, faintly, as she stepped onto the porch. She was tired, and her feet hurt in the high-heeled shoes, and the waistband on her pantyhose was chafing her waist. She wouldn't go out with John again, she thought, fumbling in her purse for the key. He was a nice enough guy, but . . .

A slight creak brought her gaze around to the deep shadows at the far end of the porch where the swing hung.

She gasped, her hand flying to her throat as her heart skipped a beat.

A man was sitting on the swing, legs spread, smoking a cigarette and watching her. She could just make out the bulky shape of his shoulders above the back of the swing, and the outline of his head. The tip of the cigarette glowed brightly as he brought it to his mouth, then dimmed as it fell again.

CHAPTER 27

"You scared the life out of me," Grace said furiously, recognizing Marino.

"I didn't know you had a boyfriend." It was an idle observation. He took another drag on his cigarette, making the tip glow bright red again.

"I didn't know *you* smoked," she retaliated, walking toward him. He was wearing his leather bomber jacket, she saw, which was zipped almost all the way up to his throat, and jeans. Cigarette smoke, white and wispy, curled around his head. Its acrid smell was in the air.

"Seems like there's a lot we don't know about each other, then, doesn't it?" He eyed her and put the cigarette to his mouth again. "Nice outfit, by the way."

"What are you doing here?" A thought seized Grace by the heart. "Jessica . . ."

"She's fine." He took a final drag on the cigarette and then flipped it over the railing, into the big snowball bush by the steps.

"You shouldn't do that. You could start a fire," Grace protested, distracted.

"It's too wet. Anyway, you probably should know that the cigarette wasn't mine. I used to smoke, a long time ago, but I quit. I found a pack with two cigarettes and a lighter in it hidden under the cushion here when I sat down. I decided to smoke 'em for the hell of it, to see if they tasted as good as I remembered. They didn't."

"Whose? . . ." Grace began, but the snorting sound he made told her his opinion as eloquently as if he'd put it into words. "You think they're *Jessica's*?"

"Unless you sit out here on the porch and smoke."

"Oh, she doesn't . . ." Grace began, then broke off under the weight of that derisive look. He was right, she realized, however much she hated to admit it. If cigarettes and a lighter had been hidden on the porch, their most likely owner was Jessica.

"What are you doing here?" she asked again, abandoning the topic of Jessica and the cigarettes for the moment. After everything she had been through with her daughter lately, discovering that she snuck cigarettes was almost small potatoes.

"I promised you I'd take this seriously, didn't I? It occurred to me that if someone really is stalking Jessica, or you, they have to be hanging around your house a lot. I thought I'd sit out here in the dark awhile and see what I could see."

That made sense. It made such dazzlingly good sense that Grace was surprised she hadn't thought of it herself. For someone to have done the things that had been done, whoever it was had to be watching the house pretty closely. It should not be all that difficult to catch them in the act.

"Have you seen anything?" she asked, suddenly feeling much better.

"Not a creature's stirred," he said. "That is, until your boy-friend pulled up."

At the thought that he had witnessed that kiss—Grace snuck a quick look over the porch rail, trying to gauge exactly how much he could see, and decided that, as the kiss had taken place right in the pool of lamplight, he could see plenty—she felt a squirmy kind of embarrassment. Which was silly, she told herself firmly. She was a grown woman, and she had a perfect right to kiss whomever she wished.

"John's a fellow judge, not my boyfriend," she said, then realized that she shouldn't be explaining things to him at all.

"Oh. I guess I didn't realize that judges go around kissing each other good night. Cops don't, as a general rule, but then, judges may be different."

"Funny," Grace said, with an intonation that meant the opposite.

"I try."

"How was your niece's christening, by the way?"

"Good. The whole family turned out for it, twenty-seven strong. The baby cried all the way through it. The rest of us were properly reverential, though."

"There are twenty-seven people in your family?"

He shrugged. "I'm one of six brothers, all cops, all Catholic. What can I say?"

"Oh my God."

"That about sums it up."

"Are your parents still living?"

"My mother is. My dad died twelve years ago. He was a cop, too."

"Does your family all live here in town? Your mother and brothers?" Grace was fascinated by the idea of a family that large, and close enough that all would turn out to attend an infant's christening. And all boys who grew up to be cops. His poor mother, was her crowning thought.

"Robby, the youngest, lives in Dayton, but he and his family drove up for the occasion."

"Where are you in the group?" Grace asked.

"Number two. After Dom."

"He's three years older than you. I remember." Grace smiled faintly.

"Do you, now?"

"So how old is he?"

"Dom? He's forty-two. That makes me thirty-nine, if you were wondering."

That was precisely what Grace had been wondering, but she wasn't going to admit it.

"You want to come in and have a cup of coffee?" she asked, changing the subject.

"Nah." The swing creaked again as he moved it slowly back and forth. The wind chimes tinkled briefly, and then fell silent. It was not a windy night, just damp and not quite cold.

"I've got to go in and let Linda go."

"Fine."

Grace hesitated, then turned and walked away. Extracting her key from her purse, she let herself into the house. Warmth greeted her, and the familiar smell of home. The downstairs lights were off except for the ones in the family room, at the very back of the house, where Linda was curled cozily on the couch watching a movie on HBO.

"Oh, hi, Judge Hart," Linda said, uncurling herself and standing up when she saw Grace in the doorway. "I didn't expect you this early."

Grace smiled. "I was tired. Where's Jessica?"

"She went to bed right before ten."

"Everything go okay?" Grace walked back into the kitchen, where she had left her purse on the counter. Linda followed her, yawning and nodding at the same time. As Grace made fresh coffee, then paid her, they chatted. When Linda left, she used the kitchen door, and Grace doubted that she was even aware of Marino sitting on the front porch, keeping watch.

She went upstairs to change clothes and check on Jessica. Jessica's door was locked, Grace discovered as she turned the knob, then knocked softly with no result. She could hear the bass beat of a rock band thumping from inside the bedroom. From that Grace deduced that her daughter had fallen asleep while listening to her stereo. It wasn't like Jessica to lock her bedroom door, but then, she herself had locked her bedroom door earlier this afternoon.

This thing was spooking them both.

Grace changed her dinner suit for the navy sweats she had

worn earlier, went down to the kitchen, poured coffee into two mugs, and added to one of them the spoonful of sugar that she remembered Marino preferred. Grabbing a brown wool jacket from the coatrack, she pulled it on and returned to the front porch. Marino still sat on the swing, she saw, his head resting back against the cushion, his face turned so that he had a clear view of the yard.

He looked around as she stepped out onto the porch. It was about a quarter after twelve now, Grace guessed, and the air was definitely cold. The wind had picked up, and the wind chimes tinkled in perfect, mournful accompaniment to the ghostly sounds of rustling leaves and rubbing branches and dripping eaves.

"I brought you some coffee." Grace held the mug out to him.

"Thanks." He sat up, taking it from her.

"I appreciate this," she said quietly, still standing in front of him. "You coming out here like this, I mean. I know you have better things to do."

"No problem." He took a sip of coffee, then looked up at her. "I'm a cop, remember? That's what we do."

Grace sat down in the rocker closest to the swing, so close that his knee fell just short of brushing her thigh when the swing moved. She cradled the coffee cup in both hands, savoring its warmth and fragrance.

"You're not planning to sit out here all night, are you?" she asked, sipping.

"Whatever it takes," he said.

"It's cold. You'll freeze."

"No, I won't."

"Where's your car?" She suddenly realized that the driveway was empty. Her Volvo was in the garage.

"A couple of blocks over, parked on the street. I wanted it to look like you and Jessica were here alone."

"What if whoever it is comes tomorrow night instead of tonight?"

"I plan to be out here tomorrow night, too."

"You can't spend the rest of your life sitting up nights on my porch!"

"I don't intend to. You get your locks changed and that security system put in on Monday, right?"

Grace stared at him through the darkness. And she realized something. He wasn't sitting on her porch thinking he would catch anyone. He probably didn't believe that anyone was even out there to catch. He was sitting on her porch in the wee hours of a cold, damp Saturday night simply because he knew that she and Jessica were afraid to sleep in the house alone.

"Sometimes you're actually a pretty good guy, Detective, you know that?" Grace sent him a singularly sweet smile, the type that was seldom seen on her face anymore.

He met her gaze for a moment, then responded with a crooked smile of his own. "You want to put that in writing, Your Honor, I'll frame it and hang it on my wall. It's the nicest thing you've ever said to me."

For a moment they sat there smiling at each other. Then Grace remembered something and mentioned it almost reluctantly, regretting having to spoil the mood. "After you left today, I discovered that there was a picture missing from the arrangement on the wall going up the stairs. A picture of Jessica and me."

He took a sip of coffee and looked at her meditatively. "So what are you trying to tell me?"

"I think he took it. The same person who left the cake and wrote on the mirror. I think he took the picture."

The sound Marino made was very much like a not-quite-perfectly muffled, long-suffering sigh. Grace bristled, then decided to give him the benefit of the doubt. He was, after all, sitting on her porch in the middle of the night, when he didn't have to be.

"You want to show me?"

Grace put her coffee cup down on the table between the rockers and stood up. Marino did the same thing, then followed her inside. Grace was very conscious of his presence behind her as she led the way to the stairwell. Only a small amount of light from the kitchen reached the hallway. With a quick flick she turned on the chandelier that hung above the stairs, and blinked for a moment at the sudden brightness. She then climbed the stairs to the place where the bare nail stuck out from the wall.

"It was here," she said, touching the nail's small flat head as she turned to look at him. The side of her hand accidentally brushed his chest. The leather of his jacket felt slick and cool, the body beneath reassuringly solid. She was surprised to find that he was so close, close enough to allow her to see every individual whisker in what must be, when he forgot to shave, a heavy beard, close enough for her to feel the heat of his body and smell the aroma of leather and cigarette smoke that clung to him. With that single glance she took in the small vee of black chest hair just visible at the base of his throat, the fullness of his lower lip compared to his upper one, the slant of his thick black eyebrows as the inside corners were drawn toward his nose in a faint frown. Though he was two steps below her, their eyes were almost on a level. His were faintly bloodshot, as if he needed more sleep than he was accustomed to getting, and slightly narrowed as they stared at the place she indicated.

Grace was conscious, suddenly, of a strong desire to touch him, to place her hands on those broad shoulders and lean forward and . . .

Then he was looking directly into her eyes, instead of at the nail as he had been. His gaze dropped, and Grace realized that his focus had shifted to her mouth. Had something in her expression revealed what she was thinking? she wondered, embarrassed at the thought. Flustered, she turned quickly back to the wall and prayed her face wouldn't turn red.

"It was one of three," she said, conscious that she was babbling a little but unable to help it. "See, the other two are still here. They were a series of the two of us together, taken about three years apart. The one that's missing is about a year old. You can see from the nail that it really was here."

"Grace . . ." He drew her name out in a way that was pained and exasperated in equal measure.

She looked at him again, recognizing from his tone that he considered the missing picture meaningless, and felt herself start to get mad.

"I think whoever left the cake took the picture away with him," she said firmly.

He glanced from her to the nail and back.

"I'm not saying it's not possible, but . . ."

"I thought you said you were going to take this seriously, Detective!" Mindful of Jessica asleep upstairs, her voice was low but fierce.

He sighed and met her gaze with a slight but unmistakable twinkle in his eyes. "There you go trying to bully me again."

His amusement was too much. Grace sucked in her breath and glared at him. "Forget it. This is useless. You've made up your mind, haven't you? None of this is happening. It's all just a figment of my overactive imagination!"

"I'll add the missing picture to the case file, okay?" His voice was soothing, and that was almost more maddening than anything else.

"Forget it! Just forget it!" Brushing past him, nearly knocking him down the stairs in her anger and not much caring if she did, Grace stalked to the light switch and flicked it off. "Go back out on the porch!" she snapped over her shoulder. "Better yet, go home! If none of this is happening, I certainly don't need you hanging around playing bodyguard, do I? You . . ."

"Hush!"

Two bounds brought him to the foot of the stairs. Grabbing her from behind, he wrapped his arms around her and pulled her tightly against him as he clapped a hand over her mouth. His action was so urgent, so unexpected, that Grace did exactly as he ordered: She hushed, hanging in his arms with the limp lack of resistance of a bean-bag toy.

"Look there!" He whispered the words into her ear as he lifted her clean off her feet and turned her around to face the living room. Clutching the hard, leather-clad arm around her waist for balance, she could feel the faint sharp stubble of five o'clock shadow scratching her skin as his jaw pressed close against her cheek. "Look at the window on the right!"

For a moment Grace was bewildered. Then she saw it. The glowing lamplight outside had caught someone in the act of walking between the lamppost and the house. Thrown in sharp relief against the closed curtain, the shadow was visible for only a few seconds before it vanished from sight.

CHAPTER 28

"STAY HERE!" MARINO LET HER GO, PULLED A
gun from the back waistband of his jeans and ran on silent feet for
the front door.

Stay here nothing! Grace ran, too, for the kitchen, and her
own gun. She would go out the kitchen door, and they would
have him trapped between them.

The idea of catching the criminal who had been preying on
her daughter filled Grace with a kind of savage triumph. She had
always wondered if she would be capable of shooting someone if
she had to. Now she had the answer, she thought as, pistol in
hand, she slipped out the back door. She could.

The kitchen door opened onto a cement-floored, covered
walkway that led to the door to the garage. The walkway was
about twelve feet long by five feet wide, and it was wet and
slippery. Roof-high verbena grew the length of it on both sides,
so that the passage itself formed a kind of sheltered tunnel. There
was an opening on either side just wide enough to permit a person to pass through, to the front and backyards. Grace stepped
cautiously through the opening onto the flagstone path that led
around to the driveway, unmindful of the shower of icy raindrops
she dislodged or the rush of cold air that hit her in the face. She

held the pistol stiffly in her right hand, and her glance darted all around.

The night was dark except for the round pool of yellow lamplight some thirty feet in front of her. Flanked by the house on one side and the garage on the other, the area where Grace stood was deep in shadow. She could see clear down to the hedge on the driveway side of the yard, but the house blocked her view of the rest. Moving carefully forward, she was conscious of the acceleration of her hearbeat.

Where was Marino? Where was the intruder? Remembering the direction in which the shadow on the curtain had seemed to be heading, the answer was obvious: in the backyard.

Grace turned and beheld a figure on the roof of the walkway. It was darker than the charcoal sky against which it was silhouetted, and it crouched low as it scrambled along. Whoever it was obviously meant to gain entry by the roof of the house, which slanted down almost low enough to meet the walkway roof over the kitchen door. From there the figure would, perhaps, seek out an unlocked second story window.' . . .

Never afterward could she remember the next few seconds. without a shudder, she raised her pistol and pointed it at the figure. . . .

"Freeze!" Marino yelled from the backyard. His voice sounded muffled and distant, but the order was unmistakable. The figure on the roof straightened like a puppet whose string had been pulled abruptly upright, and jerked around to look in the direction of the voice. In the process it seemed to lose its footing. Its arms windmilled, its feet danced, and then with a little cry it fell from sight.

Grace stopped breathing. All the blood seemed to drain from her face, her body. She would recognize that voice anywhere, any time, under any conditions, even as high-pitched and frightened as it had sounded then.

"Jessica!" she cried, horror in her voice, and ran toward the backyard.

When Grace reached her, Jessica was lying, arms outflung, in the grass, with Marino kneeling beside her. In the background, the tree house from her childhood looked down from the nearly bare branches of the sturdy oak where it had been built so many years before. Beneath it, the bright yellow plastic swings of her swing set were visible even through the darkness, swaying gently back and forth with the wind. A shower of droplets blew down from somewhere above, sprinkling Grace's face.

"Jessica, Jessica!" Grace threw herself down on her knees beside Marino, uncaring of the wet grass that quickly soaked through her sweatpants. She leaned over the supine figure, unmindful of the gun, which she still clutched in her right hand. "Oh, my God, is she hurt?"

"Jesus!" Marino muttered, as Grace's hand holding the pistol landed almost in his lap. Without another word he removed the weapon from her grasp. Grace barely even noticed. Her attention was all for the white-faced girl who, thankfully, was staring up at her wide-eyed.

"Hi, Mom," Jessica said feebly.

Grace felt heat in her face as the blood returned to it in a rush.

"Hi, Mom?" she repeated disbelievingly, her voice a couple of octaves higher than normal. That answered her question for her, she thought. Jessica was not hurt. "Jessica Lee Hart, what were you doing on the roof?"

"At a guess, I'd say she snuck out again," Marino said dryly when Jessica failed to answer.

Grace stared down at her daughter without speaking. For an instant, in an attempt to gain control of her emotions, she closed her eyes. When she opened them again, Jessica was already scrambling to her feet, brushing off her clothes.

"I'm really sorry, Mom," Jessica said in a tiny voice.

"Are you hurt?" Grace's voice was sharp. Jessica shook her head.

"Go into the house." Grace knew she sounded preternaturally calm. What she felt was—blank. Nothing. Just icy cold. She was in shock, she decided dispassionately. Which was probably a good thing, for the moment.

Jessica slunk into the warm, brightly lit kitchen, with Grace at her heels and Marino bringing up the rear and closing the door behind them. With the section of her mind that remained available to register such things, Grace saw that he carried her pistol, and only her pistol. His, she assumed, was once again tucked into the waistband of his jeans.

Jessica walked past the table, tracking mud and bits of grass across the floor, to turn and face her mother at the center island. She rested one hand with its green-tipped nails on the counter by the sink while the other flipped long strands of straight fair hair back from her face. The hot-pink strand in front was now purple, Grace noted, to match the earrings that dangled from her ears; Jessica must have recolored it while Linda was here. Grace also saw that Jessica's hair and clothes were wet and covered with grass and mud, and she was dressed in jeans and the black leather jacket she had worn to the mall earlier. She flicked a glance to the coatrack, remembering Jessica removing the garment and hanging it there when she had come in from the mall. How had she failed to notice that it was missing? she wondered. How had she failed to sense that Jessica was not, after all, safe inside the house?

"Where have you been?" Grace's voice was soft and controlled, and sounded unnatural even to her own ears. She moved to the end of the center island, her hand lying along the cold tiles just as Jessica's was, staring at her daughter as if she were observing with curiosity a creature from a different planet.

How could Jessica have snuck out of the house *again*? Did nothing they had experienced mean anything to her? The mere idea that her daughter had been out roaming around in the dark, unprotected, when she knew that someone was out there who wanted, at the very least, to scare her badly, terrified Grace. Did Jessica have absolutely no sense at all? No notion of self-preservation?

"Mom, I'm *sorry*," Jessica said. Her face was as white as

paper, her eyes were huge, and she looked on the verge of tears. For the first time since she could remember, Grace found that the sight of her daughter's distress did not move her. Not one bit.

"Where have you been?" This time there was a force to the question that made Jessica blink.

"I've been to a party, okay? A *party.* I knew you would never let me go so I snuck out. I'm sorry." Truculence laced Jessica's voice now. Her chin was up, and her hands were clenched into fists. Grace felt her muscles tense.

"Your bedroom door was locked. You crawled out your window, didn't you? You deliberately locked your bedroom door and turned on your stereo so that I would think you were in your room when I got home, and you crawled out your window, along the roof to the walkway, and down the trellis on the back of the garage, didn't you?" Now that she was alerted to the general idea, Grace could picture the route as clearly as if she'd seen a map of it. "To begin with, do you know how *dangerous* that is? I had a gun; Detective Marino had a gun. We thought you were that creep who's been breaking into the house. What if one of us had shot you? What if the creep was out there watching somewhere and grabbed you? What if you fell off the roof? What if? . . ."

"Oh, Mom!" Jessica interrupted. "You think everything I do is dangerous! Everywhere I go, everything I eat, all my friends! You just want to keep me ten years old for the rest of my life! Well, you can't! It's my life, and I'll live it the way I want!"

"Young lady, with that attitude, you'll never get out of this house again!"

"What are you going to do, ground me forever? It won't do any good. I'll just sneak out."

"If you do . . ."

"What, Mom? What are you going to do? What can you do, huh? Nothing, that's what!" Jessica was yelling at the end, thrusting her face toward Grace's, her eyes flashing.

Grace got a whiff of beer from her daughter's breath.

"You've been drinking!" She could not believe it. Not *again.*

"I had some beer! So what? It was a party, and there was a

keg, and I had some, just like all the other kids! You know what else I did? I smoked a couple of cigarettes, and part of a joint— you hear that, Detective? *part of a joint*—and made out with a really cute guy! And I'll do it again any time I want and you can't stop me! So there!"

Grace lost it. For the first time in years she completely lost control of her temper.

"Want to bet?" she bit out. Then, before she even knew what she meant to do, she drew back her hand and slapped Jessica's face.

The sharp sound of the slap and Jessica's resultant gasp echoed through the room. Grace's hand stung in the aftermath of the blow. Her face drained white at exactly the same rate that Jessica's did.

Only Jessica's left cheek was slowly pinkening as the blood rushed to fill in the imprint of Grace's hand.

For a moment mother and daughter simply stared at each other.

"I hate you," Jessica choked out, her hand pressed to her abused cheek. "I want to go live with my dad!"

Grace felt as if there were no bones left in her body. She felt sick, literally sick to her stomach. But there could be no backing down now, no gathering her daughter into her arms and apologizing and crying with her as she promised her that everything would be just as Jessica wished. She had to remember what was at stake here—for Jessica's sake.

"Go to your room," she said steadily. "We'll talk about this tomorrow."

"The door's locked, remember?" Although tears were running down her face now, and her hand was still pressed to her cheek, Jessica still managed to look, and sound, defiant. "I can't get in."

"I'll get it open for you. Come on." Marino, who'd been a silent presence in the background during this tender mother-daughter exchange, intervened in a quiet voice before Grace could reply, which was just as well. Grace was so upset she could barely talk. She must have done a million things wrong for them to come to this, she thought. And she was afraid, so terribly afraid, that the situation might be beyond repair.

What did a mother do, when her half-grown daughter wouldn't listen? Chain her to the wall?

Marino left the kitchen, with Jessica still rubbing her cheek, stomping in his wake. Grace watched her go, aching for the sweet little girl who had once thought her mommy was the most wonderful being on earth.

Then she turned, leaned her upset stomach against the counter, gripped the tile edge with both hands, rested her forehead against an overhead cabinet, and closed her eyes.

She was still standing like that when Marino returned to the kitchen. Five minutes could have passed, or fifty. She heard him enter the room, knew by the sound of his footsteps on the hardwood floor that it was him, but still she could not bring herself to open her eyes or look around.

She felt tired, and sick, and utterly drained. And sad. So terribly, terribly sad. As if she had lost Jessica forever.

"You okay?" He came up behind her and put his hand on her arm. Grace felt his touch as just the slightest of pressures and realized that she was still wearing the bulky, brown-wool toggle coat that she had put on what seemed like hours earlier. She realized, too, that her sweatpants were wet from the knee down, her feet were soaked, and she was crying.

She never cried. She had learned long ago, in a very hard school, that crying was a waste of time. The only thing that ever came of it was a stuffed-up nose.

"Fine," she said, only her voice sounded strange.

"Grace . . ." His hand tightened on her arm.

"I'm okay." Her voice was sharp. He released her arm and stepped back. Still she could not face him.

Grace realized that she was hot and started to undo the wooden fastenings that closed the front of her coat. It gave her something to do, while she struggled to regain her composure. Shrugging out of the garment, she was surprised to find it being lifted from her shoulders and set aside. This small kindness made more tears well up. She closed her eyes tightly, willing the tears to stop, determined that he should not see.

"Did you . . . get the door open?" she managed with only the slightest hesitation in her voice. Still she could not turn around or open her eyes. The thrice-damned tears would not go away.

"Yeah," he said. "Credit card. Easy as pie. Grace . . ."

His hands curled around both her arms above the elbow. Grace could feel the solid presence of him close behind her.

"Just leave me alone. Please," she said when he started to turn her around. She opened her eyes, blinking rapidly, trying by sheer dint of will to dissipate the tears, when she realized he wasn't going to do as she asked.

"Hey, it's not that bad." He turned her to face him despite her resistance, his hold gentle but unbreakable. Pride compelled her to look up at him, and she had to look up, she found. It was always a surprise to her to discover that he was so tall. The top of her head did not reach his nose. His shoulders were wide, blocking her view of much of the kitchen. His head was bent toward hers, and his face was close enough so that she could see every vein in the slightly bloodshot brown eyes and every tiny line surrounding them. His hair looked very black with the bright kitchen lights shining on it, while his skin looked very bronze. He was frowning down at her, his mouth tight with concern. His lower body was mere inches from hers, almost trapping her against the cabinets. She could feel the solid strength of his legs in front of her, while in back the hard edge of the counter pressed into her flesh just above the base of her spine.

"Yes, it is." Abrim with tears or not, her eyes met his defiantly as she lifted her hands to brush the moisture away. "It is that bad. I just slapped my daughter for the first time in our lives. It's worse than bad."

"You lost your temper. It happens."

"Oh, God, I feel like such a . . . rotten mother." To her annoyance, she gave a mighty sniff and felt a tear spill from her right eye. She hadn't meant to say such a thing, to make such a confession to him of all people, when she knew he had disapproved of her mothering skills from the first. But she couldn't seem to help it. She felt wretched, absolutely wretched, and he was there and being sympathetic when what she needed more than anything on earth right at that moment was a shoulder to cry on. . . .

"Oh, let me go, Marino," she said, avoiding his gaze and trying, without putting much real force into the effort, to pull her arms away from his grip, "before I make a total, utter, and complete fool of myself."

"You're not a lousy mother, Grace." His voice was soft, while the hands on her upper arms were firm as they refused to let her go. "Know what I've seen since I've met you two? I've seen a woman who loves her daughter and is doing her very best for her. And I've seen a daughter who loves her mother, but is grappling with a few issues of her own right now. For God's sake, she's a teenager. They do these things. It's nothing to beat yourself up over."

Grace looked up then, met his eyes, and despite her best efforts gave another sniff.

"Who are you, Dr. Mom?" she asked, trying to lighten things up.

"Something like that."

The expression on his face was her undoing. He looked as if he cared.

Tears welled into her eyes anew, and spilled down her face. She was not accustomed to having anybody look like that for her.

"Oh, God," she said miserably, giving up and letting her head drop forward so that her forehead rested against his chest. He had removed his jacket; her skin touched the soft flannel of his shirt. "I told you I was going to make a fool of myself."

"Go ahead," he murmured, his body curving around hers. "I've got all night."

CHAPTER **29**

GRACE GRIPPED THE SOFT, MUCH–WASHED COT-
ton flannel—it smelled faintly of Downy—with both hands and
hung on as if for dear life. His arms were wrapped around her,
gentle and strong and protective, holding her close. It was such a
luxury to lean against him, such a luxury to be comforted, to feel
as if her troubles mattered to someone besides herself, that she
could not bring herself to pull away.

"So talk to me," he said, and she sniffed and gulped and held
on tighter and complied. She talked about Jessica, about what a
sweet little girl Jessica had been and how Jessica hated her diabetes
and how she suspected that Jessica was rebelling against her by not
injecting her insulin on time or eating properly or taking care of
herself in general. She talked about her guilt about being a working mother and her particular guilt about working so much when
Jessica was young. She talked about her divorce and the effect it
had had on Jessica. She talked about her terror that Jessica was
getting into trouble with drugs and her fear that Jessica had been
targeted for revenge by a drug ring. All the while he held her, and
listened, and made sympathetic noises. When at last Grace ran out
of words, she just rested in his arms, her head against his chest,
feeling strangely at peace.

"Do you realize," he said at last, the bristles on his chin

scratching along her cheekbone as he bent to speak in her ear, "that you have been talking to me forty-five minutes straight about Jessica? What I want to know is, what about Grace?"

Grace looked up at him then, lifting her head away from his chest and tilting her chin so that she could see his expression. She still held on to the front of his shirt, but less desperately now. His face was very close, his eyes warm and touched with humor as they met her gaze, his mouth twisting up at the corners into a wry half-smile.

"What do you mean, what about me?" she asked, frowning.

"Your whole life revolves around her, doesn't it?"

"To all intents and purposes, she is my life."

"Maybe she shouldn't be. Maybe that's the problem. Maybe you need to live for yourself just a little for a change."

Grace felt herself getting angry—what did he know about her and her daughter?—but the anger died almost at birth. After all, what he was saying was no more than what she had been telling herself for some time: she needed to let go of Jessica, at least to a certain degree. But what she knew with her head was not all that easy to convey to her heart.

"It's been so long, I wouldn't even know where to start." This confession was offered up with a flickering smile as she released her grip on his shirt at last, splaying her cramped fingers flat against his body, enjoying the juxtaposition of the softness of the flannel over the hard resilience of the muscles beneath. Her hands rose and fell with the rhythmic rise and fall of his chest, and she liked that, too. In fact, she liked everything about him, from the way he smelled—she had never before realized what an aphrodisiac the scent of Downy could be, when mixed with the underlying aroma of man—to the physical facts that he was taller than she was, broader than she was, harder than she was, and stronger than she was, to the concern and genuine human caring he showed her. Taken all together, it was a dangerous combination, and she knew it. What she really needed to do, if she was smart, was move out of his arms and recover her equilibrium on her own. But she couldn't quite bring herself to do it, not yet. She felt warm and comfortable and cared for, the latter for the first time in years.

"You could start with me."

Meeting his gaze, she frowned, not comprehending. "Start with you? How?"

He smiled down at her, his expression rueful. He really was very handsome, she decided, whether one liked the type or not, with his brown eyes twinkling and his mouth twisted up into that self-deprecating smile. "Has it even occurred to you that I find you very attractive?"

Grace's eyes narrowed suspiciously. Her fingers curled into the front of his shirt again. "No-o."

"You don't think I'm on twenty-four-hour-a-day call for everybody in the city, do you?" The question, and the smile that accompanied it, were wry.

"I . . . hadn't thought about it."

"Then I suggest you think about it, Your Honor." With exquisite sensitivity, his hands slid up her back. Grace tracked their movement even through the thickness of her sweatshirt. Her fingers tightened on the folds of flannel she held, and fascinated, she watched his eyes as his head bent toward her. His lids drooped and the golden-brown depths darkened until they were mere rings around the blackness of his pupils. Grace felt her lips part with anticipation as she realized that he was going to kiss her.

God, she wanted him to kiss her!

Her hands slid up to rest on his broad shoulders, and she rose on tiptoe to meet his mouth. When their lips first touched, the contact was gentle, almost clumsy, but the sheer heat of it made Grace gasp. She pressed her body against his with sudden, fierce need, and she slid her arms around his neck.

His mouth lifted from hers for an instant and their gazes met.

"I've been wanting to do that since I first laid eyes on you," he whispered, kissing her again, his lips hard and sure as they closed over her mouth. His tongue slid between her lips, and Grace felt fire shoot clear down to her toes.

"You have not," she protested breathlessly, pulling her mouth away from his, striving to keep things under control, to keep a clear head. He smiled down into her eyes, then pressed another quick, hungry kiss on her mouth, and the idea of her clear head went right out the window.

"I have too. Bossy women turn me on." It was no more than a murmur, spoken as he lifted his head. Grace only smiled a little in response, feeling almost dizzy with anticipation. Their mouths touched, and then she was kissing him greedily, her lips and tongue as hot and hungry as his. Aching and yearning, she pressed tightly against him, desperate for more, for the feel of his hands on her skin and his body joined to hers and . . .

"Wait! Wait!" she whispered frantically, pulling her mouth from his, her hands lying flat on both sides of his bristly jaw now as she sought to put a little distance between them. She needed to slow things down, to think. . . . "I don't even know—are you married?"

He lifted his head, and his eyes met hers. She found warmth and humor and an intense, burning desire for her in their depths.

"No, I'm not married." His voice was low, husky with passion, with a little thread of amusement running through the words.

"Oh. Good. Uh . . ." Grace knew there were other things she needed to know, questions she needed to ask, matters that needed to be discussed between them before this progressed any further, but she couldn't think while he was kissing her and his body was pressing hers back against the cabinets and his hand was sliding up the front of her sweatshirt—

Jessica's scream was as sudden and shocking as a deluge of icy water.

His hand stilled, his mouth lifted, and for a moment the two of them merely stared at each other, so dazed with passion that they weren't quite sure what, if anything, they had heard.

Then Jessica screamed again.

Grace pushed free at the same moment that he let her go, and they both ran for the stairs. He was ahead of her, bounding up the steps, drawing his pistol from the back waistband of his jeans as he went, with Grace racing at his heels. Jessica burst from her bedroom while they were still only halfway there. Grace could hear her feet pounding along the upstairs hall. Sweet and childish-looking in a pale-blue nightgown, her hair hanging loose around her face, she hung over the upstairs railing, gasping and sobbing hysterically.

"Are you okay? Are you hurt?" Marino was shouting the questions at her as he gained the top of the stairs.

"Jessica! Jessica!" Grace was right behind him.

"Mom! Oh, Mom! It's in my bed!"

"You two stay here." It was an order—he was good at giving orders, Grace thought—tossed out as he ran past Jessica toward her bedroom. Grace was at the top of the stairs then, and Jessica fell into her arms.

"Sweetie, what is it?" Grace wrapped her arms around her sobbing daughter and hugged her close, their earlier contretemps temporarily forgotten. Jessica clung, weeping and trembling, as if she would never let her go.

"Oh, Mom, it's so sick! Why would anybody do that?" Jessica was crying noisily, her face buried in Grace's shoulder, her arms wrapped around her mother's neck. Grace could barely understand her words.

"Baby, what? . . ."

"Grace." Marino stood in Jessica's bedroom doorway, beckoning to her. His gun had been tucked out of sight again, which gave Grace to understand that whatever crisis had occurred, they were in no immediate danger. "I think you need to see this."

He looked, and sounded, grim. Hard to believe that this was the man who had been kissing her so passionately just a few scant minutes before. Hard to believe that *she* had been kissing *him* so passionately just a few scant minutes before.

She had been kissed by two different men tonight, and she could barely remember the first. The second was to the first as the sun was to a candle.

"Jess, let me go look. . . ." Grace tried gently to disengage herself.

"I'm coming with you!" Sobbing, clinging, Jessica would not let go. Mother and daughter moved with arms around each other toward the bedroom. Marino watched their approach, his face set in harsh lines, his eyes hooded and difficult to read. As they reached the doorway, he shook his head at Grace.

"She doesn't need to see this again," he said quietly. Grace met his gaze, read the warning there, and nodded.

"Wait here, baby." Disengaging from Jessica, she left her leaning against the doorway as she crossed the room to join Marino, who stood at the foot of Jessica's bed.

"I was in bed. I turned over and stretched out my foot and . . ." Jessica said from the doorway, the explanation ending with a sob and a shudder.

Only the small bedside lamp was lit. Shadows shrouded the corners of the room. Jessica's discarded clothes lay in a heap on the floor—another bit of defiance from a child who had been taught to hang up her clothes or put them in the hamper as soon as she took them off, Grace thought. A soft circle of golden light touched the pillow with its lace-trimmed, pink-striped case that still bore the imprint of Jessica's head. Her headphones lay near the pillow, silent evidence that Jessica had been listening to music in bed. The covers had been pulled all the way back so that they hung over the footboard, puddling on the carpet.

"Look there."

Grace reached the bed and looked where Marino indicated, down at the very foot of the mattress, which was cheery in its pink-striped sheet. For a moment she did not comprehend what she saw. Then she did, and gasped.

There, at the very bottom of the mattress, in a sealed plastic freezer bag filled with water, lay Godzilla. He was dead.

CHAPTER **30**

"**O**H, NO!" GRACE CLAPPED A HAND TO HER mouth and took a step back from the bed. Her gaze remained fixed on the horror at its foot. "Oh, no!"

"Somebody killed him," Jessica said in a choked voice from the doorway. Barefoot, looking very thin and fragile in her blue nightgown, she was leaning against the jamb, tears streaming down her face. Grace backed away from the bed until she reached her daughter's side. The two of them came together, clinging to each other for support.

Marino looked around at them, his expression grim.

"Somebody killed him." Almost disbelievingly, Grace met his gaze and repeated Jessica's words.

"Poor Godzilla." More tears spilled from Jessica's eyes. Grace, her heart aching for both her daughter and the dead pet, hugged Jessica close. "Why would anybody do something like that to him? He was just a—just a hamster."

"Oh, baby, I don't know." Contemplating what had been done to the hamster was horrifying. Contemplating the kind of person it would take to do such a thing, then deliberately put the grisly evidence in Jessica's bed for her to find, was even worse.

It was downright scary.

"All right, ladies, let's go downstairs. I don't want to disturb anything until the crime unit gets here." Marino came up behind them, wrapping an arm around their shoulders, hugging them, giving what comfort he could as he urged them toward the stairs. Even in this moment of crisis, even as sick at heart and upset as she was, Grace was conscious of his welcoming touch. Jessica seemed to accept the hug as natural under the circumstances, Grace was pleased to see.

"I *told* you these things weren't pranks!" she said fiercely over her shoulder to him as they moved toward the stairs. At the top of the steps he let them go, and they proceeded downward on their own, with Jessica going first. A thought assailed Grace half-way down, and she looked back at him with narrowed eyes. "You can't possibly think this is a prank, can you?"

"I don't think this is a prank, no," he said as they reached the bottom of the stairs. "I'm not sure what it is. The first thing that needs to be ascertained is how the hamster actually died: did it drown in that bag or did it die of natural causes before someone put it in there? That will determine the arc of the investigation. What I need to do first is make a few phone calls."

Grace turned to face him, her gaze suddenly steely. Jessica's safety was at stake; she knew it as well as she knew her own name. No matter how she felt about Marino—and she would have to work that out in her own mind at a later time—Jessica's well-being was her first priority.

"No, *I* need to make a phone call. I'm going to call the district attorney. I want police protection for my daughter, right now. And I mean to see that it happens."

"What do I look like, chopped liver?" The question was dry.

"*Official* police protection."

"Are you talking about going over my head, Your Honor?" The look he gave her was narrow-eyed.

"That's what I'm talking about, Detective." Her gaze met his, and held. An awareness of the passion that had burned so hotly between them was there, silently acknowledged by both. But overriding that was the fact that she was a judge and he was a cop, and in the local authority rankings, that gave her the upper hand.

"Fine. Call anybody you want."

"Mom, do you think somebody's really after me?" Jessica sounded frightened. Sliding a hand into Grace's, she huddled close against her mother's side.

On the verge of denying it, Grace hesitated. It would not do, under the circumstances, to give Jessica a false idea of her own safety. Tonight's trip out the window still blazed vividly in Grace's mind. Under the circumstances, they could not afford a repeat.

"I don't know, baby," she admitted.

"I'm scared." Jessica's voice was small and squeaky.

"I'm scared, too."

Marino looked from one to the other of them, exasperation and concern mingled in his expression. "Grace, take Jessica in the other room and let me handle this, will you please?"

"I told you, I want police protection for my daughter." Grace was absolutely determined.

"I'll see that she gets it."

They exchanged measuring looks.

"Fine. Then do it," Grace said shortly.

"Thank you. I will."

He stepped past them into the kitchen, picked up the phone, and started dialing. Somewhat against her better judgment—she had learned long ago that trusting others to do a necessary job was a bad idea—Grace took Jessica on into the family room and left him to it. Mother and daughter curled up together on the couch while Marino made his calls. Jessica had stopped crying, but she was shivering, and Grace wrapped the afghan that always lay along the back of the couch around her shoulders. Grace was sitting on one corner of the couch, her shoes kicked off and her feet tucked up under her, her daughter's head on her shoulder, when Marino finally entered the room.

"Well?" Grace asked, the single word a challenge.

"The cavalry's on the way," he said. He was carrying two

mugs and had Jessica's pink chenille bathrobe thrown over one arm.

"What does that mean?"

"It means you get the whole nine yards. Total police protection for both of you." He sounded a little terse as he set the mugs on the low wooden table in front of them. "In the meantime, coffee for you, *Your Honor*"—he looked at Grace—"hot chocolate for you"—he looked at Jessica—"and your robe." He handed Jessica her robe and the sugar-free cocoa. "They're going to be wanting to ask you some questions when they get here," he said to Jessica. "You probably want to put this on."

"Thank you," Grace said, not missing that pointed *Your Honor,* and she was not referring to just the coffee. For a moment their eyes met and held. Grace smiled slightly, conciliatingly, and his eyes softened just a fraction.

"No problem." Marino turned and went back into the kitchen. Grace took a sip of coffee while Jessica sat up and shrugged into her robe. Jessica's face was pale and splotchy. Her nose and eyes were red from crying. Even now, with the worst of the storm over, her breath came in intermittent hiccups.

"Don't you want your hot chocolate?" Grace asked, when Jessica ignored her cup. In general, Jessica loved hot chocolate. Thus reminded, Jess picked up the cup, looked at it, and put it down again with a little shudder.

"Do you suppose Godzilla suffered?" Jessica asked in a subdued voice.

Grace's heart turned over with sorrow for her daughter and her pet. "I don't know, baby. I hope not."

Marino walked back into the room carrying his own mug. The family room was simply set up, with the couch placed along one of the two long walls, flanked by a rocker on one side and a navy-blue leather chair with a matching ottoman on the other. An oval coffee table sat in front of the couch, with the TV directly opposite, in a multiple-unit walnut entertainment center that also held tapes and books. More bookshelves lined one of the shorter walls, while the other was a bank of windows, with curtains drawn now to keep out the night. Round brass lamps on either side of the couch were turned on, as was the overhead light, making the room very bright.

"Somebody wants to kill me, doesn't he?" Jessica asked him, her voice tiny now, as Marino sat down in the blue leather chair. "Is it something to do with that drug thing at school?"

"I don't think so," Marino answered, before Grace could reply. "And I don't think anybody wants to kill you. I think somebody's just trying to scare you a little, for whatever reason. We're going to find out who, and why. In any case, we'll keep you and your mom safe, I promise."

Grace and Jessica both looked at him as he sipped from his mug. She believed him, Grace realized, and felt her tense muscles marginally relax. Whatever was or was not between them, she absolutely believed that as long as he was around, they would be safe.

For her part, Jessica frowned as if something had just occurred to her.

"What are you doing here in the middle of the night, anyway?" she asked him. Her glance slid around to her mother. "Did you call the cops on me?" Her voice was equal parts disbelief and outrage.

"I didn't even know you were gone until you fell off the roof," Grace said with some asperity. "I would have called the police if I had known, believe me, but I didn't. Detective Marino was very kindly following up on the other things that have happened when we saw your shadow sneak past the window."

Grace's gaze was drawn to Marino as she finished that speech, and for a moment their eyes met. The memory of the kisses they had shared shimmered in the air between them, as tangible as a heat wave on a hot August afternoon, and then was gone. He was still exactly the same obstinate, exasperating, thick-headed macho lug she'd been dealing with for weeks now, Grace realized. But with those kisses, everything between them had changed.

A knock, muffled, since it came from the front of the house, interrupted the conversation.

"I'll get it," Marino said when Grace instinctively started to rise. "It's probably a couple of uniforms. They're usually the first to arrive. Jessica, we're going to need to know exactly where you were tonight and who you were with, and the same for any other times you've snuck out lately, so be prepared."

Having delivered this warning in an unexpectedly stern voice, Marino left the room. Reminded of Jessica's transgression, Grace glanced at her daughter, her expression chiding.

"Mom, I really am sorry about sneaking out," Jessica said, having no trouble interpreting that look. "I shouldn't've done it. I know it. I shouldn't've done any of the things I did. It's just— there's this boy I like and he invited me to a party and I knew you wouldn't let me go and . . ."

"If you wanted to go to a party, you should have asked me, Jess." Grace met her daughter's apologetic gaze over the rim of her cup as she took another sip of coffee.

"Would you have let me go if I'd asked you?" Jessica asked, the challenging note in her voice softened by a hiccup.

Grace sighed. It really was difficult for her to stay angry at this person she loved more than anyone else on earth. She could feel her wrath softening over Jessica's escapade.

"Probably not," she admitted.

"Then what good does it do for me to ask?"

"You wouldn't be grounded for the rest of your life for sneaking out, for one thing," Grace pointed out.

Jessica grimaced. "Is that what you're going to do?"

"I'm thinking about it. I'll let you know."

"All the other girls get to go to parties. Why can't I? It's not fair!"

"I can't believe that all your friends—Emily Millhollen, for example, or Polly Wells—are going to parties with boys at age fifteen. Especially parties where there are kegs of beer, marijuana cigarettes, and obviously no parents present." Grace's voice was dry.

"That's only because nobody ever asks them," Jessica muttered, but had the grace to look away as she said it.

"Jessica—" Grace was interrupted by Marino's reentrance into the room. With him were his brother Dominick and another man, who was not wearing a uniform but who, Grace assumed, was also a police officer. From sounds elsewhere in the house, Grace guessed that others were now on the premises as well.

"Grace, this is my boss, Captain Gary Sandifer."

"Judge Hart."

"Captain Sandifer." Grace stood up and shook hands with the tall, thin balding man in the tan trench coat, who was regarding her with the respect generally accorded to her office. Grace felt the mantle of authority that she wore primarily on the job settle over her. Her voice was crisp, her handshake firm.

"I understand you've had some problems—" Sandifer began.

"If you don't mind, I'd prefer to talk about it in the kitchen. My daughter's been upset enough." Grace gestured toward the doorway behind them.

"Oh, of course."

As Sandifer turned back toward the door, Marino detained Grace with a hand on her arm. In a low voice, he said, "Dom's going to take Jessica's statement. He's got a daughter about that age, and he's good with kids, so I'm hopeful he'll get something useful out of her. We're treating this as a threat against you in your capacity as a judge, by the way. Jessica, as a private citizen, wouldn't be able to command the same degree of protection that you do."

"All right. Good idea." So he *had* handled it. As upset as she was, Grace wasn't sure she would have thought to work it that way. The idea that he had perhaps done a better job getting something done than she could have was both novel and, in a way, reassuring. Having someone she could lean on was a new thing for her.

With a single glance toward Jessica, who was replying with a small smile to something Dominick had said to her, Grace went into the kitchen after Sandifer. Marino followed, then walked on past the two of them, presumably to supervise what was going on upstairs.

"I understand that there have been a number of frightening incidents, including your daughter's pet being killed," Sandifer said, when he and Grace were alone. "Here in Franklin County we don't take kindly to somebody threatening one of our judges and her family. What we are going to do, with your permission, is make this a top-priority investigation and assign twenty-four-hour protection to both you and your daughter until we get this situation resolved. We'll have someone with both of you everywhere you go and someone posted here in the house at night. Detective Tony Marino has been heavily involved in this case from the beginning, I know, and he has volunteered to be the protection officer in your house at night. I assume you have no objection to that?" The look he gave her was a little searching, and for a disconcerting moment, Grace wondered if Marino's kisses were branded in neon on her mouth. Which was ridiculous, of course.

"No. No objection." Grace shook her head.

Sandifer nodded. "That's fine, then. As for your daughter, I assume she'll be maintaining her usual activities, going to school and so forth?"

"I . . . haven't had time to really think about it. At this point, I would answer yes."

He nodded again. "We'll have someone with her everywhere she goes, even in class. We've got several young-looking women officers who would be ideal, I think."

"Jessica is the priority. I want her kept safe. All the incidents have focused on her."

"That's what Detective Marino said. Don't worry, we'll take care of her. We'll take care of both of you, until we get this resolved."

"I appreciate that."

"Pardon me, Judge Hart."

Grace looked around inquiringly at the uniformed officer who had just appeared at her elbow. According to the badge on his breast pocket, his name was George Becker. He was a small man, about Grace's own height, portly in build, with thinning black hair and a bristly black mustache. What caught her eye, though, was something else altogether: he was wearing what appeared to be surgical gloves, and carrying a small, zip-top plastic bag in one hand and a long handled Q-tip in the other.

"If you don't mind, Your Honor, I need to get a tissue sample from you. I'll be taking one from your daughter, too."

Grace crossed her arms over her chest and frowned. "Why?"

"So we can compare the results with those from any physical evidence we find, and thus eliminate you or your daughter as sources."

"What kind of physical evidence?"

"Hairs, body fluids such as blood, saliva, or semen, possibly a sliver of skin if someone has been scratched or cut, that type of thing."

"Oh. Certainly."

"If you'll just open your mouth . . ."

Grace did.

As Becker inserted the swab between her teeth and the inside of her cheek, and swished it around, Sandifer asked, "Has any physical evidence been found?"

Becker withdrew the swab. "I really couldn't say, sir. I just take the samples." He put the swab into the plastic bag, sealed it shut, and headed toward the family room.

CHAPTER **31**

TONY WAS STANDING IN FRONT OF ONE OF THE long windows in Jessica's room, arms crossed over his chest, watching as Randy Zoller of the crime unit meticulously vacuumed the carpet. The contents of the vacuum bag would be examined for evidence such as hairs or textile fibers not consistent with the room or its inhabitants. Charlene Young, also of the crime unit, was performing the same service for the bottom bed-sheet, using a smaller, hand-held vacuum.

Dom entered the room, distracting Tony's attention. He walked over to join his brother by the door.

"Still think I'm taking her complaints too seriously?" Tony gibed in a low voice.

"It's a freakin' dead hamster, Tony, not murder one. The most we could convict the perp on if we caught him red-handed is cruelty to animals and trespassing."

Tony shook his head. "You're missing the big picture, brother." He held up his hand, counting possible charges off on his fingers as he spoke. "What we got here is possible terroristic threatening. Obstruction of justice. Interference with a public official in the performance of his—in this case, her—duties—"

Dom interrupted. "Let me point out, this was aimed at the daughter."

"If somebody wanted to intimidate you, what would be the best way to go about it? Threaten you, or threaten, say, Christy?"

Christy was Dom's teenage daughter.

Dom looked at him. "Point taken."

"Did you get anything useful out of Jessica?"

"The daughter? Where she was, who she was with, any enemies she might have—apparently half Hebron High School, she thinks. I got it all down. One interesting thing. She was on her porch late one night just after this started and thought she saw someone in the yard, watching her. She ran into the house, so scared she slept with her mother."

"You think we got something?" Tony knew his brother well. He could tell that Dom was starting to believe there might be some substance to Grace's fears after all.

"Maybe." Dom shrugged. "Okay, there's probably something here. But it looks to me like what it might be is somebody stalking the daughter, not the mother."

Tony and Dom both watched as Charlene Young bagged the bottom sheet.

"Like I said, if somebody wanted to get to you . . ."

"Okay, okay. The only thing is, we can't justify an investigation of this scope or twenty-four-hour police protection if the perp is just some kind of weirdo targeting the daughter. We're only able to do it if the target is your girlfriend, because she's a public official."

Tony gave Dom a sour look. "Would you quit with the girlfriend crap? And I'd say there's a good possibility that Grace *is* the target. We need to check out the cases she's working on, people she might have sentenced lately, that type of thing."

"Well, gee, I guess I'll just let you go over all that with *Grace*."

Tony's sour look lightened fractionally. "When's the last time somebody told you to go fuck yourself?"

Dom pretended to ponder. "A couple of days ago, I think. And I think it was you."

Tony laughed. "Yeah, well, this time I mean it. Anyway, let's get to work."

By the time the police finally left, it was after four A.M. Jessica lay on the family room couch, nearly asleep. Grace sat in the blue leather chair nearby. She was yawning when Marino walked into the room, having seen out the last of the contingent of police officers who'd scoured the house from top to bottom looking for evidence.

"You look beat. Both of you. Go on to bed," he said, looking from one to the other of them with a crooked half-smile.

"What did . . ." Grace began, and yawned again.

"Anything you want to know, I'll tell you tomorrow. Go to bed."

To Grace's surprise, she found the thought nearly irresistible. "All right then." She got to her feet, walked over to the couch and pulled Jessica up as well. "Let's go, sweetie."

"Oh, wow, I'm tired," Jessica said.

"You need any help?" Marino asked Grace, as Jessica swayed on her feet. Grace put an arm around her.

"No, I can manage. There's a daybed upstairs in my office. It's all made up, all you have to do is throw the little pillows off it. If you need extra blankets . . ." She yawned again.

"I'll find them. Don't worry about me. Good night." His voice was faintly dry.

"All right. G'night." In truth, Grace was too tired to worry about him. She was so tired her eyes felt gritty, and every other breath was a yawn.

But as she settled into bed—she and Jessica were in her bed, because Jessica could not bear the thought of returning to her own—she did reflect, with one of her last, conscious thoughts, that being able to surrender so fully to sleep was a luxury she had not enjoyed since the night she had found Mr. Bear down by the road. And the only reason she was able to do so tonight was because she was perfectly confident that she and Jessica would be safe as they slept.

And the reason she was so confident that they would be safe was that Marino was in the house, spending the night.

CHAPTER 32

T HE ONLY GOOD THING ABOUT HIS MOM WAS that she made the best rice pudding in the world. With a spoon, he scraped out the last creamy remnants from the big white mixing bowl and ate it with leisurely enjoyment. Then he carefully pulled the Saran Wrap back over the empty bowl and returned the bowl to the refrigerator, in a kind of revenge of the nerd thing, he thought with a snicker. His dad was going to be home before lunch tomorrow, which was Sunday, and his mom had made the pudding special for him. Which had made eating it just that much more fun.

The house was completely dark, except for the glow of a single TV and the light from the refrigerator, which he now shut. His mom was in bed. She had fallen asleep partway through Jay Leno, and it was her TV that was still on. Even in the kitchen he could hear little bits and pieces of some dumb late-night movie. Donny, jr., having just finished humping Caroline on the couch down in the basement, was at that moment hustling her out the basement door. Through the kitchen window he could see them sneaking up the outside steps, then heading hand in hand for Donny's car. Listening to them getting it on had been fun, too. No, exciting was more the word. *Real* exciting.

Lately he'd been heading over to Caroline's at night to watch her undress for bed. Not that she knew he was there, of course. But her bedroom was on the ground floor and her curtains didn't quite close in the middle and if he got up real close and put his eye to the glass he generally got quite a show.

He debated whether he wanted to go over there tonight. It was only a block away, and he could cut through the yards in about three minutes, but he'd already had a really big day and he was dead beat.

It had been a good day. A full day. He'd dropped off his present for Jessica—his *two* presents—and picked up his memento and then hung around to watch as the judge lady, true to form, called the police. He would have hung around longer, maybe come back at about eleven or so that night to see if his second present had been discovered—the judge lady would be calling the cops twice in one day, a record—but it was raining and so he'd decided to go to a movie instead. In the end, he'd sat through three for the price of one and gotten home just in time to listen to Donny, jr., and Caroline in the basement while he finished off the rice pudding.

The rain had stopped, though, so he guessed he could amble on over to Caroline's. He would only be gone maybe twenty minutes max, and then he could come back and go to bed in happy anticipation of his mom's explosion in the morning, when she found out that somebody had eaten up all the pudding.

She would know who, too. Donny, jr., didn't even like rice pudding.

What the hell. He grabbed a baseball cap and jacket from the closet in the hall, just in case it should start raining again, and headed out the back door.

The air was cold, the grass was wet, and every time he accidentally brushed against a bush he got showered with icy droplets. The one fence he had to climb—it was one of those wood, four-board, farm-type fences—was slippery. His left foot slid off the bottom rail just as he straddled it, causing his groin to crash painfully into the top board.

He was still limping and cursing under his breath by the time he got to Caroline's house.

Squeezing through the opening in the hedge into her backyard, he saw that she and Donny, jr., were standing on the sidewalk in front of her house, kissing and groping as they said good night. He watched envyingly until Donny managed to drag himself away and head back toward the street where his car was parked. While Caroline was waving at Donny, Little Brother got himself in position to get a bird's-eye view of the peep show.

Sure enough, Caroline went inside, went into her bedroom, and turned on the light. With his eye to the window, he was able to get a pretty clear view of most of the far side of the room, including her closed door and the light switch. Fortunately her closet was in his line of vision, as was the foot of her bed. Tonight her cat, a fat white Persian, sat on the foot of the bed. Like himself, the cat watched with rapt attention as Caroline began to undress.

God, she was pretty. Just like Donny, jr., to get the prettiest girl in school for a girlfriend. He always got the best of everything, always had, all their lives. If his mom was cooking steaks for supper, she'd always give Donny, jr., the biggest one. *He* needed it, she'd say. She bought him the best, most expensive clothes, because *he* looked so good in them, she'd say. They'd paid for half of Donny's car, and all of his insurance. He'd had to scrounge up the funds for his own motorcycle, and he had no insurance. Everything Donny wanted, Donny got. Little Brother got the leavings, if he was lucky.

Caroline's room was painted blue, which he knew was her favorite color, probably because it matched her eyes. Her bedroom furniture was white, with little bits of gold around the edges that was probably some sort of fancy style, though he didn't know what it was called. He could see her dresser, which was on the wall opposite the window, with its attached mirror. She stood in front of the mirror, brushing her hair.

Although her back was turned to him, he could see her face

through the mirror. Actually, he could see the whole front of her body to the waist. He hoped she stayed there while she undressed.

She didn't, of course. She turned away from the mirror, and walked to the left, out of his line of vision. When he could see her again, she was just wearing her bra and jeans. God, she looked good like that, so slim and sexy, with her tits swelling up over the silky blue bra and her skin all creamy.

The only thought that marred his pleasure as Caroline reached for the fastening of her jeans was that Donny, jr., got to do more than watch. He got to . . .

She stopped, with her hands on her waistband, staring like she heard something that startled her. It couldn't have been him, he hadn't made a sound, and anyway she was looking to the left, toward her bed. He shifted a little, so that he could see what she was looking at.

The big white cat was sitting on the end of her bed, just like it had been before, *only now it was staring fixedly at the window.* At him.

Just like it knew he was there.

Shit. Before he could get away, before he could jump back or duck or anything, the curtains whipped apart in front of him and there was Caroline, staring through the glass at him.

He almost pissed in his pants.

He dropped like a stone to the ground, hoping she wouldn't be able to see him through the glass, through the darkness. A slice of light from the window cut across the grass just in front of his head. Then the slice turned into a sliver as she let the curtains fall together again.

He took a deep, shaken breath. Getting caught playing Peeping Tom would be bad. It would be worse than bad, in fact. Everyone would think he was some kind of pervert. His parents would shit. . . .

"Donny? Donny, is that you?"

Unbelievably, she was outside, coming around the corner of the house, looking for him.

Looking for Donny, jr.

Scrambling on all fours along the side of the house away from her, he realized something: He was wearing Donny, jr.'s, Chicago Bulls baseball cap—the one made of black suede with a big red bull on the front—and Donny, jr.'s, jacket. She must have seen enough of him through the window to think he was his older brother.

Thank God she didn't know who he really was. If he could only get away . . .

"Donny? What are you doing?"

A prefabricated metal tool shed adjoined the house in back, and he crouched in its shadow, in the angle it made with the house. He huddled there with a coiled hose and a bunch of over-turned flower pots and a hoe and shovel and a sack of fertilizer as big as he was, his heart pounding, the lower part of his jeans getting all wet from the grass. If he tried to run across the yard, she would see him. His only hope was to hide until she was gone. If he was lucky, she would just walk on by. . . .

But when, in his whole life, had he ever been lucky?

"Donny?"

He dared to glance up, and he saw that she was coming right toward him. It was obvious that she saw him, saw Donny, jr., rather, because she was approaching without any kind of hesitation at all.

"Donny?" Her voice was soft and sweet and mystified. She'd put her sweater back on, he saw, before she'd left the house.

There was nothing to do but stand up. He did, and she came right up to him.

"I thought you went home. Did you forget something? I . . ." Her words broke off at the same time as her hand touched his arm. Her eyes widened.

"You're not Donny," she said accusingly.

The story of his life.

"I . . ." he began, but his throat closed and he couldn't say another word.

He didn't have to. She was mad now that she knew who he

was, jerking her hand away from his arm, her face screwed up as if she smelled an awful stink, her voice harsh and hateful.

"You were spying on me, weren't you? Peeping in my window, watching me undress! Weren't you? Weren't you? You're sick, did you know that? Sick and gross and disgusting and. . . . Wait till I tell my parents. They'll call the police. They'll call your parents. Donny'll beat the crap out of you, believe me, and that's probably the best thing that will happen, you little worm." She turned to head back into the house, tossing her hair, fury in every line of her slender body.

"Caroline, wait. . . ." He caught her arm. He couldn't let her go, couldn't let her tell her parents and the police and everybody. He had to stop her, had to make her see reason, but he couldn't think of anything to say.

"Get your hand off me, you pervert!" She jerked her arm out of his hold and stomped off toward the front door.

He couldn't let her go, couldn't let her do it, had to stop her somehow. . . .

Panicking, casting his eyes wildly around for help, he spotted the shovel. Only if he had to . . .

"Caroline . . ." He ran after her, caught her just as she got to the corner of the house, grabbed her arm again and spun her around. "Caroline, please, don't tell anybody. . . ."

She laughed contemptuously in his face, and that's when he knew he'd have to do it, he had no choice or she *was going to tell.* . . .

In the last seconds, as he swung the shovel up and brought it down right on top of her head, he could see in her eyes that she knew what he was going to do, knew that she was dead, that he was going to kill her. And she was afraid. . . .

When the shovel hit she was just opening her mouth to scream. It hit so hard that it bounced back up off her skull of its own volition, like a rebounding ball. The *thunk* was solid, sick sounding, like a pumpkin splatting open on concrete. He was still listening to its echoes as she crumpled to the ground.

Then, for good measure, he hit her in the head again.

For what seemed like an eternity he stood there, looking at her as she lay limply at his feet, blood trickling from her nose and mouth and ears and pouring from the open wounds in her head. Then he shook himself out of his stupor, took off Donny's jacket, and wrapped it around her head. He couldn't leave a trail of blood for the cops to follow.

He'd have to hide the body until he figured out what to do.

Sweat was pouring off him, rolling down his face like rain, dampening his shirt, but he didn't feel hot, he felt cold. Picking Caroline up—limp, she weighed a ton, far more than he would have expected for such a slender girl—he carried her flaccid body away from the house, in case her parents should wake up and come looking for her.

First things first.

Setting her down beyond the hedge, he went back and dug up the bloody spot where her head had rested on the ground, then covered it with fresh sod unearthed from a remote corner of a neighbor's yard.

By the time that was done and he got back to Caroline, he knew exactly what he was going to do.

He was smiling, not upset at all, because as black as things had looked in the beginning, they were going to work out for the best in the end.

Little Brother had finally figured out a way to win.

CHAPTER 33

Usually, on Sunday mornings, Grace got up early to enjoy the peace and quiet. Her modus operandi was to schlep downstairs barefoot in her nightgown, make coffee, retrieve the paper from the front porch, drink two cups, eat a bagel, and read the paper before going back upstairs to shower and dress. Today, however, mindful that Marino was somewhere in the house, she showered and dressed first, in pale khakis, a black turtleneck, and black flats, and if truth be told took extra care in putting on what little makeup she wore.

Thus it was almost ten before she walked into the kitchen.

He was sitting at the table with a half-eaten bowl of cereal and a glass of orange juice in front of him, one section of the paper propped against his coffee cup, the others strewn haphazardly across the tabletop. His black hair was curling at the ends, wavy on top, and still damp, making it obvious that he'd taken a shower. He was frowning slightly as he concentrated on whatever article he was reading. A heavy growth of beard shadowed his lean jaw, and he still wore the same flannel shirt and jeans he'd had on the previous night.

He hadn't really come prepared for a sleep-over, of course. It occurred to Grace to wonder what he'd slept in, but she banished the thought almost at once.

Dwelling on the tantalizing possibilities was not going to help her composure.

"Good morning," she said briskly, walking into the kitchen as if there were not the slightest awkwardness in the situation, and heading toward the coffee pot. As his cup attested, he'd already made coffee. The welcome aroma wafted through the air.

"Morning." He looked at her over the top of the paper, ate cereal, and tracked her movements as she poured herself a cup of coffee; then he smiled at her as—after taking a reviving sip of the hot, strong brew—she finally looked his way again. "I helped myself to breakfast. I hope you don't mind."

"No, of course not." She returned his smile with a quick, slightly impersonal one as she crossed to the refrigerator. Just because he had kissed her yesterday—no, correction, they had kissed each other, and so hotly that her heart pumped faster every time she allowed herself to recall the details—did not mean that they were in the throes of some deathless romance, she cautioned herself, as she had done about half a dozen times since awakening. Those kisses might mean a lot, or they might mean very little. She was not even sure how she felt about them herself, and for all she knew he might be the kind of man who made a pass at every halfway attractive woman he thought he had a chance with.

It would be a mistake to read too much into something that might mean nothing at all.

"I'm going to have a bagel. Would you like one?" she asked politely.

"No, thanks. I've got cereal." He was being polite, too, Grace reflected as she extracted a single frozen bagel from the bag in the freezer and popped it into the microwave for the required forty-five seconds. When the *ping* sounded, Grace hesitated only a moment before carrying her bagel, a jar of strawberry preserves, and her cup of coffee to the table. Instead of her usual place—that would mean sitting right beside him—she chose a chair on the opposite side of the table and sat down.

"The women's section is around here somewhere," he said

with an air of abstraction, glancing around over the pages scattered across the tabletop as though he would help her find it.

"What are you reading, sports?" Grace inquired with perfect affability, locating and retrieving the front, general news section that she always started with.

He grinned, his attention suddenly all on her, his eyes twinkling. He looked handsome, charming, and very endearing smiling at her like that, she thought with a worrisome pang in the region of her heart—and with conscious effort she did not smile back.

"I knew that would get you. It was a joke, Grace."

"Not funny, Detective." Using her professional facade of cool detachment as a shield, she took a sip of coffee as she checked out the section he held. "And I see you *are* reading sports."

"I'm a Pacers fan, what can I say?" Still grinning, he returned his attention to his paper, then glanced at her again a moment later. "By the way, if you need an engraved invitation to call me Tony, consider you just got one."

Not calling him by his first name had been a deliberate choice on her part. She had tried to avoid even thinking of him that way. If she kissed him and called him Tony, she was well on her way to sliding down a very slippery slope. Their relationship was forever changed. Instead of being professional, it became personal, and she wasn't sure she was ready for that.

So she avoided answering.

"What did you do with my gun?" She hadn't seen it since he'd taken it from her last night.

He looked over at her speculatively. "You really want to know?"

"It would be nice, yes."

"Then say, what did you do with my gun, *Tony*."

Grace met his look with a frown. "Are we childish or what?"

"Probably. Say it."

If she balked, she made a bigger deal out of her use of his

first name than she wanted to. She hadn't expected him to make an issue of it.

"What did you do with my gun, *Tony.*" She gave him a little, ironic smile.

"That was hard, wasn't it?" He *tsk-tsked* sympathetically. "You said it real well, though."

"My gun?"

"It's on the top shelf of the closet in the dining room. Unloaded. The magazine with the bullets is on top of your china cabinet. While I'm here, do me a favor and leave it there, would you, please? The thought that you're going to grab a gun and come running if trouble strikes gives me the willies."

Before Grace could reply to this, Jessica walked into the kitchen. Damp hair pulled back from her face and secured at the nape with a barrette, obviously fresh out of the shower, she was dressed, too, in jeans, and an oversized purple sweatshirt with the legend *Where are you, Leo?* scrawled across the front in pink. Glancing from her mother to Marino and back, she headed toward the refrigerator with a wan "Hi."

Both returned her greeting. Grace even managed to hold her tongue when Jessica sat down with a Diet Coke, a piece of cheese, and a quick, challenging look for her mother.

Jessica had to learn to manage her own disease.

"Did you sleep well, sweetie?" was all Grace said.

Jessica nodded, then shook her head. "Kind of. I woke up a couple of times, thinking about Godzilla." Her gaze went to Marino. "What . . . happened to him? His body, I mean. Did the cops take it?"

Marino nodded. "Some tests need to be run on it. Why?"

"I want to bury him. In the backyard, under the forsythia in the corner. I don't want him to just be . . . thrown away."

Jessica had taken neither a bite of cheese nor a sip of her soft drink, Grace saw. Her daughter was obviously hurting, and her heart ached in sympathy. *But she needed to eat.*

"I'll make sure you get the body back for burial, if you like," Marino said.

Jessica nodded, and took a small sip of Diet Coke. Grace concentrated on eating her bagel and drinking her coffee. After a moment, Jessica ate her cheese, then went to the pantry for a box of cereal. When her daughter returned to the table with a bowl of healthy grains, Grace took care not to appear the slightest bit interested.

"What homework do you have for tomorrow?" she asked instead.

Jessica shrugged, spooning cereal into her mouth. "Not much. Spanish vocab. An algebra sheet. I'll do it tonight."

Grace nodded, finishing her bagel. Tonight, too, they would have to talk, and by then she hoped she would have come up with some kind of effective punishment for her daughter's transgressions. So far, she'd been too tired and too preoccupied to think about it.

Obviously discipline was not one of her strong points.

"Okay, ladies, how about we talk about today's agenda for a minute," Marino said, glancing from Grace to Jessica and back as he folded the sports section and laid it on the table. "I have to go to my house, feed the dog, pick up some clothes and other necessities, and that kind of thing. Since I can't leave you two, I suggest you come with me. Any objections?"

"You have a dog?" Jessica looked interested. "What kind? A police dog?"

"No, Kramer's a mutt."

"Kramer?" Grace looked at him, fascinated. She realized that she was curious to see his home, and his dog, and anything else that might tell her something about his character. Eager, in fact.

"Remember *Seinfeld*? I named her that because her life is one perpetual bad-hair day." He looked faintly sheepish. Grace grinned.

"We'd love to come meet Kramer," she said.

"Yeah, we would," Jessica echoed.

"Anytime you're ready, then." He rose, picking up his dishes and carrying them over to the sink, where he rinsed them and put them into the dishwasher. Grace and Jessica followed suit.

"Where's your car?" Jessica asked curiously when they were backing out of the driveway some fifteen minutes later. It was a beautiful October day, sunny and crisp, with a cloudless blue sky. The only reminder of the last several days' rain was the occasional puddle that dotted the pavement. Grace felt her spirits lift as the trio left the house behind, and only then did she realize just how worried and upset she had been. In the car, Jessica was in the backseat. Grace drove. Marino was in the front passenger seat. He had volunteered to drive, but Grace, with a superior lift of her brows and a negative shake of her head, had turned him down.

"Did anybody ever mention to you the possibility that you might be kind of a control freak?" he had murmured in Grace's ear then, while Jessica climbed into the back and just before he'd walked around to the passenger side. Grace hadn't had a chance to reply.

"I parked it around the corner," Marino said in answer to Jessica's question, craning his neck both ways as Grace pulled into traffic, just as if he were the one doing the driving. Noting that, Grace made a face at him. *Talk about control freaks,* she mouthed silently, because of Jessica in the back. That he understood was clear by the sudden quirking of his mouth into a smile. "We'll pick it up later, maybe on the way back."

The house Marino directed them to was in Victorian Village near the university. Undergoing a revival, it was a thriving community of hundred-year-old houses. The area was an interesting mix of residents and housing values, with everyone from corporate vice presidents with families—in huge, completely restored brick homes that sold in the mid–six figures—to small, shotgun-style frame houses favored by singles and students who could most politely be described as fixer-uppers. Marino's house was one of the latter. It was a one-story, gray-frame house, with a covered concrete stoop and a single, large, many-paned window looking out onto the street. Similar houses were close on either side. An elderly woman swept the stoop of the porch next door. As Grace pulled up to the curb and parked—there were no driveways—the woman turned, paused with her sweeping, and watched the three of them get out of the car.

"Out all night again, huh, Tony?" she called with a wave and a cackle as he followed Grace and Jessica up the short, cracked concrete walk that led to his stoop.

"Working, Mrs. Crutcher, always working," he yelled back with a good-humored grin.

"That's what you always say," Mrs. Crutcher retorted with an answering grin and a dismissive gesture; she returned to her sweeping as Marino unlocked the door and they entered the house.

Grace's first impression was that it was shabby but neat, with the faintly musty smell of a place in need of a good airing. The walls were plain white and largely unadorned. The furniture—a brown tweed-upholstered couch and a tan Naugahyde recliner in the living room—was worn but serviceable. A braided rug covered the floor, a TV stood on a stand in one corner, and a non-functioning fireplace was fronted by a brass and wire screen. Paperback books filled the shelves built into alcoves on either side of the fireplace. A mirror had been hung over the mantel, which except for a single small, framed photograph, was devoid of decorative bibelots.

"Where's your dog?" Unlike Grace, Jessica evinced no interest at all in the house or its contents.

"In the backyard," Marino said with a glinting smile. "Go out through the kitchen."

He led the way through a second room directly behind the living room—originally intended as a dining room, Grace thought, but outfitted with a desk, a chair, a computer, and overflowing bookshelves as a den or office—to the kitchen, a small square room with three walls given over to white formica cabinets, white counters, and white appliances. The fourth wall, covered with red-and-white windowpane-plaid paper, contained a door with a glass pane and a tall rectangular window, both topped with a red-and-white-gingham frill. A glass-and-wrought-iron table and two wrought-iron chairs with red seat covers stood in the middle of the room. The tabletop was piled high with mail. Beyond the kitchen, Grace got a glimpse of what looked like two bedrooms, with white walls and beds and not much else.

"Out there." Marino smiled at Jessica, pointing to the door. Without waiting for any further permission, she crossed to the door, opened it, admitting a gust of fresh air, and stopped on the threshold as she was greeted by a sharp bark.

Marino moved to stand behind her for a moment, said, "Yo, Kramer, I'm home," over her head to the unseen denizen of the yard, and then headed toward the bedrooms.

"I'm going to shave real quick and throw some things into a bag. Make yourself at home," he said over his shoulder to Grace.

"A puppy!" Jessica exclaimed rapturously at the same time, and disappeared down the steps into the yard.

Grace followed Jessica and stood in the doorway for a moment looking down. The kitchen door opened onto three gray-painted wooden steps, which led down into a narrow, grassy side yard. This part of the yard ran along the length of the house before expanding into the backyard proper, where from her vantage point Grace could see part of a detached frame garage painted gray like the house. A door in the back of the garage opened onto the yard, while the front, with what she assumed was the car entrance, opened onto an alley that ran behind the house. In one corner of the yard, a small, apparently dead rose garden reached with bare, thorny branches toward the sky. A chain-link fence covered with weedlike vines surrounded the property, making a right angle into the side of the house just beyond where Grace stood at the top of the steps. Directly below her Jessica knelt. She was being jumped on and slavishly licked by a pair of dogs who were carbon copies of each other except for the fact that one was knee-high while the other was about a fourth the size. Both were brown and white and so furry that just about the only way to tell one end from the other was that the back of each had a wag to it. Grace's second glance found small, pointed ears attached to the tops of their heads, and busy pink tongues at work on any part of

Jessica's person they could reach. Long tufts of white hair spring-ing from where, in humans, eyebrows would be, allowed only an occasional glimpse of two pairs of liquid-brown eyes.

"Oh, Mom, aren't they sweet?" Jessica exclaimed with a glance up at her mother. Jessica was wreathed in smiles, and Grace had an idea that Marino's stock had just soared sky-high in her estimation. Having never owned a dog—her father had equated dogs with mess when she was growing up, so their family had never had one, and later she had been too busy with school and work and Jessica to even consider acquiring one—Grace was not so sure about the sweet part. In fact, she had never felt really comfortable with pets at all. Jessica, on the other hand, adored all animals. She was holding the puppy on her lap while Kramer rolled onto her back, legs kicking in the air, for a tummy rub, which Jessica gladly supplied.

"Mom, ask Detective Marino what the puppy's name is," Jessica requested with another upward glance. She was grinning from ear to ear, looking happier than Grace would have thought possible, considering the trauma she had suffered through the pre-vious night.

Grace nodded and withdrew from the doorway. In the near bedroom she caught a quick glimpse of movement through the partially open door, confirming Marino's location.

Moving over to the door, she knocked softly while taking care not to look inside. After all, as she had discovered herself, a bedroom was a private thing, and anyway he might be changing clothes. . . .

He was. At least, his lower face was covered in shaving foam and he was shirtless as he pulled the door open to look down at her with raised brows. A lightning glance told Grace that his shoulders and upper arms were heavy with muscle. His chest was broad and solid looking, with a triangle of thick black hair that tapered down over a ridged abdomen to disappear in a thin trail beneath the waistband of his jeans. And the whole of his upper torso was a shade paler than the outdoorsy bronze of his throat and face and arms.

Shirtless, he looked so sexy that she caught her breath.

Her gaze flew to his, and once again the memory of those shared kisses flared between them. Her mouth went dry as she contemplated lifting a hand to his bare chest and tilting up her face. . . .

Jessica was in the yard. *No.*

Grace was so unnerved at her reaction to his bare chest that she hurried into speech. "Jess—Jessica wants to know the name of your puppy."

He shrugged. "I just call him puppy. He was one of three. I've already found homes for the other two. I'm still looking for somebody to take this one." He smiled at her.

Grace forgot—well, largely forgot—about his state of undress as she stared up at him suspiciously. "I hope you're not thinking that Jessica . . ."

"Nah." His smile broadened into a grin. A shirtless man with his face half covered in shaving cream could be a very beguiling as well as sexy creature, Grace discovered. "I just thought that, instead of grounding her, which clearly doesn't work, you might consider resorting to a bribe of sorts to keep her out of things she shouldn't be into and in the house at night."

"A bribe . . ." Grace frowned after him as he turned away from her and headed back into the bathroom. His bare back was just as sexy as his chest, she noted, watching him walk away from her. His shoulders were wide and his hips were narrow and. . . "Are we talking *dog* as bribe?"

"It was just a thought," he said, pausing on the bathroom threshold to look at her.

"Not a good one," Grace said positively.

He shrugged. "Your call."

Stepping into the bathroom, he reached for the taps on the sink. As steam began to rise from the water pouring out of a silvery spout, he picked up a black, T-shaped razor and lifted it to his face. Tilting up his chin, he scraped away a narrow swath of foam and whiskers with one practiced swipe along his throat. Then his gaze met hers through the mirror above the sink. To her embarrassment, Grace realized that she had been watching, fascinated, as he shaved.

Quickly she turned away.

"Tell Jessica she can name it anything she wants," he called after her.

She could hear the amusement in his voice. Her only question was whether it was directed at her for watching him with hungry eyes through the mirror, or for her reaction to his suggestion about Jessica and the dog.

CHAPTER 34

T HE TELEPHONE RANG WHILE GRACE STOOD IN
the doorway watching Jessica play with Puppy—she had passed on
the non-name—and Kramer.

"Grace, get that, will you?" Marino called from the bedroom.

Grace did as she was asked, although with some trepidation.
She did not feel enough at home in his house to answer the
phone.

"Tony Marino's residence," she said in a clear, crisp tone.

There was a leaden pause. "Who is this?" It was a woman's
voice, unmistakably suspicious.

"Uh, who's calling?" Grace riposted, not wanting to give
her name under the circumstances.

"I am calling for Tony." The suspicion in the voice grew
more pronounced.

Grace abandoned the battle. "Just a minute, please." She put
her hand over the mouthpiece. "It's for you," she called, thinking
what a surprise. Then, when he didn't answer, she raised her voice.
"Tony, believe it or not, it's for you."

"See, Tony's an easy name to say, even when you're being
sarcastic." He grinned at her as he appeared in the bedroom doorway, wearing a navy sweatshirt over a white T-shirt that showed

just at the neckline, and faded but clean jeans. His face was clean-shaven now, too. "Who is it?"

"A woman." Grace was careful to keep any inflection from her voice.

"Yeah?" He looked interested, taking the receiver from her.

"Hello?" he said into the mouthpiece. For a minute or two he said nothing else, listening to what must, from his reaction, have been the torrent of words that greeted him. Then he glanced at Grace, who had forgotten that she still stood nearby watching him. Under the influence of that twinkling gaze, she was recalled to herself and turned away. Moving to the door again, her back to him as she ostensibly watched Jessica play with the dogs, she could not help but overhear every word he said.

"Yes, it's a woman. Yes, she's in my house. Yes, she's very pretty. Yes, that's right. Her name is Grace."

While Grace grappled with the pleasure-pain of the fact that he had described her as very pretty while talking to another woman, he paused again. This pause lasted several minutes. Finally Marino laughed.

"I'll try. I'm not promising anything, though. Yes, I will. Okay. 'Bye."

He hung up. Grace, her muscles rigid with the effort not to turn and look at him, continued to stare out into the yard. The only problem was, she was so attuned to what was going on behind her that she saw nothing at all.

"That was my mother," he said. "You and Jessica have been invited to lunch."

The sheer surprise of that brought her swinging around. He still stood with one hand on the phone.

"Your mother?" She must have gaped at him in amazement, because he laughed as he headed back into the bedroom.

"Remember her? The mother of six cops?"

"Yes, but—I was picturing her as some frail old woman in a nursing home, or something of the sort." Grace followed him, almost unaware that she was doing so. "The woman on the phone didn't sound frail. She didn't even sound old."

"She'll be glad to hear that. She's sixty-five and prides herself on being as strong as an ox and as tough as shoe leather." He was in his bedroom now, pulling the rope tight on an army-green duffel bag stuffed with belongings. Without his naked chest to distract her, Grace was able to form an impression of the room. In pride of place was a comfortable-looking king-size bed topped with what appeared to be a hand-pieced quilt in shades of red and blue. Four pillows in a motley array of cases rested against the simple oak headboard. A nightstand in the same oak as the headboard was beside the bed, with a lamp, a clock, and a pile of paperback whodunits on it. A tall chest in some kind of dark wood stood against the far wall, with a straight chair beside it. The one window was covered in discount-department-store-quality antique satin drapes in off-white. The walls were white and unadorned. Like the rest of the house, his bedroom was clearly intended to be functional, not beautiful, to the eye.

"Every Sunday afternoon my mother cooks, and everybody who can make it stops by to eat. This Sunday's special, because Lauren—my niece—was christened yesterday, and Robby and his family are still in town. All my brothers are going to be there, and their families, and my granny, too. Mama wants me to bring you."

"Me?" Grace's mind reeled at the thought. "She doesn't even know me."

"She liked the way you sounded over the phone."

"Oh, *right*."

He laughed, slung the duffel bag over his shoulder, and headed toward her. Grace automatically moved out of his way, and he passed her on his way through the house. She followed again, a little helplessly, as he set the duffel bag down by the front door.

"So, do you want to go or not?" He straightened to look at her.

"Jessica and I can't just barge in on a family gathering." Grace frantically dredged her mind for excuses. The truth was, she both wanted to go and didn't. Even more than his house, his family would tell her a lot about the man. It would be both interesting and informative to meet them. But for her and Jessica to go with him to such an intimate event—that made it personal. Very, very personal. And their relationship really wasn't.

She didn't even know if she wanted it to be.

"Sure you can. Mama invited you. Look, Dom's told her about the lady judge and she wants to meet you, okay? Lady judges are not all that common in her experience. But we don't have to go if you don't want to."

"*You* go. Jessica and I can just go home and . . ."

"Grace." His voice was very soft and his gaze as it met hers across the room was suddenly intense. "You forget that to all intents and purposes we're Siamese twins for the day. Where you go, I go, and vice versa."

Grace groaned. His eyes darkened, and he was moving purposefully toward her when Jessica bounced into the kitchen, both dogs at her heels. Jessica was smiling, her eyes sparkling, the end of her ponytail flipping from side to side. At her advent, Marino stopped where he was, looking faintly rueful as he thrust both hands into the front pockets of his jeans and rocked back on his heels.

"Mom, I had this really great idea: Since Detective Marino's going to be staying at our house for a while, do you think Kramer and Puppy could come and stay, too? That would be so cool. I mean, if it's okay with you, Detective." Her gaze went questioningly to Marino.

Grace groaned again, foreseeing what was about to happen. Marino's intense expression vanished, and he grinned at her teasingly before directing his gaze toward Jessica.

"Call me Tony, Jessica. Detective Marino gets to be a mouthful after a while. And sure, I don't care if the dogs come. You've got to get your mom's permission, though."

"Mom, please." Those big blue eyes turned on Grace. Marino—Tony—was looking at her too, his expression amused.

"Fine." Realizing that she had no chance against the two of them, Grace gave up the fight and mentally surrendered to the whole enchilada: name, dogs, and afternoon at Mama's. If it was all too personal, well, then, so be it. She would just have to deal with the consequences, if any, when they came. "Bring the dogs. I don't care. By the way, Jess, Detective Marino—*Tony*—wants us to go to his mother's house for lunch and a big family get-together. What do you think about that?"

Jessica looked at Tony, considering. "Are there going to be kids? Like my age?"

"I've got a thirteen-year-old niece, a fourteen-year-old niece, and two sixteen-year-old nephews, besides tons of younger ones. They're great, you'll like them. And every Marino that was ever born plays killer basketball."

"Oh, yeah?" Jessica's eyes lit up. Tony nodded.

"Sounds good to me." Jessica looked at her mother. "What do you say, Mom?"

"Fine," Grace said again, mentally throwing up her hands. She felt as if she were getting ready to jump into water way over her head. The question was, could she swim?

"Great." Tony grinned at her, the twinkle in his eyes faintly devilish now. "Lock the back door, Jessica, please, and we'll be on our way."

Tony's family was, as advertised, warm and welcoming and boisterous and really, really big. Five brothers, all of whom resembled each other except for degrees of taller, shorter, fatter, and thinner, plus wives—all were married except Tony—and fifteen children ranging in age from the sixteen-year-old twin boys belonging to his brother Rick, who was two years younger than Tony, to the four-week-old daughter of his youngest brother Robby, were present, as were his mother and grandmother. The house was an arts-and-crafts "cottage"—really a large, rambling affair with a sloping roof, shed dormers, and huge front and back porches—set on ten acres in a rural area just north of Columbus on Farm Road. The driveway was gravel, the grass clogged with weeds, and cars of all different makes and descriptions were parked everywhere. The overall impression the property gave was distinctly shabby but, Grace thought, a good kind of shabby. The kind of shabby that comes from lots of children and little concern for grass—not much money, but visitors galore. The place showed the wear and tear of a house that had been lived in and loved, which gave it a beauty all its own.

From the moment they walked around back, where what seemed like throngs of people swarmed around half a dozen picnic tables loaded with stacks of paper plates and cups, plastic utensils, bags of ice, and cases of soda, Tony was greeted with exuberance on all sides. He was the recipient of so many hugs and kisses that Grace lost track. Grace was hugged, too, indiscriminately. Jessica was luckier: she was immediately whisked away by the teen-agers—Christy, fourteen; Susan, a year younger; and Joe and Ja-mie, the sixteen-year-old twins. As Joe and Jamie, in the gangly way of adolescents, were as darkly handsome as the older male Marinos, Grace wasn't surprised by her daughter's willingness to leave her side. Even Tony's dogs got into the act, barking and racing madly around the picnickers' feet. At least four other canines were present as well, adding to the general air of carnival-type confusion.

Even as his relatives were greeting Tony, Grace found herself the focus of attention. Everyone, it seemed, was staring at her, not just when they were introduced, as might be expected, but before and afterward as well, some openly and some out of the corners of their eyes. She got the feeling that they were talking about her, too, under their breath and in asides so that she couldn't quite hear what was said. To her surprised dismay, she started to feel almost shy. As *shy* was a trait she had purposely worked very hard to eliminate from her character years before, she was nonplussed by its reappearance. Lost in the sea of Tony's family, exchanging hellos with plump blond sister-in-law Beth and brother Mike, then tall, slender blond sister-in-law Meredith and brother Kyle, Grace was almost grateful to come face-to-face with Dominick, whom she at least knew by sight.

Almost grateful. It was also a little embarrassing.

"Glad to have you join us, Judge Hart." His voice was a shade too hearty as he also appeared to feel some of the moment's awkwardness. He had been to her house several times now, but always in his official capacity as a police officer. Now the occasion was social, a gathering of his family with her as his brother's guest, and he seemed just as uncomfortable as Grace was with the transition.

"Please. Call me Grace," she said with a smile as she held out her hand, determined not to betray any embarrassment. "It was kind of your mother to invite Jessica and me."

Dominick took her hand in his big, warm one and almost snorted. "*Kind* of her? She's been dying to get a look at . . ."

He broke off abruptly, dropping her hand as he apparently got an elbow in the ribs from the petite brunette at his side.

"Oh, ah, yeah, this is my wife, Jenny," he said, casting a guilty glance down at the round-faced, pretty, brightly smiling woman beside him. The top of her head didn't quite reach his shoulder, she was wearing strawberry-pink slacks and a striped blouse, and her dark brown hair was just a tad too bouffant for fashion, but Grace liked her instantly. She had laughing brown eyes the warmth of which matched her wide smile, and a pronounced motherly air.

"We're all glad you could come, Grace," she said smoothly. "And Jessica, too. The kids were excited when they found out they were going to have some fresh blood among them today."

"Especially since they heard she plays a mean game of basketball," Dominick chimed in, nodding his head at the paved area in front of the detached garage, where Jessica was already playing H-O-R-S-E with the others. Wondering where they had heard any such thing, Grace turned a questioning gaze on him. But before she could ask, Tony was beside her.

"Mama'll skin me if I don't take you in and introduce you," he said easily.

"In?" It was a delaying tactic. But Grace couldn't help it. Now there was no *almost* about it: she did feel shy. She felt like a new girlfriend being vetted by the family, when she was no such thing, not really. Her involvement with Tony was only slightly personal, just a few kisses exchanged under stress. It was *not* the type of relationship that all the interested glances and whispered remarks seemed to imply.

"She and Granny are in the kitchen. They do the cooking," Tony explained.

"She won't let her daughter-in-laws anywhere near the stove on occasions like this," Jenny added with a smile. "She tries to make us think it's because she wants to give us a break. But the truth is, none of us can cook like she does and she knows it."

"You're a good cook," Dominick protested loyally.

"I'm glad you think so." Jenny's smile widened as she looked up at him. Love shone out of her eyes, and she placed an affectionate hand on his arm.

"Catch you two later. Come on, Grace." Tony's hand curved around her elbow, and before she could say anything else she was being pulled by him, willy-nilly, toward the back porch.

Her nerve failed her. "Oh, I can't," she said faintly, and stopped just as they reached the foot of the steps. They were momentarily alone, with the milling family some twenty feet behind them and Mama still to be faced beyond the porch.

"What?" He stopped, too, and looked at her, frowning. "Why not?"

"They all act like they think I'm your new girlfriend. They're . . . checking me out. Your mother—I'm worried that she'll think the same thing."

He studied her for a moment in silence.

"You worry too much," he said finally. He caught her hand, pulling her, not exactly willingly but without any further overt resistance, up the stairs and after him into the house.

CHAPTER **35**

"**M**AMA, GRANNY, THIS IS GRACE." TONY
still held her hand as he pulled her after him into the hot, humid
environment that was his mother's kitchen. Clinging to that
warm, strong hand as though to a lifeline, Grace was immediately
assaulted by an olfactory cacophony of smells—rich, savory smells
tinged with garlic and spice—from a quartet of pots bubbling on
the stove and from what looked like at least a dozen steaming
casserole dishes lined up on dish towels spread out over the sturdy
pine table.

"Tony!" His mother turned from stirring a pot on the stove
to embrace him, and he dropped Grace's hand to enfold her in a
great bear hug. Her hand felt suddenly cold, and Grace herself felt
almost as if he had abandoned her, which was ridiculous, she
knew. When his mother finally let him go, he was hugged by his
grandmother, while his mother turned to look at Grace.

"So you're the one I talked to on the phone, in Tony's
house." His mother's gaze moved over Grace from top to toe, her
eyes narrowed critically. She was about Grace's height but built
along queenly lines. Her iron-gray hair showed occasional black
threads, rather like Tony's in reverse, and Grace realized that his
hair would look like that in twenty years' time. She wore it in a
curly, chin-length style that, at the moment, was pushed back

behind her ears. Her face and features bore a remarkable resemblance to Tony's, which meant that she was handsome rather than pretty. Her skin was more olive than his, without the bronze he had acquired from time spent outdoors, and it was relatively unlined. Her eyes were a rich chocolate brown, set beneath winged brows as gray as her hair. She wore a loose black dress of indeterminate age that hit her at midcalf, with an apron—gray with dancing fruit—tied over all.

"It was nice of you to invite Jessica and me to come today, Mrs. Marino," Grace said politely. Though she was nervous—the woman was openly studying her—Grace was determined not to let it show.

"You are welcome, Grace." Mrs. Marino's rather stern face relaxed into a smile, and suddenly she looked so much like her son that Grace blinked. "Do you mind if I call you that? Dominick says you are Judge something, but that seems very formal to say."

"Judge Hart, Mama," Tony supplied. "Grace, this is my grandmother, Rosa Marino. My mother is Mary."

Unlike Mary, Rosa was a tiny woman, slightly stooped, with snow-white hair drawn back from her face in a bun. She had to be in her eighties, Grace figured, and she looked it, with a pale crumpled face and bony hands, though she still had the bright curious dark eyes of a bird. Like Tony's mother, she was dressed in a midcalf-length black dress, with an oilcloth apron tied around her middle.

"I hope you like good food"—Rosa Marino said to her, and Grace recognized Tony's twinkle in her eyes—"because that's what we have, and plenty of it."

"And now is the time to eat it, while it is hot," Mary Marino concurred, turning to Tony. "You! You may make yourself useful and start carrying out these dishes. Call your brothers in to help, too."

"I'll be glad to help." Along with Tony, Grace turned toward the table, eager to grab a dish and escape from the kitchen. She felt uncomfortable under the weighing eyes of his mother and grandmother, rather as if she were partaking of their hospitality under false pretences. After all, their obvious conclusions to the contrary, she had not come as Tony's date.

"No, no, those dishes are heavy and hot. Let Tony carry those. You may carry the bread, Grace, if you will." Mary Marino handed her a pair of handleless baskets piled high with bread and covered with cloth napkins, as Tony, laden down with casserole dishes, thrust a head out the back door and bellowed for his brothers, who came running to help.

A short time later, chaos had quieted into relative calm as the entire family sat down to eat. Grace was seated some distance from Jessica, who was grouped with the teens. The food, as advertised, was wonderful, though Grace could sample only a small portion of what was offered. Veal and chicken dishes and various kinds of pasta and salads, vegetable casseroles, garlic bread and plain bread and rolls, two kinds of homemade cake and an apple pie, all vanished at an amazing rate. Unable to monitor what Jessica was eating, Grace gave up trying and concentrated on her own meal. Tony consumed enormous amounts of food, she saw, and clearly enjoyed bantering with his brothers and their families. At his side, Grace said relatively little but listened with some amusement to the round-robin of family stories that most often cast one or the other of the brothers as goat.

Later, after the dishes had been cleared—Mary's prohibition on daughter-in-laws in the kitchen did not extend to the washing up, it seemed—Grace sat on a folding lawn chair at the side of the paved area by the garage watching as Dominick, Tony, and Rick—the three oldest brothers, who made up one team—went down in defeat to the team of little brothers Kyle, Mike, and Robby in the championship game of their cutthroat basketball competition. Jessica, whose team had been knocked out in the previous round—she, Joe, and Jamie made a surprisingly good team, defeating everyone except the older Marino males—played fetch with the dogs nearby. Rosa sat down in the chair next to Grace, which had just been vacated by Jenny, who had jumped up to console a crying child.

"It is good for Tony that you are here, Grace," Rosa said

earnestly, after a few preliminary remarks that mainly concerned the astounding ability of her grandsons with a basketball. "You must not mind if we all seem to be very interested in you. It has been hard for him, you see. Very hard. You are the first real sign that he is coming out of it."

Not understanding, Grace frowned. "What has been hard for him?" she asked carefully.

The old woman shook her head. "Losing Rachel, of course. Oh, it was a terrible thing! We all wept a thousand tears. But Tony—his mother feared he would die. It has been over four years now, and he has been alone all that time—except for the chippies who come and go, of course, the little cheap women, for he is a man after all—always alone in his house, always alone when he comes here to his family. Alone in his life, and that is not good for a man, especially one like Tony who has the gift of love and laughter as all the Marino men do. You are the first decent woman he has shown an interest in, the first woman he has brought to meet his family, since then. We are very glad to know you for that reason."

Grace's hands rested on the chair's armrests. Rosa patted the one nearest her clumsily.

"You musn't read too much into my being here," Grace cautioned. "Tony and I—we're not—that is, we don't really have a relationship, as such. I . . ."

Rosa laughed, and patted her hand again. "Dominick has told his Mama all about you and Tony, don't worry. He knows his brother well, and he could see what was happening. It made Mary very happy to know that Tony was finally moving on from the terrible thing with Rachel."

Grace swallowed, but with the best will in the world she could not keep herself from asking the obvious question. "Mrs. Marino—"

"You must call me Rosa."

"Rosa, then. Who is Rachel?"

Rosa gave her a sharp look. "So he has not told you about Rachel." She shook her head, looking troubled. "You must ask him, then. Rachel is the key to Tony, and he must tell you about her himself."

Rachel. The name seared itself into Grace's mind. Who was she? A former girlfriend? A wife? Tony had said he was not married, but had he been? *Rachel is the key to Tony.* Whoever she was, her relationship with Tony had obviously been serious.

As illogical as it was—and she knew it was illogical, when she herself had been married and divorced and she and Tony *had* no relationship as such—she did not like to think of Tony just getting over a previous, extremely serious relationship. With a sense of shock, Grace realized that where he was concerned, she was starting to feel—possessive.

She was still brooding over the discovery and its implications when they left.

They arrived home at twilight, dogs and all. As soon as the car pulled into the driveway, it was as though a dark cloud had fallen over the previously merry party. Even the dogs were subdued as they sniffed around the yard and house. Tony immediately became all business, turning on all the lights and checking out the rooms one by one while Grace and Jessica stayed, not quite huddling together, in the kitchen until he gave the all clear. With a sense of waiting for the inevitable other shoe to drop, Grace was tense as she moved through the house. Jessica was openly crabby, ostensibly over the need to do her homework but really, Grace thought, simply because just being in the house where so many frightening things had occurred was now so stressful. When Jessica went upstairs to give herself her shot—the supplies were kept in her room—Grace automatically went with her. Jessica had not been in her room since the horror of the previous night, and Grace did not want her to face it alone. To her distress, she realized upon entering the room that Godzilla's cage still stood in its accustomed place. Determinedly matter of fact, she removed the cage and set it out in the hall, then completely stripped and remade the bed, even turning over the mattress. Meanwhile Jessica rolled the vial of insulin in her hands to warm it, filled the syringe, and injected herself in the thigh.

Later, Tony made some phone calls to verify the next day's arrangements for their protection, after first having discreetly removed all reminders of Godzilla from the house, at Grace's request. Grace and Jessica sat at the kitchen table reviewing Spanish vocabulary. Then, taking heart in the company of the dogs, who followed her wherever she went, Jessica chose to brave her room alone to do her algebra in the familiar environs of her desk. Grace, cup of coffee in hand, stepped out on the front porch for a breath of fresh air, preparatory to going upstairs and meting out punishment—extended grounding, she supposed—to Jessica. The house she had once loved so much felt almost claustrophobic to her now.

The crisp afternoon was gone. The night was dark, and cold, and smelled of lingering dampness. A light wind had arisen, gusting through the trees, rattling the leaves of the snowball bush, setting the wind chime dancing. Shadows shifted and blended, came together and separated. Something seemed to move in the far corner of the yard.

Grace froze and then had to laugh at herself as a piece of someone's Sunday paper, abandoned to the elements, blew close enough to be identified.

But she did not step into the yard to pick up the paper, which she once would have done without thought.

It was this that had been taken from them by the creep who was preying on them, Grace thought. Their sense of security, hers and Jessica's. Where once the small world they inhabited had seemed familiar and safe, now everything, even the home they had lived in for years, was a strange and frightening place. Little things like a sheet of newspaper blowing across the yard in the dark had the power to send her heart leaping into her mouth.

Grace shivered and went back into the house, taking care to lock the door behind her.

Thank God Tony was there. The knowledge caused her tense muscles to relax a little. Until the creep was caught, she and Jessica were protected. She did not like to think how she would have felt if they had been alone.

She still could not get the thought of Tony's Rachel out of her mind.

Grace went upstairs, reluctant but resolute, and found Jessica sprawled out on her bed fast asleep. Both dogs were curled up next to her, lying together right against her side. They lifted their heads as she entered, but did not bark and made no move to jump off the bed.

Lips tightening with disapproval—how sanitary could it be to sleep with dogs? didn't they all have fleas, or something?—Grace looked the animals over, wondering how to shoo them from the bed without waking Jess in the process. They looked like brown-and-white dust mops cuddled close beside her daughter, Grace decided as they lowered their heads to their paws again. Watching them seemingly prepared to sleep the night away at Jessica's side, Grace felt a sudden, totally unexpected rush of appreciation for them. After all, their presence had made what would have been a hard day much easier for Jessica. Their presence had emboldened her sufficiently to do her algebra in her room. And their presence had comforted her enough so that she could fall asleep in her bed. Not only that, but they would guard her while she slept.

A few fleas were a small price to pay for all that.

Grace withdrew a small quilt from Jessica's closet and gently covered her with it. The dogs never moved, and when she was done Grace rather clumsily patted each one on the head.

The puppy licked her wrist.

Rubbing the damp spot against her pants, not sure whether to be pleased or disgusted, she turned off the light, closed the door, and went downstairs.

The dogs stayed where they were.

It was after ten now, and Grace's usual practice was to be in bed no later than eleven. Before she could retire, though, she had a case full of briefs to look over, clothes to lay out for the morrow, a shopping list to make, and several loads of laundry to do.

Instead of doing any of that, she went looking for Tony.

He was in the family room, lounging comfortably on the

couch, his feet in their white athletic socks crossed at the ankles and resting on her coffee table. He had taken off his sweatshirt—the house was warm—and wore only the snug white T-shirt tucked into his jeans. His gun lay on the end table beside him, next to the lamp which, besides the TV, was the room's sole source of illumination at the moment. The remote control unit was in his hand, and he was casually flipping channels. He looked up as Grace entered the room.

"Your idea about dog as bribe is beginning to grow on me," Grace said by way of a greeting, crossing the room and sitting down in the rocking chair. His gun, black and lethal looking, lay on the end table between them. "Would you really let Jessica have the puppy?"

"Sure." He smiled lazily at her and turned the volume down on the TV. "She was a big hit with my nephews, by the way. They were impressed."

"Probably because she's got a heck of a jump shot," Grace said with a lurking smile of her own.

He laughed. "Well, that, too."

"I liked your family. Everyone was very nice to a couple of strangers in their midst. And the food! Your mother and grand-mother are wonderful cooks. They should open a restaurant."

"I'll tell 'em you said so. They'll love you for it."

"All your brothers seem to have made very happy mar-riages," Grace ventured.

"Yeah, they all picked out nice girls."

"Except you."

He cast her a sideways glance. "Except me," he said agreeably.

Grace took a deep breath. Obviously, if she wanted him to answer her question, she was going to have to ask it first.

"Tony," she said, "who's Rachel?"

CHAPTER 36

HE LOOKED AT HER FOR A MOMENT WITHOUT saying anything. His body stiffened, and his eyes widened slightly as if he were absorbing a body blow. Then his jaw hardened and his face closed up, leaving it absolutely blank except for a disquieting shadow in the backs of his eyes.

"Who told you about Rachel?" he asked carefully, as if he had to concentrate to enunciate the words.

To her surprised dismay, Grace felt jealousy like a gnawing pain in her chest as she saw how much he cared. Whoever this Rachel was, he had obviously loved her—did still love her—desperately. No way was she ever going to be able to compete with that, she thought, and then was surprised and depressed to discover that she would even want to.

"Your grandmother mentioned the name. She didn't tell me anything. She told me I should ask you."

"Ah, Granny." Tony closed his eyes, then almost immediately opened them again. He looked directly at Grace.

"Rachel was my daughter," he said.

Was. Grace caught that word, assimilated its meaning, and felt her blood freeze. For a moment she simply stared at him, appalled.

"Oh, Tony," she said at last, her voice hoarse with sympathy. "I'm sorry. I had no idea."

"That's all right." He looked away from her at the TV. Some shoot-'em-up flick was playing on the channel he'd stopped at when she'd come into the room. Along with Tony, Grace watched as an enormous, muted explosion blew a car into smithereens.

"I should be over it," he said then, his voice very steady, cool, and collected. "It's been more than four years now. Life goes on."

The pain he took so much care not to express screamed silently at her through the emotionless words.

"I don't think anyone ever gets over losing a child," Grace said, her heart aching for him. Standing, she took the few steps needed to bring her to the couch, too, then sat down beside him, automatically kicking off her shoes and curling her legs up beneath her so that her shoulder butted into his side and her knees brushed his thigh. The cozy resilience of the couch gave beneath her weight; the hardness of his body was unyielding. She put a hand on his shoulder, which was warm and solid feeling beneath the softness of the cotton T-shirt, and pressed closer against his side in a wordless gesture of comfort. "Four years, forty years, four hundred years. I don't care how much time had passed, I would never, ever get over it if something happened to my child . . . to Jessica. . . ."

Her eyes filled with tears.

He flicked her a sideways glance. "For a tough-acting judge, you're pretty softhearted, aren't you? The reality is, no matter how much you love something, you don't own it, you know? Sometimes you just can't keep it no matter what you do, and it goes away and you're left behind. And you gotta deal with that, and if you do, if you keep breathing and eating and sleeping and counting sunrises and sunsets, it'll get better. It's been getting better for me for a while now; I can think of her sometimes and smile, just at something silly she said once or something we did. I'm glad I can do that."

He broke off and stared at the TV, as if he were concentrating hard on the program. As a Tums commercial had taken the place of the movie, it wasn't hard to guess that he was focusing so intently without really seeing anything at all, trying to conceal what he would consider an excess of emotion.

"Was it an accident?" The question was hardly more than a breath, and Grace patted his shoulder in a silent offer of comfort as she asked it. "If you'd rather not talk about it, just don't answer."

For a moment she thought he wasn't going to. Then he flicked her another one of those sideways looks and his arms slid around her waist. His hands gripped her hipbones, lifting her up and across him with easy strength so that she was sitting on his lap. His arms wrapped around her, and in answer her arms slid up around his neck. Seen at such close quarters, he looked tired and drawn—his eyes bloodshot, with tiny lines fanning out around them, deeper lines scoring his bronzed face from nose to mouth, and a day's growth of beard darkening his lean jaw. Closing his eyes, he leaned his head back against her encircling arm and the back of the couch and took a deep breath. After a moment he lifted his head again and opened his eyes, meeting her gaze.

"She had cystic fibrosis," he said. "We—my wife and I—found out when she was just a little kid, hardly more than a baby. I was a cop then, too, just like now, a rookie on the force, and we lived in Cleveland at the time because that's where Glenna—my wife—was from. They told us Rachel wouldn't live but we couldn't believe it; she was so full of life, such a happy kid, such an absolute joy. But there was this mucus that would fill up her lungs and we had to pound on her, literally beat her little thin chest and back with our fists so that she could breathe. Glenna couldn't take it. She left us, left Rachel and me, divorced me, just came to see Rachel sometimes. After a while, Rachel didn't care, I didn't care. We had each other. We were tight. Then one morning, at the end, when Rachel was really sick, she sat straight up in her hospital bed and said, 'Listen, Daddy, do you hear the angels singing?' I was sitting there on the bed beside her, and she smiled right past me like there was somebody else there, and then she just slumped against my shoulder and died. I couldn't believe it. Just like that, and she was gone."

He broke off, and took another deep breath. "She was eleven years old."

Tears that he wouldn't let fall glittered in his eyes, and Grace's heart swelled so with his pain and her sorrow for him and his little girl that she felt it would burst.

"Oh, Tony," she whispered, hugging his neck, snuggling closer, kissing his bristly cheek. "I'm so sorry."

His arms tightened around her so fiercely that for a moment Grace couldn't breathe.

"I lost it then. Just completely lost it. If it hadn't been for Dom, who came and got me and brought me home to Columbus and basically put me back together again, I don't know what I would have done. I quit the force, started drinking, didn't care if I died too. In fact, I hoped I would. I couldn't bear to think of Rachel, my Rachel, in a dark cold grave all alone. She didn't like to be alone, especially toward the end, when she was so sick. After she died, all I could think of was, now she's alone in that grave for eternity." His jaw clenched, and he stopped talking abruptly. Then his head dropped to her shoulder, and his chest expanded against her as he drew in a mighty breath, and then another. In Tony's world, real men didn't cry, Grace realized, but he was crying nonetheless, silently, without tears, drawing in deep, harsh breaths and slowly releasing them. Helpless to alleviate his grief and knowing it, she did her best anyway, holding him close and kissing his cheek and his ear and whatever other parts of him she could reach, murmuring soft, broken things while tears coursed down her own cheeks.

After a few moments he lifted his head and looked down at her. His eyes were red-rimmed and damp, the golden-brown irises suspiciously bright, but with her gaze on him he managed a quirky half-smile.

"What are *you* crying for?" he demanded huskily. His gaze touched on her wet cheeks and brimming eyes and shaking mouth, then met hers. His voice went absurdly gentle. "Never say you're crying for me?"

"Oh, Tony . . ." She couldn't help it. Her voice broke and she couldn't continue, not that it mattered anyway because there was really nothing to say. More tears coursed down her cheeks, and as he watched them fall his mouth tightened.

"Grace," he said, his voice deep and low; and then he kissed her.

At the touch of his mouth, more tears flowed from her eyes, and she was crying openly as he kissed her, sobbing in his arms when he was the one who had suffered the loss, who had been dealt the near-mortal blow of losing a child. She wept for him and his child, and for herself and her child, and for the terrible tragedy of love ripped asunder. All the while he kept kissing her, whispering her name as if he would offer *her* comfort. And finally she kissed him back, clinging to him as she realized that she had no more defenses left, that her heavily armored heart had swelled so with emotion that the armor had finally cracked to let him in.

His kisses turned hard and fierce then, as he felt the change in her response, and his hold on her deepened. His tongue was wet and scalding hot as it thrust into her mouth. Raw emotion consumed them, and they pulled at each other's clothing, greedy for the warm, life-affirming contact that was sex. Grace tugged at the edges of his T-shirt, pulling it from the waistband of his jeans, her hands sliding beneath the thin cotton to find and stroke the chest she had so admired earlier in the day. Warm, faintly damp skin over steely muscles, the silkiness of fine chest hair, the rough raised bumps of his nipples: Grace gloried in each and every sensation. Cradled by his arms, her hands caressed him with sensuous delight.

Then his hand slid beneath her turtleneck and bra and found her breast, closing over it, touching her nipple, rubbing it with his thumb, and she forgot everything else in a fiery burst of pure erotic hunger.

Gasping, arching her back, Grace shivered and clung to his shoulders as his large warm hand moved from one breast to the other, playing and teasing, arousing with each touch. When his mouth left hers to trail hot kisses along her jaw, she moaned.

Thwarted by the turtleneck protecting her throat from his mouth, he gripped her top with both hands and pulled it over her head, and then with his next movement reached between her shoulder blades to unclip her bra and tug it off.

Grace had a moment of clarity when his hands were not on her body, and she opened her eyes and took in the scene. She saw herself, slender and fine-boned, with small pink-tipped breasts and pale skin, bare from the waist up in the warm pool of lamplight, curled up on Tony's lap. He was fully dressed if a little mussed, the hem of his T-shirt out of his jeans, his black hair tousled, his eyes more golden than brown now, agleam as they were with desire for her. His shoulders in the plain white T-shirt were broad and thick with muscle. His skin looked very brown against her paleness as his hand found her breast again.

For a moment she just looked at that large brown hand splayed out possessively against the creamy smoothness of her skin. Then his hand moved, and she couldn't think at all.

Her last relatively clear image was of the muted eleven o'clock newscast flickering across the TV screen in the background, and of one of his feet, clad in a snug white athletic sock, shoving the coffee table out of the way.

Then he bent his head. She caught just a glint of silver as the lamplight struck the thick black and silver waves of his hair.

Hot and wet and hungry, his mouth closed over her nipple. Grace gasped, and her hands moved up to clutch the back of his head, holding him to her. Her eyes closed, and she arched her back, offering him her breasts with abandon.

When his mouth finally left her breasts, her nipples felt cold and wet and hard as pebbles in air that seemed arctic after the heat of his mouth. She whimpered in protest at the loss, only to find herself being gathered into his arms and lifted.

She opened her eyes. He had turned off the lamp and TV, she realized groggily, so that the room was dark except for the light spilling in from the kitchen. The only sounds were the harshness of his breathing and her own softer gasps. He lowered her onto the rug, the rose-and-blue-and-tan oriental carpet that she had picked up for a song at a flea market years before and never thought to put to such use. Its texture was rough against her bare back, and the hardness of the floor beneath was readily apparent.

A measure of sanity returned to her.

"Tony," she whispered. He loomed over her, stripping off his own T-shirt and tossing it aside, so that her hands, as she lifted them to hold him off, encountered the warmth of his bare shoulders. Sliding her hands along the muscular width of those shoulders, almost lost in the blaze of his eyes, she nevertheless managed to murmur: "I don't think—not here in the house, I . . ."

But she never finished her protest, because as she spoke he unbuttoned and then unzipped, with an audible sound, her khakis, and pulled them down, along with her panties, so that when he was finished she was naked, lying on the oriental rug in her darkened family room *naked,* with him in his jeans on his knees beside her and his hand sliding with slow, hot intimacy up one soft inner thigh.

He touched her, finding the tiny moist bud that quivered desperately beneath his caress, and then he bent over her and his mouth followed his hand and the wet heat of his tongue touched her, too—and she was lost, totally lost, to conscious thought.

Under the scalding tutelage of his mouth, her nails curled into the roughness of the carpet, scratching over its surface, clawing for some sort of grip to keep her anchored to earth. Her thighs fell open helplessly under his ministrations, allowing him free rein, and he took full advantage, his mouth and hands stroking and caressing, delving and withdrawing, wickedly teasing until she was gasping and writhing and moaning his name.

And then he bit her, softly, gently, but it was enough, in that particular spot, to send her over the edge, to send her hips arching up off the rug to press hard against the source of her torment as her body exploded with passion, sending her spinning, her mind whirling away while her body quaked and shook and shuddered.

Finally she collapsed limply back against the carpet, drawing in great gulps of air, feeling light-headed and peaceful and in urgent need of sleep.

But what she had reckoned was finished was not. He was between her legs now, hard and hot and urgent with need, sliding inside her, stretching her and filling her and demanding her response when she weakly tried to close her thighs only to find them firmly pinioned apart by the muscular strength of his.

Grace opened her eyes in protest—all she wanted to do was rest—to find him bearing down on her, his face and body deep in shadow. She could just make out the muscular outline of him, limned as his body was with light from the kitchen, and the bright glitter of his eyes. Even as she prepared to utter some variation of "uncle!" he kissed her, his tongue as hard and hot as it invaded her mouth as that other part of him. His hands found her breasts, her nipples, at the same time as he started to move. He thrust fiercely, taking now instead of giving, blatantly intent on satisfying his own need. To her surprise Grace found her body awakening again, found herself responding to his urgency, found herself quivering and clutching and cleaving to the hard body that swept her along with it on a tide of driving passion. Her nails dug into his back instead of the carpet. Her legs wrapped around his waist.

"Tony," she gasped as her world exploded for a second time. He groaned in response, thrusting deep, and found his own release, burying himself deep inside her quivering body.

CHAPTER 37

In THE BRIGHT LIGHT OF MORNING, GRACE BLUSHED
to remember the night. They had made love again and again, until
they were both exhausted. In between lovemaking sessions, they
talked. Tony told her about his childhood, about what it was like
to be one of six boys—a cross between a world championship
wrestling round-robin event and the close camaraderie expressed
by Shakespeare's "We few, we happy few, we band of brothers"
bit, as he described it. And Grace told him about her much lone-
lier childhood, which to all intents and purposes ended with the
death of her mother. They described their respective marriages—
bad, they both agreed—and enumerated the positive and negative
points of their jobs. One thing they did not talk about was Rachel. Grace got the feeling that Tony could not bear to have that
wound touched on again so soon, and she respected his reticence.

She fell asleep at last, dozing off in his arms while they were
talking, and then awoke sometime near dawn to find herself
wrapped in a blanket and apparently levitating up the stairs. It was
a frightening moment before Tony's face came into focus and the
situation in which she found herself became clear. Maneuvering
carefully through the almost pitch-dark house, he was carrying
her up the stairs to bed.

"You don't want Jessica to find you asleep in the family

room in the morning," he whispered in her ear when she blinked at him sleepily, his eye on Jessica's closed door.

No, she didn't. In fact, it was one of her hard-and-fast rules never to make love to a man in her own house, and certainly not when Jessica was present, even if she was asleep. But what had happened with Tony transcended all the rules. It was like nothing that had ever happened to her before.

She had been consumed by lust.

The thought shocked Grace, and then she had to smile at the idea. For the first time in her thirty-six years of life, she realized, she finally "got it" about sex. Before, when she had heard her friends raving about this or that sex act or this or that man, she had smiled politely and secretly pitied them for their lack of self-control. Now she knew better. She had learned over the course of one night just how earth-shattering, mind-blowing, and life-altering sex with the right man could be.

And to think that Tony Marino was the right man. That was almost the most mind-blowing thing of all.

Grace was still smiling over it when she fell asleep. And when the alarm went off and she slept right through, she had no doubt that she was smiling still.

Jessica came and woke her, twenty minutes late. Thus began a mad rush for school and work that gave Grace no time to do more than flash Tony, met at the breakfast table, a semiembarrassed smile, gulp a cup of coffee and snatch up the day's paper from the porch before she and Jessica were on the road with the police officers assigned to protect them for the day. Tony would relieve both day officers at five o'clock, when he would be back on duty at the house.

Jessica's officer, Gloria Baer, was a blond woman who looked no more than seventeen. Dressed like Jessica, in jeans and a loose sweater (with, Grace presumed, a gun concealed beneath), she would be introduced at school as Jessica's cousin, visiting from out of town, and would stick with her like glue throughout the day. The officer assigned to Grace was Barry Penick. He was in his early thirties, a slim man of medium height with thinning brown hair. He wore a sport coat and tie, the better, Grace guessed, to blend into her courtroom.

As early as lunchtime, she was heartily sick of having a protection officer. Penick followed her everywhere, even to the rest room, waiting outside like a faithful basset hound until she reappeared. When she called the lunch break and stood up to head to her chambers, he stood too, prepared to come along.

Unable to stop herself, she gave him a disgruntled look. The thought that ran through her mind was, let's call the whole thing off.

Jessica was in danger, not she.

Grace bit her lip and headed for her chambers. After allowing him to check the room for possible hidden assassins, Grace shooed Penick out the door, under the pretext that she had work to do, and locked it. For a moment she leaned against it with a sigh of relief. Then she headed for her desk, on which waited a deli fruit plate brought in at Grace's request by one of the secretaries. Pouring herself a cup of coffee, Grace sat down to read her newspaper and eat.

When she got to the comics page, her eyes widened, and then she frowned. Although she had picked the newspaper up off her porch that morning in what she had assumed was a pristine state, she had apparently been wrong. Someone had gotten hold of her paper before she had.

Three horoscopes were circled in bright red marker, impossible to miss with even the most casual glance at that page. One, Virgo, was her own. The second, Pisces, was Jessica's. The third ringed horoscope was Capricorn.

Grace stared at it and for a moment forgot to breathe. Capricorn. January 21. That date was one of the most significant in her life.

When she read the horoscope itself, she felt like breaking into hysterical laughter: *A message from someone in your past could have you lost in memories.*

It was coincidence, of course. It had to be.

Maybe Tony was a Capricorn, and he had gotten to the paper before she had and circled the horoscopes.

In bright red marker? And how would he know her birthday, and Jessica's? Oh, he might possibly have gotten them from a police report, she supposed. Was that kind of information routinely recorded on police reports? Grace couldn't remember.

It was kind of a stretch to picture Tony even interested in horoscopes, much less ringing three of them with a red marker so they would not fail to catch her eye.

But what other explanation could there be?

Maybe there was absolutely no meaning to it at all. Maybe the paperboy had been reading the horoscopes.

Because the only explanation that made sense was impossible. Grace could hardly bring herself to think about it.

Heart pounding with anxiety, Grace instinctively reached for the phone. She would dial Tony's pager number. He needed to know about this.

Her hand stopped and drew back. She couldn't call Tony. She could hear him saying, in that pained way of his, it's a *horoscope,* Grace.

In other words, it's nothing at all.

That's exactly what he would think, unless she explained to him the significance of that particular date.

Which she couldn't do.

Wouldn't do.

Couldn't even bear to think about.

She had put it behind her years ago, released the past like ashes in the wind and vowed to go forward and make the best life possible for herself and, later, Jessica.

The only time she ever allowed herself to remember was on January 21. Of every year.

Nausea churned in her stomach.

It was not possible.

It was not possible.

Possible or not, Grace was upset to the point of being

physically ill for the rest of the day. Not only upset, but afraid. If the impossible should be true, she needed to tell Tony, urgently.

But this was something that she had never told anyone. It was the deep, dark secret of her life.

As Rachel was the key to Tony, this was the key to her.

And no one knew.

Maybe the horoscope meant nothing.

Please, God, let the horoscope mean nothing.

Please, God. Please, please, please.

When Grace got home that night, with Penick in the passenger seat of her car—she had refused to allow him to drive, although he had tried to insist—Jessica and Tony were playing basketball in the driveway. It was such a pleasant sight, such a homey sight, that Grace felt the tension that had been with her since lunchtime begin to ease.

It was a beautiful fall day, sunny and crisp. The leaves on the big oak in the center of the front yard were a vivid burnt orange. The other trees in the yard and along the street were shaded in all variations of red and bronze and gold. By the garage, the trio of burning bushes blazed scarlet. As the car pulled in, the dogs jumped up from where they had been lying and rushed forward, barking excitedly and wagging their tails.

Breathing deeply of the smoke-tinged air, Grace got out of the car to the accompaniment of the slapping sound of the basketball against the pavement and the insistent *woof* of the dogs. Both animals jumped on her, big hairy paws waist-high on her navy-blue hopsack blazer and little hairy paws just above the hem of her matching skirt. Rather gingerly, Grace patted Kramer, then Puppy, on the head. Puppy licked her wrist again as both dogs dropped to the ground.

Still not sure how she felt about being licked, Grace wiped the damp spot on her sleeve.

"Good dogs," she said. In almost comical unison, they rolled over on their backs in the grass, their feet waving in the air in a nonverbal but eloquent request for tummy rubs.

"Hey, Mom!" Jessica greeted her, taking advantage of Tony's momentary distraction to sneak in a dunk.

"Not fair!" he yelled, his attention forcibly recalled by the swish of the ball through the net and Jessica's triumphant *yes-s!* complete with fist pump as she scored.

Walking toward them, Grace caught the runaway ball, holding it as Tony jogged to claim it.

"Hi," he said, taking the ball in both hands and smiling at her. He was wearing jeans and a ratty, short-sleeved gray T-shirt with a hole just above his navel, and he looked so good that it was all she could do not to fall into his arms there and then.

"Hi." She smiled back at him. With a start she realized that several seconds had passed and they were simply standing there looking into each other's eyes and smiling without speaking. She quickly turned away in confusion, not wanting Jessica—or Penick, for that matter—to notice any change in their relationship.

What was between them was so new, so tenuous, that Grace was wary of letting anyone else find out until it had had at least a little time to grow.

"Homework, Jessica?" she called over the rhythm of the bouncing ball, trying to sound like business as usual, as Tony dribbled back into the game.

"Study for an algebra test tomorrow. Social studies. Spanish." Jessica flung her arms up in the air, waving them, trying to stop Tony in his drive toward the basket.

"How much have you done?" Grace skirted the game and turned down the sidewalk, heading toward the front door. She knew the answer but asked the question anyway, which illustrated the triumph of hope over experience, she supposed.

Jessica grinned without answering. That meant *none,* which was exactly what Grace had known before she asked.

As a young mother with a daughter just starting kindergarten, one of the vows she had made was that her child would do her homework every day immediately after school. Now, as an older, pretty well worn-down version of that same mother, she was just thankful homework got done at all.

"I'm going to change my clothes and start supper," she called. Tony had stopped playing for a moment and was talking to Penick, rather earnestly Grace thought. No fool he, this time he held the basketball in his hands. Jessica's protection officer was nowhere in evidence, and Grace assumed she had left when Tony had arrived.

The thought of the circled horoscopes intruded again, sending a chill racing down her spine, as Grace walked along the sidewalk. She needed to ask Tony his birth date. . . . Maybe he *had* done it, and she was worrying for nothing.

"Two points! I am *skunking* you!" Jessica's whoop told the story about which way the game wind was blowing and made Grace smile. Jessica was never so fully herself as when she was playing basketball.

Still smiling, trying to shake off her almost certainly unfounded worry over the horoscopes, Grace climbed the steps to the porch, crossed the porch to the door, turned the knob, and discovered that the door was locked. Her smile turning to a frown, she put her key in the lock. Or at least she tried to. Her key wouldn't fit.

Of course, the locks had been changed. And the security system had been installed, too. Pat had come today instead of Wednesday and let the workmen in.

There was no way to put this stalker thing out of her mind. It had taken over every aspect of their lives. She could no longer go to the bathroom alone, read a newspaper in peace, or even get into her own house.

Grace took a deep, calming breath. She was not going to allow one sick individual to poison her life.

And she was not going to dwell on circled horoscopes that were almost certainly of no significance. It was just her own guilty conscience that made them loom so large in her mind.

"Hey, I'm locked out," she called plaintively to the group on the driveway.

All three of them looked at her. The ball was in Jessica's hands now. With a word to the other two, Tony came jogging to

Grace's rescue. Reaching the porch, he grinned at her and pro-
duced a key from his pocket. As he inserted the key into the lock
and opened the door, a tinny little siren went off inside the house.

"Your code number is 3227, and you have forty-five seconds
to punch it in before all hell breaks lose," Tony told her as he
stood back so that she could precede him into the house. "The
box is in the dining room closet. Come on, I'll show you how to
do it."

"I'm going to feel like I'm living in a prison," Grace
groaned, following him into the dining room through the mahogany pocket doors that matched the ones leading into the living
room opposite. Both reception rooms opened off the front hall,
the dining room to the left and the living room to the right.

"Lots of people around here have them. Between the security system, the new locks, the dogs, and me, I think we've pretty
much got your stalker beat."

"I hope so," Grace said fervently, watching while he
punched out the code number on a keypad mounted on the closet
wall. With an acknowledging little beep, the tinny noise was
blessedly silenced. The tiny red light on the top left went off, and
a tiny green light on the top right came on. There were two
square buttons at the bottom of the keypad. One was blue with a
picture of a fire truck. The other was red, with a big *E* on it.

"What's your code number?" he asked her.

"3-2-2-7."

"Good. Remember, you've got forty-five seconds to punch
it in before the alarm goes off. See these buttons here?" He
pointed to the buttons Grace had been studying. "The blue one's
a direct line to the fire department. The red one's a direct line to
the police. All you have to do is hit either one for instant help.
Got it?"

Grace nodded. The question about his birth date almost
popped out of her mouth of its own volition there and then. But,
she scolded herself, she needed to be a little more subtle. . . .

"Good."

Then Tony turned to her, his mouth quirking into a little

smile. Before Grace knew what was happening, he had her pinned against the dining room wall, his body weight holding her there, his hands on either side of her waist. His eyes were a twinkling golden brown as he looked down at her. Meeting his gaze, Grace was easily able to put the horoscopes out of her mind.

Her hands went automatically to his shoulders.

She smiled up at him.

"Miss me?" he asked, and kissed her before she could answer. Grace wrapped her arms around his neck and kissed him back, which, she supposed, was answer enough.

She was still kissing him when the front door flew open with a bang. Immediately they jumped apart.

"Aunt Grace! Are you here?" The voice belonged to Paul. He was stomping through the front hall. With a single speaking look at Tony, Grace turned and fled through the second dining room door, the smaller swinging one that led into the kitchen.

"Hi, Paul! Where've you guys been?" Grace greeted her nephew as he arrived in the kitchen scant seconds after she did, via the entry hall route. His hair was standing on end, and he was wearing jeans and a Cincinnati Reds T-shirt. Trying not to look or act flustered, Grace resisted the urge to lift her hands to her overwarm cheeks or smooth her hair and hoped that Tony's kiss hadn't left a mark. Her lipstick was gone, of course, but it was the end of the day and that could have occurred quite naturally. And Paul was only six, after all. He was unlikely to notice anything different about his aunt's appearance short of the sudden appearance of flaming-red hair or the growth of an elephant's trunk where her nose usually was.

With a quick ruffle of Paul's hair, she headed for the refrigerator. Supper on short notice—she hadn't had time to put anything into the Crock-Pot that morning—usually consisted of chicken breasts and rice, with a salad and possibly another vegetable and bread.

Maybe she should try to do something more. After all, Tony would be eating with them tonight.

Remembering his mother's and grandmother's cooking, Grace gave up on the thought. As far as cooks went, she could not compete.

He was going to have to take her as she was, or not at all.

Maybe she could somehow work the topic of astrological signs into the dinner-table conversation. Grace pictured herself leaning toward Tony over their plates of chicken and rice, fluttering her eyelashes, and cooing that bar pickup classic, "I'm a Virgo. What's *your* sign?"

The picture thus conjured up was irresistible. Grace had to smile.

"We've been to see Mamaw. Aunt Grace, Jessica won't let me play with her dogs! She threw a basketball at me! It just missed hitting me, too! It went right over my head."

"Oh, dear."

"I think Jessica can be forgiven. He was trying to teach the little one to stand on its head. Forcibly." Jackie walked into the kitchen with a purple sweat suit–clad Courtney at her heels and a sack from Kentucky Fried Chicken in her hand. Dressed in an oversized black T-shirt with multicolored buttons sewn onto it, and matching black stirrup pants, she looked very pretty, Grace thought.

"Hi, Jax. You've been to Cincinnati?" That was where Stan's parents lived. "You should have let me know. I've been trying to call you all weekend."

"I left a message with Jessica on Friday."

Trying to remember everything that had happened on Friday was too much. Grace shook her head. "She didn't tell me. We've had a lot going on."

Jackie looked at her. Then, instead of saying any more, she jiggled the bag in her hand so that it rattled enticingly, with the obvious intention of attracting her children's attention.

"Anyone who wants chicken tenders and fries, follow me," she said, heading into the TV room.

Whooping, Paul and Courtney followed her.

By the time Jackie got back, Grace was already brushing barbecue sauce on chicken breasts preparatory to putting them under the broiler.

"I guess you *have* had a lot going on," Jackie said with meaning, leaning back against the counter and regarding her older sister with a fascinated gaze. "Fill me in. I find it hard to believe, but from something Jessica said—is the handsome cop *living* with you now?"

CHAPTER 38

"**H**IS NAME IS TONY. TONY MARINO. AND YES,
he is staying with us for a while, but it's not what you think." As
she spoke Grace filled a pan with water and set it on the stove,
turning the burner on high.

"You've got a hunky guy living with you, and it's not what I
think? What are you doing, then, running a shelter for homeless
cops and their dogs?"

"Ha, ha," Grace said, opening the freezer and extracting two
small boxes of frozen broccoli casserole. After looking at the packages for a reflective moment, she took out a third. She didn't have
any real knowledge of the amount of food Tony generally consumed for supper, but from the size of him she guessed it was
substantial and the amount of food he had consumed at his
mother's house was truly phenomenal.

"Grace, *tell me.*"

"Oh, for goodness' sake." Setting the icy boxes on the
counter, Grace started to rip one open. Then, with a glance at
Jackie, she scooted them toward her sister. "Here, make yourself
useful. Put these in the microwave while I make the salad, would
you, please?"

"Sure." Jackie began prying at one of the boxes.
"Grace . . ."

Grace sighed. As she made salad and put rice on to boil and slid chicken under the broiler, she told Jackie an abbreviated version of what was happening with the stalker. She left out a few things, like the exact nature of her relationship with Tony and any mention of Rachel, and she glossed over a few others, such as the true extent of Jessica's misbehavior. But by the time she was done, Jackie had a fairly accurate picture of the situation.

"Oh, my God!" Jackie was appalled. At Grace's direction, she was transferring nuked broccoli casserole to a baking dish so that it would look a little more appetizing as a single unit. "Why didn't you tell me?"

Grace was adding shredded carrots from a supermarket packet to the salad. "You already have so much to worry about, with Stan out of work and all. I didn't want you to have to add Jess and me to the list."

"You know, sisterhood is a two-way street. You're always worrying about me. Why shouldn't I worry about you for a change?" Jackie frowned down at the shapeless green mass in the casserole dish. "Do you have any shredded cheese or something I could put over this to make it look better?"

Without Grace saying a word—which she wouldn't have done for any amount of money—Jackie seemed totally in sync with the goal of making the meal as presentable as possible since Tony would be joining them.

"In the refrigerator." Grace tossed the salad and judiciously added a few drops of lemon juice. "I know it's a two-way street, but there wasn't anything you could have done to make the situation better, so I didn't see any point in upsetting you. I just told you now so you would understand why Tony's staying here."

"You should have told me anyway. That thing with the hamster, that's *scary*." Jackie opened the refrigerator and peered into the depths. She ducked, then emerged holding a half-full bag of shredded cheese. "Ah-hah!" she said, brandishing her find and closing the refrigerator door.

"The worst thing is, it seems to be directed at Jessica." Grace was so used to keeping her problems to herself that she felt strange, discussing the situation with Jackie. But she was glad her sister knew. It was a relief to be able to talk about it.

"If you'd told me, the kids and I could have moved in with you for a while. God knows, Stan wouldn't have objected." There was a bitter note to Jackie's voice as she said that last.

As Grace pulled the chicken from under the broiler, Jackie popped the broccoli into the oven for a few minutes to melt the cheese.

"How's his job hunt coming?" Grace inquired sympathetically, transferring the chicken breasts to a serving plate.

"Same as always. The truth is, all he wants is his old job back, and since that's not going to happen I expect him to be out of work for a while." Jackie shrugged and removed the broccoli from the oven. The cheese had melted into an attractive golden layer on top, effectively hiding the mess underneath. "I wish I'd been smart like you and finished my degree. Life would be a lot easier for the kids and me."

"That looks good," Grace said, eyeing the finished product appreciatively. "You know, you could always go back to school."

Jackie made a face as she set the dish on a trivet. "Maybe some day."

"I could help you out financially. . . ." Grace tasted the salad and added a little more lemon juice.

"I couldn't do it, not with the kids. And Stan would have a fit."

"Screw Stan." Grace tossed the salad one last time.

"I'd rather screw the hunky cop," Jackie said wickedly.

"Jackie!" Grace was scandalized.

"Grace!" Jackie mocked her.

"Here," Grace thrust the salad bowl at her. "You set the table and I'll finish the rest."

"Want to use the good china?" Jackie teased, carrying the salad bowl to the table and setting it down in the middle. Grace threw her a look.

"Just set the table."

Jackie laughed. "Okay, fine. Listen, maybe I should take the kids and go home, if you and the hunky cop want to be alone."

"Just set the table," Grace said again, carrying the pan of rice over to the stove and draining it.

Jackie stuck her tongue out at her sister and proceeded to set the table.

While the children watched TV in the family room, the three adults and Jessica ate in the kitchen. The food wasn't of the same caliber as Tony's family's feast, but it was decent and healthful and there was enough of it. Tony and Jessica talked basketball, arguing the relative merits of the Pacers (his favorite) versus the Boston Celtics (hers). Meanwhile, Grace and Jackie, neither of whom had the least interest in professional basketball, talked children and personalities, while Grace tried to think of a way to work birth dates into the conversation. Finally the four of them moved on to general topics. Jessica excused herself to go upstairs and do her homework, while the adults lingered over coffee.

"Jax, what do you want for your birthday?" Grace asked, having given up on coming up with some brilliant way to introduce the topic. Stupid would have to do, but at least she was not batting her eyelashes at Tony.

"It's not until the end of February," Jackie said, eyeing her with some surprise.

"I know, but I was thinking about starting my Christmas shopping soon, and I thought I might as well get all my gift-buying over with. So what do you want?"

"Anything." Jackie shrugged and gave her one of those sister looks that said, what on earth are you babbling about?

Grace ignored it.

"When's your birthday, Tony?"

"November 16. I'll be forty."

Scorpio. He was a Scorpio. He hadn't circled the horoscope. Had she ever really thought that he had?

Her stomach tightened around the just-consumed meal, and she started to feel sick.

"Grace, I'm serious about the kids and me staying here with you until this thing is over," Jackie said earnestly while Grace fought to keep her distress from showing. "There's safety in numbers, you know."

"That might just make you and your children targets, too," Tony said. "And we'd have three more people we'd have to protect."

"But if Jessica's the target, why would the creep be interested in us?" Jackie argued.

"I'm not sure that Jessica is the target. Grace may well be the target, with the perp using Jessica to get at her. He could get at her through you and your children, too."

"We'll still stay." Jackie looked at Grace. "I hate the idea that you and Jess have been going through this all alone."

"Thanks, Jax." Her emotions largely under control now, Grace smiled at her sister. "I appreciate the offer, I really do. But since Tony's here . . ."

Instinctively she glanced at him, and their gazes met across the table. He smiled at her, and she must have smiled back, and for longer than she realized, because when she looked at her sister again Jackie was shooting the pair of them covert glances, her eyes bright with rampant speculation.

"Okay. But if you need me, call," Jackie said, smooth as silk. "I'll come running with bells on."

She and the kids left shortly afterward. Grace went upstairs to touch base with her daughter about the progress of her homework. Worry over the horoscopes tried to raise its ugly head, but Grace resolutely forced it back.

What she feared could not be true. She refused to stew over it any longer.

Like harmless shadows in the dark, shaped into ghosts by a fertile imagination, the specter was almost certain to be nothing more than a product of her own mind.

The dogs, Grace saw when Jessica opened the door in response to her knock, were once again lying on Jess's bed. Both
looked up as Grace came through the door. Both wagged their
tails. Neither jumped to the ground.

"Jess . . ." Instead of talking homework, Grace realized
that the time had come to mete out discipline over the latest
sneaking-out incident. The trauma of Godzilla's death was all that
had saved Jessica so far, but the transgression had to be dealt with,
shock and sorrow over the loss of the pet notwithstanding. "Jess,
sit down. We need to talk about what you did Saturday night."

Jessica groaned. "Mom, I'm right in the middle of Spanish. . . ."

Grace used her best I-mean-it voice. "Jessica. Sit. Now."

Making a face, Jessica plopped down on the edge of the bed.
The dogs raised their heads as the mattress bounced, and crawled
over to lie, one on each side, next to Jessica. Looking at her
mother all the while, Jessica absentmindedly played with their
ears.

"Mom, I'm really sorry. I won't do it again, I promise."

Standing in front of her daughter, arms crossed over her
chest, Grace gave her a level look. "Saturday was the fourth time
you've snuck out. That I know of."

"I'm sorry."

"You were drinking alcohol. And, by your own admission,
smoking pot."

"I'm *sorry*."

"Jessica, *I'm sorry* just doesn't cut it in this case. If it was the
first time it had happened, maybe. But not now."

"What do you want me to say? I *am* sorry."

Grace looked down at her reflectively. "Pretend I'm you,
and you're me. I'm the fifteen-year-old daughter who, even
though grounded, was caught sneaking out in the middle of the
night for the fourth time, and I drank alcohol and admitted to
smoking pot and making out with a boy. You're the mother,
remember. What would you do?"

Jessica looked up at her, wide-eyed.

"I'm really sorry, Mom," Grace whined, in almost perfect imitation of Jessica. Then she reverted to her normal voice. "Now, what do you do?"

"Ground you for the rest of your life, I guess," Jessica said glumly after a brief pause.

Grace pursed her lips. "Jess, you need to understand something. I am the mother, and you are the child. I will do what I have to do to keep you safe until you're old enough to live on your own. I control the money. Clothes, CDs, movies, all the good stuff—I can cut you off from them just like that. You'll be sixteen in March. I have to sign for your driver's license. I can choose not to, you know. In other words, there are many options open to me other than, or in addition to, grounding you. I want to make that very clear."

Jessica's eyes were wide on her face. It was obvious that she had never considered the matter in that light before.

"Do you understand?"

Jessica nodded. Puppy nudged her thigh as though in silent sympathy, and Jessica patted the dog.

Grace sighed. "I love you. You know that. I don't want to do any of those things. All I want is to keep you safe. I'll make you a deal."

"A deal?" Jessica looked and sounded both hopeful and wary.

"How would you like to keep that furry beast?"

Jessica looked down at the dog beside her. "Puppy?"

"Yes."

Her eyes flew to Grace's face. "You mean I can have Puppy for my own?"

"Under certain conditions. Number one, no sneaking out of the house ever again. If you want to go somewhere, you ask me, and if I say no, that's the end of the matter. Number two, no alcohol. Number three, no pot, or any other illegal substance. If you promise to abide by those rules—and they are absolute—you can keep the dog. If you break any one of them, even once, the dog goes back to Tony."

"Oh, Mom!" Jessica jumped off the bed and threw her arms around her mother. "Oh, Mom, yes! I've wanted a dog so much—I'll do anything!"

Grace hugged Jessica back, but she deliberately kept her voice stern. "We have a deal, right?"

"Yes!"

"Okay. As long as you stick to the deal, he . . . she—whatever it is—is yours."

"Oh, Mom, thank you! And Puppy's a boy." Jessica was practically jumping up and down with excitement as she turned back toward the bed. Puppy and Kramer were sitting up now, looking toward Jessica in identical, head-cocked-to-one-side inquisitive mode. Jessica scooped Puppy up in her arms and swung back around.

"I'll never sneak out again, or drink beer, or smoke pot, I promise. Oh, Mom, I thought you didn't like dogs!"

"They're starting to grow on me," Grace said, watching as the small furry creature bathed Jessica's chin with a moist tongue. Jessica bounced over to hug her again, and Puppy, also in on the hug, seized the opportunity to lick Grace's cheek.

When Jessica released her, Grace wiped the damp spot away. The dog's mouth was open. If she hadn't known better, Grace would have sworn the animal was grinning at her.

"Finish your homework," Grace said dryly, knowing it would be some time before Jessica settled down enough to comply. But still, as she left her daughter's room, Grace felt good. That kind of positive discipline was easy to apply.

And she felt surprisingly confident it would work. A dog was something Jessica would value enough to change her behavior for.

She went downstairs and found Tony loading the dishwasher. Stopping short in the doorway, she watched.

"You're pretty handy to have around, aren't you?" she said after a moment. Her macho cop kept surprising her.

"With six boys and no girls, you think we didn't learn how to keep house?" He grinned at her. "Want to know my guilty secret?"

"What?" Grace asked, picking up the dishrag to wipe down the counter and table.

"I can cook."

"Oh, wow!" Grace widened her eyes in exaggerated delight. "Now you've found the way to my heart."

"Have I?" His voice was husky as he pushed the buttons to turn on the dishwasher. Then he turned toward her. He was reaching for her, and she was coming into his arms, dishrag and all, when they heard Jessica bounding down the stairs.

Immediately they were six feet apart.

"Mom, Tony, I've thought of the perfect name!" Jessica said the instant she saw them. Both dogs were at her heels, and it was obvious she had no thoughts on any subject other than her recent acquisition. "Chewie! What do you think of that?"

"Chewie?" Grace said doubtfully, while Tony looked at her instead of Jessica and grinned.

"It's short for Chewbacca! You know, from *Star Wars!*"

"Great name!" Tony said appreciatively, while Grace nodded.

"Sounds good. Chewie."

"I'm going to take them out and start potty-training him. I didn't want to tell you, Mom, but Chewie's had a couple of accidents on the rug in my room."

"Has he?" Grace shot Tony a darkling look. She hadn't thought about the subject of accidents, but surely he had known his dog wasn't house-trained.

Tony grinned, shrugged, and looked a bit sheepish. "I'll come with you, Jess. He'll be really easy to housebreak. His mom was. But you'll have to cut him a little slack for a while. He's only ten weeks old."

That remark, Grace felt, was directed at her. "As long as he *gets* housebroken."

"He will!" Her daughter and Tony replied in chorus. They looked at each other, grinned, and headed out the back door in perfect harmony, with the dogs pattering at their heels.

Raising her eyes skyward as the door closed behind them,

Grace mentally asked of heaven, *what have I let myself in for?* But she was smiling as she finished wiping down the counters, and she continued to smile as she headed down into the basement to put in a load of laundry.

And when the thought of the mysteriously circled horoscopes entered her head, she immediately drove it out again.

CHAPTER **39**

GRACE WAS ON HER WAY OUT THE KITCHEN DOOR the next morning when she noticed it: a key stuck in a gooey pink blob of chewing gum, right in the middle of the door's glass pane.

"Wait," she said to Penick, who was in front of her. Jessica and Gloria Baer had just left for school. For a moment Grace simply stared numbly at the key. It was, she was almost certain, a key to her house, one of those that the new locks had rendered inoperable. Then she turned back and stuck her head in the kitchen.

"Tony," she said in a small voice. He still sat at the table drinking coffee. As a protection officer, she had discovered, he didn't sleep: he was on duty, and thus stayed awake all night, to watch over them. Consequently, he had been bleary-eyed at the breakfast table that morning.

He glanced up. One look at her must have told him something was up, because he got immediately to his feet. He was wearing a gray sweatshirt over jeans, with white athletic socks but no shoes on his feet. He needed a shave, and his black hair was tousled.

Even bleary-eyed, unshaven, and tousled, he was sexy.

"What?" he said, padding toward her. Penick was behind her now, frowning, looking mystified.

Grace stepped back out onto the walkway and waited for Tony to join her.

"Look," she said, pointing.

He looked, and his face tightened.

"At least he couldn't get in," Grace said. She crossed her arms over her chest, feeling suddenly very cold despite the sunny brightness of the morning and her new bone-colored wool suit. All the uneasiness she'd managed to suppress since arriving home the previous evening sprang to renewed life.

"Go on to work. I'll take care of it," Tony said in a clipped voice. He glanced at her then, and smiled. That smile was almost as intimate as a kiss. If it hadn't been for Penick standing behind her, he would have kissed her, she knew. But he didn't, and she felt the loss. "We'll get him, don't worry. In the meantime, you and Jessica are safe."

"I know." She smiled back at him, rather wanly. But as she followed Penick out to the car she felt dread, cold and suffocating, settle over her like a cloud.

The memory of the circled horoscope was heavy as a lead ball in her chest.

January 21st. She could not get the date, with all its implications, out of her mind.

Should she tell Tony? Or not?

The question troubled her so much that she had difficulty concentrating in court. It was Tuesday, and she had the usual run of cases: divorces, custody disputes, incidents of domestic violence, child abuse, juvenile delinquents. By eleven o'clock she was as tired as if she had worked a full day—and Colin Wilkerson was standing in front of her arguing on behalf of a mother trying to deny joint custody or even any visitation by her husband. He was not the biological father of the child in question, although he had married the mother when the child was six months old and raised it as his own. Now, after nine years of marriage and stepfatherhood, the mother wanted a divorce, and, further, wanted to deny her soon-to-be-ex-husband all future contact with the child.

"Legal precedent is clear," Colin said, citing cases. "Mr. Harvey has no right to even see Lisa, much less sue for joint custody of her. The fact is, he is neither the child's biological nor adoptive father, and thus has no standing in this case."

Having already listened to Mr. Harvey's side of the story and to the report of a court-appointed psychologist who had examined the child, Grace looked at Colin, who appeared coolly confident of the merit of his client's legal position.

"The child's name is Lisa Harvey, is it not?"

"She has gone by that name, yes. But Mrs. Harvey is planning to remarry, and at that time the child's name will be altered to that of her new stepfather."

Grace looked at Mrs. Harvey. A big-boned blonde of perhaps thirty, she was attractive in a bosomy, big-haired kind of way.

"So what Mrs. Harvey is basically proposing is that her child be raised by a succession of fathers?"

Colin looked taken aback. Mrs. Harvey's eyes widened.

"The child has been raised as Lisa Harvey from infancy, is that right, Mrs. Harvey?" Grace asked.

"Yes," Mrs. Harvey said in a soft voice.

"She considers Mr. Harvey her father, is that right?" Grace continued.

"Well, yes, but . . ." Mrs. Harvey began.

"The fact is he is not," Colin quickly interceded.

Grace had heard enough. "In this case, I think that raising a child as its father from infancy to age nine gives Mr. Harvey certain rights. I rule that he is to be awarded joint custody of the child known as Lisa Harvey. Schedules are to be worked out between the opposing parties and presented to this court for approval." She banged the gavel down on her desk. "Case dismissed."

"Wh–what?" Mrs. Harvey's mouth dropped open. Eyes and mouth formed almost perfect O's. "Colin, you told me that he had no chance!"

A plump, dark-haired man in a too-small suit, Mr. Harvey slumped in his chair, disbelief quickly replaced by a huge grin. His attorney patted him on the shoulder.

"Margaret, it's all right," Colin said swiftly to his client, and looked daggers at Grace. "Your Honor, may I approach the bench?"

No, is what Grace wanted to say. She really wasn't in the mood for Colin Wilkerson. But, as usual, he didn't wait for her permission. He seemed to feel that their one-time relationship gave him a special dispensation of formality where she was concerned.

"All right, this is too much," he said in a furious undertone when he stood before her. "You are taking personal vindictiveness to an extreme. Under the law, that man had no case, and you know it. You found against my client strictly to get back at me."

Grace looked at him and mentally counted to ten. The courtroom was emptying behind him, and new people were coming in. Just one more case, and she would call the lunch break.

Thank goodness.

"Colin, believe me, you overrate your importance in my life," Grace said coldly.

"It is obvious to anyone what you are doing. You are punishing me every time I stand before this court for some offense I'm not even aware of committing. But let me tell you, your ruling in this case will not stand! It is absolutely without legal precedent!"

"You are welcome to appeal."

His face turned red, and his fingers curled and uncurled at his sides.

"I warn you, Grace: I'm not going to put up with this. You are hurting my practice by denying every case I bring into your court. I'm telling you now, whatever it takes to get you off the bench, I am prepared to do. Do you hear me? Whatever it takes!"

Before Grace could open her mouth to say *contempt of court,* a hand fell on Colin's shoulder. Clean-shaven now, dressed in his leather bomber jacket over a flannel shirt and jeans, Tony stood behind him, his eyes narrow and his jaw hard. Penick, courtroom ready in a sport jacket and tie, came out of his seat at the side of the courtroom at this sign of trouble and headed toward the bench. So too did Walter Dowd.

"That sounds like a threat, Counselor," Tony said.

"Who the hell are you?" Colin turned to glare at the other man, his face so red now that Grace half-expected to see steam start pouring from his ears. Only the size and style of his opponent kept him from letting fly with his fists, Grace surmised. Although Colin was tall, it was obvious at a glance that he was no match for Tony's hard, muscular frame.

"Cop," Tony said succinctly. "And you're threatening an officer of the court."

"What's the problem?" Penick asked, ranging himself alongside Tony. Walter shifted to one side, so that he stood nearest to Grace.

"I've seen you before," Colin said to Tony, his eyes narrowing. Then he glanced at Grace, his mouth curling into a sneer. "He your new boyfriend?"

Tony stiffened. Penick, clearly sensing the imminent escalation of the conflict, shifted his weight, appearing to balance on the balls of his feet as he glanced from one would-be combatant to the other. Walter's hand settled on his gun. Grace looked at the four men in front of her bench and sighed.

"Colin, do me a favor: Go away. If you want to try to have me removed from the bench legally, fine. If you threaten me again, or in fact, say one more word, I'm going to find you in contempt of court and have you locked up. Don't make me do it."

Colin glared at her, his hands opening and closing at his sides, his face bright crimson now. His furious gaze transferred to Tony and then to Penick, who was standing just behind Tony, and finally to Walter, whose hand still rested on the gun holstered at his side. Then his lips thinned, and without another word he turned on his heel and took himself off.

Tony looked after him thoughtfully, then glanced at Grace.

"Who is that guy?"

"His name is Colin Wilkerson. He's an attorney," Grace answered.

Tony moved closer to the bench so that they could talk without being overheard by anyone except, perhaps, Penick and Walter, who still stood nearby. "I've seen him here before. In fact, weren't you having a disagreement with him then, too?"

"Probably. Colin thinks my rulings against him are personal. At one time, we . . . went out."

"I see." Tony's gaze met hers, and there was something—a hint of disgruntlement, maybe?—in the depths of his eyes that had not been there before. It was obvious to Grace that he did not like the thought that she had once dated Colin Wilkerson.

Was he, perhaps, just a little jealous? Grace was surprised at how much she liked the idea that Tony Marino might be jealous of a man she had dated briefly months before.

"What are you doing here, anyway?" Grace asked.

"I thought I'd take you to lunch." His gaze met hers again, and the anger at the backs of his eyes faded away.

They were speaking quietly enough so that not even Penick and Walter could overhear. They could be seen, though, and both Penick and Walter, along with several others seated in the court-room, were watching them curiously. Though she knew they were being observed, Grace couldn't help it. She smiled at him. His expression softened in response, and he smiled back at her.

"I have one more case to hear before I can call lunch."

"I'll wait."

Grace listened with some impatience to her final case of the morning, which was, thankfully, a simple divorce that only needed finalizing, and then called the lunch break. Tony and Penick had been sitting side by side on the far right side of the courtroom, and they approached her together as she stepped down from the bench.

"I'll take over watch-dog duties until after lunch," Tony said to Penick as Grace joined them. "Feel free to go grab a sandwich or something." He glanced at his watch. "We'll meet you back here at one o'clock."

Penick looked doubtful. "I'm on duty. . . ."

"I'm officially relieving you until after lunch." Tony out-ranked Penick, but that didn't make the other officer look any happier about the situation.

"Don't worry, I'll be perfectly safe with Detective Marino," Grace said with a smile for the younger man.

"Think so?" Tony said in her ear as Penick, still looking doubtful, took himself off.

"As safe as I want to be," she amended, and grinned at him. He laughed. Grace stopped for an instant in her chambers to remove her robe, and then they hurried through the secretaries' big office and headed down the back stairs toward the parking lot.

As much as she wanted to, they didn't touch, not even to hold hands. As long as she was in the Franklin County Court-house, she had her dignity as a judge to uphold, and Tony seemed as conscious of that as she was.

Once inside his car, though, he kissed her, a quick hard kiss, then inserted his key into the ignition and started the engine. Conscious that it was broad daylight and they were in the parking lot of the courthouse with people all around, Grace refrained with some mental effort from wrapping her arms around his neck and returning the favor with interest.

But she wanted to, and her expression must have told him so, because his eyes heated as he looked at her.

"How hungry are you?" he asked, pulling out of the parking lot into the heavy traffic of downtown Columbus at midday.

"Not particularly."

He grinned at her. "We could go to my house."

His house was less than five minutes away, Grace knew. She had called the lunch break at 11:15. It was now 11:25. That gave them about an hour and a half before she had to be back on the bench.

"Okay." Even as she said that one little word, her body began to quicken. The night before, when he'd started kissing her on the couch during the evening news, she'd been forced to tell him her rule, about no sex in the house with Jessica present. He had agreed that it was a good rule, and very important for Jessica's well-being, and then kissed her again and sent her to bed before, he said, he took back everything he had just said.

She hadn't even been surprised that he'd been understanding. Besides being mouth-wateringly sexy, Tony Marino, she had learned, was a decent and honorable man.

When they reached his house, Mrs. Crutcher next door was on her porch watering the plants with an old-fashioned tin watering can.

"Hi, Tony!" she called, waving, as they stepped out of his black Honda, which he parked at the curb.

"Hi, Mrs. Crutcher." Tony waved back. Grace felt her face pinken as the old woman, watering can in hand, studied her with open interest as she and Tony headed, without touching, for the house. It was silly, but she was sure that the woman knew precisely why they were there.

"Out all night again, Tony," Mrs. Whiting chided.

"Working, always working," he replied with a grin.

"Nice work if you can get it," she retorted, chuckling, and looked pointedly at Grace, who smiled feebly in response. She was still watching them as Tony unlocked his door and pulled Grace inside the house.

"She's better than any watchdog I've ever seen," Grace said with fervent relief as the closing door blocked the woman's prying eyes.

"Isn't she? She's my own personal security system." He grinned at her as he locked the door, then pulled her into his arms. "I wouldn't be surprised if she has my house bugged."

On that pleasant thought, he kissed her.

CHAPTER 40

HIS MOUTH WAS HOT AND URGENT AND TASTED
faintly of coffee. Her purse landed on the floor with a faint thud.
Wrapping her arms around his neck, Grace kissed him back with
greedy intensity, plastering her body against his.

Conscious of the ticking clock, her hands slid down the
smooth leather front of his jacket to find its zipper, which she
pulled down and disengaged at the bottom. Moving her hands to
the soft flannel beneath, she started work on his shirt buttons even
as he shrugged out of his jacket.

"Jesus, I want you," Tony breathed the words in her ear as
his mouth slid down to her neck and his hands dispensed with,
first, the single button that held her blazer closed and then the
blazer itself, which fell to the floor to join his jacket and her purse
at their feet.

"Mmmm," Grace said, her teeth occupied in nibbling his
earlobe.

His palm flattened over her breast, and Grace released her
victim to draw in a ragged breath as her nipple hardened instantly.
The white silk shell and flimsy nylon bra she wore were no protection against the heat of his touch. His hands slid all over the
fragile fabric, front and back, exploring and titillating, caressing
even such unlikely erogenous zones as her shoulders and the

length of her spine and her waist. Meanwhile, her hands dealt with the last of his shirt buttons and then moved inward to find the warm, hair-roughened flesh beneath.

His chest felt so good, so warm and firm and masculine, to her touch.

"How does this damned blouse-thing come off?" Tony's stroking hands stilled on her rib cage, and he lifted his head from where he had been kissing the sensitive area at the side of her neck to look down at her. Frustration, bafflement, and blazing desire combined in his face.

Realizing the purpose behind his exploration of new erogenous zones, Grace had to smile.

"There's a button at the back of the neck."

Lifting her arms, she demonstrated, dealing with it for him. Before she could return to her journey of discovery across the hard contours of his chest, he caught the hem of her shell and pulled it over her head, then dropped it on the floor, leaving her standing before him in her delicate white bra and bone-colored wool skirt and conservative heels.

He touched her breasts, caressing her through the thin nylon. His hands were large and warm and hard, and her nipples stood up like soldiers called to attention under his ministrations. Her hands lay flat against his chest, her fingers curling into his skin like a nursing kitten's as she experienced an onslaught of desire so intense that her knees went weak.

Her bra had a traditional double hook-and-eye fastening that was located between her shoulder blades. He seemed to have no trouble finding *that,* because he unclipped it in a matter of seconds. Her bra slid down her arms, then was tugged free and tossed aside. Grace first glanced down at herself, bare now from the waist up, and then looked up at him.

Her breasts were small but firm, with pinkish-brown areolas and nipples that stood stiffly erect. His jaw hardened as he looked down at her body, and his eyes darkened until they were almost black.

His hands, large and bronze against the ivory of her skin, rested on either side of her rib cage just above the waistband of her skirt. Against her skin, she could feel the faint abrasiveness of the calluses on his palms.

Grace's heart started to pound, and a hot rhythmic quickening began in her loins.

"You are the sexiest thing I have ever seen in my life," he said, his voice husky.

This drew a shaky laugh from her. "I was just thinking the same thing about you."

He glanced up and met her eyes. "Were you now?"

Before Grace realized what he meant to do, he bent and picked her up in his arms, lifting her as easily as if she weighed nothing at all. Arms automatically looping around his neck, eyes widening, she met his gaze as he carried her toward the door that led into the dining room.

"Now that's what I like in a man: muscles," she said teasingly, her voice low and throaty with the passion that was already causing her bare breasts to swell longingly against his chest, and her nether regions to pulse and burn. But her eyes were smiling into his as he maneuvered her through the narrow doorway.

He smiled back at her, his eyes hot.

"You're what I like in a woman," he said. Bending his head, he kissed her nipple, which made her gasp, and then her open mouth. "All of you. Every single inch."

He kissed her again and was still kissing her as he carried her through the dining room and kitchen and into his bedroom. When he lowered her to his bed and followed her down, Grace had a fleeting realization that the hand-pieced quilt that covered it was as soft as it had looked the other day. Then his hand was sliding up the inside of her panty-hose clad thigh beneath her skirt, trailing fire behind it, and she ceased thinking of anything at all except him.

She kicked off her shoes as he pulled off the rest of her clothes and slid his shirt down his arms. Then he pulled away from her, standing up and stripping off the remainder of his garments with hands that were not quite steady. His eyes flamed as they moved over her, sitting naked as she was in the center of his bed.

She felt naked, too, she thought, erotically naked in a way she had never before felt, even though she was sitting as modestly as it was possible for an unclothed woman to sit, her knees drawn up to her chest and her arms wrapped around her legs.

Her body tingled in greedy anticipation of what was to come.

Watching him as he pushed his jeans and shorts down his legs and then straightened to stand naked before her, she felt a rush of purely wanton desire that made her feel as if she were melting in that place between her legs. She no longer felt like the thirty-six-year-old woman, mother, judge, and divorcée who had been around the block more times than she cared to remember.

She felt like a girl again, a young and beautiful girl just becoming acquainted with the wonder of desire. No, she corrected herself, she felt like a woman.

A woman in love.

Her lips parted on the thought, and her eyes widened on his face. But before she could react in any other way, he was coming down on the bed beside her, his weight denting the mattress as he pushed her back into the softness of the bed and covered her body with his.

Grace met his kiss with her own, curling her tongue around his and her arms around his neck, opening her mouth and parting her legs for him instantly. There was no need for any preliminaries, no desire for any foreplay, she wanted him inside her instantly and he must have wanted that, too, because even as he settled on top of her he thrust deep and hard, groaning into her mouth. Grace moaned an answer as she wrapped her legs tightly around his waist.

"Tony, Tony, *Tony*," she cried as he took her with a fierceness that was exactly what she craved.

She bucked and writhed and clung and then, finally, went exquisitely, quiveringly still, beneath him as he buried himself inside her one last time, holding himself there as he found his own release.

When it was over, when Grace had at last floated back to earth and remembered all the whos and whats and wheres of the situation, she first smiled a sleepy, contented smile at the black head buried against her shoulder. Next she cocked an eye at the alarm clock beside the bed.

12:35. Grace groaned.

"Tony." She shoved at his shoulder. He was lying atop her, hot and sweaty, his big body still joined to hers. All that muscle weighed a ton. She was, to all intents and purposes, pinioned beneath him, unable to move.

"Mmm?" he responded, turning his head a little so that his lips could nuzzle her neck.

The touch of those warm lips on such a sensitive spot sent a little thrill all the way to her toes.

"Tony, we have to get up! I have to be back in court in about twenty minutes."

He groaned and lifted his head, looking down at her with an expression in his eyes that was not quite a smile. The rest of him stayed just where it was.

"You—are—beautiful—and—sexy —and—" he said, punctuating his words with butterfly kisses dropped on her mouth.

"Late," Grace finished for him tartly. She shoved at his shoulder again. A woman in love or not—and she would have to consider that more carefully later—she was also a judge, and she had to be back in her courtroom by one o'clock.

He grimaced comically and rolled off her, lying on his back, with no apparent concern for his nudity, and crossing his arms beneath his head as he watched her scramble off his bed with scant dignity.

"Whoever said women were the romantic sex obviously never made love to one," he said in a complaining tone.

"In, out, thank you, lout," Grace replied pertly over her shoulder, grinning at him and disappearing into his bathroom for a quick shower to the accompaniment of his shout of laughter.

He appeared moments later, while she was rinsing off the soapy lather she had quickly applied, and stuck his head around the curtain, watching her ablutions with interest.

"I could join you," he suggested with an exaggerated leer. That he was still naked was obvious from the triangle of bare arm and shoulder, chest and hipbone that she could see.

"What time is it?" she demanded by way of a reply, turning off the taps. He obligingly handed her a towel, then glanced at his watch.

"12:39."

Grace groaned again. Wrapping the towel around herself, she stepped out of the tub.

Tony was standing there naked, just as she had surmised. He caught her by the shoulders, dropped a quick kiss on her mouth, grinned at her, and stepped into the tub, pulling the curtain shut.

"Hurry!" she urged as he turned on the water.

Walking into the bedroom, she saw that he had thoughtfully gathered up her clothes from the various places where they had been dropped. Everything—bra, panties, hose, shell, and suit— was in a neat little pile on the bed. Her shoes had been placed side by side on the floor nearby.

Hurrying into her clothes, watching the clock with one eye, Grace thought, who in her right mind wouldn't fall in love with a man like that?

She felt a warm tingling kind of glow rush over her skin from her head clear down to her toes.

She was stepping into her shoes when he emerged from the bathroom, body gleaming wet and a small white towel clutched modestly around his waist. With his broad-shouldered, narrow-hipped, hairy-chested athlete's body, he looked so hunky she would gladly have fallen on him a second time—if she didn't have to be in court at one P.M.

"Hurry," she admonished him again. The time was 12:43.

"I already did. That's why they call it a quickie," he observed with a wry smile as she rushed by him on her way to the living room, where she had left her purse.

"Get dressed," she hissed, ignoring his lame attempt at humor. Fortunately, men tended to be speedy about pulling on their clothes, she thought, and all she had to do was run a brush through her hair and apply lipstick and powder and she was as good as new.

Her purse was just inside the door, where she had dropped it when Tony had first kissed her. Snatching it up, she hurried to the mirror over the fireplace.

She was applying the finishing touch—a thin layer of a translucent lipstick in a shade called all-spice—when her gaze was caught by the framed picture on the mantel. The frame was dark wood, the picture itself was small, and it was positioned to the far left, which, she thought, explained why it had not caught her eye earlier.

Because, as she picked it up, she realized that it *should* have caught her eye. It was a candid summer snapshot of a girl of perhaps ten or eleven, pretty but way too thin, dressed in a filmy white dress with smocking on the bodice and a white ribbon tied in her hair. She had long straight hair as black as Tony's, and huge, shadowed, dark eyes. She was smiling—grinning hugely, actually. Her arms were lifted and opened wide as though to show off the flowers that surrounded her. They were roses, and the child stood in the midst of a huge circular garden in full bloom. The flowers were lush enough so that Grace, looking at the picture, could almost smell their perfume. Every blossom was a beautiful, creamy white.

It was in color, but the child's black hair and dark eyes and the white of her dress and the velvety cream of the roses gave the impression of a black-and-white print. The effect was haunting.

The child, of course, had to be Rachel. It could be no one else.

Looking at it, Grace felt a lump rise in her throat.

Tony walked into the room then, fully dressed in a sweatshirt and jeans. He was smiling, his face warm and relaxed, his eyes bright and teasing.

His expression changed in the space of a heartbeat as Grace met his eyes across the room and his gaze fell to the picture she held in her hand.

He stopped walking and, for the space of a pair of heartbeats, simply looked at her. Grace could tell from his eyes that he was absorbing the psychic equivalent of a fist to the stomach.

"She was beautiful," Grace said at last, in a very soft voice.

He moved then, coming to stand beside her. When he reached her side, he looked down at the picture in her hand and gently lifted a finger to touch the image beneath the glass.

"She was, wasn't she?" Grief was there in his eyes, and in the white lines bracketing his mouth, but his voice was steady.

"She looks so happy. Whose garden was it?" He needed to talk about his pain, Grace thought, if he was ever going to move beyond it.

"Hers. Rachel loved roses. That was taken the summer before she died. She and I went to a nursery near where we lived and bought all the white rosebushes they had in stock. When we got them home, I dug up a garden for her in the backyard of our house in Cleveland and planted them. That whole last summer, I watered and fertilized and sprayed the damned things and did everything but pray over them to keep them alive. Hell, I probably prayed over them, too. They were still blooming when she died. When I left Cleveland, I dug them up and brought them with me. Because she had loved them, I couldn't bear to leave them behind."

Grace thought of the circle of scraggly, dead-looking rose bushes in the backyard of the house they were standing in.

"Are they here?" she asked.

He nodded. "Once in a while I remember to water them, but they've never bloomed since I moved them. I ought to dig them up and throw them away, but I can't bring myself to do that to—Rachel's roses."

If there was a slight break in his voice before he said his daughter's name, that was all.

"Oh, Tony . . ." Paradoxically, it was Grace who had tears in her eyes as she looked up at him. Going up on tiptoe, she kissed his cheek and then his mouth, her lips soft and comforting. He wrapped his arms around her, and for a moment, without speaking, he held her tight.

Then she felt his hold shift and realized that he was looking at his watch.

"It's 12:54," he said, letting go of her and taking the picture from her hand to place it back on the mantel. "If we leave right now, you'll only be a few minutes late."

"Oh, gosh." He seemed okay, or at least as okay as it was possible to be under the circumstances. But she hated to just rush away, when he might need to talk or something.

"I'm fine," he said firmly, apparently getting some inkling of what she was thinking from her expression as she looked at him. "Let's go. You've got a courtroom of people waiting on you."

But he wrapped his arm around her waist and kept it there all the way to the car and, Grace thought as she returned the favor, to heck with what nosy Mrs. Crutcher might think.

CHAPTER 41

"WHAT ARE YOU DOING HERE IN THE MIDDLE
of the day?" It was a little after three. Dominick, having apparently just arrived at the station, stopped by Tony's desk on the way
to his own. Traffic in the squad room was light at that time of the
day, with only one other detective, Joe Gonzalez, at his desk.
"You're on night duty. You're supposed to be home sleeping."

"Working on something." Deeply absorbed in what he was
doing, Tony was slouched in his chair, his chin resting on one fist,
and he barely glanced up at his brother. In fact, he was comparing
fingerprints on his computer screen. A thumbprint taken from
Grace's house was on the left. On the right, a series of thumb-
prints flashed past as the computer trolled for a match. He had
already run through the files of drug-related arrests associated with
Hebron High School with no luck. Now the computer was comparing prints taken from the files of individuals who had appeared
before Grace in court over the past two years. Of course, not
everyone who had appeared before her had fingerprints on file,
and a number of other people who might have a reason to want to
scare her or Jessica probably also didn't have fingerprints on file,
but still the exercise was necessary.

Detective work, Tony had discovered, was largely a process
of elimination, assisted by common sense and luck. His standard

operating procedure was to rule out everything he could, then go with what was left.

Over the years, it had proved to be a surprisingly successful strategy.

"How's the girlfriend holding up?" Dom asked.

Wary of what the brother who knew him so well might be able to read in his eyes in answer to that, Tony didn't even glance up.

"Fine." If he had hoped the monosyllable would deter Dom, well, he hadn't really expected it to.

Dom laughed and said, "Mama likes her."

"She told me."

"Did she?"

"At length." Tony did glance up at his brother then. "What do you two do, gossip about me over the phone all day long?"

"Nah. No more than fifteen minutes a day, at the most." Dominick was grinning.

Despite his displeasure over being the subject of his family's interested speculation, he had to smile at the picture thus conjured up: his mother and Dominick with telephone receivers pressed to their ears, yakking away.

Dominick was getting more old-womanish all the time. Tony told his brother so and received a punch in the shoulder for his pains.

"Afternoon, gentlemen." Gary Sandifer walked into the squad room, the tan trench coat that was his trademark swirling around his legs as he moved.

"Captain," Tony and Dominick both said. Under his breath, Tony added to Dom, "Good God, is everybody coming in early now?"

"We're short-handed, what with you and Penick and Baer having been pulled out for the babysitting gig. Lots of things are going down."

"Yeah?" Tony glanced at Dom with interest.

Before Dom could reply, Sandifer stopped by his desk.

"How's the Judge Hart thing coming?" he asked.

"It's coming, and that's about all I can say."

"Tell me what you got."

The computer continued its endless blinking as Tony held up his fingers, counting off points as he enumerated them.

"Number one, I got an allegedly stolen and recovered teddy bear, no prints, no nothing. Number two, I got oil on a mirror, pure mineral oil, generic, no recoverable prints on the mirror but one unidentifiable one lifted off the bedroom doorknob. I'm trying to find a match for it. Number three, I got a cake made by Holliman's Grocery in Westwind Shopping Center, telephone order placed by a 'Stanley,' according to the bakery's records, with a phone number that turned out to be a fake. It was a distinctive cake that one guy remembers decorating. Nonpoisonous, standard ingredients, no crime committed in ordering it or purchasing it, no reason for the clerk who rang it up to remember anything about the person who picked it up. It was paid for in cash. Number four, I got a dead hamster on ice at the morgue, drowned in a plastic bag. City water. No fingerprints on the bag. Some fibers on the animal that we have not been able to match to anything."

"In short, you got zilch." Sandifer sounded resigned.

"But," Tony continued, "this morning we caught a break. Number five, the bozo left a no-longer-functional key to the house stuck to the kitchen door with chewing gum."

Sandifer looked at him with an arrested expression.

Tony nodded. "Yep. Whoever this guy is, he made a mistake. Now we got DNA. From the saliva in the gum."

Sandifer frowned. "That's not going to help you run him down."

"No, but it means we'll be able to make a positive ID when I find him."

"Sure you'll find him?"

"Positive."

"Hurry this up as much as you can, then. We can't keep Judge Hart and her daughter under guard indefinitely. The powers that be tell me that the D.A.'s already started bitching about the costs. And we need you back on the job."

"We're going after Lynn Voss," Dom said.

"Jesus, I want to be in on that." Tony grimaced. Much as he wanted to get Voss, he wanted Grace kept safe more. The only problem was, he wasn't sure in his own mind that she or Jessica was actually in any physical danger. It was possible that they were, but it was more likely that the perp would turn out to be nothing more than a crank. He'd exaggerated his sense of their imperilment for the sake of obtaining the protection that Grace wanted.

Tony meant to do his best to see that the guy had the book thrown at him when he was caught. Especially if, because of him and his antics, he missed out on the operation that would finally nail Voss.

"Keep at it," Sandifer said, and moved on toward his office.

"Hey, at least your babysitting job has perks," Dom said suggestively, prodding Tony's shoulder with an elbow.

"Don't you have work to do?" Tony shot his brother a quelling glance.

"Yeah." Dom grinned, and headed for his desk. Tony returned his attention to the flashing fingerprints.

Nearly an hour later, he still had nothing. No matching fingerprints. No lab report on the DNA in the chewing gum, although they'd promised to rush it. He'd even run a check on that attorney, Colin Wilkerson, who had been giving Grace trouble, and had come up empty.

Not that he had expected anything else. His gut instinct still told him the perp had to be a kid. But he would have liked it to have been Wilkerson.

He stood up to leave.

"See ya," he said to his brother, who was busy working the phone.

Dom looked over at him, receiver to his ear, his finger poised over the keypad. "Hey, you wanna shoot some baskets for a little bit before you go?"

There was a basketball goal set up at one edge of the parking lot behind the station house. He and Dom had shot a lot of ball there over the years.

Tony shook his head. "No, not today. I've got to go take care of my girls."

It was only as he saw the arrested expression on Dominick's face that Tony realized what he had said.

He turned and walked out before Dom could comment.

If his brother made a joke, he would throttle him.

The last time he'd said that—*my girls*—had been about ten years ago.

Then, he'd been referring to Glenna and Rachel.

My girls: that's what he had called them, with easy, affectionate familiarity. The phrase had been part and parcel of the lost, bright years before his life had been consumed by pain.

He couldn't believe he'd used it again.

For Grace. And Jessica.

My girls.

CHAPTER 42

Tony had something on his mind. Over the next few days, Grace could sense the difference in him, although there was no outward change in his behavior. He was there every day when she and Penick arrived at the house. If he and Jessica weren't playing ball in front of the garage, they were in the backyard with the dogs, or in the kitchen starting supper. True to his word, Tony was a good cook, and Jessica, to Grace's astonishment, proved to be an eager and an apt pupil. As basically a noncook herself, Grace was surprised but pleased to discover this latent talent of her daughter's.

Tony picked Grace up every day at around eleven-thirty, and every day, without even bothering to discuss it, they adjourned to his house for what he termed, with a teasing grin, "lunch."

The sex was fantastic, and in the evenings, when they did no more than talk about everything and anything, he was a charming, interesting, and sensitive companion.

Sometimes they went over different facets of the investigation, twisting and turning possibilities like pieces of a puzzle as they tried to make the facts fit into certain scenarios. Sometimes they talked politics. He was no admirer of Bill Clinton, whom he called "the president after Bush," laughing when it took several repetitions for Grace to get the joke. Sometimes they talked about one of Tony's cases, and sometimes they talked about one of Grace's.

Grace told him about her marriage. The reason for the breakup—Craig's infidelities—no longer hurt, but his increasing lack of interest in Jessica infuriated Grace. She, too, had been the child of a father who had started a second family and subsequently lost all interest in the children from his first, so she knew what it felt like. As a consequence, she did her best to fill in the gap left in her daughter's life by Craig's lack of interest. But the one who suffered, of course, was Jess.

Tony talked about his wife, Glenna, but only briefly. The last time he had seen her had been at Rachel's funeral, and he would be perfectly content never to see her again. Her mother's defection in the face of Rachel's illness had been a pain that she should not have had to suffer. Tony would never forgive Glenna for it.

Grace didn't blame him.

They talked about books and TV shows and movies, and public personalities, and the foibles of their relatives, particularly in-laws. No matter what the topic was, they never seemed to run out of things to say.

Grace realized that the fear she had lived with since finding Mr. Bear by the road had largely dissipated. At night, with Tony in the house, she felt completely and utterly safe. Her main continuing source of anxiety was Jessica. She could not help but worry when her daughter was away from her during the day. But she trusted Gloria Baer. So far, thankfully, no attempt had been made to bother Jessica at school.

She worried, too, about the origin of the circled horoscopes, although she tried not to. Convincing herself that they had to be pure coincidence had been difficult, but to a large degree she had managed it. Stamping out the niggling "what if" factor entirely, though, was proving almost impossible.

If it had not been for the threat of danger to Jessica, whose safety she valued more than her own life, she would have been content to let the investigation drag on forever.

Because when it was over, Tony would move out of her house.

Thinking about that, Grace realized that she didn't want it to happen.

Tony's presence was something she had come to count on.

He fit into the fabric of her life, and Jessica's, as seamlessly as if he had always been a part of it.

She did not want him to go away.

But there was something on his mind, something bothering him. Grace could see it in his eyes when he looked at her, hear it sometimes in the timbre of his voice. Once she had even asked him if anything was wrong. Of course, being a man, he had denied that there was.

She knew better. But she didn't know what it could be, or how to pry the truth out of him.

On Wednesday, they had fantastic news: Jessica made the varsity basketball team. The roster was posted on the school bulletin board at the end of the day, and Jessica called her mother from the school office before she and Gloria even started home.

Grace had interrupted the case she was hearing to take the call on her cell phone—Jessica never called her at work unless it was an emergency—and rejoiced with her daughter when Jessica told her.

Emily Millhollen made the team, too.

Finally, at the end of the conversation, Jessica had said something startling.

"I want to call Tony, too," she said, as casually as if calling Tony with her good news was the most natural thing in the world for her to do. "Do you have his number?"

Masking her thoughts—not even sure what her thoughts were, because Jessica's request had put them in such a jumble—Grace gave her Tony's pager number.

That night, she and Tony and Jessica went out with the other varsity members and their families for an impromptu, celebratory dinner. As they ate, Grace realized that it felt right to have Tony there with them. He seemed as excited about Jessica's triumph as she and Jessica were.

He was becoming a part of their family, Grace thought. But she wasn't quite sure how she felt about that.

She was in love with him. The time had come to acknowledge that, at least to herself.

But was it the kind of love that would last? Or was it a short-term thing, fueled by great sex, that would burn itself out by the sheer blazing intensity of its heat?

Before she allowed Jessica to grow too attached to him, she had to make sure that Tony wasn't going to just go away when his investigation ended. She didn't want Jessica to be hurt.

She didn't want to be hurt.

On Friday, when Tony came to pick her up for lunch, he was frowning. One glance at him told her that something had happened.

"What's wrong?" she asked, as soon as she slid into his car and they were alone. He was wearing a charcoal-gray sweatshirt and jeans and, from the smoothness of his chin, had shaved within the last hour. He looked tired—he couldn't be getting more than three hours of sleep a day—and faintly grim.

He looked at her then, as he pulled the car out into traffic.

"We got the DNA results on the gum back from the lab this morning."

"That's good—isn't it?" A single glance at his face told her that the answer was negative. "What's wrong? Doesn't it help?"

"Whoever chewed that wad of gum has DNA that's compatible with yours."

"What?" For a moment Grace didn't understand. "What does that mean?"

"I mean the saliva that was tested could only have come from a relative of yours."

"What?" Grace felt panic, cold as ice water, start to flow through her veins.

"It's not Jessica. We compared the sample with the sample

we got from her. They're similar, but not a match. I want to take a sample from your other relatives. Jackie, for example, and' her children, and your father and his second batch of children."

"My father? But—we hardly have a relationship. You know that. I told you." Indeed, she had told him how her father, influenced by Deborah, had grown increasingly distant from her over the years. He lived in Minnesota with the three children he had fathered with his second wife and had, to all intents and purposes, forgotten about his oldest daughters. Grace was lucky to see him once a year. He would be hard put to pick Jessica out of a lineup. She barely knew her three half-siblings, who were all under twenty.

"Whoever chewed that gum is a close relative of yours. From what you told me, your only close relatives are Jessica, Jackie, her children, your father, and his children. Jessica's out; her sample is close, but not a match. That leaves the others as possible suspects, and I'm going to need a sample from each to determine which one it is."

Grace was so cold by now that she was surprised her teeth weren't chattering.

"Tony—Paul and Courtney are too young. They couldn't possibly have broken into my house and left that cake, for example."

"I don't really consider Paul and Courtney suspects."

"Who, then? Jackie? My father?"

They reached his house before he could answer. Tony parked at the curb, and as he came around the hood toward her Grace stepped out of the car into the bright sunshine of another beautiful fall day. It was warm for October, but she was freezing despite the black wool suit she wore. All around her the foliage blazed with brilliant colors. Falling leaves drifted lazily through the air, littering the streets and piling up on the lawns. A pair of gray squirrels chased each other through the yard across the street, chittering noisily as leaves swirled in their wake like rustling miniwhirlwinds. Mrs. Crutcher was in her yard, her gray hair curling tightly about her head, wearing what in the fifties would have been called a housedress as she raked her leaves into neat piles. Tony took Grace's hand, steering her past his nosy neighbor.

"Hi, Tony. Working again, I see."

"Always, Mrs. Crutcher. Always."

Grace was only vaguely aware of any of this. She felt as if she were in a dream. Nothing seemed quite real.

Except for that long ago January 21st.

Oh, God, she couldn't believe it. It made her sick to even consider the possibility. But it—almost—had to be true.

They were inside his house now, in his living room. Tony shut the door and turned to take her into his arms, which was their modus operandi for "lunch." But something in her expression stopped him. He frowned down at her.

"Grace . . ." His voice was sharp.

"Oh God, Tony. I need to sit down." Her knees felt as if they would buckle at any second. Her sensible two-inch heels suddenly felt like stilts; her ankles wobbled as she fought to keep her balance. He caught her elbows, his expression alarmed, and half carried her the few steps to the couch. Sinking down on it, she buried her face in her hands.

"What's the matter? Are you sick?" He hunkered down in front of her, one hand on her thigh. Although he sounded ready to resort to drastic measures, she could do no more than shake her head no.

"Jesus God, are you pregnant?"

This horrified question was enough to raise her head from her hands.

"No!"

"Then what?" He looked, and sounded, baffled and worried at the same time.

Grace took a deep breath. There was no help for it. She had to tell him.

"Tony." She stopped. Her throat closed up. She physically could not go on. For a moment she simply sat there, concentrating on remembering to breathe as she stared into his frowning eyes. If he was in love with her now, he wouldn't be when she finished talking, she knew.

She tried again. This time her vocal chords worked.

"I had—have—another child. A son."

There, it was out. The secret that she had guarded all her life, that she had meant to take with her to her grave. Just blurted out in the time it took to take a breath, just like that.

Something so momentous should have taken longer to say.

But now he knew.

His eyes narrowed on her face. Grace lifted her chin and met his gaze with challenge in her own. She had done what she had done. There was no changing the past now. If she was ashamed and regretful and sick with guilt and sorrow, she would die before she would let anyone know. The truth had to be shared, for Jessica's sake. The emotions were her own.

"You have a son?" Tony asked carefully, his eyes searching hers.

"Yes." Bald statements seemed to be all she could manage today, Grace thought. But she supposed she should be thankful that she could speak at all.

"Okay." He stood up abruptly, towering over her for an instant. Then he moved, scooping her up off the couch, and walked over to the shabby old recliner with her in his arms. Clinging to his shoulders was a reflex reaction on her part. She felt no pleasure in being in his arms. In fact, she felt nothing at all, except cold. She was so very, very cold.

"So talk to me," he said, sitting down with her on his lap. "I told you about Rachel. You tell me about this."

Grace sat stiffly in his hold, refusing to surrender to the warm comfort of his arms around her or the tempting proximity of a strong shoulder to lean on. Her story was different from his. In his, he was both hero and victim. In hers, she was the lowest of the low.

He would despise her when he knew. But she had to tell him, for Jessica's sake.

"I had a baby boy when I was a teenager and gave him up for

adoption." It seemed that all she could do was blurt out bald facts. If she said more, if she gave voice to the torment inside her, she feared that she would shatter into a million pieces, and like Humpty Dumpty, no one would ever be able to put her back together again.

"The chewing gum," he said, as if an issue that had troubled him was resolved.

Grace nodded jerkily. "It almost has to be him. I—I—there's something else I haven't told you."

He said nothing, merely lifted his eyebrows at her. He was sitting comfortably in the recliner, his head resting against the curved back, his gaze on her face, while she perched rigidly in the loose circle of his arms. She did not look at him fully, only glanced at him from time to time. Her arms were crossed over her chest to ward off the chill that threatened to freeze her blood. Her feet did not quite reach the floor. In the center of the room, golden sunlight streamed through the open curtains, dust motes dancing in its path. The corner where they sat was gloomy with shadows. The faint musty smell of the place warred with the scent of soap and clean clothes and man.

"On Monday morning, I picked the newspaper up off the doorstep. It has a . . . horoscope column on the comics page." She took a deep breath. "Three horoscopes were circled in red. Virgo—that's mine, August 30th. Pisces—that's Jessica, March 8th. And, and Capricorn. January 21st. My son was born on January 21st." She took a deep breath. "I suspected then, but I prayed it wasn't true. But it's obvious, isn't it? He's found me. God, he must hate me to do this!"

Grace closed her eyes, her fingers digging into her upper arms. Her grief was beyond tears. It was a dry, burning sorrow, so intense that she felt it as a physical pain, as though a giant fist were squeezing her heart.

His arms tightened around her, pulling her closer. Grace resisted for a moment, but then her spine went as limp as cooked spaghetti and she sagged against his chest, her head resting tiredly against his shoulder, her hands splaying against the front of his sweatshirt. She drew a deep, shuddering breath. It was an effort to fill her lungs.

"No one knows—but you," she said. His face was turned toward her so that she was looking up at him at an angle. Her gaze touched on the hard, clean lines of his features with a sense of loss. "All these years—I never told anyone. Not my father, not Jackie, not Jessica. No one. It was as if, once I gave him away, he ceased to exist. Except I could never forget that he did."

Tony's eyes darkened on her face, and he pressed his lips to her forehead in the kind of gentle kiss he might have bestowed on a hurt child. When he drew back, Grace's fingers curled in the folds of his sweatshirt, clutching it desperately.

"You want to talk about it?" he asked.

Grace shook her head because no, she didn't. But then she began to talk anyway, the words spilling out of their own volition.

CHAPTER **43**

"MY MOTHER DIED WHEN I WAS FOURTEEN. I loved her so—we were so close. I felt as if my whole world had been blasted to smithereens. I was angry. Angry at myself, for not being able to save her, angry at my father for living while she had died, angry at God, even angry at my mother for dying and leaving me. It was as if my life had lost its center. I just—went nuts. I got hooked up with a wild crowd and started drinking and partying and staying out late and doing anything and everything under the sun. Jackie was little, she didn't know what was going on, and I don't think she even remembers much about those years now. My father—my father remarried within a year of my mother's death and didn't have time for me. I was a huge source of trouble in our home. My stepmother hated me. To be fair, I hated her worse. My father sided with my stepmother in everything. Our house was in a constant state of warfare, and nothing they did made any difference to me: I was going to do what I wanted and to hell with the consequences. Then one night I went to a party and got so drunk I passed out. In the morning, when I came to, I was sprawled in the backseat of somebody's car, with no idea whose, or of how I got there. My clothes were all messed up, and I realized—I realized that someone had had sex with me while I was unconscious. I didn't remember anything about it, didn't know who or even how many. It bothered me enough so that I never got drunk again after that—but there was worse to come. It took a while—I was young and dumb in those days—but after about four months I realized I was pregnant."

Grace took a deep breath. "The truth is, if I had figured it out any sooner, I probably would have had an abortion. But it was too late. I was scared to death. Terrified. I knew my father would probably beat me half to death—he believed strongly in physical discipline, especially for me—and then disown me. My stepmother would gloat. All her predictions about the way I would end up had come true. I couldn't face them. When I was almost seven months pregnant and couldn't hide it any longer, I ran away. It was about a month before Christmas." She laughed mirthlessly. "Needless to say, I had a rude awakening into what life without a family was like. I had just what money I'd been able to save, a couple of hundred dollars, and nowhere to go. I couldn't face my friends. Their parents would have called my parents in any case. I walked the malls, looking at all the lights and decorations and crying because it was Christmas and I was all alone. I slept in cheap hotels for a while, and ate as little as I could, and still I got down to my last twenty dollars unbelievably fast. When I was almost at the end of my rope, I saw an ad for abortion alternatives in the newspaper, and I called it. They told me to come on in. I did, and they gave me a place to stay and, when the time came, delivered my baby." Grace stopped, swallowing. When she continued, her voice was low. "I never even held him. He was born, and they took him away. I signed papers consenting to his adoption, and that was that. The only reason I know he was a boy is because of something I overheard one of the nurses say."

She stopped again, and Tony's arms tightened around her. He didn't say anything, just held her close. After a moment she was able to go on.

"I went back home. I had nowhere else to go. I went back home and took my father's punishment for running away and finished high school—I only had a few months to go. I didn't want to party anymore, not ever again. I applied for loans, and got them, and went to college. I concentrated on studying and made top grades. I met Craig when I was a junior and married him the summer between my junior and senior years. Then Jessica was born. When I held her in my arms for the first time, that's when I really understood what I had done. I loved Jessica so much. I hadn't understood how much I would love a baby. Before Jessica, my son was—I guess you'd say an abstraction. He didn't seem real. There was so much fear and shame and pain surrounding his birth that I had just wanted to make it all go away. But after Jessica— after Jessica, I knew. From the moment they put her into my arms, I loved her from the bottom of my heart, and I knew what I had done in throwing away my son." She shuddered. "If I could do one thing over again in my life, it would be that. I would not have given away my child."

Her voice broke, and her eyes closed. Her throat ached with the pain of unshed tears, but still she did not cry. All the tears in the world could not wash away the pain she felt. She did not deserve the heart's ease of tears.

"Grace." Tony's voice was low, his arms warm and strong around her. She curled more tightly into his lap, wrapping her arms around his neck, ashamed of needing him so desperately but unable to help it. He knew the worst of her now, was seeing her emotionally naked, and she was terrified that he would find her ugly. If Tony wanted nothing more to do with her now that he knew, she would not blame him. He had loved his own daughter so, only to have her wrenched from his arms by fate. She had deliberately walked away from her son.

"Grace," he said again, when she did not respond. "I want you to think about this: What would have happened if you had kept your son? Realistically, now. What would you have done? Would you have gone back home?"

Grace shuddered. "No. I could never have gone home again. My father and stepmother would not have let me in the door."

"So you would have been on your own with an infant,

right? You, a teenager without a home or anyone to support you or even a high school diploma. Where would you have taken the baby? Back to one of those cheap hotel rooms? No, you were out of money. A homeless shelter? Maybe you could have applied for welfare and gotten it, although it takes awhile to get on the rolls. There you would have been: an unwed teenage mother without a high school diploma, surviving on welfare. And that's absolute best-case scenario."

His hand came up to stroke her cheek, and then a finger tilted up her chin. "Open your eyes, Grace, and look at me."

Unwillingly she did as he said. His eyes were warm with tenderness for her. Tenderness she did not deserve.

"I almost backed out of marrying Glenna, you know. I got cold feet at the last second and almost left her at the altar. If I hadn't married her, we wouldn't have had Rachel, and I would have been spared the pain of watching a child die by degrees. Rachel would have been spared all the agony that damnable disease put her through. But she—and I—also would have missed the greatest joy." He was looking at her intently. "The point is, we all come to forks in the road, and we all make our choices and live with them, for good or ill. If you had chosen to keep your son, you would not have had Jessica. You wouldn't be the woman you are today. You came to a fork in the road, and you made the best choice you could at the time, under the circumstances you were faced with and using the information you had. You have nothing to beat yourself up over."

"Oh, God, Tony, what kind of mother gives a baby up for adoption?" It was a cry from the heart.

Callused fingertips stroked the underside of her jaw. "A very young and frightened one, in your case. Grace, do you know what first attracted me to you? I loved the way you were with Jessica. I loved the way you were ready to take on the whole world, including me and the whole damned police bureaucracy, for her. I loved the way you loved her, so fierce and protective and yet, gentle, too. You're a great mother, Grace. A wonderful mother. Just because you made a hard choice when you weren't much older than Jessica is now doesn't take away from that. You did the best you could, and that's all any of us can do."

Grace looked deep into his eyes and was comforted by what she saw there. The lump in her throat was still present and still painful. But the horrible ache in her chest was easing, slowly, by infinitesimal degrees.

"I love you, Tony Marino," she said clearly. And then, to her own surprise, she burst into tears.

CHAPTER 44

I T WAS PROVING HARDER TO TRACK DOWN GRACE'S
son than Tony had anticipated. He was at his desk in the squad
room later that afternoon, squinting at his blinking computer
screen and coming up with zilch. The fact that the baby had been
born in a private clinic was slowing things down. Tony could find
no record of his birth. There was, simply, no baby boy Douglas,
which was Grace's maiden name, listed as being born on the
correct date in Franklin County, where Grace said he had been
born.

Tony didn't even consider the possibility that Grace had gotten some of the vital information wrong. The events surrounding
the birth of the child were seared into her soul.

He would find the kid, though. Now that he knew what he
was looking for, it was just a matter of doing a little police work.
Since he'd come up dry with the birth certificate, his next stop
would be adoption records. Sooner or later, he would hit pay dirt.

The question was, what would he do with the kid when he
found him? Grace would not prosecute the boy, Tony knew. In
fact, she was likely to prostrate herself at his feet, begging for
forgiveness.

The kid had to have some major problems to have done the
things he had done, from breaking into Grace's house to killing

Jessica's hamster. And he was probably harboring a major resentment against Grace as well.

As he thought of the hell Grace had been through, not just recently but during years of condemning herself for what she had done, Tony felt a slow-building anger start to burn inside him. If the kid gave Grace any more grief, his first inclination would be to throttle him, poor abandoned baby or not.

Tony foresaw trouble with a capital *T* when the kid was found. Grace would be in anguish, Jessica—who would have to be told—would be thrown into even more turmoil, and the kid himself sounded like the next Ted Bundy.

He meant to pay a call on Grace's son and do his best to put the fear of God in the kid, before ever telling Grace where he was. Terroristic threatening was the least of the charges he would threaten the kid with, if he didn't behave.

Funny enough, he never even considered the fact that, once the criminal aspect of the case was over, it was really not his problem. If it affected Grace and Jessica, it affected him.

My girls.

His mouth quirked into an ironic half-smile. That's what they were to him, he realized. His girls, mother and daughter. His. Funny how his life seemed to be coming full circle.

Grace had told him she loved him. After that, she'd been too busy crying and he'd been too busy mopping up her tears to have any rational discussion at all. With her sense of duty, Grace had of course insisted on keeping that damned one o'clock deadline.

Tonight they were going to have quite a talk.

"How's it coming?" Gary Sandifer was standing beside his desk, looking down at the computer screen, which was trolling automatically through adoption records looking for a baby boy adopted in Franklin County within a year of the birth date of Grace's son. The child had been born in Franklin County and obviously still lived here, or he would not be able to prey on Grace as he had been doing. It was not much of a stretch to assume the adoption had taken place in Franklin County, so Tony included that in the parameters he had typed into the search program.

"It's coming," Tony said noncommittally. Without even really thinking about it, he came to the lightning decision that Grace's secret was going to stay just that: a secret, at least as far as the department was concerned. He would locate the kid, put the fear of God into him, haul him off to counseling, do whatever it took to make things easier for Grace. As far as the department was concerned, the investigation would be wound up with a "perp unknown" designation.

Nobody would care. The department had bigger fish to fry than the hamster-murdering stalker of a local judge and her daughter.

"I can give you maybe another week, at best," Sandifer said, shaking his head apologetically. "Then I'm going to have to pull you guys off."

"You already working on Voss?" Tony asked. Tied up with this investigation, he felt like a kid in a school classroom, sitting impatiently as he waited for the dismissal bell to ring so he would be free to do what he really wanted to do. In this case, that was to get Voss.

"We're getting started."

Tony grimaced. Knowing how he felt about Voss, Sandifer patted him on the shoulder.

"I don't think we'll get him in a week," he said consolingly, and headed for his office.

Fifty-five baby boys of approximately the right age had been adopted in Franklin County during the time frame Tony was looking at. He had not expected that there would be so many. Printing out the list, he folded it, tucked it into his pocket, and then stood up. Grunt work was what it would take to run all those kids down, but then, grunt work was, by and large, what he did.

But not right now. It was four-thirty and he had to be heading home.

There were four or five girls playing basketball in the driveway when, having parked his car in its customary spot two streets over, he let himself in through the side gate. They did not notice him as he walked across the yard, which was ankle deep in fallen leaves. To Tony's surprise, he saw that Jessica was not among them. He was still pondering the implications of that as he entered the house.

Jessica and Gloria Baer were in the kitchen. Gloria was standing with both hands flat on the countertop, looking at Jessica with concern, while Jessica, face abnormally pale, sat on a bar stool sipping orange juice. The dogs were sprawled at her feet. They came toward Tony, toenails clicking, tails wagging.

"Hi, Tony." Gloria looked around at him almost with relief. Hers was a tough job, babysitting Jessica during the day. With an inward grin, Tony conceded that he would far rather have his own task of babysitting Jessica's mother.

Of course, even if Gloria *had* been assigned to watch over Grace, she would not have gotten nearly as much enjoyment out of it as he was getting.

"Is there a problem?" Tony patted both dogs and looked at Jessica.

Jessica made a face. Her eyes met his and then slid away. "Nothing major. I just forgot to take my insulin this morning. My blood sugar got a little low."

"She looked like she was going to faint out there playing basketball," Gloria said severely.

"Did you call her mother?" Tony asked Gloria.

"No! *No!*" Jessica's reply was sharp. "I told her not to call my mother, and you're not to either, Tony, do you hear? I took my insulin, and I'll drink this orange juice, and I'll be fine. Just leave my mother out of it."

Tony said nothing for a moment. The ridiculous colored streak in her hair was lime green today, he saw, which had the effect of making her eyes seem very blue. She really looked an awful lot like her mother, Tony thought, which would have endeared Jessica to him even if he had not grown to appreciate her for herself.

"Fine," he said mildly, and hung his jacket on the coatrack before opening the refrigerator door to help himself to an orange juice, too.

Since Tony's advent rendered her off duty, and she seemed to sense trouble brewing, Gloria left with a quick good-bye. Jessica drained the last drops of her orange juice and eyed him with some resentment.

"You're going to tell Mom, aren't you?" she demanded.

Tony sighed, and rested a hip against the counter opposite where she sat as he chugged his orange juice. "Don't start, Jess. You know I have to. You don't want people telling your mother you didn't take your insulin, then take your insulin. It's as simple as that."

Jessica glowered at him. "God, I hate this damned disease!" she burst out.

"You don't know how lucky you are to have it."

"What?" Jessica stared at him in disbelief.

He nodded. "Yeah. Lucky. You know why? Because it's treatable. All you have to do is take your insulin when you're supposed to, and watch what you eat, and you'll be fine."

"And that makes me *lucky*?"

Tony looked at her for a long moment. Then he said, "Did I ever tell you about Rachel? My daughter? No? Well, I had a daughter. She would be about your age if she had lived, but she didn't. She died when she was eleven years old. She had cystic fibrosis. Now there's a disease that's not treatable. She hated cystic fibrosis just like you hate diabetes, but there was nothing she—or I—could do. No treatment could save her. I would have given anything I possessed—everything I possessed—my life, even, without a second's hesitation, if we could have treated her disease with two shots a day and a special diet."

He broke off. Jessica stared at him, wide-eyed. After a moment he managed a crooked smile. "So, you see, you're lucky. So damned lucky."

"Tony, I'm sorry." Jessica looked appalled.

Tony nodded and took another swig of his orange juice.

"Does Mom know?"

Tony nodded again. It was funny, he reflected, the more he talked about Rachel the easier it became. It still hurt, but he no longer felt he might die from the pain.

"Tony?"

"Hmmm?"

"You like Mom, don't you?"

Immediately he felt a little wary—Jessica and Grace had been alone together for a long time, and who knew how she might feel about the addition of a third party, even one she liked as much as she did him—but he nodded.

"Have you ever thought about—well, maybe dating her, or something?"

Tony cocked an eyebrow at her and did his best to keep his face suitably bland. "You wouldn't mind?"

Jessica shook her head. "Some of the guys she dates, if she married them, I'd have to run away from home. You'd be okay, though."

This time Tony knew his face was anything but bland. He was amused, surprised, curious, even a little touched, and there was no way to hide all that. "Are you by any chance trying to marry your mom off?"

Jessica shrugged. "Not to just anybody. But—I'm a freshman in high school. In four years, I'll be going away to college. I hate to think of going off and leaving Mom all alone. I wouldn't mind so much if she had somebody like you."

"You *are* trying to marry your mom off!" Tony couldn't help it. He grinned from ear to ear, picturing what Grace's reaction would be if she could hear this conversation.

"You're not going to tell her, are you?" Jessica looked suddenly anxious.

Tony laughed out loud. "Now, would I tell your mother that her daughter practically proposed to me on her behalf?" He shook his head. "I appreciate the thought, though, Jess. I really do."

As it happened, Jessica's friends stayed until supper time, and then Jackie and her children stopped by and ate with them. Used to the casual closeness of his own large family, Tony accepted the presence of Grace's sister and children philosophically. The only problem was, he had no chance to have any private conversation with Grace. He hadn't even managed to kiss her hello.

After Jackie and her brood left, Grace and Jessica chatted as they cleaned up the kitchen. Watching them from his spot on the couch in front of the TV, Tony was struck once again by what a good relationship they really had.

As he had told Jessica earlier, she was lucky.

Kramer and Chewie were at the back door, wanting out. He got up and opened it, and they streaked across the backyard, barking in furious answer to the yapping of a dog down the street. Tony glanced up at the clock over the pantry. It was five minutes after ten o'clock.

On a Friday night, Jessica could stay up as late as she chose.

Here he was, dying to get Grace alone, and it looked as if it wasn't going to happen, at least not any time soon if the way mother and daughter were gabbing was any indication.

Wasn't that the way life always worked?

"I'm going to take out the trash," he said, heading for the full trash can on the far side of the refrigerator.

Grace nodded, so caught up in something Jessica was saying that he wasn't even sure she heard. With a wry smile, Tony reflected that he felt like the father in a family sitcom, kind of third-wheelish.

But it was good to feel like part of a family again.

He pulled the plastic liner from the can, knotted the top of it, and set it down while he put in a fresh liner. Then he picked up the bag of trash and headed out the door.

Kramer and Chewie were over behind the garage, snuffling at something. It was impossible to tell what it was in the dark. Tony dropped the trash bag in the big metal garbage can in the garage and went to investigate. It was a beautiful night, warm and clear, with a huge orange moon hanging low in the sky and thousands of twinkling stars spiraling around it. Indian summer. He loved it. It was his favorite season of the year.

Rachel had died in an Indian summer.

The memory brought bittersweet sadness with it. She had loved Indian summer, too.

When he returned to the house, he was going to march Grace and Jessica out into the backyard so that they could enjoy the beauty of the night.

If he had learned nothing else in his life, he had learned the importance of squeezing all the goodness possible out of each day.

The dogs were whining and pawing at something in the shadow of the garage. It was darker there, so dark that Tony could not quite make out what they had found. Whatever it was had not been in the backyard earlier, he was certain.

The object lying in the grass at the base of the garage wall was black and sort of cylindrical and large, more than five feet long. Frowning, Tony realized that he was looking at something wrapped in the same kind of oversized garbage bag he had just deposited in the garage, with duct tape wrapped around it, striping it with gray every few feet.

Then Kramer hit pay dirt. His paw ripped through the plastic—and what looked like an overstuffed white glove flopped out. Both dogs snuffled at it, whining.

To his horror, Tony realized that he was looking at a pale, bloated human hand, still attached to its arm.

Alarm bells went off like gangbusters in his mind. The hairs rose on the back of his neck. Kramer looked around, snarling at something just beyond him even as Tony whirled, reaching for his gun—

Something that felt like a baseball bat hit him with the force of a home run–caliber swing right in the side of the head, and stars exploded before his eyes. Then everything went black.

CHAPTER **45**

K ILLING HIS MOM WAS FUN. HE HAD MEANT TO
do it later that night, do the whole family at once after his dad got
in from Indianapolis and Donny came home from handing out
more flyers about Caroline being missing. But at about nine
o'clock, his mom caught him eating the rice pudding she had
made for his dad, just like he had done the week before. She had a
major cow, screaming that somebody as fat and zit-faced as he was
had no business eating sweets.

He walked into his bedroom, got his dad's pistol from where
he had hidden it under his bed, and returned to the kitchen with
it. Man, had she shut up fast when she saw the gun. Her mouth
had popped open like a fish's, her hand had clutched her throat,
and she'd said his name in this weird kind of voice that told him
she knew what he was going to do.

" 'Bye, Mom," he said, and shot the ugly bitch right in the
face.

Of course, she was even uglier after that.

She'd bled like the pig she was. In a matter of minutes,
there'd been a big puddle on the kitchen floor where her head
rested. There were splatters on the walls, too, kind of like spaghetti sauce with mushrooms and noodles in it. He couldn't have
that, couldn't leave the mess although he didn't feel like cleaning

it up, because he didn't want Donny and his father to realize what was going down until it was their turn to bite the big one.

He got a bunch of towels from the linen closet, wrapped a couple around his mom's head—on second thought, maybe she did look better with only half a face—and then wrapped trash bags around that. He'd already discovered how handy trash bags were for streamlining the handling of a dead body. He had wrapped Caroline in trash bags before he'd stashed her in the basement freezer of a neighboring family that had gone on vacation—he would retrieve her tonight, and leave her in the house with the rest of them. Caroline had frozen up real good, kind of like hamburger. He'd checked on her a couple of times, and she didn't even stink.

Killing his mom first had kind of upset his schedule, though. He'd meant to off the judge lady and her daughter first, and then come home and do his mom and dad and Donny while they slept. But his mom had really pissed him off. He was fucking tired of being called fat.

Bundling the body in more garbage bags, then wrapping duct tape around it in strategic areas so the bags wouldn't separate, he pondered what difference this slight change would make in his plans. Finally, as he wiped up the blood on the floor and on the walls with his mom's best towels—boy, would that piss her off if she knew—he concluded that, like everything else that had happened, killing his mom first had probably been for the best.

Still, what if the cops were too damned dumb to connect the murdered mother and daughter in Bexley with his own murdered family in Upper Arlington? After watching them screw around with his modest little forays into the judge lady's house over the last few weeks, and then try to solve the mystery of Caroline's disappearance, he wasn't too impressed with their intelligence. It was, he thought, entirely possible that they might miss the connection.

But not if he left his mom's body in the judge lady's house as a calling card.

Smiling, he picked his mom up—the fat pig weighed like

lead—slung her over his shoulder, and carried her out to her car, which was parked in the attached garage. It was a new car, a Maxima, and his mom loved it. She would never let him drive it, though she loaned it to Donny every time he asked.

He would drive it tonight, and she would ride in the backseat, dead.

He went back into the house to stuff pillows under the covers on her side of the bed so that it would look, to anyone like Donny who might casually check, as though their mom was asleep in bed. Then he took the keys to the Maxima from her purse, grabbed a couple of dollars in case he ran low on gas, got the gun, and picked up the bag he had already stocked with the other items he needed for tonight.

Finally he got in the car and drove away. He'd had to bend his mom's legs to make her fit in the backseat. Too bad she was dead. He liked to think about how uncomfortable she would be.

At the judge lady's house, instead of parking a few blocks away as he usually did with his motorcycle, he parked on the next street over so that he'd just have to go through the front and rear yards of the house that backed up to hers before climbing over the fence into her yard. By now, he knew the lay-out around here as well as he knew his own neighborhood. He felt a pang of regret as he reflected that this was the last time he'd have reason to visit the judge lady's house. It had been almost a year since he had discovered her identity with the help of an Internet search group dedicated to reuniting adoptee's with their biological parents. In that period of time, watching her and her kid had almost turned into his hobby, or something. Oh, well, all good things must come to an end, he thought.

Getting out of the car, he glanced through the windows and realized that his mom's body was too easy to see on the backseat. All anyone had to do was peer in—even wrapped in garbage bags, the bundle looked odd enough that it might prompt a call to police.

He hadn't realized that the streetlight on the corner provided so much illumination. For a moment he considered moving the car. Then he decided he'd just take his mom with him. He'd meant to come back for her anyway, so he'd just be lugging the body to the house a little earlier than he'd planned.

Man, she was heavy. He stuck the gun into his jacket pocket—well, Donny's jacket pocket—and hoisted her onto his shoulder, after first making sure that there was no one around. In just a few minutes he was safe in the dark, out of reach of the street lamp's illumination, just him and the moon and the stars and the rustling leaves underfoot and the creaking branches overhead.

Bexley was really a lovely community, he thought. Almost as nice as Upper Arlington.

Somewhere not too far away, a dog began to bark. The little yappy dog he'd heard almost every time he'd visited the judge lady's house.

Tonight he might do the universe a favor and off the dog, too.

When he got to the fence around the judge lady's backyard, he lowered his mom to the ground on the other side—he was afraid that just dropping her might split the plastic bags open and leave him with another mess to clean up—and then climbed it himself.

Most of the windows in the judge lady's house were lighted up. He wondered what she and Jessica were doing in there. Well, he'd know pretty soon.

His plan was simple. The security system they'd installed meant nothing to him; changing the locks wasn't even going to slow him down. And the judge lady's cop boyfriend? Piece of cake.

They didn't turn the security system on until bedtime. He knew because he'd been watching through the windows ever since they'd gotten it put in.

And he wouldn't need a key, because he was going to do the one thing they'd never expect.

Knock on the door. And when they answered it—which

one of them would, because people everywhere always answered their doors just like there was a law that they had to or something—were they ever going to get a surprise.

Knock, knock. You're dead.

He smiled at the thought.

CHAPTER **46**

" "H E'S REALLY NICE, MOM. I THINK HE'S GOING
to ask me out. If he does, can I go? Please?"

Grace looked at her daughter, who was wiping off the table
while she herself loaded the dishwasher. Jessica was wearing jeans
and a black sweatshirt with the sleeves pushed up past her elbow,
and her eyes were wide with entreaty.

Was fifteen really old enough to date? Intellectually Grace
knew it was, but in her heart and mind Jessica was still a little girl.
But, as Tony would say, time to let the little girl grow up.

"We'll see," Grace temporized. Tony or no, there was no
point in crossing that bridge until they actually came to it. But
when it came right down to it, she guessed she would let Jessica
go.

"Mom! . . ."

A frantic scratching sounded at the back door. Jessica turned
to open it, and Chewie bounded in. While Grace and Jessica both
watched with amazement, the pup scuttled across the kitchen
toward the stairs like a grizzly bear was after him, ears flat and tail
between his legs.

"What on earth? . . ." Mother and daughter exchanged
bemused glances. Closing the door, Jessica hurried after her dog.

"Chewie! Chewie! Here, Chewie!"

Jessica vanished into the hall, and seconds later Grace heard her footsteps pounding up the stairs.

Frowning, she closed the dishwasher, then headed toward the kitchen door. Tony was in the backyard. . . .

The door opened before she had taken more than three steps. For an instant, Grace felt relief, thinking that Tony was coming in. Then she froze as she realized that the person who stood there was not Tony.

He was a young man of perhaps seventeen, wearing a Chicago Bulls baseball cap, a black nylon jacket with some kind of school insignia on it, and jeans. Stocky in build, he was about five-ten, with short black hair and a square pale face with acne on his chin.

He was carrying a gun, a gleaming silver pistol, the mouth of which was pointed straight at her heart.

Grace knew who he was, knew it instantly. Her blood froze, her heart contracted, and though she tried to draw in air her lungs refused to expand.

"S-son," she croaked. One hand covered her mouth as the other reached out to him in instinctive entreaty.

The horror of the moment, the hideous perfection of a fate that brought her abandoned son back to her armed with a gun, was something she had subconsciously expected since she had seen those circled horoscopes, Grace realized. Or maybe even longer than that, perhaps from the very moment when she had given birth to him and then given him away, on that long-ago January 21st.

Retribution at last.

He smiled, a slow taunting smile, and stepped on into the kitchen, closing the door softly behind him.

"Hi, there, Mommy," he said, his voice low and husky. Her son's voice, she thought dazedly. She was hearing her son's voice for the first time. She was looking at her son, hearing his voice, and he was going to kill her.

That's what he had come to do, she knew instinctively. And she deserved it, for what she had done. She wouldn't even try to run away.

He came toward her, the gun leveled at her middle. "Mommy, Daddy's out there in the backyard with his skull split open. The family dog, too, what a shame!"

Tony. Oh, no. Tony didn't deserve to die for this. This was her sin alone, no one else's. Only she deserved to pay. . . .

He reached her then, roughly grabbing her shoulder with the hand that wasn't holding the gun, his short, blunt fingers digging into her flesh in a way that would have hurt if she had been capable of feeling physical pain. But she was beyond that. Her body was numb with shock.

She looked up into his face and saw, as she had expected, that his eyes were blue.

"Where's little sis?"

Jessica. Jessica. He had come for Jessica, too. No. No. . . .

"No!" she screamed. Galvanized by terror for her daughter, she shoved him with all her might. Caught by surprise, he stumbled backward, almost falling on the slippery wood. Whirling, she ran for her daughter's life.

"Mom?" Jessica called from the top of the stairs. Jess was already on her way down, Grace saw, as she darted into the hall.

"Run, Jess, run!" Grace cried, flying up the stairs. Her terror was instantly communicated to her daughter. Jessica's face changed, and then she was running, too, leaping for the upstairs hall while Grace bounded after her. Just as Grace reached the top of the stairs, she heard him behind her. Glancing down, she saw her son in the hall, the gun he held pointed straight at her back.

"Mom! Mom!" Jessica was inside her room, holding onto the edge of the door, waiting for her. . . .

He fired. As she lunged toward Jessica, Grace felt the bullet whiz by her ear. It hit the wall with a sound like a hand smacking flesh. The echo of the explosion rang in her ears.

Jessica screamed. There was another scream, and Grace realized that she was screaming, too.

She leaped through Jessica's door, and her daughter slammed it shut and locked it.

It would hold him off for only a moment, Grace knew.

CHAPTER 47

R AINDROPS FROM HEAVEN. THAT WAS THE FIRST
conscious thought that ran through Tony's mind as icy-cold droplets sprinkled over his face. His eyes blinked open, and immediately a blinding pain made him close them again. The whole right
side of his head felt as if it were on fire. Just opening his eyes made
his head hurt so badly that he almost passed out.

More freezing raindrops splattered on his skin. Tony gritted
his teeth and opened his eyes again. It was night, a moonlit, clear
night with nary a cloud in the sky. Warm, too, with no more than
a gentle breeze stirring the leaves that lay on the ground. How,
then, was cold rain falling on his head?

He looked up, straight up past the dark, shadowy eave of the
garage roof, into the tangled branches of a nearly leafless oak tree
overhead. The droplets appeared to be blowing down from the
tree.

But there had been no rain for the last few days, so how
could that be? And why were they landing just on and around
him, as though he had his own personal rain cloud, although there
was no such thing that he could see.

It hurt to think. His eyes closed again, and he sank back
toward oblivion with a feeling of relief.

A muffled sound, like a car backfiring or a firecracker going off some distance away, broke into his slide into unconsciousness. It spoke to him urgently, and he struggled to make sense of it despite the overriding pain in his head.

A gunshot. From somewhere in the mists of memory, identification sprang.

Right on its heels came terror.

Terror was a tangible thing, cold like steel, sharp as a knife sliding through flesh, he discovered. He felt it lodge in his heart.

My girls. The phrase popped into his brain. Blurry images, a woman and a girl. The first pair were a young, pretty brunette and a black-haired toddler with huge, haunted eyes. They were swallowed up by darkness, and he was conscious of an aching sense of loss. The second pair, another woman, with short blond-streaked hair and worried blue eyes, and a rail-thin teenage girl who looked like the woman, stayed in his mind's eye. He got the feeling that the darkness threatened them, too.

My girls. A gunshot.

Abruptly Tony remembered. Grace's son. The dead hamster. The cake. The mirror. The teddy bear. He'd screwed up, thinking the kid was harmless. The kid was here, now, this moment, in the house with Grace and Jessica, and meaning to kill.

Tony moved, and pain exploded inside his skull. He kept moving, rolling onto his side, knowing that it was urgent that he get into the house and stop what was happening before it was too late, before Grace and Jessica were swallowed up by the same darkness that had stolen Rachel from him.

Rachel. He could almost see her. For a moment her image was so real that she seemed to be flesh and blood again, standing there in the darkness beside him, looking down at him. She was rendered in exquisite detail, her delicate, fine-boned face pale with illness, her wide mouth smiling a little, lips together, the ends of her long black hair stirring in the breeze. She was wearing the white smocked dress she'd been buried in. Her eyes locked with his, and she seemed to extend a hand to him as though she would help pull him to his feet.

"Rachel?" he choked out. But of course she didn't answer, because of course she wasn't really there. She couldn't be.

Tony never knew afterward how he got upright, but he did, compelled by the image standing before him. Once on his feet, he staggered sideways until his shoulder hit the garage wall, gaping at his daughter as a thousand and one agony-spewing grenades seemed to go off inside his head. The pain was hideous, unbearable almost, but he scarcely noticed because Rachel was there. His vision blurred, from pain or tears he didn't know, and when he could see again she was gone, vanished as though she had never been there at all. Which of course she hadn't been. He knew that, but still, for just a moment, he could have sworn . . .

He had no time to dwell on it, though, no time to look for Rachel, or to mourn her loss. He had to get into the house. That was the one driving thought that kept him from passing out again. Grace's life was at stake, Grace's and Jessica's. He knew it as surely as if someone had shouted the warning into his ear.

He did not think he could bear to lose another person that he loved.

Pushing off from the garage wall like a swimmer from the side of a pool, he staggered toward the house, passing Kramer whose poor limp body lay near the passageway. His eyes touched on the dog, a brown-and-white fur rug sprawled on his side in the grass, but he could not stop to check whether or not Kramer still lived. As he neared the door, he reached for the gun that he always stashed in the back waistband of his jeans and was both surprised and not surprised to discover that it was not there. The kid had taken it.

Grace's son.

She would not want him to kill her son.

He might have to.

God, he couldn't even walk straight. Whatever the kid had hit him with, he was hurt bad. He could feel blood pouring down his face, warm and sticky, with a noxious sweetish smell that he recognized.

Three doorknobs instead of one. Concentrating, Tony grabbed for the one in the middle. Bingo.

The effort of turning the knob was so great that he broke out in a cold sweat.

But he turned the knob, and the door opened, and he was inside the kitchen, watching the fat red drops of his blood splatter onto the hardwood floor almost abstractedly, as though it wasn't his blood at all. From upstairs, he heard a rhythmic jarring thud, almost like the beat of a giant drum. *Thud*—pause, one two three—*thud*—pause one two three—*thud*—

The kid was trying to break in a door. Grace and Jessica must have locked themselves in a bedroom. Good for them. That gave him a little extra time.

He was too broken, too weak, to bound up the stairs and take down the sniveling little turd like he wanted to do. He could barely walk, barely see, and his blood was splashing down all around him like rain.

The dining room. In the closet was the security system with its panic button feature that would call the cavalry, and Grace's gun. The bullets were on top of the china cabinet. He had put them there himself.

Now if he could just stay conscious long enough to reach the dining room . . .

Everything was spinning around him. Floor and wall were tilting crazily, and he felt like he was caught up in that old Fred Astaire dance scene where Fred tapped merrily across the walls and ceiling as well as the floor.

Gritting his teeth—God, it hurt to do that!—and concentrating fiercely, Tony lurched from the kitchen through the door that led into the dining room. Grabbing the table for support as his knees threatened to buckle, he took a deep breath. Pain like a knife stabbing through his lungs told him that he probably had a few broken ribs. The kid must have worked him over good. . . .

Fool, he called himself bitterly for not having been more careful. He lurched toward the closet in the corner.

The rhythmic thudding continued upstairs.

His hand was slippery with blood, he discovered with surprise as he tried to grip the closet doorknob. Swiping his palm over his jeans, he tried again. The knob turned, the door came open, and he almost fell on the wall that held the keypad. A thin plastic cover protected the panic button. Leaning heavily against the wall, he clawed at it. It came open.

Crash! The sound of splintering wood. Screams, high and shrill. Grace. Jessica. The kid had broken into the room. . . .

His finger found and pressed the panic button. Once, twice, three times for good measure. Then, summoning all his dwindling resources, he reached up toward the shelf where he had hidden the gun.

CHAPTER **48**

J ESSICA WAS ALREADY OUT THE WINDOW WHEN THE
door crashed open and Grace's son burst into the room. Chewie,
who stood beside Grace, began barking hysterically, his tail low,
the hair on his spine standing up so that he looked like a razor-
back hog.

From the roof, Jessica screamed like a siren, over and over
again, in automatic, instinctive reaction, Grace knew.

"Go, Jess!" Grace cried. Instead of following her daughter
outside, she slammed the window shut and turned to face her son.
To get to Jessica, he would first have to go through her.

The lamp was lit beside the bed. Its cheerful yellow glow
provided the room's only illumination. Outside the window, the
night was incongruously beautiful, alight with moon and stars.
Jessica would be scrambling across the roof to safety. . . .

Chewie continued to bark ferociously, for all the good it did.

"Got you, Mommy," her son said, loud so that he could be
heard above the dog, pointing the gun at her. Grace's heart leaped
in her chest. She did not want to die. . . . He smiled. "Bang,
bang."

Grace threw herself to the floor just as he squeezed the trigger for real. The bullet slammed into the wall where she had been
standing. Plaster exploded outward, tiny bits of it striking Grace's

cheek. Chewie yelped, and darted behind Jessica's pink tweed chair. Grace wished that she could find safety so easily. The bed shielded her for these few seconds, but he would be upon her in an instant and then . . .

She would die. What would happen to Jess? Craig, and more particularly Craig's new wife, wouldn't want her, but he was her father. Jessica would go to him and be resentful and miserable and, most likely, impossible to control. Would the whole grim cycle start all over again?

Please, God, no.

Grace saw his shadow coming first, looming larger on the wall where the bullet had hit. Chewie must have seen it, too, because he started to bark again, hysterically. Grace tried to wedge herself under the bed, but the frame was too low and she didn't quite fit. For an instant she considered pulling the dust ruffle over her head and cowering beneath it, but he knew where she was. She couldn't hide.

Her breathing was rapid, shallow. Her heart was beating so fast she could feel it pounding in her chest. She broke out in a cold sweat as she turned over to face . . .

Her son. And, through him, her own death.

She took a deep breath and stared up at him as he came around the end of the bed. There was a weird smile on his face and, she thought, hatred for her in his eyes. She was lying on the plush rose carpet at his feet, lying helplessly, looking up at him as he pointed the gun at her chest. Any second, he was going to pull the trigger and she would die with the sound of the gunshot that killed her and the dog's high-pitched barks ringing in her ears.

Suddenly, like a film speeding at fast forward through her head, she remembered the day that he had been born. The fear, the pain, the newborn's mewling cry. Like Jessica, he was her baby. Her child. Flesh of her flesh, bone of her bone. Her son.

And he was going to kill her.

Jessica. The window was opening behind her son, silently, carefully. Jessica's foot and lower leg, clad in a sneaker and baggy, raggedly hemmed jeans, appeared.

No, Grace wanted to scream, realizing that her daughter was coming back to try to aid her. Jessica was sliding through the window. . . .

Thank God for Chewie. His hysterical barking masked any sounds.

"You don't want to do this," Grace said loudly to her son, wanting to make sure he stayed focused on her. Her nerves had suddenly turned to ice, she was no longer afraid to die, no longer afraid at all except for Jessica, who was in the room now. He would kill Jess.

"Sure I do, Mommy. You ruined my life." He was speaking loudly, too. "Did you know that? You ruined my life. Little Brother. Second best. Not good enough. That was me, always. Because of what you did."

"I'm sorry," Grace said, and meant it. She stared up at the gun, and her son, and prayed that Jessica would slip out of the room and just leave her to her fate. The fate she had always felt she deserved.

But she knew, as well as she knew her own name, that Jessica would not leave.

"Sorry don't catch it this time," he said. His arm straightened as he aimed the gun. Of their own accord, Grace's teeth clenched and her muscles stiffened as she prepared for the slam of the bullet into her body. "I don't have time to talk to you anymore. I've got to go catch little sis. I figure if I go back through the house, I'll just about be in time to watch her coming down that ladder-thing on the garage, like she's done before. So say night-night, Mommy."

His finger tightened on the trigger. Grace watched it with horror, feeling as though everything was happening in slow motion now. She screamed, rolling toward the wall, just as a flash of blue—Jessica—appeared behind him. Rolling, she caught quick glimpses of Jessica's hand clutching something as it rose high above his head and slammed down into his back. He screamed, the sound high-pitched, surprised. The gun exploded, and a bullet thudded into the carpet not half an inch from Grace's nose. He grabbed at his back and whirled on Jessica. The gun tumbled to the ground.

With his back turned to her, Grace could see the hypodermic needle still sticking out of the meaty part of his neck.

Jessica had stabbed him with her own insulin syringe.

"You bitch! You fucking little bitch!" He screamed, cursing, as one hand snatched the syringe from his neck and the other grabbed Jessica. She was screaming now, too, clawing at his face. Chewie, still barking, apparently emboldened by Jessica's peril, darted from behind the chair to grab the hem of one of his jeans-clad legs. He kicked the dog off, with one hard, vicious jerk of his leg, and Chewie slammed into the wall with a yelp. Jessica screamed again as he threw the syringe to the floor. Her scream ended in a choking gurgle as he locked both hands around her throat.

Grace snatched up the gun he had dropped and fired. Just like that, with no time to think.

Boom! The gun exploded. For a moment everything seemed to freeze in a hideous tableau: Jessica, blue eyes huge, clawing at the hands wrapped around her neck, gasping for breath; her son, choking the life from his sister, a curse on his lips; and herself, on her back on the carpet, holding the gun in both hands. Then a red stain burst onto the back of his black jacket between his shoulder blades and spread.

Slowly, slowly, his fingers opened. His hands dropped away from Jessica's throat, and, like a toppling tree, he fell to the carpet.

For a moment no one moved. The last echoes of Jessica's scream, like the sound of the gunshot, died away.

Then Grace, on hands and knees, scrambled to her son's side.

CHAPTER 49

Tony SURVEYED THE CARNAGE FROM THE DOOR-
way, where he leaned heavily against the jamb. He'd arrived, gun
in hand, just a split second after the kid had been shot, in time to
watch as he released Jessica, and tumbled to the floor.

He couldn't see Grace, and his heart gave a great, terrified
leap. Then she scrambled out from behind the bed, on all fours,
reaching the kid and turning him over, her face as white as Ivory
soap.

Of course she would feel bad, killing the kid. But it sure beat
having it happen the other way around.

Jessica crouched beside her, an arm around her mother's
shoulders. The two exchanged a quick hug, and then Grace said
something to Jessica as she placed two fingers beneath the kid's
ear. Checking for his pulse, Tony surmised.

Knowing himself no longer needed, since the damsels in
distress had managed to save themselves without his help, he
sagged to his knees, still clutching the jamb to keep from pitching
flat on his face on the floor. A trail of smeared blood was left on
the white paint of the door frame in the wake of his slide, he
noticed with woozy disinterest. Chewie appeared from somewhere, limping toward him on three legs, his left rear foot held off
the floor, his tail wagging faintly nonetheless.

Tony dared not let go of the jamb to pat the dog, who sniffed at him doubtfully, reminding him of poor Kramer. Jessica glanced up then, spotting him, and from the horror on her face Tony surmised that he was not a pretty sight.

"Mom, look at Tony!" Jessica gasped, jumping to her feet and rushing toward him.

Grace looked up then, and the expression on her face mirrored Jessica's. Seconds later both of them were beside him, grasping his arms as they eased him onto his back on the carpet. Grace gently removed the gun from his grasp, and set it on a bookshelf just inside the door.

"Get me a towel," Grace said to Jessica, her voice urgent. Jessica jumped to her feet to comply. Her face was as white as Grace's.

"Dear God, Tony." Grace's hands were gentle in his hair, and then he thought she touched his face, although he couldn't be sure; the whole right side of it was numb. Jessica came back then with the towel, and Grace pressed it to his head just above his right ear.

"There's so much blood. . . ." Jessica sounded almost awe-stricken as she stared at him. Tony supposed, with a tiny flicker of humor, that he must be a pretty gruesome sight.

"He's going to be okay. Head wounds always bleed a lot." Grace's voice was slightly sharp, as if she were daring her words not to be true.

Tony could hear sirens in the distance. The cavalry was near at hand, still welcome even if, like himself, they were arriving just a little too late.

"Are either of you hurt?" he managed, panting as he fought to keep unconsciousness at bay.

"We're fine, and you're going to be fine, too," Grace said, pressing the towel harder against his head. From the quick looks mother and daughter exchanged, Tony deduced that both of them thought the last part of that statement was either wildly optimistic or a flat-out lie.

"I love you," he said to Grace, in case he didn't get another chance. He wanted to reach for her hand, but he found he didn't have the strength to do much more than bat an eyelash. The funny part about it was, this was the conversation he'd meant to have with her this evening. Only he'd pictured the occasion as having more to do with moonlight and kisses than bloody, battered bodies.

She smiled at him, a little crookedly, and bent to kiss the uninjured side of his mouth.

"I love you, too," she said, straightening and pressing the towel harder against the side of his head.

Behind her, Jessica was watching and listening, eyes wide. Tony met her gaze and would have grinned if the mere thought had not brought with it a premonition of nauseating pain. For a moment she stared back at him, the current teenage variation of the phrase *fast worker* stamped on her face as plainly as if it had been printed in ink. Then she blinked, smiled, and gave him a thumb's up behind her mom's back.

There was a pounding on the door downstairs.

"Cavalry," Tony mumbled. Grace nodded and said to Jessica, "Go let them in."

CHAPTER **50**

THE IMPRESSIONS THAT STAYED WITH GRACE long after that night was over were this: hordes of cops, two ambulances, a small crowd of neighbors on the lawn. Kramer, found by the garage, still alive but severely beaten, rushed to a veterinary hospital. The weapon, a tire iron taken from Grace's garage, discovered near the dog, covered with congealing blood. Another body, a woman found not far from Kramer, wrapped in garbage bags. Bright lights, flashing cameras, and questions, dozens of questions.

Her son, badly wounded but alive, loaded into one ambulance with a battalion of police guards. Tony, semiconscious, loaded into the other ambulance. His hand clinging to Grace's until they made him let go, because she was not allowed to ride with him to the hospital. She and Jessica following in her Volvo. Irony of ironies, both Tony and her son taken to the same hospital and bundled into the emergency room one after the other.

Both rushed into surgery. Tony, at least, was expected to live.

A lifetime's worth of guilt like a huge pile of stones crushing down on her chest.

Finally, Grace and Jessica were left to stare at the clock in the surgical waiting area.

"Mom," Jessica said after a while. "Why did that guy keep calling you Mommy?"

Grace looked at her for a moment without replying. How could she tell her daughter the truth? For Jessica, she had always tried to make everything—herself, their home, their life—so perfect. Her daughter was very young to have her illusions so thoroughly shattered.

And yet, there was no help for it. Jessica deserved to learn the truth from her, instead of reading it in a newspaper, or seeing it on a TV newscast, or, if she missed those, hearing it as gossip from her friends.

Grace told her. The complete, unvarnished truth. And then sat there, as she had with Tony, emotionally naked, waiting for the verdict from this person whom she loved.

"How awful," Jessica said, saucer-eyed, after staring at her mother for a long, silent moment. "Why didn't you ever *tell* me? You must have felt so bad!"

Grace looked at her daughter and saw nothing but love for her in the blue eyes that were so like her own.

"Jess," she said, enfolding her daughter in a hug, "you are totally incredible."

"I know." Jessica hugged her back, then released her. Seeing that her daughter looked worried, Grace tensed, waiting. Was the verdict not yet completely in?

"Does Tony know?" was what Jessica asked.

Relief washing over her, Grace nodded.

"Oh." Jessica seemed to ponder. Then her gaze sharpened on her mother's face. "You two have been dating behind my back, haven't you?"

Grace squirmed a little in her seat and shrugged. "Sort of. Not exactly dating, but . . ."

"Why, that dirty dog!" Jessica said indignantly. "He never said a word!"

While Grace stared speechlessly at her daughter, Jessica elucidated. "I asked him if he'd ever thought about dating you, and he said—he said—well, I can't remember exactly what he said, but he certainly didn't say you were already dating!"

"Do you mind?" Grace asked, almost diffidently.

"*That's* what he said," Jessica said triumphantly, her memory apparently jogged. Then, looking at her mother, she shook her head. "I think Tony's great. In fact, I kind of asked him to marry you."

"What?"

"Hey, Mom, you can't get too mad. I heard you tell him you love him, and I heard him say the same thing to you."

Grace was still staring speechlessly at her daughter when Dominick walked in.

"Tony?" he asked without preamble, the moment he spotted Grace.

"He's in surgery." She stood up. "The doctors say it's not life threatening, but he was hurt pretty badly. He had a gash on his head as long as my hand, and they think he might have a skull fracture, among other things."

"Jesus. What happened?"

Grace told him, all of it, including the identity of the attacker. She refused to live with any more secrets. This particular one had already cost one person her life.

Her son, now known as Matt Sherman, would be going to prison, or worse, after he was released from the hospital, she knew. The body found in her backyard had been identified as that of his mother, Sylvia Sherman. He had killed her, shot her at point-blank range in the face with a large caliber weapon.

He had killed his adoptive mother, and then come after his biological mother.

Grace knew that she would live with the horror of that for the rest of her life, as well as the guilt that went along with it.

But she was thankful, so thankful, that he had not succeeded in killing Jessica and Tony and herself.

They all three had so much to live for. A new beginning, maybe, after tonight.

More Marinos walked in then, and after that, they kept coming until the whole gang, from Mary and Rosa to youngest brother Robbie, crowded the waiting area. The noise level was deafening. The comfort level was immense.

When two other, unrelated, individuals entered, Grace felt almost sorry for them. Both men, a father and son, she thought—although they did not really resemble each other—were pale, and the son's eyes were puffy and red-rimmed as if he had been crying. The father wore a conservative navy suit, and the son, who looked about twenty, wore jeans and a sweater. They kept to themselves, almost seeming to huddle together in one corner of the large room that no longer seemed large, filled as it was with Marinos.

A man in a white lab coat whom Grace assumed was a doctor came to the door about fifteen minutes after the newcomers joined them.

"Donald Sherman?" the doctor called. Grace realized who these two had to be and stared at them, transfixed.

The adoptive father and brother of her son.

The father stood up and walked to the door, and the son followed him. Grace's eyes widened on the son. He reminded her irresistibly of someone, though she could not, for a moment, think whom. He was tall and thin and athletic looking, unlike his adoptive brother. His hair was the kind of light brown that had once been blond.

The color of Jessica's hair and her own before she had taken to highlighting it.

And the way he moved . . .

Grace stood up, leaving Jessica deep in conversation with Dominick, and moved jerkily toward the pair, who were talking to the doctor.

". . . just missed his aorta," the doctor said. "He's lucky to be alive."

"It might be better if he wasn't," Mr. Sherman said heavily.

"Dad," the son remonstrated, gripping his arm.

"Oh, God, Donny, he killed your mother. . . ."

"He's sick, Dad. He couldn't have been in his right mind."

A nurse hurried down the hall and said something in a low voice to the doctor.

"He's conscious and asking for you, Mr. Sherman," the doctor said.

Mr. Sherman shook his head. "I can't talk to him."

"Dad"—Donny's voice was urgent—"we can't just abandon him. He needs us now more than ever."

Mr. Sherman looked at Donny and shook his head again. "You were always a good brother to him. This isn't your fault. You're the best son a man could have."

"Dad, please . . ."

"All right. All right. For you." He nodded at the doctor, and then, in response to a gesture from the nurse, father and son followed her down the hall.

Grace, fascinated, followed too.

For what seemed like an eternity she hovered in the hallway outside the room they were shown into, but in reality it could have been no more than twenty minutes. The occasional passing nurse cast her a curious glance, but no one bothered her. When Mr. Sherman and his son emerged at last, she was studying the room charts posted on a bulletin board just down the hall and trying not to hope for the impossible. The physical resemblance might be just a fluke. . . .

"Mr. Sherman." Grace walked up to the father before she lost her nerve. He looked shaken, she saw, while the son was white as a ghost. "I'm Grace Hart. Judge Grace Hart. The boy in there—that is, my house is where—where he broke in. Where they found your wife." She took a deep breath. Donny's eyes, she saw, were blue. And his nose was long, with a bump in the middle of the bridge. She tore her gaze from his face. "I'm—I'm very sorry," she finished lamely.

For a long moment the three of them simply stared at one another. Grace's heart was racing. She felt almost sick with hope.

"It is I who must apologize to you," Mr. Sherman said heavily. "Matt—my son in there—tried to kill you and your daughter. I don't know what to say."

"He did it because he was jealous of me," Donny said in a stunned tone. "He said so."

Mr. Sherman grimaced as though in pain, then looked at Grace directly.

"I believe you must be the biological mother of my son," he said.

Grace almost gasped. To have the truth that she had striven so long to hide spoken aloud so matter-of-factly was—unsettling. But the question remained—which son?

Donny was staring at her. Her gaze met his, and it was all she could do to pull it away to focus on his father.

"If—is—I was under the impression that it was my son who attacked my daughter and me," Grace could not bring herself to ask the question directly.

Mr. Sherman shook his head. "To my never-ending sorrow, Matt is my biological son. My wife and I had decided not to have children, because of . . . of certain psychiatric problems on her side of the family that we feared might be passed on genetically. We adopted Donny here as an infant, and a year later Sylvie accidentally got pregnant with Matt." He let out his breath in a short, bitter sigh. "She thought it would be nice for Donny to have a younger sibling. When she found out the second child was a boy, she was ecstatic. She wanted Donny to have a little brother."

Grace barely heard the last few sentences. She stared into the eyes of her son. For a moment she could not speak. He appeared to be similarly affected, because he in turn stared in silence at her.

"Hello, Donny," she managed after a moment.

He said nothing, and Grace braced herself to be snubbed. But then he held out his hand. "I . . . don't know what to call you," he said.

"Grace," Grace said swiftly, taking his hand. Mom was too intimate and, for a child, could belong to only one person in the world. Donny's mom was dead, under dreadful circumstances that very day, and he must be heartsick with horror and grief. But Grace was his mother, and he was her son, and he was alive and well and she was holding his hand.

"Grace," he said.

One of the hardest things she had ever had to do was let his hand drop. But she did it.

Dominick and Jessica appeared around a bend in the hallway and came toward them.

"This is my daughter," Grace said when they reached her. "Jessica."

The physical resemblance between Jessica and Donny was striking. Even Jessica noticed it, blinking at the young man in apparent confusion.

"Hi, Jessica," Donny said, and Grace realized that his adoptive parents—no, his *parents*—had taught him excellent manners. "It's nice to meet you."

"This . . . this is . . ."—Grace almost said *your brother,* but again, that suggested a relationship beyond the biological tie that connected the two. She didn't want to take anything for granted, or seem to go too far, too fast—"the baby I was telling you about. The one I gave up for adoption nineteen years ago."

"My brother?" Jessica gasped. Grace almost had to smile. Trust Jess to get to the heart of the matter. She glanced at Grace. "You mean—the guy who broke in wasn't? . . ."

As Jessica broke off, apparently afflicted with belated delicacy, Grace shook her head.

"Thank goodness," Jessica said devoutly. It was all Grace could do not to clap a hand over her daughter's irrepressible mouth.

"Mr. Sherman," Dominick said, interrupting the awkward moment, and offering a hand first to Mr. Sherman and then to Donny, "I'm Detective Dominick Marino, Franklin County Police. First, let me express my condolences on the loss of your wife.

I know that this is a very difficult time for you and your son." His glance flicked to Donny and back. "I understand that you were able to talk to your other son. Did he tell you what prompted his actions? Why he killed your wife?"

Mr. Sherman cleared his throat. "Donny, why don't you take this young lady here—Jessica?—for a little walk up the hall, okay?" He waited while Donny, frowning but obedient, did as he was asked. The two moved out of earshot, but remained visible just up the hall. Mr. Sherman looked from Dominick to Grace and back. "There's no need for him to hear all this. Matt did . . . talk about that. He and my wife never got along, never. They were . . . alike in every way, too much so. Matt said he was jealous of Donny, because he thought my wife and I loved Donny better than him. He meant to kill my wife and me, and Judge Hart and her daughter, and blame it on Donny, whom he also meant to kill after making him write a note confessing to the crime. Apparently he planted some evidence at your house"—he glanced at Grace—"implicating Donny. And he meant to plant more. He was wearing Donny's shoes, so the footprints would be consistent with Donny's, and meant to leave a glass Donny had drunk from and some of Donny's hair and a few other things like that at the scene of the crime."

"Oh, my God! The gum!" Grace gasped. When Dominick and Mr. Sherman looked at her with incomprehension, she waved their inquiring looks aside. "Never mind. Tony knows."

"There is one other thing," Mr. Sherman said grimly. "And this is the part I didn't want Donny to hear. He was in the rest room when his brother told me, thank God." He took a deep breath. "Apparently Matt also killed Donny's girlfriend, who disappeared from her house last weekend. Her name is—was—Caroline Staples. You'll find her body in a freezer in the basement at 327 Maple in Upper Arlington."

CHAPTER **51**

A WEEK LATER, TONY WAS RELEASED FROM THE hospital. It was about 5:30 P.M., and Grace had swung by to pick him up after work. Jessica had basketball practice until six, and after that she was spending the night with Emily Millhollen.

So they had the whole night alone. Unfortunately, Grace thought, Tony was still too weak to make it worth their while.

His head was covered by a wrap-around white bandage that looked, Grace told him, like a turban. Beneath it was a hairline skull fracture and two deep cuts, one requiring twenty stitches and the other thirteen. He had two broken ribs, which were taped, and huge, intermittent bruises from the top of his head to his ankle on the right side of his body.

His face, which had been swollen to the size of a basketball the day after the beating, now looked fairly normal, if one discounted the gash on his right cheekbone, which had required six stitches, and a blackened right eye that was now fading toward normal in shades of purple and yellow.

"So you're having lunch with Donny next Wednesday?" Tony inquired. He was leaning back in the passenger seat of her gray Volvo, looking perfectly content.

"Yes. He called me." Grace beamed at him with transparent delight. "He said he wants to get to know Jessica and me."

"Things have a way of working out, don't they?"

"I feel like this enormous weight has been lifted from my shoulders. He's a nice boy, Tony."

"He seems to be. Wait, you're missing the turn!"

They were heading toward his house so he could pick up some things, as he would be staying with Grace and Jessica until he was completely recovered. Grace whipped the car down the street Tony indicated, and grinned as Tony hung onto the armrest with an alarmed expression.

"Chicken," she teased when the maneuver was completed.

"Are you ever going to let me drive?"

She pretended to consider. "Probably not."

He shrugged. "Just asking."

Grace pulled up in front of his house.

"You sure you don't want to wait in the car while I go in and pack you a bag?" she asked anxiously, turning to look at him.

"I may not be up to full strength, but I think I can manage to walk in the house," he said, his voice dry.

"Fine." Grace got out of the car, and so, more laboriously, did Tony. Dusk was falling, and Grace watched the streetlights flicker on in the alley behind his house. Here on the street, long purple shadows stretched across the leaf-strewn lawns as the last remnants of daylight faded away.

Tony stood beside the car, one arm resting on its top, and Grace hurried unobtrusively to his side. Wrapping his arm around her waist, he permitted her to help him up the walk.

"Hey, there, Tony! You feelin' better?" From her front window, Mrs. Crutcher must have seen them pull up, because she came hurrying out onto the porch.

"Yeah, Mrs. Crutcher, thanks."

"What about your dog, what was his name? Is he doin' okay?"

"Kramer, Mrs. Crutcher. She gets out of the hospital on Monday."

"His bill'll probably be as big as yours," Mrs. Crutcher chortled.

"Yeah, probably." Tony didn't sound quite as amused.

"Well, you folks take care."

"You too, Mrs. Crutcher. Good night."

" 'Night."

They had reached the stoop now. Grace took Tony's key from his hand and opened the door. The old woman was still watching as they went inside.

"You'll never have a stalker," Grace said with certainty, reaching to turn on the light. "I don't think anyone could get past Mrs. Crutcher."

"I wouldn't want to be the one to try," Tony agreed. His hand caught Grace's, keeping it from reaching the switch.

"Tony . . ." she protested.

"Grace," he said, gently mocking, then bent his head to kiss her mouth.

To all her protests that he couldn't, he replied that he could, and demonstrated it, too. True, he wasn't up to a lot more than just lying on his back in the middle of the bed, but that proved perfectly satisfactory to them both. She undressed him, and herself, and then amused herself by teasing him until he was groaning, and she suddenly didn't find the activity quite so amusing any more. He had lots of injured parts she tried to be careful of, but in the end the passion that flared between them was so hot and fierce that she forgot all about his damaged state, and rode him until the world exploded. Then she collapsed on top of him, gasping and replete.

At that he groaned, in a different timbre from the lewd noises he'd been making just moments before, and winced palpably. Recalled to a sense of his disabilities, she immediately rolled off him.

"Oh, Tony, I'm sorry!" She reached for the bedside lamp. Switching it on, she looked at him contritely. "Are you all right?"

"I think you broke my few remaining whole ribs and . . ." he said, then started laughing at the horrified look on her face. "I'm fine. You just came down on a tender spot, is all."

"We shouldn't have . . ." she began, conscience-stricken.

"Yes, we should have. In fact, if you give me a minute, we're probably going to do it again. And again. And . . ."

"Oh no we're not." Grace rolled off the bed, and stood, arms akimbo, looking down at him severely. He was still her handsome Tony, broad of shoulder, narrow of hip, and long of leg, but the white bandage circling his head and rib cage, plus the massive contusions that marred almost his whole right side, made him look like a refugee from a horror movie. "If you could see yourself . . . You need to rest."

His eyes moved over her, their quick heating reminding her that she was naked. He reached out, caught her hand, and tugged.

"Tony, no."

"Just come and lie down here beside me for a minute. I won't do anything, I swear."

"Oh, yeah, right."

"There's that paranoid nature of yours again."

"I am *not* paranoid."

"That's a matter of opinion."

He tugged at her hand once more, and despite her protests, she allowed herself to be persuaded to stretch out beside him, on his uninjured side, her head on his shoulder, her hand resting just above the layers of white bandage that circled his rib cage. And then he proved, very thoroughly and once and for all, that she did *not* have a paranoid nature, that every suspicion she had ever harbored in her life had, in fact, been well-founded, including the one about his true intentions when he had coaxed her down on the bed.

She would have told him so, too, and very pithily, except when she finally caught her breath enough to yell at him, he distracted her by the simple but uncharacteristic gesture of raising her hand to his mouth, and kissing the back of it.

"I love you," he said then, looking deep into her eyes. "Marry me?"

To shorten what in reality proved to be a very long and physically tiring answer, she said yes.

. . .

It must have been around midnight before they were ready to go. Grace insisted on carrying his duffel bag out to the car, and Tony let her, number one because his ribs were really hurting like hell—not that he meant to admit as much to Grace—and number two because he needed just a minute or two alone.

He was moving on in his life now, putting the past behind him, and he felt just the smallest twinge of guilt about that. He would love Rachel forever. She would be a part of him for as long as he lived, but he knew now that he could be happy again, that life still held sweetness for him, like surprise packages just waiting to be found and unwrapped along the road.

Her picture was already stowed in the duffel bag, so he did the next best thing and walked out into the warm, breezy night to say good-bye to Rachel in her garden. Off behind the garage, the gauzy yellow light of the street lamp was swarming with bugs as it illuminated the alley. Overhead, a pale quarter moon rode high in the sky, surrounded by dozens of tiny stars that glittered like diamond chips on a field of midnight blue. Closer at hand, the grass and fallen leaves beneath his feet looked almost black. A faint scent wafted through the air.

Roses?

Tony frowned, and then his eyes widened as he stared at Rachel's rose garden. Unless he had completely lost his mind, it was in bloom, in full, glorious bloom, each bush lush with large white blossoms that released their perfume into the night.

In four years, those bushes had not sprouted so much as a bud. And it was late October yet. Warm still, admittedly; Indian summer, yes; but—roses in October?

Tony was not convinced until he was close enough to reach out a hand and touch a velvety flower.

Roses. In October.

Tony stood there transfixed, staring at Rachel's roses, in full bloom now where, only a week before, there had been nothing more than a circular patch of leathery, almost leafless branches and thorns.

A white moth came straight at him, swooping out of the darkness seemingly from nowhere, and he ducked away instinctively as its soft wings brushed his cheek.

It felt almost like a caress.

A horn honked from the street. Grace. He had to bring her back here, to show her—no.

If he showed her, maybe she would tell him that she'd had the rosebushes replaced. Maybe she knew why the bushes were blooming, and there was nothing mysterious about it at all. She'd had them fertilized maybe, and watered. Something.

If that was the case, he didn't want to know.

This he was going to take as a sign of benediction from the daughter he would love until he died.

Very gently, he plucked a single bloom, inhaling the sweet fragrance before placing it in the pocket of the leather bomber jacket he wore. He would press it in a book when he got home.

He smiled faintly to think that Grace's house was now home.

The horn sounded again.

"I've got to go," he said aloud, to no one in particular.

Then he turned and headed toward the street where Grace waited behind the wheel of her Volvo. Jessica would be home tomorrow, and the thought made Tony feel oddly complete.

His life had come full circle, he thought. He was going home to his girls.

In the darkness behind the house, a small white moth hurtled joyfully upward, this time racing without regrets toward the light.